W9-BLG-733

THE
SECRET
CHAPTER

BY GENEVIEVE COGMAN

THE
SECRET
CHAPTER

AN INVISIBLE LIBRARY NOVEL

GENEVIEVE
COGMAN

ACE
NEW YORK

ACE
Published by Berkley
An imprint of Penguin Random House LLC
penguinrandomhouse.com

Library of Congress Cataloging-in-Publication Data

Names: Cogman, Genevieve, author.
Title: The secret chapter: an invisible library novel / Genevieve Cogman.
Description: First edition. | New York: Ace, 2020. | Series: The invisible library; book 6
Identifiers: LCCN 2019033034 (print) | LCCN 2019033035 (ebook) |
ISBN 9780593197844 (hardcover) | ISBN 9781984804761 (paperback) |
ISBN 9781984804778 (ebook)
Subjects: LCSH: Librarians—Fiction. | Secret societies—Fiction. |
GSAFD: Alternative histories (Fiction) | Adventure fiction. | Fantasy fiction.
Classification: LCC PR6103.O39 S43 2020 (print) |
LCC PR6103.O39 (ebook) | DDC 823/.92—dc23
LC record available at https://lccn.loc.gov/2019033034
LC ebook record available at https://lccn.loc.gov/2019033035

First Edition: January 2020

Printed in the United States of America
1   3   5   7   9   10   8   6   4   2

Cover design and image composition by Adam Auerbach
Book design by Laura K. Corless

To my godparents—Judy, James, and Angela.
Thank you for everything.

ACKNOWLEDGMENTS

There had to be a heist at some point in the story, didn't there? And there are certain tropes that consistently occur in a heist narrative, whether the protagonists are trying to get away with the *Mona Lisa*, a casino's earnings, or the entire gold stocks of Turin and Fort Knox...

Many thanks to my editors, Bella Pagan and Rebecca Brewer. Have I said lately that I appreciate you? I appreciate you very much. You're great at helping me work out what needs to be done to improve the book, and how to do it.

Thanks also to my agent Lucienne Diver for all her support and for being constantly in my quarter and one hundred per cent behind me. (Which sounds rather like putting your nose to the grindstone and your shoulder to the wheel at the same time, but you know what I mean.)

Thanks to all my beta-readers and all the people who supplied information for the story: Beth, Jeanne, Phyllis, Anne, Stuart, Crystal, and everyone else. Your help makes a difference, and I'm very grateful for it.

Thank you to all my friends at work and in leisure, who supported my tendency to make marginalia plot notes on minutes and who didn't run away when I spent ten minutes trying to explain the plot to them. It's good to know that everyone understands the significance of Chekhov's shark. (Like the gun, but for some reason less frequently used.)

Thank you to the city of Vienna, which I have visited and loved. (I do know *The Raft of the Medusa* is in the Louvre in Paris—in this world, at least. Don't shoot me.) Vienna is a beautiful, fascinating place, and really didn't deserve me driving a plot lorry through the middle of it. Any errors in my depiction of a CENSOR-managed Vienna are my fault entirely.

And thank you to all the fans of the Library out there. Stories matter—telling them, sharing them, preserving them, changing them, learning from them, and escaping with and through them. We learn about ourselves and the world that we live in through fiction just as much as through facts. Empathy, perception, and understanding are never wasted. All libraries are a gateway into other worlds, including the past—and the future.

THE
SECRET
CHAPTER

LIBRARY UPDATE TO ALL OPERATIVES—TOP PRIORITY

A truce has finally been agreed between the dragons and the Fae.

This is neither a hoax nor a test of your intelligence. Nor is it a drill to check whether you are aware of what to do in a crisis.*

This formal peace treaty has been signed by His Majesty Ao Guang (Dragon King of the Eastern Ocean, representing all eight dragon kings and queens). The signatory for the other side is the Princess, a high-ranking representative amongst the Fae. This treaty requires non-interference, by each side, in the other's declared territories. It also calls for mutual non-aggression where potentially delicate situations arise.

(In other words, hands off and *no* starting fights.)

This is wonderful news. I would like to remind everyone that we are not here *just* to obtain books for our personal reading lists. The Library is tasked with maintaining the balance between order and chaos, between the dragons and the Fae, and is bound to protect the alternate worlds they claim—and the humans living in them. Peace is a positive step—even a very minor and carefully defined peace such as this one. It should cut down on accidental human casualties during larger conflicts. It will *save lives*.

Now, I need to make the following point absolutely clear . . . As a co-signatory, Librarians are bound to act as neutral parties. As such, we are committed to helping resolve disagreements and—most importantly—to *not* stealing books from anyone who's signed up to these accords.** We can't risk breaching the treaty which we ourselves helped organise.

Technically *all* dragons are subjects of the eight dragon monarchs and have therefore signed up to the treaty in principle—which means that it is now out of the question for us to steal from any dragon. Fortunately we have never been caught doing such a thing and would certainly never consider it . . . If you do remove a book from a place that wasn't listed in the treaty but turns out to be from a dragon's personal fief, then—assuming you survive—the situation can be negotiated and reparations arranged by the Library representative for the treaty. But since the Fae don't have the same rigid hierarchies, it can be much harder to determine whether or not an individual Fae has signed up. In practice, check details *first*, "acquire" books *second*, and be aware that negotiation may be an option. But please be careful.

The full text of this treaty and a list of all current signatories, and the worlds that they consider to be their personal property, is attached to this message. You are strongly advised to read and memorise it. Be aware that ignorance of the new situation will not be an excuse, unless you are very, very, *very* lucky.***

All irregularities will be handled by a tripartite commission. The Fae representative has not yet been appointed, but the Library delegate is Irene, Librarian-in-Residence on world B-395. And the dragon representative is Prince Kai, son of His Majesty Ao Guang.

Librarians, please understand that this may be the most significant chance we've ever had to stabilise the alternate worlds we visit. And let's not confuse the *means* by which we maintain the balance between order and chaos—collecting books—with our ultimate *ends*. Getting hold of a book to cement peace for one world may breach the overall peace treaty for multiple worlds. Now more than ever, we have to maintain our neutrality.

Times are changing. Let's help them change for the better.

Coppelia, Senior Librarian

* We note that the Library has not had fire alarm drills for the last two hundred years. This is because we found the two default responses unhelpful. These being "running away screaming" or "resigning yourself to death while clutching your favourite books." Librarians with more useful suggestions should contact Yves via email and attach a full benefit-threat analysis.

** I'm aware that if the owner doesn't know that the book has gone, then consent is not an issue. Under some circumstances I might be sympathetic, but the current political situation is very unstable. Let's not push our luck.

*** We have had it pointed out to us that this sort of repetition is poor style. But we feel it's necessary to make our point.

CHAPTER 1

S mile and circulate," Irene said through gritted teeth, drawing her skirts back from the blood that had spattered by her
feet. She watched the brightly coloured mob in front of her.
"It might be messy, but it was only a duel to first blood. It's not as
if anyone was killed."

Servants in spotless white and black had come scuttling out
like cockroaches to wipe the floor clean and provide fresh cocktails for the onlookers. The height of London's fashion mingled
with the cream of its notoriety, assisted by a wide selection of
drink and drugs. The chandeliers, sparkle as they might, did very
little to light up the corners of the room. Here, the more serious or
depraved of the Fae present smoked opium, sipped absinthe, or
even discussed the latest novels.

It was, in short, one of Lord Silver's best-ever parties.

"It's not the duel I'm complaining about, it's the calligraphy
challenge that started the quarrel," Kai muttered. He hadn't left

Irene's side so far this evening, and she was grateful for it. This wasn't a party for them to enjoy: it was one where they needed to be seen. It was a political event and a lion's den. But even here, Kai had his sense of aesthetics. "The choice of ink colours available was completely unsuitable, she should have demanded a steel pen, and frankly the whole thing ought to have been called off until both parties could get better paper. No wonder they came to blows instead of competing as planned. It simply wasn't possible for either to produce work representative of their skills."

"Yes," Silver said, sweeping into place behind them. "I have to admit I'm embarrassed. At one of *my* parties, anything that a guest demands should be available there and then. I will simply have to lay in better supplies for the future."

"Well, it is the latest thing," Irene answered, trying to calm her heartbeat. She had never been comfortable with anyone mysteriously appearing behind her. And running for her life would be a challenge, in her highly expensive but restrictive silk dress. "I hear it's hit aficionados as badly as the Dutch tulip craze. Remember when everyone *had* to own the latest bloom? And is it true that there was an ink robbery at Harrods?"

"Your friend the detective would know better than I," Silver said. He was barely six inches behind Irene, and she was painfully conscious of his presence—his height, his warmth, the curve of his lips . . .

Fae were dangerous. Even when they were technically now allies.

She faced Silver, her dress rustling. "Lord Silver. When you invited us, we had expected a smaller occasion. Something more . . ." She considered the word *intimate* and rejected it hastily. "Discreet."

"You aren't enjoying it?" Silver said, amused. The light from the ether-lamps made a halo of his pale hair, but nobody would have classed him as anything other than the most fallen sort of angel. His shoulders and build—and overly tight trousers—were enough to make anyone think of sin. And the lingering curve of his lips, and glint of his eyes, suggested that he was far more interested in debauching mortals than saving them. He fitted perfectly into this alternate Victorian England as a libertine and man about town; like many powerful Fae, he was a personification of certain types of stories. But the ones that involved his sort of character definitely weren't meant for children. "But you're drinking my champagne . . ."

"It's very good champagne," Irene said, in an attempt to find something on which she could honestly compliment him. Also, there hadn't been anything non-alcoholic on offer. "But as I just said, *discreet*. There are at least a hundred people here."

The music from the string quartet in the corner speeded up, and a space cleared on the floor. Two guests, a man in stark white and a woman in black, began to tango. At least two possible duels and one assignation broke off, as guests turned to watch and applaud.

"My dear little mouse," Silver said, using the pet name that he knew most annoyed Irene. "You were aware I was going to show off you and your dragon prince to my kind tonight. It might not have been *said*, but there was certainly an *understanding*. And your princeling isn't objecting to any of this."

"I'm letting her do that for me," Kai said equably.

In the dramatic lights and shadows thrown by the trembling chandeliers, he had the perfect beauty of a classical statue. His hair was black, with just a touch of blue. His eyes were dark blue, with a hint of underlying fire. And his skin was as pale as marble, but comfortingly warm to the touch. Since his recent selection as dragon representative in the newly built dragon-Fae truce, he had thrown himself into politics. Or at least, he'd thrown himself into choosing the most appropriate clothing for political occasions. Irene had to admit the effort wasn't wasted.

"Agreeable as well as handsome. The perfect partner." Silver's smile made the implication of *in the bedroom as well as out of it* quite clear, and Irene felt Kai's arm tense under her hand. "Nevertheless, if you want my help in a certain matter, you'll stay at this party for at least another couple of hours."

Irene knew exactly what he meant. She had been named as Librarian representative for this same truce. She would be the mutual point of contact for both Fae and dragon queries and new signatories. And—it was unspoken, but clearly visible in her future—she'd be the person responsible for sorting out any problems. However, the Fae representative had yet to be chosen. And as Silver was on one faction's selection committee (or whatever mechanism they had for choosing a representative), she wanted his assistance.

She sipped her champagne. "I know we're both trying to help each other here . . . Our presence increases your prestige among your own kind. And in return, you could influence the selection of the Fae representative—choosing someone who won't make our lives a living hell." She smiled politely. "However, no one will benefit if Kai or I are killed in a duel on your home ground."

"That won't happen," Silver said categorically.

Irene raised an eyebrow.

"Anyone who challenges you will never be invited to one of my parties again," he clarified. "Now if you'll excuse me, I have a tango to interrupt."

Irene watched him go. "It really is very good champagne," she said with a sigh.

"What *did* Vale say when you asked if he'd show up?" Kai enquired.

Irene couldn't help smiling. "That he found his current researches into ink-smuggling far more rewarding than another pointless party thrown by Lord Silver. He felt he'd already done his bit for the dragon-Fae peace treaty in Paris. And if he did attend, it would be to search the upstairs rooms for evidence of crimes, while everyone else was downstairs. Also, if he had shown up, Mu Dan would have shown up too, an uninvited dragon at a Fae party . . ."

"I don't know why she's spending so much time in this world," Kai muttered petulantly. "As a judge-investigator, surely she's got important business elsewhere. Anywhere elsewhere."

"It's because she wants to recruit Vale to work on some of her cases." Mu Dan had helped Vale and Irene catch a murderer during the signing of the peace treaty in Paris. And she'd been making veiled offers of employment to Vale ever since. "You can't blame her for wanting the best. But don't worry. He's not going to agree." They were both protective of their friend.

Kai nodded. "We should both try to relax," he suggested. "You're prickly because you thought this might be a polite social occasion among neutrals. I'm less concerned because I knew we'd be among enemies."

So much, Irene thought, *for the truce.* "I live in hope," she said. "We have to start somewhere. And any other generic platitudes that spring to mind."

Kai's eyes narrowed abruptly. "I know that face. What's she doing here?"

"Politics too, I imagine," Irene said. The woman approaching was Fae—and she was a secretary, minion, and cat's paw of one of the most powerful of their kind. "Sterrington, how interesting to see you here."

Sterrington smiled and raised her glass in salute. "How nice to see you both. Stolen any good books lately?" Her dark hair was smoothed back into a low knot at the base of her neck, and her grey watered-silk gown was appropriate to the late Victorian period of this alternate world. Gloves concealed the fact that her right hand was largely cybernetic.

"We've been living quietly lately," Irene answered. "It's been very pleasant. I've actually managed to catch up on my reading."

It had been a relief to have a few weeks in which she was out of danger and able to do mundane things such as move house, renegotiate her relationship with Kai—and even brush up on some of her foreign languages. Acquiring works of fiction for the Library from alternate worlds was her vocation, and her job, but it was rarely peaceful or easy.

"I see." Sterrington's enigmatic smile suggested disbelief, as if Irene had actually been arranging the downfall of monarchs or thefts from imperial fortresses. "How . . . surprising."

"And I'm surprised to see you here," Kai said. "I'd thought that your master wasn't on good terms with Lord Silver."

"If the Cardinal waited to be on good terms with people before dispatching emissaries, he'd never send anyone," Sterrington countered. "Why didn't you visit me in Liechtenstein? I sent an invitation . . ."

Liechtenstein was the major centre of Fae activity on this

alternate world. But as such, it was one of the places Irene *least* wanted to visit. "I must apologise for that, but I would have been . . . uncomfortable. You know we Librarians can't tolerate too high-chaos an environment."

"You managed Venice well enough last year," Sterrington said.

"Yes," Kai said. The faint shadow of scale-patterns blossomed across his cheekbones and the back of his hands, like frost-ferns on a window, and a brief flare of draconic red glinted in his eyes. "Where I was kidnapped by the Guantes. I believe you were working for them?"

"Water under the bridge," Sterrington said lightly. "I thought that under the new peace treaty we were going to be much more understanding . . . about little things like that."

Irene passed her still half-full glass to Kai. "Please could you fetch me some more champagne?" she said quickly.

Kai inclined his head in a gesture not unlike a duellist's salute and stalked off on his errand.

"I seem to have made a strong impression," Sterrington commented. "I can't remember him being that easily offended last time we met."

Irene searched for a way to change the subject. But Sterrington beat her to it. "Would you care for some cocaine? Locally sourced."

"I didn't know you took cocaine."

"I don't, except on rare occasions, but Lord Silver thinks I do. I didn't like to disappoint him." She winced at a clashing noise that almost drowned out the tango. "What *is* that?"

"Russian sabre dancers." Irene had demanded a look at the bill of entertainments before agreeing to attend. "With tame Afghan hounds."

"No white stallions?"

"They were held up at Customs."

"I'm glad to hear you're not involved in anything more alarming than *this* sort of affair." Sterrington's elegant gesture took in the scene.

A little warning flag raised itself at the back of Irene's mind. "*Is there something more alarming going on, apart from our mutual treaty?*" she asked mildly.

"Only the usual," Sterrington said with a shrug. "Deaths, violence, bloodshed, assassinations, murders, thefts. You and I should have a get-together to discuss it all. Have your PA call mine—you do have one, don't you? I can recommend an excellent firm if not." Her tone didn't change, but her eyes searched the crowd as she went on. "By the way, Silver did screen the guest list, I hope?"

"He did," Irene said. She followed Sterrington's gaze as surreptitiously as she could. "But you were waved through, so clearly whoever's checking names at the door isn't as reliable as they might be. Is there a problem?"

"Possibly. Do you see that Fae, the man with the green cravat?"

The cravat in question was a particularly toxic shade of emerald, the sort associated with mambas and poisonous frogs. Otherwise, the man looked average enough—for Silver's parties—and he was within five yards of Kai. "You know him?"

"Know of him. Of course, I haven't met him personally—"

"Get to the point . . ." Irene almost rolled her eyes.

"His name's Rudolf," Sterrington said. "He lost his mother in some business involving a dragon takeover of her world. The Cardinal heard he was planning to publicly revenge himself against the new dragon delegate—and so I dropped by. I suppose desperate people will do desperate things."

Irene's glance swept the room. There was no sign of Silver. And the general press of guests was thick enough that it'd take her at least five minutes to get round the edge of the dance floor, now occupied by waltzers, to reach Kai. "I need your *word* that you're being truthful about this," she said.

"The Fae have as much to lose as you have," Sterrington said. "Why else would I have bothered to tell you about this? In fact, I think you might owe me a favour for warning you. Can you stop him?"

"Not from across the room." The Librarians' private Language could do a great many things. It could boil champagne, redirect electricity, freeze canals, and generally affect reality. But if it was being spoken, then it had to be audible.

"What are you going to do?"

Not *what do we do*, Irene noted with an inner sigh. "I'll stop him," she said, and approached the nearest male. "Excuse me, but would you care to dance?"

His eyes widened in surprise. "Ma'am," he began, "this is a most unexpected pleasure, and I can only—"

"Dance," Irene said and forcibly spun him onto the dance floor—in Kai's direction.

"I never dared hope for the honour of your acquaintance, ma'am," her partner began.

But Rudolph was even closer to Kai now—and she saw an opening through the crowd. "You must tell me more about it later."

"Why not now?"

"Because I'm—" She disengaged smoothly and spun round to the next pair. "Changing partners," she finished, hooking the woman out of her partner's arms and shifting her path closer towards Kai.

"Thank you," her new partner breathed, settling against Irene's shoulder. "I've always dreamed of being rescued like that. Did you *see* where he was putting his hands?"

Irene looked down at the blonde head trying to nestle itself against her chest. This was the problem with operating in a high-chaos world. Everything kept on trying to settle itself into standard narrative patterns. She hadn't *meant* to be a chivalrous rescuer. "Don't worry," she said soothingly. "Everything will be all right in a moment." In approximately thirty seconds, when she'd reach Kai. With a final swirl she reached the edge of the dance floor and released the blonde, giving her a pat on the shoulder.

But her eyes were on Kai. His hands were full—a champagne glass in each. And Rudolf was behind him, one hand already reaching into his jacket to pull out a pistol.

One step. Two. Three, and she was grabbing Rudolf's shoulder. As his eyes widened in surprise, she sent a sharp-knuckled jab into his guts with all the strength that anger and fear gave her.

The gun fell from his hand and clattered onto the floor as he dropped to his knees. He was still struggling to get up, so Irene lifted her skirts and kicked him in the stomach for good measure, wishing for once that she'd worn shoes with a more pointed toe. He collapsed to the floor, gasping for breath.

Fighting fair was for exhibition matches and formal competitions.

Irene glanced up to see an expanding ring of gawping onlookers. Especially given the treaty, she needed some sort of excuse for what she'd just done—and Sterrington had vanished. At least Kai was still holding the champagne. She could do with a drink.

Inspiration came as a driving wedge of waiters pushed through the crowd towards her. "He's not on the guest list," she said, indicating the groaning Rudolf. "Lord Silver will wish to deal with him . . . personally."

"I will?" Silver said, stepping out of the throng and refastening his cravat.

There was a crash of drums as the Cossack sabre dancers took to the floor, giving Irene the chance to step closer and mutter, "Sterrington told me he was here to assassinate Kai. It would have rather dominated your party."

Silver's eyes sharpened, and he caught her hand to press his lips against it. "As I have always said, you are my particularly *favourite* little mouse—"

"Excuse me," Kai said, detaching Silver's grip—with what looked like a rather painful twist—and pressing a champagne flute into her grasp instead. "Am I missing something?"

Irene resisted the urge to touch her hand where Silver's lips had brushed her skin. He'd lost none of his powers of seduction, unfortunately. "Just an assassination attempt," she said. "As you said, we are among enemies. Let's smile. And circulate."

In the carriage on the way back to their lodgings, Irene finally let herself relax. But even through the thick wool and silk of her cape, she could feel Kai next to her, as taut as piano wire.

"You're brooding," she said.

Kai was silent for a while before he finally spoke. "I can defend you against rational threats," he said. "I can even protect you against the Fae, and heaven and earth both know that they're irrational. But how am I supposed to keep you safe from fanatics?"

"It was *you* he was trying to kill," Irene pointed out.

"Yes, and you threw yourself into his path to stop him. And how do we know that the next killer won't be after you? Some sort of murderous loon who's sworn vengeance against all Librarians because one of you once stole his favourite book?"

"Well, yes," Irene had to admit. "Some people can go in for quite disproportionate vengeances . . ."

"They are meant to be disproportionate to set an example," Kai said. "That's the *point*."

"And so it goes throughout history." She sighed. "No doubt it would be exactly the same if we could go back to the dawn of time, to the birth of the first Fae, or the first dragons . . ."

Kai seemed glad to be diverted from his brooding. "That's the sort of historical record you *might* find in the Library," he said. "Less so among my father's histories. Technically he must have had parents himself, of course, but that sort of thing is lost in the distant past. We tend to focus on the future."

Irene pricked up her ears at Kai discussing his people's past, even in such a guarded way. He almost never did that. "Do you think that your dragon monarchs inspired Chinese mythology?" she asked. "Or mythology in general? I couldn't help noticing that the names of the kings are often the same as in fable."

"Well, obviously," Kai said. "There aren't any other dragon monarchs around, after all."

"But looking to the future, not the past . . . you're right. We do have a problem. What do we do about assassins? Especially since we're supposed to be available, known to be based here for anyone who wants to talk to us . . ."

Irene tugged her cloak tighter against the damp cold. Spring might be on the way, but it was taking its time, and London's fogs were wet and bone-chillingly bitter. Her mood was shifting to match the weather. "Kai," she said, "would it sound childish if I said that I wish we were off acquiring books somewhere, rather than trying to be politicians?"

She felt him relax, and he squeezed her hand through her layers of cloak. "The word, Irene, is stealing."

"Oh, *semantics*. '*I* acquire,' '*you* borrow,' '*she* steals,' '*they* invade and loot . . .'"

The carriage drew up outside their new lodgings, a fringe benefit of their positions as representatives of the treaty. Kai stepped out and helped Irene down before paying the driver. Irene looked up at the windows. Light showed round the edge of the lounge curtains. "Vale may be here," she said. "Perhaps he's finished that investigation after all."

Kai perked up and bounded up the steps. Irene followed more slowly.

The house was quiet and dark, except for a single lamp burning at the end of the hallway, but light was leaking out from underneath the lounge door. It was two in the morning; the housekeeper would long since have gone to bed.

Thoughts of the night's earlier events flickered through Irene's mind, and she laid a warning hand on Kai's wrist. The house was currently warded against Fae intrusion (which was going to make matters awkward when they *did* get a Fae colleague). And a cage around the letterbox should have prevented anyone from inserting bombs, globes of poison gas, or giant venomous spiders . . . Short of a twenty-four-hour armed guard, it was difficult to make the place more secure. However, Vale had a key. Logically it would be him and nobody else.

Yet something made Irene uncertain. Something was . . . off balance.

Whoever it was in the main room would have heard them entering the house too. There was no point in trying to hide.

She opened the lounge door and froze in the doorway. A man was occupying the sofa, and several reference books lay open around him in a detritus of notes and scribblings. The woman, tucked up in the big wingback armchair that Irene herself liked to occupy, was busy doing the *Times* crossword.

"Irene?" Kai asked, his tone sharp.

"Kai," Irene said, her voice rather strangled, "please allow me to introduce my parents."

CHAPTER 2

K ai's reaction was much faster than Irene's. *No doubt because they're my parents*, she reflected sourly. *If it had been his father or mother sitting there, I'm sure he'd still be standing around with his mouth open . . .* He bowed politely, but his eyes were bright with curiosity. "We're honoured to receive you in this household," he said. "I know Irene has been hoping to see you."

"For a while now, actually," Irene said keeping her voice calm but feeling rage focus itself to a needle. "You didn't write."

She sensed Kai stiffening at her tone. She *was* glad to see them here, safe and well. But a month ago they'd been hostages, in danger of their lives, and there hadn't been a single whisper of communication afterwards. She'd sent emails on the Library system—even physical letters when she could.

Didn't it mean anything that she was their daughter and that she cared about them?

Except . . . that might be the problem. A huge unanswered

question lay between them. She'd found out that she was adopted, and she didn't know how much that changed things. Certainly it had left a lot for her to consider.

Her mother unfolded herself from the big armchair in a confusion of skirts and newspapers. "You must be Prince Kai," she said. "I've heard so much about you! Not from Irene, of course, she never writes . . ."

"I've written three times in the last month," Irene cut in.

"Not about Kai here," her mother said. She smiled. Her hair had been blonde when Irene had last seen her, but it had returned to a more natural grey now and was pinned back in a suitably matronly bun. Her dress was dark green, one of Irene's own favourite colours, and her glasses were set with little crystals in the curves of the frame.

But there were tiny wrinkles at the corners of her eyes, in the hollow of her throat; the marks of growing age and weariness. Irene looked at her father, who was carefully setting aside the books he'd been using. He looked unchanged, unchangeable, with badger-streaked hair, wide shoulders, and gentle eyes. But when Irene scrutinised him as if he were a target, rather than as a child looking at her parent, she could see the same traces on him as well. Concern collided with rage and knotted painfully in her chest.

"Kai," she said. "This is my mother, whose chosen name is Raziel. And my father, whose chosen name is Liu Xiang." Not that either name had anything to do with their origin or nation of birth. Librarians were extreme cultural appropriators when it came to names they liked or found thematically resonant. "My parents, please allow me to present Prince Kai, son of Ao Guang, Dragon King of the Eastern Ocean."

She was wondering what to do next, when Kai politely offered to put together some refreshments. The door shut behind him, leaving the three of them alone.

Something in Irene snapped. She threw her arms around her mother, conscious of how fragile she felt. "If you ever," she muttered, "*ever* drop off the radar like that again . . . for heaven's sake at least let me know you're all right."

Her mother smelled of cedar. It had always been one of her favourite scents. Irene could shut her eyes and imagine that no time had passed—except that now she was the taller of the two.

"I *am* here too," her father said with a smile.

Irene hugged him tightly. "Are you both all right? I was told you were hostages at one of the dragon courts, during the peace conference—held to guarantee the negotiators' good behaviour . . ."

"It was the court of the Queen of the Western Lands," her father said. "Terribly nice people, but we were parked at a country house in their equivalent of Texas, with absolutely no books. And a great many apologies for there being no books. They'd been removed in case we tried to use them to escape, no doubt. We had to spend most of our time watching movies instead."

"Or going for healthy walks," Irene's mother grumbled. "I despise healthy walks."

Irene tried to imagine weeks without books, then took a deep breath. "We've only a minute or two before Kai comes back, and I have a question I don't want him to hear."

Her mother settled back down into her chair, shaking out the newspaper again. "Can anyone think of a good word for *double ace*, seven letters, last letter *e*?"

Irene was about to say *ambsace*, when something about the

question penetrated. The newspaper wasn't a distraction for her mother any more; it was a shield. And her mother was trying to distract *her*.

"There isn't time for questions," her father said. "There isn't even time for crosswords. I'm afraid we didn't come for a family catch-up. You're needed at the Library—now, Irene. Coppelia sent us to pass the message on."

Her trained reflexes had Irene immediately calculating how she could reach the Library if she left at once. But something made her hesitate. She had so many questions, and now she was about to lose the chance to ask them. *Again.*

Unless she asked them now.

"Why did Coppelia send *you* to tell me?" she asked. "A junior Librarian could have done the job. Or she could have sent a physical message." The Library had ways of getting word through to its agents—admittedly destructive ways, but Coppelia had used them for emergencies before.

Her mother shrugged. "We volunteered to take her next message to you. We wanted to make sure you were safe and well. And now we know."

Irene felt a deep stab of anger at the airiness of the brush-off, and she was about to snap something suitably withering and distant in response . . . But no, they were both trying to distract her from personal questions, from getting closer to them. Again.

She bit her lip, determined to stay calm. "I need to ask this one question," she said. "Before I go. While you're still here. I *know* I'm adopted . . . You wouldn't have done it if you hadn't wanted me. I accept that. I understand that. I'd just like to know . . . how. How it happened."

"Strange," her mother said, after a long, shocked pause. "You spend thirty years rehearsing the answer to a question, and then when it comes . . ."

". . . all the words are gone," her father finished.

"A few simple, straightforward ones would do," Irene said tartly. "Was I a random selection from a local state orphanage? Did you find me floating down the river in a basket?"

"Trying to make us feel guilty will *not* work, Ray," her mother snapped. It hurt, as always, to hear a childhood pet name used in anger. "Do you want me to say that I hoped this day wouldn't come? Fine. It's true. I hoped you'd never find out. Is that so strange?"

Irene paced a few steps, listening to the crackling of the fire. "This would be easier if you hadn't taught me all your tricks," she said, trying to find the words that would make them understand. "You were the ones who taught me how to divert a question, how to change a subject. How to answer a question with another question. You taught me all of this, and now you're trying to do it to me. I accept that it really would have been easier for all of us if I'd never suspected. But please, Mother, Father . . ." She tasted bitterness, and her eyes stung with a childish urge to cry. "Please understand that now I *do* know, I have to know the truth."

"Do you really?" her father asked. And it was a sincere question. "Would it actually make any difference if I were to tell you that . . . we stole you from a palace and you're actually a princess?"

Irene put aside the image of herself in archetypal dress and coronet. "No," she finally said. "No, it won't really make any difference *what* you tell me. I just want you to *want* to tell me. I'm sorry, that probably doesn't make sense . . ."

"Stop apologising," her mother said. "You're an adult now, Ray. *Irene.* You shouldn't be apologising all the time."

"You forgot to say that we were proud of her," her father noted quietly.

"Oh." Irene's mother looked embarrassed. "Darling, we *are* extremely proud of everything you've done, and we want you to understand that before we leave. You *do* understand that?"

"Um, thank you," Irene said. It was something she'd *always* wanted to hear from them . . . but now that her mother was finally saying it, she couldn't think of any better response. "I'm glad. But you're still not answering my question."

Her father began to speak, then fell silent as Kai opened the door. "I beg your pardon," he said, "but may I borrow Irene for a moment?"

"Of course," her father said, waving her towards the door. "We aren't going anywhere—though Irene probably should . . ."

Irene bit back the urge to ask Kai to leave them for just a moment. But she joined him in the corridor, closing the door behind her.

There was a glint of anger in his dark blue eyes, a flash of dragon-red. "Someone else has entered this house," he said. "Our rooms have been searched."

"Oh, hells," Irene said. She realized what must have happened, and flushed. "Just to check—was it a serious search, or did whoever it was just turn the place over casually?"

"The second," Kai said. He frowned. "But they left *my* belongings alone . . ."

"That would be my parents," Irene admitted, feeling embarrassed as well as angry.

"They searched your *room*? *Why*?"

"Probably not in detail," Irene said, trying to reassure him. "They'd just have wanted to know what I was up to."

Kai looked at her. He opened his mouth, closed it, then tried again. "Irene, we've never talked that much about your parents. Is there something you want to tell me?"

Irene wished there were a corner to retreat into. "I have a complicated relationship with my parents. It's a good relationship, but . . ." But now she had to hurry back to the Library—and they'd finally been about to answer her questions about her adoption. Why did everything have to happen at once?

"You hardly ever see them!"

"Yes, that's why it's a good relationship." Somewhere in between her parents wanting to know about everything she did, and her not wanting to tell them, they'd started checking her rooms while she wasn't there. Not her rooms at the Library, of course. Those were locked. Those were *hers*.

Was it that surprising that a daughter of spies had developed trust issues? she thought wryly.

"They do it because they worry about me," she finally said. "And they don't actually search in depth . . . Look, this is sounding worse by the minute. Possibly our relationship does have a few problems. All families have issues. I don't ask about what goes on in your family, do I?"

She saw him recoil as she retaliated, and was meanly satisfied for a moment. "I've been called to the Library," she said, trying to smooth over the bad feeling. "But . . . I need to ask my parents something urgent before I go. Maybe we can discuss this later?"

The door opened before Kai could answer—or disagree—and her father leaned round it. "Is anything the matter?"

"We're just discussing the brandy," Irene said, before Kai could interject.

"There won't be time for brandy," her father said. "The thought is appreciated, but you really need to go, so we'll leave you to it."

Irene couldn't let them get away. "I need to talk to them," she said again. "And I apologise for them intruding like that. Because *they* won't."

"I think we need to have a serious talk about a few things," Kai said, quietly. "Once your parents have left."

Irene re-entered the lounge and shut the door behind her with a thud. "I warded this place," she said. "I thought it was safe from enemies. I did *not* expect to have to defend my privacy from other Librarians."

"If you're sleeping with a dragon prince, then that's something that concerns us," her father said mildly. As always, his surface calm was smooth and firm. An Olympic ice-skating team could have used it as a rink. "I think any parent would be worried about that."

Irene felt the flush creeping into her cheeks again, but this time it was anger as much as embarrassment. "And if Kai mentions to his father that Librarians have been going through his belongings? What then?"

"We left his stuff alone," her mother said. She was shrugging her coat on and doing up the fussy little gilt buttons. "Irene, you are about as communicative as granite underneath a glacier. So far in the last year, you've faced off against Fae, dragon kings, and Alberich himself. You were worried about us. Try to understand that *we* were worried about *you*."

"But *I* wouldn't go through your belongings!" Irene retorted.

"You would if you had the chance," her mother said.

Irene would have liked to deny that, but . . . if it were the only way of making sure they were safe, she wouldn't hesitate. And if it were a choice between their safety and her ethics, her ethics would lose. They might be dysfunctional, but they were still a family.

Even if she had to know more about her origins. "Before you walk out on me—please answer the question this time. How did you adopt me?"

It was her father who answered, his words slow and unwilling. "Other Librarians knew that we wanted a child. We couldn't have one. There was no medical reason . . ."

Alberich had already told Irene it was impossible for two Librarians to have a child, but she wasn't allowing them to get off topic again. So she simply nodded, willing him to continue.

"Another Librarian was pregnant. It wasn't her fault or her choice—we don't know the full details, we didn't ask. She was going to bear a child that she didn't want. She offered the child to us. It was that simple."

"Who was the Librarian?" Irene asked. She stepped forward, her hands clenched around the back of a chair. "Who was she?"

"Nobody you know," her mother said, voice raw. "And I heard that she died since."

Irene felt a distant shock as the facts were laid out. Anger surged in her, rather than grief, at the way this last link to her "true heritage" had been snatched away, if she could call it that . . . for if she'd never known her biological mother, how could she feel genuine grief for her death? And yet shouldn't she feel *something* for her?

She didn't even know if her parents were telling the truth.

"And that's all?" she finally said.

"What do you *want* to hear?" her mother demanded. "Something more romantic? Everyone tried to do the best they could. Do you blame us for it? Were we that bad as parents?"

"No," Irene said. She didn't hesitate. "No, you weren't bad parents. You never were." It might have been a lie, for neither she nor they had ever been perfect. But it was what she wanted to say, what she wanted to believe. They were only human, after all.

Slowly her mother lowered her head. "Then do you forgive us?"

Again the words came without thinking. "There's nothing to forgive. You are my parents. That's all there is."

"You need to get going—Coppelia will be waiting." Her father picked up his hat. He paused to give Irene a hug, but it felt more perfunctory than their first embrace, as though the conversation had drawn an invisible line between them. Was it their history as spies making them this emotionally unavailable—and was she in danger of making the same mistakes? "Urgent Library business won't go away just because you have personal issues, Irene. You should know that by now. We should talk later . . ."

"Running off to war like a coward!" The words drifted through Irene's mind, a relic of some long-forgotten film, but she bit them back. "Absolutely," she agreed. "We *should.*"

Her mother looked at them. "Get in touch when you've had time to think things over, Irene. You know how to reach us."

"When you have the leisure for it," Irene said, unable to stop the sarcasm from leaking into her voice. She tried to remember they'd volunteered to see her, to check that she was safe, but it was hard.

"If you want leisure, then you shouldn't have become a Librarian," her mother retorted.

"Fine," Irene muttered, feeling her teenage years surge back on her in an unstoppable tidal wave. Shoulders hunched defensively, she exchanged a brief hug with her mother before dragging the door open. "Just . . . take care."

"And you, Ray darling," her mother said briskly, trotting out into the hallway and heading remorselessly for the front door.

"Ah . . . did I miss something?" Kai enquired.

"Everything," Irene sighed, repressing the urge to snap. "Kai, I'm really not good company at the moment, and I have to go. I'll be back as soon as I can."

For a moment he looked as though he was about to object, but instead he hugged her. "I'll be here when you get back," he said.

CHAPTER 3

As usual, the Library was haunted by the susurration of night-owl Librarians going about their work. The vast weight of books overhanging Irene rose above her until the ceiling was lost in darkness. A few Librarians were sorting books, high up on the steel steps that criss-crossed the shelves like complicated filigree. Irene could hear their shoes ticking against the metal, and the occasional thud of books being shelved. The sound was oddly soothing.

She hurried along the walkway beneath the rows of shelving, conscious of time passing by. Normally she would have expected Coppelia to issue a transfer shift request, which would allow Irene to travel near instantaneously across the Library to Coppelia's office. Especially as this was *supposed* to be urgent. But apparently it wasn't urgent enough to justify the energy expenditure, and instead she was left to make her own way. At what was now three—

no, four o'clock in the morning. *And* Coppelia's office had apparently shifted to a position deeper within the Library, which meant a longer walk.

The only upside was that it gave her time to calm down after meeting her parents. And it also gave her a chance to consider the assassination attempt against Kai. She and Kai desperately needed a Fae counterpart on the treaty commission. Someone who could keep the Fae in check—if that was even possible.

She turned left and sped through a tunnel. Here, the walls were lined with books in Russian stacked two copies deep, their gilt titles flashing as lamps above swayed in the draught of her passage. Irene noted them as she would note any nearby book—*Prisoners of Asteroid, A Planet for Tyrants, Alisa Selezneva and Her Lens*—but most of her mind was busy.

The longer Fae committees spent trying to find the most politically suitable candidate, the more they were risking the treaty—leaving her and Kai open to rogue Fae threats. And it had been a month now. Perhaps, as Library representative, it was her *duty* to report the vacillating committees to their leaders. If the Cardinal and the Princess, among others, wanted this treaty to last, then they needed to do *their* bit.

And she'd saved Lord Silver's party, which meant that he owed her a favour too . . .

She turned right three more times, climbed a set of steps so high and narrow as to be practically a ladder, and ducked through a pair of rapidly revolving doors. Finally, she reached Coppelia's office.

Strictly speaking, there was neither day nor night in the Library. While the windows in some rooms looked out on an outside world, there was no logic to the time of day beyond the glass panes. Sometimes a Librarian might go from one room to another and find that the view had changed from a stormy mountainside to a sunlit landscape. Or they might see a cityscape under a cloudy night sky, with a foreboding moon beyond.

However, owing to the necessity of actually *communicating* with each other, many of the Library's inhabitants woke and slept at roughly similar hours. And while one could certainly stay up all night researching like the Librarians she'd just passed, studying, or simply reading, this didn't absolve them from the next day's work.

Only senior Librarians were able to set their own hours. Or sleep in. So even though it was the middle of the Library's "night," Coppelia, Irene's mentor, was still awake. She was wrapped in one of her favourite thick blue velvet robes, like a particularly luxurious nun who was going to do any repenting at a much later date, with a pair of scarves twisted around her throat. And her desk, unusually, was almost clear.

Here in Coppelia's study Irene could finally relax. The night outside the window (for this room looked out onto a city in darkness) was peaceful and quiet. A desk lamp burned between the two of them, illuminating the polished surface of Coppelia's wooden hand and striking gleams of light from the gilded icons on the walls.

"My parents said that it was urgent," she said, breaking the silence. "Though I'm assuming there are degrees of urgency, since you didn't authorise a rapid transit?"

Coppelia coughed and took a sip from her steaming mug. Irene was unable to identify the drink, except to note that it smelled herbal and unpleasant. "Yes," she said. "We have a week, perhaps two, before the world under threat moves into a very dangerous phase indeed. But we can't be sure how long we have—or how long it will take you to get the book needed to stabilize it."

"Is it a straightforward retrieval mission?" *Retrieval* was a much friendlier word than *theft*. Some of Irene's jobs were even legal. Though admittedly not many.

Coppelia took her time before answering, long enough for all Irene's mental alarm bells to go off. "It's a little different from your usual sort of job. In a way, it's taking advantage of the current political climate."

"Dancing round the subject isn't going to make me more enthusiastic about it."

"It's human behaviour. Like being polite to your elders," Coppelia said pointedly.

Irene considered her tutor's words. Carefully, she said, "I apologise if I'm a little touchy at the moment. I've just come from speaking with my parents—and, well, you know that we have some issues."

"Very good. Apology accepted," Coppelia said. "Now where were we? Yes, the new job. You're looking for a copy of the Egyptian text *The Tale of the Shipwrecked Sailor*. It's a Middle Kingdom work, which puts it somewhere between 2000 and 1700 BC. Very roughly. Do you know it?"

"The name's vaguely familiar . . . I think my father probably mentioned it at some point, given his area of expertise." Her father was one of the Library's specialists in hieroglyphs and Egyptian texts, but Irene herself had never really been interested in the language or the literature. "Are you sure I'm the best person for this job?"

"In terms of your scholarly areas of expertise, no," Coppelia said, "but in practical terms, yes. There are a few wrinkles . . ."

Of course there are. "Please go on."

"The version we are seeking is from Gamma-17," Coppelia said.

Irene sat bolt upright in her chair. "That's where I was at school!"

"Yes, that Swiss boarding school with the language specialisation. You've told me about it often enough. For reasons we haven't yet managed to confirm, they've had an extreme swing towards chaos over the last week. We urgently need a copy of that book to restabilise the world."

"My past seems to be coming home to roost," Irene said drily, thinking of her parental visit. "Is *this* the practical reason why I'm getting this job? Because I know the world from personal experience? I'm assuming there isn't already a Librarian-in-Residence."

There hadn't been one when she was in boarding school there, after all. And there were never *enough* Librarians-in-Residence. In fact—and the thought wasn't a comforting one—there weren't enough Librarians, full stop. She'd been told that by someone she'd come to distrust, but Coppelia had confirmed it later. They really *were* that thin on the ground. And they couldn't afford to let it be known. If the Fae or the dragons should suspect that the Library was weak—well, peace was all fine and good, but weak neighbours were an open invitation to exert political pressure. Or worse.

"No," Coppelia said. She coughed again and drank some more of her tea. "That wasn't the reason you were selected. This particular copy of *The Tale of the Shipwrecked Sailor* that we're after is insanely rare, which is why it's so vital in terms of its ability to stabilise the world. There's a chapter in the Gamma-17 version which doesn't occur in any other worlds' editions. But all copies of this version have been lost—except for this one copy that made it off-world. It's possible that with time and effort we might be able to locate another copy on Gamma-17, but we simply don't have time. Our best projections are that in ten days the world will move into the conglomerative stage of chaos—where it will be irreversibly trapped in that state."

Flashes of memory twitched through Irene's mind, like the turning pages of a book. People she'd known when she was a child, and then a teenager—teachers, friends, even enemies—and places she remembered. Worlds swallowed up by chaos became places where stories came true. But the human beings who lived in those worlds might as well be dolls, moving through the steps of those stories. Their personalities became nothing but changing masks to suit the whims of the great Fae who ruled them.

She would *not* let that happen to people she had known and cared about.

"Well, you clearly see an alternative to eternal chaos," she said, her voice brisk and very nearly cheerful. "So what happened to this one copy that went off-world?"

"Nine out of ten for a positive attitude," Coppelia said. "Try to keep it that way. So we're aware of a particular collector who owns this book, which he somehow acquired from Gamma-17. In keeping with the current new world order of peace and negotiation and all that, we—the Library, that is—are giving you clearance to go and negotiate with *him*."

Irene considered what that implied. "It's clearly not someone resident on Gamma-17," she said, "or you wouldn't have said the book was 'lost' on that world. And you've mentioned the treaty, so it's a dragon or a Fae aficionado. And you must think it's *possible* to negotiate with him, or we wouldn't be trying. What's the catch?"

"The Fae in question is eccentric. All powerful Fae are, of course, but this one is even more so than usual."

Irene nodded. The more powerful a Fae was, the more they fell into narrative tropes and stereotypes. It gave them unpredictable abilities—a seducer became nearly irresistible, a manipulator could convince anyone of anything, a gunman could pull off impossible shots. But that also made it nearly impossible for them to perceive reality, except through their own specific archetype. The trick, as she'd learned from experience, was to find out what that archetype *was* and somehow use it against them. "Do I know him?"

"You may have heard of him, but probably not through Library channels. His name is Mr. Nemo."

Irene searched her memory and came up blank. "No, I don't know him," she said. "But any Fae who goes round calling themselves Nemo is probably going to be enigmatic and secretive. Even if they don't own a submarine."

"Correct. Ten out of ten." Coppelia refilled her cup from the samovar on a corner of her desk. "Anyhow, this Mr. Nemo is a . . . collector. A billionaire. The sort of person who has their own Caribbean island and fills it with illegally obtained treasures. Who throws around the sort of money that makes governments forget he even exists, causing them to wipe his criminal records clean. Except there aren't any criminal records, because Mr. Nemo never existed, and anyone who looks too closely at the evidence—which also doesn't exist—will be feeding the fishes. He favours piranhas, I'm told, or sharks. It depends on the climate."

"Interesting. I can see how that persona might work inside a given world, if he's tied in with organised crime. But if he's a Fae, how does all that translate into influence among his own kind?"

"He's a fixer," Coppelia said. "That is the current term, isn't it? He can put person A in touch with person B, and takes a commission from both of them in the process. He's not a manipulator like the Cardinal . . ." She tactfully ignored Irene's grimace. "But, as they say, he *knows people*. And he collects things. And people too. He's also been carefully staying unaligned for several centuries now."

"And among other things, he obtained this book," Irene said. "How did we find out?"

"My dear Irene, there are two sorts of collectors. One is satisfied by simply owning the treasured item and doesn't care whether or not the rest of the world knows. But the other sort—they absolutely *have* to brag about their possessions. For them, half the pleasure comes from the thought of acquaintances gnawing their guts out with envy. Even if it increases the risk of theft, they can't help themselves."

"I suppose we do make the ideal audience too," Irene said. "So did he brag to a Librarian?"

"Not precisely." Coppelia slid open a desk drawer, her wooden fingers clicking on the handle, and pulled out a thick pamphlet. "He sent us a catalogue of part of his collection."

"Ooh," Irene said with appreciation, extending her hand for it hopefully.

Coppelia rapped her knuckles with the closed pamphlet. "Not so fast. I know it's late at night for you, but think it through first."

Irene pulled her fingers back, considering. "Does he *want* his collection stolen for some reason? Or is this a convenient lure for

Librarians—a baited hook with a net at his end?" She frowned. "Or is it a shopping list specifically aimed at us? Because he really, *really* wants to have the Library in his little black book of contacts . . . and he's willing to wait until we can't find a particular text any other way than by coming to him?"

"Partly the second, but mostly the third," Coppelia said. "That's why we don't let junior Librarians know about his collection— they'd get *ideas*."

"And have we never dealt with him before?"

"A few times," Coppelia admitted. "At very senior levels, and on a very specific quid pro quo basis. No open-ended bargains. It was felt that if we never, *ever* made any deals with him, he'd realize that he had us over a barrel if we finally showed up. Better to have him think that he's one of our many resources—rather than an abso- lute last-ditch option, with the prices that go with it."

"Right," Irene said thoughtfully. "So item one on the list of things not to mention is how much we want *The Tale of the Ship- wrecked Sailor*. As far as Mr. Nemo's concerned, it's just another item on a semi-regular shopping list from us?"

"Exactly. And item two on the list is that you never make any *open-ended* promises. Our deals have always consisted of a book— or an item of art—for a book. Or very occasionally, a service, spec- ified and defined with fixed end conditions. *Don't* let him talk you into anything else." Coppelia folded her hands—on top of the pamphlet, Irene noted regretfully. "Given your new position as treaty monitor, he may even think that this is our way of introduc- ing you to him."

"Just how much *can* I promise him?" Irene asked. "What if he wants a particular book and we only have a single copy here?"

"That's the nice thing," Coppelia said cheerfully. "For the Library's purposes, we only ever need the actual *story* that's in a book. We don't need the original text. If Mr. Nemo does want something from our collection, then we can keep a copy and give him the original."

"I don't suppose we could offer him a cheaper deal, where we just receive a copy of our target manuscript," Irene suggested, "and he keeps the original?"

"If he'll accept that, go for it," Coppelia said. "But I suspect he won't. He's going to want to wring the maximum value out of it."

"I was afraid of that. Oh well." Irene mentally resigned herself to painful negotiations. "In that case, you just need to tell me where to find him."

"The world is Alpha-92 and the local period is the nineteen-eighties. The Library entrance to the world is in Rome, so you'll have a bit of travelling to reach his home. Lair. Private Caribbean island. Whatever you want to call it. I've put together a pack with information and a letter of introduction. The usual."

The words *private Caribbean island* danced in Irene's head. Of course this was an incredibly important mission, vital to the survival of a world she loved, and important to the Library . . . but it was also an excuse to get away from London in winter. A cold, miserable, wet winter.

Another thought struck her. "How high-chaos is Alpha-92, and will it be an issue if Kai comes too? You know that he's going to want to. And it would make the whole 'diplomatic introduction' excuse more plausible."

"It's just about the same chaos level as Vale's world. And

Kai . . ." Coppelia frowned. "I know I don't need to warn you about this, but make sure that *he* doesn't sign any deals either. I'm sure Mr. Nemo would be only too delighted to entangle him in his web."

"A very dramatic way of putting it," Irene noted.

Coppelia laughed, a wheezy cackle that dissolved into coughing. She drank more of her tisane, mouth twisting in a grimace. "This stuff is disgusting."

"Are you all right?" Irene asked. She knew from experience just how much Coppelia disliked being reminded of age or frailty, but the older Librarian had never coughed this much in the past.

"I still haven't got over winter in Paris," Coppelia said, her voice creaky. "All that damn snow. Don't worry about me, Irene. It just takes longer to bounce back when you're older. I'm not going anywhere. You, on the other hand, are off to the Caribbean." She slid a folder across the desk to Irene. "Any final questions?"

"If we know he has it, couldn't we just steal it?" Irene asked bluntly.

"Theoretically yes, but in practice probably no. His security is very, very good. And if you did try to steal it and failed, he'd raise the price."

"Fair enough. I do have one last question—has he signed up to the treaty?"

"I don't think he's even acknowledged it exists yet," Coppelia said. "He's in an interesting position. If he does agree to abide by it, it'll restrict some of his actions. But at the same time, if he doesn't acknowledge it, then he's open to attacks by either side . . . Be careful. Be diplomatic. Try not to blow anything up."

"Your trust in me is a constant comfort," Irene muttered. But she knew it was the closest Coppelia would come to expressing outright concern. "I'll be as quick as possible. Keep drinking that tea."

And if she was *really* lucky, perhaps Kai would be so intrigued by this assignment that he would forget all about her parents— and that *talk* he'd requested. Then she could get some sleep. Tomorrow was going to be a very busy day.

CHAPTER 4

Kai was positively bounding with enthusiasm in the thin morning light as it filtered through the fog. He had reacted to Irene's news about the world where she'd gone to school with genuine sympathy. However, he was clearly excited at the thought of high-level negotiations—and the possibility of demonstrating to his father just how efficient he could be in his new position. (Irene's attempt to point out that it wasn't strictly a treaty mission had been shot down on the spot.)

In addition, the thought of a private island in the Caribbean had much to recommend it. Couple this with the fact that they'd be getting away from assassination attempts and Lord Silver's machinations for a week or two, and Irene could almost share his high spirits. Several cups of coffee had helped. She'd returned at an ungodly hour in the morning, and there had been all the business of updating Kai before she could sleep.

Well, that and the fact that there were far more interesting things she and Kai could do besides sleeping.

"I'm not sure what the most appropriate garb would be, for this season in the Caribbean," Kai mused as they exited their cab outside the Liechtenstein embassy. Irene had discussed her thoughts on the Fae treaty representative, and he'd agreed to let her fight it out with Lord Silver. "You'll want to dress for your new role as a Library representative, of course."

"We can probably get something in Rome while we're booking our plane tickets," Irene said. Part of her rebelled against wasting valuable time in shopping. But if she showed up on Mr. Nemo's doorstep looking hurried and desperate, his price for the book would go through the roof. Even humans knew how to take advantage of customers who had no other options.

They were stopped at the embassy threshold by Johnson, Silver's personal servant. As usual, he was a study in dullness, almost aggressively bland when compared to his master's flamboyance, and so very good at fading into the background. "How may I assist you?" he asked. His tone was so neutral it could have been used for a demonstration of grammatical *third person, disinterested.*

"We're here to see Lord Silver," Irene said, with a coffee-fuelled attempt at a smile. "And no, we don't have an appointment. I apologise for calling in the morning . . ."

Johnson hesitated. "If you'll wait a moment, madam." He stepped back into the building, closing the door in their faces.

"I'm not sure how our current state of polite truce equates with us being left to wait on the doorstep," Kai muttered.

"Maybe it depends on what gets tipped on our heads from the windows above," Irene speculated. "Full hostilities would be boiling oil, invitation to a party would be a bottle of champagne, and a declaration of minor irritation would be just a pot of tea."

Then the door swung open and they were escorted reluctantly over the threshold.

The interior of the embassy was strewn with debris from the previous night's party. Glasses and dishes still littered the room, licentious pamphlets were scattered across the floor, and stockings dangled from the lampshades. A solitary cravat had been nailed to the wall with a gemmed stiletto, and the remnants of a game of cards were splashed with wine and blood.

When they passed the main staircase, Kai frowned. "Isn't Silver in his bedroom?"

"Not at the moment," Johnson said. "Will you be wishing to see him in his bedroom, sir?"

Kai opened his mouth to say something that would probably have scorched the walls, looked at Irene sidelong, then simply said, "I'd hate to think we'd dragged the poor fellow out of bed for such a very minor thing as our visit."

"Fortunately for you, princeling, I never went to bed." The room they entered was full of feeble morning sunlight, making the furniture and wallpaper look even more expensive and tawdry than usual. Silver was still in last night's dinner wear, sprawled in an armchair, cravat hanging loose and collar open. His jacket lay disconsolately in a corner, and his shirt was stained with lipstick—at least, Irene hoped it was lipstick. He nursed a glass full of a greenish concoction that was probably not herbal tea.

Across the card-table from him sat Sterrington, as upright as a wooden doll, still immaculately dressed and gloved. Scattered across the table between them was an ongoing game of cards. Both players had turned their hands down.

"Gambling, I presume," Kai said repressively. He raised an eyebrow, much as Irene had seen his father do once before. "I suppose I shouldn't be surprised. What are your stakes?"

"The souls of men," Silver said cheerfully. He took a sip from his glass. "Would you like some?"

"It's a little early for me," Irene replied, "and we won't keep you from your game. I called about a business matter. Oh, and to let you know Kai and I will be absent from London for the next few days."

"You can't just waltz off like that!" Silver protested. "What if you're needed here?"

"I haven't been needed so far," Irene pointed out. "And you Fae have yet to choose a representative from your side. That's the business matter."

Silver frowned. "My dear little mouse, do I strike you as some sort of vulgar businessman?"

"You're the Liechtenstein ambassador. You run one of the biggest spy networks in London. You throw parties which tie up half the city's police. All these things keep you very busy."

"True, but those are all the employments of a *gentleman*," Silver scoffed.

"Ah. So you're disclaiming all responsibility for choosing a Fae treaty representative?"

Sterrington stiffened like a hound on point, and Silver set his glass down with an abrupt click. "No, I wouldn't say that. I wouldn't say that at all. Why this sudden pressure, Miss Winters?"

The change in address was a welcome sign that he was taking her seriously. "We all know now that Rudolf was going to assassinate Kai last night. Kai was vulnerable not just because he was attending the party, but because he is the dragon representative.

And sooner or later someone else will take a shot, and they might be better at it than Rudolf. Without an appointed Fae representative on the treaty commission, any Fae may think they can take action against Kai—"

"Or against you," Kai put in.

"Yes, though I hope that there aren't *too* many Fae out there who dislike Librarians on principle."

"You'd be surprised," Sterrington said unhelpfully.

Irene tried not to stare at the ceiling and pray for strength too obviously. "Look, we need a Fae treaty representative as soon as possible. Not just for our sakes, either. You are both involved with the treaty's success. I would like to point out in the strongest terms that if something Fae-inspired happens to me or Kai, it's going to go up in *flames*. And *you* will be held responsible. I understand that there's been some debate about whom to appoint." Partly caused by the fact that Silver didn't want the job himself but was unwilling to relinquish it to anyone else. "When we return, I hope there *will* have been a decision. Without any more disruptions at your parties, Lord Silver."

"I'm still not happy about you vanishing like this," Sterrington said, betraying her own interest. "What if there's an emergency?"

Irene shrugged. "Let's hope there won't be. Besides, when I was given this post, it was *in addition* to my duties as a Librarian. Those duties are calling."

"And Prince Kai?" Sterrington said.

"I'm tagging along," Kai said, his tone cool. "Do you have a problem with that?"

"It might be inconvenient."

"Your convenience is hardly my concern."

Irene glanced sideways at Kai. She'd asked him to be firm but fair, but he was drifting into the territory of deliberate rudeness. But she remembered Sterrington *had* worked for Kai's kidnappers, so she swiftly changed the subject. "I'm not expecting anything urgent to come up in our absence. Are you?"

"Of course not," Sterrington said. But her eyes were dark with thought, and Irene wondered if she'd had other reasons for coming to this London besides stopping Rudolf . . .

"I don't suppose you'd like to tell us where you're going, my dear Irene? And why?" Silver interjected.

"No, I wouldn't. Library business." Irene smiled at Silver, showing teeth. "And since we've fulfilled our obligations—shall we leave, Kai?"

"With pleasure," he replied.

"Perhaps we'll have some good news for you when we get back," Silver called after her. "We are having the most *interesting* discussions . . ."

And that almost made Irene hesitate, in her plan to force Silver to sort out the Fae representative. Leaving those two behind, together, was a little too close to leaving cats in charge of the kitchen while the cook went out shopping.

But her mission couldn't wait. They had a plane to catch. Several planes.

Forty-two?" The customs officer looked Irene up and down. "I've always had people tell me how young I look," Irene said, smiling helpfully. The Library had provided a couple of fake passports for this world; unfortunately the age on the woman's passport was noticeably higher than Irene's own thirty-something.

The officer didn't look entirely satisfied, but there was an impatient queue growing audibly more impatient. With a sigh he stamped Irene's passport and waved her in the direction of Customs.

Kai fell into step beside her. The crowd of people moving through Miami Airport was thick enough to cover up the noise of casual conversation. "It's good to be able to stretch my legs," he said.

"Enjoy it while you can," Irene said gloomily. They joined the crowd by the luggage belt, a jostling mass of padded shoulders and linen jackets, moussed hair and ankle-socks. "I suspect we have more travelling ahead of us. The Library's directions end here— Mr. Nemo wouldn't give them any more information as to his whereabouts."

"This shows a truly ridiculous level of paranoia." Kai plucked Irene's case from the belt with casual strength, then his own a moment later. "If he's really as powerful as his reputation implies, why is this Mr. Nemo so secretive?"

Irene thought about it as they headed for a phone booth—the last instruction she'd been given by Coppelia. The Library's link to this world, Alpha-92, was via the Vatican Library, which meant they'd had to route their trip through Rome. Travelling via the Library was a wonderful thing—but it only had one fixed exit to any given world. "Maybe it helps build Nemo's reputation. If he were *easy* to reach, he'd be less sought after. Like designer clothing. It's the mystique that counts, even if you could get a good imitation at a tenth of the price."

"Well, he is Fae," Kai said. "And don't look at me like that, Irene. I *will* control my tongue in his presence. But if he has agents already watching us, then we might as well give up now."

They reached the booth. "Stand guard, please," she requested, and lined up a row of change on the top of the phone. This might be a long call.

She dialled a number—one she'd memorised from the list of instructions in the Library folder—and the phone was picked up after a single ring. "Who is this?" a voice demanded.

"A person seeking an expensive item," Irene replied.

"Can you give me any identification?"

"I speak for my organisation, and our nominated phrase is, *I could be bounded in a nutshell and count myself a king of infinite space, were it not that I have bad dreams.*" She wondered who'd chosen the *Hamlet* quotation: the Library or Mr. Nemo?

There was a pause, then the sound of tapping keys and faint murmurs. Irene fed more change into the phone. Finally the voice said, "And your own name?"

"Irene. Often known as Irene Winters."

More murmuring. "And the item you require?"

"I would rather not discuss that over an open line."

"Very good." The voice didn't sound as if it had actually expected her to give details. "Where are you currently?"

"Miami Airport, with one other person."

"Another Librarian?"

"No. A dragon. Prince Kai, son of Ao Guang, King of the Eastern Ocean."

Another pause. "*Very* good. Please hold."

Irene fed more money into the phone as she waited.

"How's it going?" Kai murmured over his shoulder. He was watching the ebb and swell of the airport crowd, casual in his new designer jacket and linen trousers. Unfortunately the nineteen-eighties in this world didn't have cheap mobile phones and laptops—but they did at least have Armani.

"All right, I think," Irene said. "So far."

The voice spoke again. "Do you have a pen and paper?"

Irene bit back a sigh of relief and propped her notepad against the wall. "Yes."

"Take the next available plane to Paradise Island in the Bahamas—that'll be the ten thirty on Paradise Island Airlines. Two seats are being held for you under the names Rosencrantz and Guildenstern. When you've arrived, go to the transport desk at the right of the entrance and say you need transport to the Golden House. You'll need to identify yourself again too—when you're asked why you're there, say it's for the shark-fishing. From there, transport will be arranged to your final destination. Have you got that?"

Irene repeated the instructions.

"We'll be seeing you soon, Miss Winters."

The line went dead.

Irene hung the receiver back up and turned to Kai. "We're in the hands of experts," she said drily. "Let's hope we can trust them."

It was late night as the small plane descended towards Paradise Island. Irene peered out of the window but was disappointed to see a well-lit but fairly standard casino and resort, rather than anything more Amazonian. Bridges below spanned the ocean, linking Paradise Island to Nassau, their lights strung across the dark waters like jewels. Beside her, in the aisle seat, Kai leafed thoughtfully through a tourist brochure.

It had only taken a few minutes on the plane to identify half a dozen men and women who were carrying guns, who were distinctive enough to be Fae, or who were just plain suspicious. Other visitors for Mr. Nemo? A convention of some sort? There was the woman with the black veil, furs, and sharpened fingernails, each nail varnished and gleaming. Another man wore formal dinner wear, and his only luggage was a pack of cards, which he dealt out and reshuffled in irritating repetition on his drop-down table. One elderly individual in first class was so withered and wrapped in coats that their gender was impossible to distinguish. But they were sipping brandy as though Prohibition would be redeclared tomorrow.

Conversation died when the plane began to descend. But it didn't lessen the feeling of danger on the plane, a raw edge that had certain individuals watching their fellow passengers. Perhaps they knew something Irene didn't and were planning counter-measures for when something—anything—happened. She and Kai weren't immune from this observation. In fact, they might be the most dangerous people there.

Hindsight had also pointed out one possible mistake. While she herself was not particularly distinctive, Kai was quite visibly a dragon to anyone who knew how to look. His features went be-yond handsome and into beautiful, capturing the perfection of an ink-drawing or a marble statue that had stepped down into life. If you could look into a human's face and see the spirit behind their eyes like a candle-flame, then by comparison a dragon was an elec-tric light or a raging conflagration. And that was only their human form. If anyone on the plane had a problem with dragons, then Kai might be a target.

However, as the plane's wheels bumped against the tarmac, she knew she had to focus on her mission. She only had nine days now. That might not be enough. And as she stepped off the plane, she knew that she'd underrated the danger of their companions. The passengers eyed each other like wolves waiting for a moment of weakness. The air was balmy and the distant sound of music echoed across the landing field, but tension sang in the air, twisting tighter with every passing moment.

Something very bad is going on, she thought. *And I don't even know what it is. How embarrassing if we end up getting shot because of someone else's drama* . . .

A man whom Irene had tentatively pegged as yakuza—the tattoos showing at his wrists, the line of the gun under his jacket, the Japanese he'd been speaking to his female companion—politely gestured Irene to go ahead. Irene smiled at him and his partner (who was camouflaging a katana in an apparently innocent golf club bag) and walked on through, past Customs and into the entrance hall.

At this time of night, there weren't that many people around, but those who *were* there were . . . lurking. There was no other word for it. They lounged on benches, apparently scrutinising books or checking their watches, but their attention was all on the new arrivals.

With a surge of relief, Irene realized that the lurkers weren't just watching her and Kai—they were eyeing all the newcomers. It was as if they knew that there was someone suspicious on the flight but didn't know their identity. In which case, this would be the wrong moment to panic and make a run for it.

She caught Kai's eye and did her best to communicate, *Act normally,* as she pulled her case over to the transport desk at the right of the entrance.

The young woman sitting there put down her magazine and looked up. "Can I help you?" she asked, her tone bored.

"I think so," Irene said. She kept her voice at a low, conversational pitch, hoping that it wouldn't carry. "I need transport to the Golden House for two."

But her precautions were in vain. As soon as Mr. Nemo's directions were out of her mouth, she heard from behind her, "Make that for three."

Irene turned round to look into the barrel of a gun.

CHAPTER 5

Irene tried to focus on the face of the man holding the gun, rather than on the gun itself. Though to be fair, it was always difficult in this sort of situation to move one's eyes from the dark circle of the barrel. He hadn't been on the plane with them. A cigarette dangled from the corner of the man's mouth. And while his clothing was expensive—silk jacket, linen slacks, a Rolex gleaming heavily on his wrist—his sunglasses were cheap and tacky.

However, the gun was the important thing.

"I beg your pardon?" she said, trying—and failing—to sound innocent.

"Me. You. Headed for Golden House," the man said. His cigarette jerked as he spoke. "And if anyone else gets any smart ideas about coming along—"

There was the chuff of a silenced gunshot. Irene couldn't tell what direction it had come from, but the gunman abruptly tumbled forward, his pistol clattering against the floor. She stepped back fastidiously as blood began to spread from the fallen body.

For a moment the room was absolutely silent.

And then figures in black came screaming down from the ceiling, dangling on uncoiling ropes. Their blades gleamed as they unsheathed them mid-drop.

A fusillade of gunfire rattled through the room as innocent-seeming tourist after innocent-seeming tourist pulled out revolvers and automatics—blasting away at the ninjas and each other. Others drew blades—swords, daggers, and even, to Irene's overtaxed eyes, a metal-edged lasso. They retreated into corners to defend themselves or took advantage of the situation to stab potential opponents from behind. The very few people who were *genuinely* innocent tourists ran screaming for the exits.

Kai caught Irene up in his arms and leapt across the information desk, dropping behind it. Irene found herself shoulder to shoulder with the receptionist. There was just about enough cover for all of them if they crammed in tight.

Irene grabbed the girl's arm. "What the *hell* is going on?" she demanded.

The girl rolled her eyes as if that was the stupidest question since *Is water wet?* with a side option on *Is fire hot?* "Don't ask me, miss, I just do the travel bookings."

Right. And you're displaying an astonishing lack of panic. If you're not working for Mr. Nemo directly, then you know someone who is. Irene pulled her instructions to mind. "We need transport to the Golden House, as I said. We're here for the shark-fishing. The names are Rosencrantz and Guildenstern." She winced and ducked farther down, as what sounded like a machine pistol stitched a row of holes in the wall above their heads. "Will that be enough?"

"That'll be fine," the girl said cheerfully. Her clothing was standard travel agent gear, but her earrings and necklace were—to Irene's estimation—solid gold and genuine pearls. The sort of jewellery that cost far more than a desk clerk's salary. *Definitely on someone's payroll.* "You'll need to go back out to where the planes are, look for the small seaplane down the end with the green banding, and speak to the pilot. He'll ask you—"

Her words were drowned out for a moment by a furious shriek.

"Tourists," the girl muttered. "He'll ask you where you want to go, you tell him Denmark, then you get on board and do what he says. You got that? And this lot won't kill you—until they've tortured you for those directions, that is."

"This is ridiculous," Kai snapped.

Irene agreed but decided to complain about it later. "Got it," she said. "Will you be all right?"

"Nice of you to ask, but don't worry. There's a trap-door under here." The girl tapped the floor. "We get this sort of thing a lot, though I have to say this is worse than usual. Good luck catching your plane!"

The trap-door opened with a click, and the girl slid through it like an eel, vanishing into the darkness below. It closed behind her before Irene had managed to do more than think it might be a good idea to follow. She wondered what this crowd wanted with Mr. Nemo, and whether she really wanted to find him herself.

But all she said was, "So, any ideas how we get through that mob?"

"Can you use the Language?"

Irene grimaced. While the Language could affect reality itself, it wasn't always the right tool for the job. "I can't tell them not to perceive us; there are too many of them. Bringing the ceiling down would hit us too. And I could tell the floor to hold their feet, but so many of them have guns, and they don't need to be able to move to shoot."

She checked briefly round the side of the desk: the general brawl had dissolved into individual fights. The weaker participants, and a lot of the ninjas, had fled the scene or died. This was actually an improvement. People focusing on a specific opponent might be less likely to spot her and Kai making a run for it. "If we move along the back wall here, staying behind the check-in desks as much as possible, that gets us to within twenty yards of the customs hall. Have you noticed the suspicious total lack of security guards?"

"Yes. Have you noticed how fresh the paint is on the walls here? And the bullet scars it's covering up?"

"I have *now*," Irene said. "This must be a regular through-point for anyone visiting Mr. Nemo. But is it normal for there to be such a crowd of opportunists? What do they all want?"

Kai coughed. "You know, Irene, usually *you're* the one telling *me* to act, not theorise . . . Besides, we need to go before the chaos level gets any higher."

There was indeed a definite sense of chaos in the air, like the tension before a thunderstorm. And if Irene could perceive it, then Kai—as a dragon, a creature of order—would be feeling it ten times as much. She glanced up to check the rafters, but there weren't any more ninjas—or at least, none she could see. They were ninjas, after all.

"Let's get to it, then," she said. "Leave the suitcases—it's only clothing. On three—one, two, three . . ."

And they bolted sideways, scuttling along with their heads

lowered. Irene clutched her small briefcase, leaving Kai with his hands free. She had no delusions about who was more effective in hand-to-hand combat.

The next check-in desk along had been deserted by its occupant, but the lines of a similar trap-door in the floor indicated where they'd gone. A knife whipped through the air above them, embedding itself in the wall.

"Damn," Kai muttered. "Spotted."

"As long as nobody yells, 'Stop them, they're getting away . . .'" Irene answered, before realizing just how *stupid* it had been to say that. Another reason to curse Fae powers: once you were in their vicinity, it was far too easy to fall into stereotypical patterns.

"Stop them!" a female voice shrieked on cue. "They're getting away!"

One of the surviving ninjas came hurtling over the desk, twin knives gleaming in his hands. Kai straightened and, with a fluidity that came from a life of martial arts training, caught the man's ankle and swung him into the wall. As the ninja slid to the floor in a tangle of black-clad limbs, they made a dash for it.

"Madam!" A short blonde man with a finely waxed moustache threw himself into Irene's path. "Name of a little blue ox, you must listen! I require your help to obtain an original icon of St. Cyril—"

Irene whacked him in the face with her briefcase and kept running.

Something—someone—came whizzing in from her left in a whirl of silk scarves and gleaming nails. Kai threw himself forward and intercepted a barehanded strike aimed at Irene's neck. It was the woman from the plane, but now there was blood dripping from her nails, and they glistened with an oily shine that screamed *poison*.

The woman feinted, then lashed out at Kai, and he parried, falling back. "Keep going," he said over his shoulder.

Irene didn't argue; she burst into a run, circling round a pair of barehanded fighters who were busy kicking each other into the nearest desks.

The room was full of screaming—and gunshots echoed from the rafters.

A gunman slid along the floor, blasting away at the other side of the room. Irene hiked up her skirt and vaulted over him before ducking a heavy-set bearded man with grasping hands like hams. He'd somehow lost his shirt in the last ninety seconds and his chest hair was smeared with blood and oil. *Do I want to know? No. I don't want to know.*

She'd nearly made it to the baggage area, when she skidded to a halt. Two women in leather trench coats had staked out the area for their personal duel. Their blades—one a katana, the other a heavy broadsword—were drawn and they eyed each other with the calm of warriors waiting for the perfect moment to strike.

And they were *in her way.*

Then yet another gun poked into her back. At this rate her jacket was going to develop creases. "Hey, dame," a male voice snarled in heavy Brooklyn Gangster, "you wanna make both our lives easier and tell me how to get to Mr. Nemo, or do I have to get nasty?"

Panic helpfully concentrated Irene's mind. **"You perceive that the woman who knows about Mr. Nemo is going that way!"** she said, pointing between the two swordswomen.

The Language took hold of his perceptions and adjusted them. With a snort he pushed Irene aside, stalking up towards the duellists. His shoulders beneath his ill-fitting jacket were as broad as his accent, and the pistol in his hand was a very real thing that would fire very real bullets. The two women both took a step back as he charged between them. Irene sprinted forward, following the big thug's tracks. Once she was past the swordswomen, she put her fingers to her lips and whistled *hard*. She saw Kai's head turn in her direction. He'd know to follow.

The baggage hall was now deserted apart from the man who'd preceded her. Luggage carousels rotated, carrying suitcases round and round in an endless quest for their owners. The noise of combat coming from the entrance hall gave Irene a renewed surge of energy, and she headed for the far door.

"Hold it—right there!" The words alone wouldn't have stopped Irene, but the bullet cracking past her did. She raised her hands and turned to see the thug stalking towards her.

He was such a truly perfect example of the genus *Thug*, species *American thirties gangster*, that he had to be Fae. The slicked-back hair, the double-breasted suit, the fedora, the polished wing-tip shoes—and, of course, the ready gun in his hand. "Now I don't see no one round here who knows a thing," he said, "except for you, lady. So you tell me who you're working for. The Cardinal? The Grail King? The Orisha? The Shogun? Or is it someone else?"

The effect of the Language hadn't worn off yet. That was good. Once he realized that she could affect his mind by talking to him—well, that was the point when people became nervous. Therefore dangerous. Unfortunately, the Language wouldn't stop a bullet mid-air. "Powerful names," she said carefully. "If you think I work for one of them, then you shouldn't get in my way."

"Yeah, yeah." He yawned; gold-capped teeth showed. But his eyes stayed on her, cold and focused. "I'll make a deal. You were with that other guy, right? So you're travelling as a pair. Drop him, take me instead, we both get to see Mr. Nemo. We both win."

"He's not the kind of guy who likes to be told no," Irene said, backing towards the grinding luggage conveyors.

"Neither am I, baby," the thug answered. He took a step towards her. "Now look, I've made you a good offer. Do I need to start shooting a few non-essential bits off you, or should I go to your friend instead?"

He sounded confident enough, but there was an edge of urgency to his words. It was only a matter of time before someone else found her and made their own offer.

She opened her mouth as if to agree, then gasped, looking over his shoulder.

It was one of the oldest tricks in the book, but it had become a cliché because it generally worked. He turned, bringing up his gun.

And Irene dived for cover behind the conveyor belt. **"Luggage, hit that man!"** she shouted in the Language.

She couldn't see with her head down, but the noises were fairly descriptive. When silence fell and she raised her head, there was just a single shoed foot protruding from underneath a heap of suitcases.

Fortunately her own small briefcase, which had been caught up in the Language's effects, was near the top of the pile. She extricated it with a yank, then turned at the sound of footsteps. Kai came skidding through the far doorway. "Over here!" she called.

Then she saw the people a few paces behind him.

There were doors between the baggage area and the exit hall. They were the heavy sort of folding metal doors that were saved for emergencies, activated by computer controls rather than by anything as simple as someone swinging them shut. At the moment they were drawn back and locked in place.

Irene set her jaw. That was about to change.

She braced herself. **"Folding doors between the luggage hall and the exit hall,"** she ordered, **"close and lock!"**

That cost her. It was harder work than changing a single person's perception or throwing suitcases. Grinding metal echoed through the room as the doors strained against their current position, screeching against the floor. They slammed together barely a foot behind Kai, shielding him from a fusillade of blows and gunfire.

Kai wiped a line of blood from his forehead. He'd lost his jacket somewhere in the brawl. "Are you all right?" he demanded.

"I'll do," Irene said, trying to ignore the incipient headache. Really, this was quite a minor use of the Language. It must be the high chaos level getting to her. "But unfortunately I've made it very clear that the Library's involved. Let's hope that doesn't come back to bite us."

Out on the tarmac, there was a row of planes—but only one had a green stripe on it. The fresh air blowing from the sea was a relief after the sweaty atmosphere of the airport interior, and Irene's headache was starting to recede. They ran to the plane, shouting for the pilot; a cockpit window slid open, and an unshaven face peered out. "What are you wanting, love?" His accent was pure London, incongruous in the middle of the Caribbean.

"A ride. For two passengers!" A sudden burst of noise came from the building, suggesting that doors had been broken through and people were about to arrive, and Irene added, "And we need it fast!"

"Where to?"

"Denmark!"

"Just you wait a minute, love, I'll be right with you."

"I'm not sure we have a minute . . ." Irene said, bouncing from foot to foot.

A hatch in the side of the plane creaked open, and a rope ladder spilled out. "Here," another unshaven man said, peering out. "And make it quick."

Irene had learned how to climb rope ladders in gym at school— the other girls had often objected, but she considered it a useful survival skill. Kai swarmed up after her, and the second crew member pulled the rope in, slamming the hatch shut. A few bullets pinged off the outside of the plane. "Better belt yourself in," he recommended, pointing at a row of seats.

Irene dropped into a seat with a sigh of relief, snapping the seat belt closed. While the seaplane was battered-looking, with pieces of cargo lashed into place on the walls and floor of the passenger area, the seats themselves were surprisingly modern—presumably a later addition. She peered out of the window, not sure whether she *wanted* to see what was going on or not.

"Get in here, Jake," the first man yelled from the cockpit.

The shouts from outside receded, drowned out by the noise of propellers as the plane lurched off the ground and clambered into the air.

Kai leaned back in his chair, ignoring his seat belt. "Well," he said. "I'm glad *that's* over."

Irene had to agree. "Though it's depressing that being chased out of an airport by a mob of gangsters, ninjas, and assorted weaponry experts can be classed as standard operating procedure. It says something about the nature of Library fieldwork. Or about the sort of Library fieldwork *we* keep getting."

"They were a very mixed lot." Kai frowned. "That woman with the poisoned nails—no, she didn't scratch me, don't worry—she wasn't bad at all. But some of them were *hopeless* fighters. What could have brought them all together in one place?"

The small plane throbbed with the noise of the propellers and the wind outside. It was oddly soporific, and Irene found herself yawning. "I think they *all* wanted to see Mr. Nemo," she offered.

"But why all at once? Is he normally in such demand?" Kai yawned as well, stretching and then relaxing. "I wonder . . . My uncle Ao Shun would sometimes conduct job interviews like that, in order to thin out the candidates . . ."

But his voice was slowing, blurring. The passenger hold was darker now. Irene couldn't keep her eyes open. "Kai?" she slurred, her voice sounding odd to her own ears.

She slipped into darkness, with sleep swallowing her up like the ocean.

CHAPTER 6

When Irene woke, she found herself laid out like an effigy in a church, her hands folded on her chest. But the softness underneath her was a comfortable bed rather than a cold tombstone, and she could hear another person breathing.

For the moment she kept her eyes closed, so as not to inform anyone she was awake. The other person was asleep or meditating, judging from the slowness of their breaths. They were right next to her too—probably on the same bed. There was a deeper undercurrent of sound in the room, the whisper of an air conditioner. Her shoes were gone and she was barefoot.

All right. So she'd been drugged on the plane. Probably Kai as well. And they were now somewhere else. Somewhere with good air conditioning.

She needed more information than she could get with her eyes shut. Simmering anger pushed out immediate fear. If they'd been abducted and were being held for ransom or sale, she was going to make some very dramatic and valid points about why that was a bad idea.

She sat up, sinking into the deep softness of the bed, and looked around. Kai was indeed fast asleep next to her. He was slumbering so peacefully that he could have been thousands of miles away in his father's court, with nothing to worry about till scurrying servants brought the morning tea. It was a double bed—an interesting assumption by whoever had put them there—and the counterpane was silk. The bedroom beyond was luxurious, with abstract paintings hanging on the walls, expensive-looking rugs strewn across the floor, and French windows facing out onto the open sea beyond. *Closed* French windows. There were two subsidiary doors too. One stood half-open and clearly led into a bathroom, while the other could be . . . more interesting. And was probably locked. A big television screen covered a solid two yards of wall, but for the moment it wasn't on, and there weren't any obvious controls, remote or otherwise.

The crook of Irene's right elbow was aching just enough to make itself felt. She rolled up her jacket sleeve, and as she'd suspected, there was the faint red mark of a hypodermic needle. That made sense. Gas her and Kai while they were belted in their seats, then deliver a more specific sedative once they were unconscious.

She reached across and shook Kai by the shoulder. "Kai, time to wake up."

No reaction.

She shook harder. "Kai, wake up. We've been *kidnapped*."

He groaned something, eyelids flickering open for a second before he relaxed back into his doze.

"Kai! There's been a palace revolution and the peasants are attacking!"

Kai gave a deep shuddering sigh and finally opened his eyes properly. "Execute them all in the public square," he mumbled, clearly still half-asleep.

"Such a pity," a male voice said. "I must apologise. We have very little information about the proper dosage for dragons."

Irene spun towards the source of the voice, her heart slowing as she realized it was coming from the television, which had silently turned itself on. Beside her, Kai shook his head as he tried to throw off the last of his sleep, his eyes clearing.

The man on the screen was seated in front of a glass pane that either fronted some huge indoor aquarium or was somehow set into the sea itself. A shoal of red and silver fish passed behind him, swooping past like a flight of birds—but they didn't distract the eye from the man in the chair. He was heavy-set, with drooping jowls, but his small, keen eyes watched her intensely. His suit was white linen, and he wore a Panama hat tilted sideways on his bald head. A whiskey tumbler and decanter rested on a small table next to him. Irene suspected that he might be powerful enough to present himself in multiple different shapes, as some Fae could, but they would all display the same keynotes of personal overindulgence and wealth. She might never know his real face—just the image that popular culture associated with manipulators and schemers. "Mr. Nemo, I presume," she said neutrally.

"And I know your identities, of course. I trust you will forgive this communication by video link, Your Highness. I do not wish to meet you in person."

"Oh, I have nothing against you," Kai said coldly, "except for the way you have drugged and kidnapped us."

"Yes. I should explain." Mr. Nemo fished out a red silk handkerchief and mopped his forehead. "My situation at the moment is a little awkward. Please believe me when I say that I have *absolutely* no desire to gain you as an enemy—either of you, or the organisations you represent. In fact, I hope you will bear in mind how quickly I arranged your visit, as a token of my goodwill."

Irene wished she had some way of knowing whether this speech was sincere, or the sort of fast talk that went with unmissable bargains and items for sale off the back of a lorry, no questions asked. "Why don't you want to meet Kai in person?" she enquired instead.

The ice cubes in Mr. Nemo's glass clinked as he picked it up. "Miss Winters, I don't like people to be able to find me. I'm sure you know just as well as I do that dragons can locate people whom they've met before. I'd rather not give him that ability. Is that acceptable?"

Irene glanced at Kai. "Is it?" she asked. She *had* to get the book off Mr. Nemo. But if Kai wasn't prepared to tolerate these conditions, then she'd have to do it without his help.

Kai paused. For a moment Irene thought that he was going to say no, but then he shrugged. "While I prefer to meet people face-to-face, your caution is understandable. For the moment I accept your conditions. But I am still waiting for an explanation for our situation."

He had donned his political, courtly persona, and Irene felt a flash of pride that he was able to behave so politely to a Fae. Of course, he was probably daydreaming about dropping Mr. Nemo into the sea from a height of several thousand feet, but that was fair enough. She was having similar thoughts herself.

"Perhaps we could discuss the reasons for your visit first?"

Mr. Nemo suggested. "There might even be a minor discount arranged, for the inconvenience you've been caused."

Kai gestured to Irene. "Miss Winters here is the negotiator. I am simply her escort."

Irene donned her own best poker face. "The Library is interested in obtaining a particular book and I've been sent to open negotiations." She knew she mustn't make her request look too urgent—even if it was. If Mr. Nemo realized just how desperate the situation was, and how far she'd go to get her hands on that book, then he'd charge an unthinkably high price. And she'd have to pay it. There were some people, some places, that she would *not* lose to chaos.

Mr. Nemo's eyes glinted, the only sign of animation on his heavy-fleshed face. "I'm always delighted to oblige the Library. What are you seeking?"

"*The Tale of the Shipwrecked Sailor*, an Egyptian text, Middle Kingdom period," Irene said. "From the world that we classify as Gamma-17. It's in your catalogue."

"Excuse me just a moment." Mr. Nemo turned to his left and an unobtrusive young man stepped forward, offering him a brochure similar to the one that Coppelia had shown Irene.

Mr. Nemo flicked through the pages, frowning slightly, then his mouth widened into a smile. It wasn't an encouraging smile— or rather, it wasn't encouraging if one hoped to negotiate a good deal. It was the sort of expression that went with the poetic tag, *And welcomes little fishes in, With gently smiling jaws*. "Ah," he said. "That one. May I congratulate you on your excellent taste?"

"You're far too kind," Irene said guardedly. So far this hadn't gone beyond the normal boundaries of bargaining. In fact, it was refreshingly familiar. She warned herself to be careful. "Have you read it yourself?"

"I'm afraid not. I really don't have time for that sort of thing. I find it far more interesting to negotiate prices for them."

Irene felt herself judging him for his slight to her beloved books. But she reminded herself that he was Fae and that his archetype as a fixer would be shaping his personal tastes and hobbies—along with the rest of his life. Why would he care about a single story, even if it was unique? "While I don't wish to seem rude, the whole kidnapping and drugging business *has* cut into my schedule. If we could discuss the price?"

"I'm sure that a well-known and well-respected Librarian like yourself has a great many resources," Mr. Nemo suggested. "I'd be glad to sign a contract for some future services or assistance on your part, to be specified at a later date . . ."

"While that does sound very tempting," Irene lied, "I've been given specific instructions to only engage in quid pro quo bargains—an object for an object, or an object for a specifically defined service. In fact, I've been told that all previous bargains by the Library were made strictly on that basis."

Mr. Nemo chuckled. "Ah well, you can't blame a man for trying."

"I wouldn't expect any less from a businessman like yourself," Irene flattered.

"I hope you'll understand that I can't give you an immediate answer," Mr. Nemo continued. "I need to consider what the Library could give me."

"Of course," Irene said. She suppressed her disappointment. This was never going to be resolved in two minutes of conversation, she reminded herself. But she was so *close* . . .

"And I'm certainly not going to ask you to stay shut up in that suite while I'm reviewing my collection for possible gaps. It could take a few hours," Mr. Nemo said affably. "Do take a stroll! Look at my aquariums!" He gestured at the wall of glass behind him, where an octopus waved distant tentacles, as if in wiggly semaphore warning. "Have a snack. My servants will be glad to bring you any food or drink you'd like. Take a swim, even! I have some excellent indoor pools. I understand that you had to leave your luggage behind at the airport, so please feel free to use the wardrobes that I've supplied. I guarantee absolutely no obligation on your part. Call it some small compensation for the inconvenience that you suffered earlier."

"Yes, about that . . . you did say that you were going to explain."

"I'm hosting a small dinner party tonight," Mr. Nemo said. "A very exclusive one. Unfortunately word's got out, and a great many people want to invite themselves . . . You must understand, I'm sure. We have similar problems in that respect. There are many who'd try to access the Library, if they thought they had the slightest chance of succeeding." His gaze moved to Kai, though he had the tact not to say, *Even dragons.* "My usual arrangements for guests have been somewhat compromised, so I'm having to take more precautions than usual."

"I see." Irene was sure that there was more to it than that, but Mr. Nemo seemed in no mood to share. "Oh, there is one more thing . . ."

"Yes?"

"I hope this suite you've arranged isn't being monitored." She waved vaguely at the walls and the microphones almost certainly hidden behind them. "I wouldn't want to destroy your property while insisting on our right to privacy."

Mr. Nemo pursed his lips. "But imagine my feelings if you had a heart attack and were unable to call for help . . . Any supervision is purely for the *benefit* of my guests. If you really want a private conversation, there are plenty of places on my island where you can have one."

Irene suppressed an image of dolphins with microphones, swimming closer to aquarium windows to pick up conversations. "I'm afraid this is non-negotiable," she said. "The alternative is that I use my abilities to destroy your monitoring systems—wherever I go here."

"Oh, very well." He sighed. "I give you my word that the suite you are currently occupying will *not* be monitored. I reserve the right to openly communicate with you while you're in there—as we're doing now."

Irene knew that Fae promises were binding but that he'd stick to the letter of the promise rather than the spirit. Which meant that everywhere *else* on this island *was* probably monitored. But it was better than nothing. "I appreciate your generosity," she said.

"Excellent. And I'll hope to have an answer for you soon. Possibly even before supper."

"Surely not that long . . ." Irene started. Then she realized, with a cold uncertainty, that she wasn't sure what time of day it was, or how long she and Kai had been asleep. All she knew was that the sun was shining outside. She glanced at the watch on her wrist; it was half past three in the afternoon. They'd lost most of a day.

"Oh, I dine early," Mr. Nemo said. "Any further questions? Are *you* looking for something from me, Prince Kai?"

"I am not," Kai said, in the most austerely icy tone Irene had ever heard him use.

"Of course, of course. Very proper. And you, Miss Winters?"

"I'm sure I'll think of half a dozen requests once we've finished this conversation," Irene admitted, "but I have nothing right now."

"Very good. There's a phone by the bed if you need anything brought to your rooms. I'll see you later."

He raised his glass in a salute, and the screen dissolved into darkness.

"Well." Irene took a deep breath. "This is probably the only place on the entire island where we can talk freely. Do you have any idea where we are?"

"Give me a moment." A flickering pattern of scales washed across Kai's skin, like frost-ferns or fractal images, then dissolved again. For a moment Irene thought she could smell the sea inside the room, even with the air conditioning on and the windows closed. "We are still within the same waters we were in yesterday. The same chain of islands, I think, the same ocean that washes them. Other than that . . . no. Sorry."

Irene shrugged. "It was worth a try. Don't worry. I don't think it makes much difference that we don't know where we are."

Kai's eyebrows rose. "That's a reason not to worry?"

"I'm not saying that our situation is exactly *good*." Irene swung her legs round and stood up, testing her balance. "After all, we're in the territory of a powerful Fae, we don't know exactly where we are, we've lost our luggage, anything that we say outside this room is probably going to be overheard—and we're on a deadline."

Kai lay back and folded his arms behind his head. "I do enjoy it when you get optimistically fatalistic," he said. "So what do you see as the good points?"

"Well, this place isn't *too* high-chaos, or I'd be sensing it more and you'd be complaining." She waited for a nod from Kai before she continued. "And let's be reasonable in our threat assessment:

while this is a gilded cage, we *can* escape from it. From that balcony out there, or maybe this island's beaches: I imagine you could take dragon form and leave that way."

"I'd need to be sufficiently far away from the centre of this island," Kai said thoughtfully. "Here in the middle of it, I'm not sure I could assume my proper form. It may not be *very* high-chaos . . . but it is high-chaos."

"But Mr. Nemo doesn't necessarily know that," Irene pointed out.

Weighing up the situation helped her calm her nerves. Her stomach wanted to tie itself into knots with urgency—she felt she should be getting hold of the book *now*, or the world where she'd been to school might be lost past saving—even if common sense told her that she had at least a week. And Mr. Nemo was never going to hand the book over on the spot. However, she still didn't like being at anyone's mercy, least of all someone who might trade in people and promises just as often as he traded in items.

"He's interested in what we can offer too—which might keep us safe," she added. "And he knows we're under the protection of the Library."

"Well, he knows *you* are," Kai interjected. "I just tagged along."

"But you're a political figure now," Irene said, trying to reclaim the point she'd been making. "You're formally accompanying me. And . . ."

"Yes?"

"What do you want to bet that dragons have dealt with him in the past?"

"Considering the protocols he's put in place for not meeting me in person, I'd say it's almost certain." Kai's tone was resigned rather than offended.

Irene nodded. "All good points. As someone once said, 'After being struck on the head with an axe, it is a positive pleasure to be beaten about the body with a wooden club.'"

"That doesn't sound like Confucius."

"No, I think it's actually Kai Lung. Come on. Let's get cleaned up and go for a stroll."

The corridors outside were currently empty. There were no people. There was no dust. There *were* tactfully unobtrusive monitoring cameras, and occasional television screens set into the wall. But apart from that they were alone in a maze that combined the motifs of *expensive hotel* and *secret villain base*. The place didn't feel deserted or barren, but Irene felt like an ant walking through it, a prisoner in someone's vivarium.

There were stairs up. There were stairs down. There were glass doorways—closed and impenetrable—looking out onto the beaches outside. There were a lot of aquariums. After an hour of wandering round and failing to get her bearings, Irene found the fish a welcome distraction, even if they weren't a useful landmark.

As they came to the latest set of locked French windows, looking out on a beach view, she turned to Kai. "Why do you think we aren't being allowed to go outside? To make sure you can't identify the location?"

"Without a doubt," Kai agreed. He looked out at the sea beyond, his eyes yearning. "There's nothing like the living water. That time in Venice, the water was polluted by chaos. And in Vale's world, it's polluted by . . . well, pollutants. But here I'm sure it would be better. Mr. Nemo couldn't taint the entire ocean. It would wake me from a thousand years of sleep to have the water touch my skin."

"I wish I could appreciate it the way you do." There were no planes visible in the sky, no boats on the water: as far as Irene could tell, they could be anywhere in the entire Caribbean, in any world. But to dragons, she knew, it was different. Especially to one whose element was water, and who could command it to obey his will. "But I'm glad that there might be something you could enjoy. I feel a bit guilty about having brought you here."

He gave her a sidelong glance. "I thought that we'd agreed that we were equals now. You didn't order me to come."

"No," Irene admitted. "But you're only here because I am." That wouldn't count as "intelligence" to anyone who knew who they were. But they both automatically glanced around for hidden cameras.

"Let's talk about something non-sensitive . . ." Kai said. A school of fish flashed through an aquarium at the end of the corridor, their long, draping fins like fireworks in shades of orange and blue. They wandered closer to watch. "Tell me about your schooldays."

Irene suppressed her immediate reaction to bristle. That was so unfair. She'd never—well, hardly ever—asked him about *his* past. About his father. About why he'd been living with his uncle instead. About his mysterious "low-born" mother. About anything particularly personal—unless there was no other choice. "Must we?" she said drily.

"I thought friendships were supposed to be built on honesty," Kai said, a little plaintively.

"Maybe," Irene conceded, "but not necessarily full disclosure."

He shrugged. "I assumed it was just, well, school."

Irene reflected for a moment on how sensitive his question really was, in the light of their mission to save that world. After all, everything they said could be overheard. And this was a chapter of her life that she had never really discussed with other Librarians either. The fish beyond the glass circled in aimless patterns, and she wondered if they were aware that they were trapped in a glass tank, or if they assumed that there were always walls and that was simply how life *was*. "Kai," she said. "I will try to be honest with you."

About some things, at least, she thought.

"The problem is that my parents are—were—very good Librarians, which means that they were excellent spies and thieves, and they brought me up to be like them. They needed to have absolute control of information, because of their training too. They had that need to know *everything* that was going on around them, in case it could be a danger. They were constantly on their guard. Always watching. Always studying. Always working, because that's what they *were*. And they were absolutely certain that whatever they did was for the best reasons—and that those reasons justified anything at all."

Kai was silent, listening to her, but she knew he understood she was also describing herself at her worst. She couldn't entirely blame her parents if she was just as careful, just as paranoid . . . even if she'd learned it from them.

Irene swallowed. Her throat was dry. "When they sent me to boarding school, at first I was furious. I wasn't *good* enough to go with them! I had a whole lot of complicated feelings, which didn't make me a very pleasant little girl. But the school was good for me. Living full-time with people who weren't Librarians—who didn't revel in secrecy and have a need to control everything around them . . . It taught me some things which aren't in the Library code of conduct."

She remembered something Melusine had said, a detail from Irene's permanent record: *You were educated at boarding school due to parents having growing problems with your behaviour.* Had living together with her been as difficult for her parents as it had been for her?

"So, now you know." She made herself look at him. "That school gave me something I badly needed. Which is why . . ." *Which is why I'll do whatever's necessary to save it.* "I sometimes find it difficult to talk about it."

Before Kai could respond, there was a call from farther down the corridor. And Irene would have sworn there hadn't been a door there a moment ago. A woman in a floral bikini was waving at them. "Honoured guests! Mr. Nemo requests that you attend for drinks and dinner."

CHAPTER 7

Their guide led them on a new route through the maze of passages. Irene wasn't sure whether to ascribe her own difficulty in navigating them to Fae magic, secret behind-the-scenes shifting of panels, or the fact that the twisting, turning corridors all looked alike. The woman padded along barefoot, her floral bikini and curling hair incongruous against the futuristic dark metal walls and polished flooring.

Irene and Kai had been allowed time to change their clothing first: their escort, as yet unnamed, had made it clear that it was Mr. Nemo's wish. Irene had been ready to comply. But she'd been less enthusiastic when she'd found out that all the evening dresses in the wardrobe—even the halter-neck Versace catsuit—were low-cut and showed the Library brand across her shoulders. While technically she knew that Mr. Nemo knew who and what she was, it still left her feeling uncomfortably exposed.

Which is probably all part of the process, she reflected. *Now what can I do to set Mr. Nemo equally off balance?*

Voices echoed from the room ahead, indistinct but clearly multiple. Irene frowned and raised a hand to stop Kai. Their guide took a few steps, realized she was no longer being followed, and glanced back.

"I wasn't aware that there were going to be so many people at dinner," Irene said quietly. A number of unpleasant possibilities were coming to mind, with the first and foremost being that she and Kai might be candidates for sale or auction.

"Mr. Nemo will explain everything," the woman said. Her face was carefully neutral, but there was a flicker of fear in her eyes. Of Irene and Kai? Or of what Mr. Nemo would do to her if they didn't show up?

"Kai?" Irene queried.

He knew her well enough to understand the question. "An acceptable risk, I think," he said.

"Very well." Irene turned back to their guide. "Lead on."

Visible tension knotted the woman's shoulders as she continued. Irene spared a moment to wonder, *When did I become a threat, rather than just being perceived as the minion or the nonentity? Have things changed that much?*

But she was here, the Library's representative under the new peace treaty, negotiating with a powerful Fae on behalf of the Library—and accompanied by a dragon prince. And the answer her mind came up with was *Yes, they have.*

The door in front of them swung open, and she and Kai walked in.

The first thing that caught her eye was the huge glass wall that made up one side of the room. They were below sea level here, and the giant window looked out into the ocean depths, into a spotlit landscape of seaweed and passing fish. The vista dwarfed the half-dozen people who sat around an oval table, cradling their glasses.

At the head of the table stood a large television set, again displaying Mr. Nemo. He looked exactly as he had done during his earlier conversation with Irene. It was as if the camera had only moved away for a second, even though the previous meeting had been hours ago. "Our last remaining guests," he said. "Welcome to our little get-together. Perhaps I should make introductions?"

"Perhaps you should." The woman who spoke set down her martini glass. Her long blonde hair fell in loose waves over her shoulders with the sort of casual elegance that took either miraculous coincidence or a team of expert hairdressers. She was in an evening dress, like Irene, and her tailored sheath was blue silk that matched her eyes. But she somehow retained a girl-next-door air—not really *trying* to look glamorous but still emphatically succeeding. "I'd thought this gathering was much more . . . exclusive."

"Well, it's not as if Mr. Nemo showed us the guest list." The man who spoke was on the other side of the screen. His dinner suit said *wealthy*, but the line of the jacket suggested a shoulder holster. An old scar seamed the line of his jaw, ivory-pale against his black skin. The artificial light gleamed on the gold ring on his right hand and the cards on the table in front of him. "And there are two chairs unfilled at this table. Isn't that so?"

"Whatever." The sturdy woman next to him was emphatically not in evening dress. A faded denim jacket made her bulky shoulders even wider, and her T-shirt and jeans were battered and stained. Her face was tanned and her dark hair was sun-paled in places to almost the same shade of brown. Someone had broken her axe-blade nose in the past. She slouched in her chair, fidgeting with her glass. "Can we get *on* with this? I didn't come here to sit around and be talked at. If you've got a job for me, then give me the details. If not, then show me the frigging door."

"We have been brought together as a crew, surely," the big man across from her said. His dinner suit didn't fit him. His blonde hair was buzz-cut, and his battered hands looked large enough to strangle bulldogs. He cradled a tiny cocktail glass between his fingers. Irene suspected that he might have been seven feet tall if he'd been standing up; seated, he made everyone else at the table look slightly out of proportion. His accent was Russian or Eastern European—Irene couldn't be sure, especially given how he dealt out his sentences as though he were being charged by the word. "And no doubt, given the different skills around this table, we will be paid large amounts of money to steal . . . *something*. The crew's membership is at the discretion of the boss."

"I'm with Ernst, let's get down to business," the fifth person at the table said. Somehow, even though he was sitting at a table in the centre of a well-lit room, he gave the impression of hunching in a shadowy corner. His hands were manicured and well-kept, long-fingered and precise. His face was harder to see clearly, hidden under a cap of dark hair. However, Irene noted smooth anonymous features and a dark suit that seemed to absorb light. He was sitting next to the man with the playing cards, and there was something in their body language that made Irene think they knew each other.

"And have we no comments from our sixth member?" Mr. Nemo asked.

All eyes turned to the sixth person at the table. Irene felt Kai go tense beside her. For this woman wasn't a Fae like the others. She was a dragon. She was pale-skinned and dark-eyed, with hair so black it went through to the other side of darkness and hit an indigo-midnight shade beyond. It was very long and straight, with some coiled up round her head and some falling to puddle on the floor beside her chair. Her clothing was brutally plain, a vest-top and trousers in white silk. A silver cuff round her right wrist was fastened to the arm of her chair. Like Kai—like all the dragons Irene had ever met—she had a flame-like quality, a *power* to her presence that forced the onlooker to reconsider what beauty was.

"No comment," the dragon said flatly. "Get on with your offer and let me decide whether or not to take it."

Something twitched at the back of Irene's mind. *This situation is familiar, and it's not just because it's a narrative trope and I'm in a Fae's private lair. Something here is being deliberately engineered . . .*

She put the thought aside to consider later and decided to take the initiative.

"My name is Winters—Irene Winters," she said, advancing into the room. "I work for the Library, and I have no idea what's going on either, but I hope our host will explain shortly."

Kai drew out a chair to allow Irene to seat herself. "My name is Kai," he said, taking the remaining place. "I have the honour to be a recognized son of His Majesty Ao Guang, King of the Eastern Ocean. And I am prepared to respect our recent truce—as is Irene Winters. Even if it means that I must sit at table with *that person*." He locked eyes with the other dragon, and they both stared coldly at each other.

"Well, well," Mr. Nemo chuckled, "it looks as if we may have some problems here with our future collaboration."

"Collaboration?" the elegant blonde said. "Are you seriously suggesting that I work with these people?"

"Bets on which people at this table she means," the gambler said. "Evens on the dragons, three to one the Librarian, five to one anyone else."

"Nadia here is the lady who has just expressed her doubts," Mr. Nemo said. "Going around the table, and continuing with everyone's favourite aliases, we have Ernst, Prince Kai, Miss Irene Winters, Tina, Jerome, Felix, and—"

"Indigo," the dragon cut in. "That is the only name I will answer to from the people around this table."

Kai snorted. "At least you show *some* vestige of proper behaviour."

"Big words from someone with *your* father," Indigo spat at him. "I'd think more of you if you boasted about your mother's heritage."

Kai went absolutely still, a red gleam of anger in his eyes. "Don't push me, madam," he said. "Nothing in the truce forbids me from dealing properly with other *dragons*."

"Maybe not," Mr. Nemo said cheerfully, "but as my guests, I hope you'll all refrain from attacking each other. In fact, I must insist on it. Any hostilities or attempts to, ahem, exert *undue* influence will cause me to withdraw your safe-conduct agreements. Are we all happy with that?"

The dead silence around the table was not precisely agreement, but it was probably the best that could be hoped for.

Mr. Nemo clapped his hands together, and the door swung open again. Servants pushed trolleys into the room. "Dinner!" he said. "I do hope nobody has any allergies."

"Only to poison," Irene remarked. She would have liked to reach out to Kai in reassurance, but that would have been a blatant demonstration of weakness. She would have liked even more to get him alone and find out who "Indigo" was, and what precisely was going on there. But that would have to wait till later. In the meantime, if things became any worse she could always kick him under the table.

Nadia put down her glass and pushed back her chair. "Come *on*, people," she said. "Are we really going to continue with this farce? I'm not complaining about Mr. Nemo here—a great man, I've always said so—but how can *we* be expected to work with *them*?" Her hand gesture took in Kai, Irene, and Indigo. With a twitch of her shoulder, her body language shifted from *complaining* to *reasonable*. "I think we should all insist that non-participants get out of this room before the discussion goes any further. Do we really want non-Fae listening in to our private talk? How far can we trust them?"

The Library brand across Irene's shoulders stung as if it had been freshly applied with hot wires, and she frowned, letting her annoyance show. "We'll leave if Mr. Nemo wants us to leave," she said curtly. "After all, we came to see *him*. I have no idea who *you* are." She neglected to mention that two days ago she'd had no idea who Mr. Nemo was either. Why spoil a good line?

Ernst grunted and shifted in his chair like a mountain preparing an avalanche. "Two pretty ladies making speeches. But neither of them's the boss. So don't take it the wrong way if I'm not listening."

Nadia looked around the room for support. When nothing came, she flounced to her feet. "Fine. I'm walking out of here, and if the rest of you have any sense, you'll follow me. I'll be ready to talk terms when you've got rid of outsiders."

"Please go with the man by the door," Mr. Nemo said equably from the television. "He will show you to your room."

The door shut with a bang behind Nadia and her guide. In the newly quiet room, the waiters set down bowls of clear soup and poured wine for Irene and Kai.

Jerome—he of the gold ring and cards—tried the soup first, winning a mental award for bravery from Irene. "Very nice," he said politely. "Shellfish?"

"Conch," Mr. Nemo answered. "I enjoy the local seafood."

"The story is that when you visited Russia, you were served meat from the local reindeer," Ernst put in. He snapped a cracker, scattering crumbs. "And you insisted it should be grilled on charcoal. Then when a man there tried to betray you, your servants forced the hot coals down his throat."

"That is a gross exaggeration," Mr. Nemo objected. "It was nothing like that."

Kai glanced sidelong at Irene, and she could see him struggling not to enquire further.

"Stories do get around," she said. The soup was extremely good. "I'm sure that everyone at this table has had a few told about them."

Felix chuckled, but there was a glint of something unpleasant in his eyes—a mixture of distrust and dislike that Irene didn't think she'd done anything to deserve. "You know how these things work . . . Not surprising, for a Librarian."

It was true that powerful Fae accumulated stories about themselves as seabird perches accumulated guano. It helped them sustain their archetypes. She just wished she knew more about these half-dozen people. It'd give her a better idea what to expect—or what to fear. "I don't doubt that you're all important ladies and gentlemen. What I don't yet know is what, exactly, this gathering has to do with us."

"We do have a Fae acquaintance in common," Jerome said. "Do you remember Lily?"

"I knew a Lily who was an expert with guns," Irene said. She recalled the woman vividly. Lily had been a gun moll, an expert sniper, and quite probably a hit-man as well. "But I wouldn't say that I knew her *well*. Is she a colleague of yours? Or, if you'll forgive me, an enemy?"

"She was hired to work as my bodyguard once." Everyone else at the table had fallen silent to listen. "Left a trail of corpses until people started taking her seriously. Impressive. I'm sure you know how that works."

"Yes," Kai agreed, "it's a *very* bad idea not to take Irene seriously . . ."

"I prefer to handle a situation with minimal damage," Irene said firmly.

"A very worthy ambition," Mr. Nemo said. "Now may I trouble you all to take a look at this screen?"

The image dissolved into two pictures, separated vertically. *Advanced technology for this place and time,* Irene noted. *And that's just what we've seen.* On the left of the screen Mr. Nemo still sat placidly: on the right, the camera showed a tanned male attendant in floral trunks, leading Nadia down one of the interchangeable corridors.

"How much farther is it to my room?" Nadia demanded. "If Mr. Nemo thinks that he can hoodwink me into returning by walking me in circles, he'd better think again. I am a professional. I don't work with *dragons* . . . with people of that type."

"Actually, Nadia," Mr. Nemo said, and her head tilted on the screen as she heard his voice, "you do recall that your safe conduct here was dependent on you not initiating any hostilities? Or trying to exert your 'influence' on me or my other guests?"

The camera focused in on Nadia, allowing the viewers to see every moment of her eyes widening, of the colour draining from her cheeks as she made some private calculation and it came to an unwelcome answer. She swallowed. "Of course, I may have been a little hasty," she said. She smiled in the direction of the camera, focusing her attention on it. Her golden hair seemed to glow as if she were lit by an inner light, and she shifted on some axis that ran from right shoulder to left hip, arranging herself into the most attractive pose possible. "I'm sure that we can come to a mutually agreeable arrangement . . ."

Behind her, in the background, her guide was quietly sidling away down the corridor.

"And that makes twice that you've tried to use your influence," Mr. Nemo said sadly. "I'm afraid that instead of working as my agent . . . you're going to have to serve as an object lesson."

Panels in the floor slid apart beneath Nadia's feet. But it wasn't like the sort of cartoon where the victim hung in the air for a moment before falling. She dropped like a stone, and the panels sealed again above her, cutting off her shriek.

"If you would all care to turn your attention to the glass window opposite," Mr. Nemo suggested.

Heads turned as though the entire room had been hypnotised. Nadia's figure spun through the well-lit waters, struggling in slow motion. Blood trailed from shallow gashes on her hands and legs—black rather than scarlet in the harsh underwater light.

Shadows circled in towards her, drawn by the blood. And Nadia opened her mouth to scream, silent bubbles flooding out, as the sharks closed in on her.

Irene deliberately turned her head away, glad that she couldn't hear the carnage. This was not an overdone rumour about a mysterious crime lord. This was real; this was actually happening. And while she had no reason to like Nadia, and every reason to preserve her own safety, she would not stare at the other woman being killed as though it were a staged performance. "You've made your point," she said to Mr. Nemo. "Is that what you consider a useful lesson?"

"No," Mr. Nemo said affably. "I consider it an *avoidable* lesson. I do hope that we can all manage to work out our differences—without resorting to violence."

Irene glanced around the table. Kai and Indigo both displayed similar looks of frosty disdain; she could practically imagine Kai's comment of *What else can you expect from the Fae?* Even if there was a peace treaty, some attitudes would take a lifetime to change. And, she had to admit, feeding someone to sharks to make a point *was* a Fae thing to do. Assuming one was following a crime-lord archetype. The others mostly looked at each other thoughtfully. But Ernst was finishing off his soup, his attitude somehow suggesting that if he'd been in Nadia's position, he would have punched the sharks.

The servants began silently setting out a new course. It involved sliced raw dark meat of a type that Irene couldn't identify, various dips and marinades, and bowls of plain rice. Glasses were refilled. Irene had yet to touch hers.

"Thank you for all being so patient," Mr. Nemo said. "I'll now be brief. There is a particular item I want. I can give you the details of *where* it is, and *what* it is, and some assistance in the set-up, but the actual theft will require . . . experts. All of you are very well known in your respective fields. Some of you were specifically hired for this job, while others are unexpected but welcome professionals."

"Professional thieves?" Irene couldn't *deny* that her job as a Librarian frequently involved removing books without the owner's permission, but she'd rather not have it stated so blatantly. Even if it was true.

"Professionals," Mr. Nemo said soothingly. "Let's leave it at that, shall we? Now first of all, the reward. I know you all want something specific from me. Even if it's just your liberty." His eyes strayed to Indigo, who was picking at her rice with the hand that wasn't chained to her chair. "Believe me when I say that I can and will give it to you. If you bring me the object I want, safe and entire, within the next week, then I will give each of you whatever prize you name. It must be an item from my collection or a deed that I can perform—there and then—and I will provide it without hesitation or delay or cheating."

The room was silent. Ernst put down his forkful of meat. "Your word on that?"

"My word," Mr. Nemo said.

A Fae's promise was binding. Of course, it was binding to the letter rather than the spirit, but Irene couldn't see any obvious flaw in what Mr. Nemo had just said. From the abstracted faces of the other people at the table, she suspected they were coming to the same conclusions.

"And allow us to safely depart with our chosen item or items, without delay or endangerment?" Jerome asked casually.

"Yes, as swiftly as you wish, without delay or endangerment," Mr. Nemo agreed. "Now can we do business?"

There were nods around the table—even from Indigo—except from Irene and Kai.

"Ah," Mr. Nemo said, "perhaps our two unexpected arrivals have issues they'd like to raise?"

Irene glanced at Kai and received a very definite *you speak first* look in answer. "Your offer intrigues us," she said. "But Prince Kai and I are both bound by the recent peace treaty. To be blunt about it, if you're talking about a theft from someone who's signed up to the treaty, it's out of the question, and we should leave the room here and now."

Her stomach twisted with nerves. Coppelia had said that any bargains with Mr. Nemo should consist of specific exchanges, not open-ended promises. But this job wouldn't be *open-ended*—it would just mean getting an item for Nemo, which technically fell within the limits of her authority. This was the *perfect* chance for her to get *The Tale of the Shipwrecked Sailor*. If she said no and backed out of this heist, would she have lost the book—and possibly doomed a world that had helped make her who she was?

But Mr. Nemo knew about the truce and their obligations, so perhaps his job wouldn't infringe upon it?

As the seconds drew out, she could only hope that she was right.

Mr. Nemo took a swallow from his tumbler of whiskey. "The item I'm after is on a world which has *not* been claimed as territory in the treaty documents, by any dragon or Fae—or Librarian, come to think of it. Equally, the item itself has not been stated to be the personal property of any dragon or Fae or Librarian. That's as far as I can go, but I think it means you're free to work for me.

And I won't say who procured it for me, afterwards. I'll make that part of the deal."

It sounded too good to be true. But it also sounded . . . doable.

Again Irene glanced to Kai, and he gave her a very slight nod.

She turned back to the television screen. "I think we can do business."

CHAPTER 8

S plendid, splendid," Mr. Nemo said warmly. "How nice to know that we can all get along. I've always thought individual gain was a much better motivator than racial prejudice, or personal morality. Now I know *your* price, Miss Winters, just as I do everyone else's at this table—except for Prince Kai. I'll be glad to discuss it with him later."

Kai made a non-committal noise. He nibbled a fragment of meat and frowned. "Is this shark?"

Irene suddenly tasted bile. She put down her own fork, unable to stop herself from looking at the huge glass window. Memory replayed the view of Nadia's twisting body, silently screaming as the sharks closed in.

"Indeed, great white shark liver," Mr. Nemo answered. "It's a delicacy. Did you know that killer whales have a habit of knocking great white sharks unconscious, biting out their livers, and leaving them to drown? Very directed, very specific. I do admire that in an orca."

"I didn't realize that you found killer whales in the Caribbean," Irene ventured. Diplomacy told her that she needed to finish this meal or risk insulting the host. Common sense told her that if she didn't have something to eat now, then she'd regret it later. But speculation, impossible to silence, whispered at the back of her mind. She'd been told Mr. Nemo enjoyed feeding people to his sharks. Even if this particular shark hadn't eaten Nadia, there was no way to prove that it hadn't eaten *other* people.

You can do this, she told herself. *You've eaten worse. And in worse company.*

It would help if she could actually remember *when*, though.

"So," Felix said, surprising everyone by joining the conversation, "what's your target item and where is it?"

"The *item* is a painting," Mr. Nemo said. "It was created by the French painter Théodore Géricault—in 1819 in the world in question—and it's titled *The Raft of the Medusa*."

Silence fell around the table. Irene noted absently that Ernst, Kai, and Indigo had gone back to eating their shark liver, that Jerome was following her own tactic of burying it under rice, and that Felix had never taken any in the first place.

"You do *know* about the painting, I hope?" Mr. Nemo finally said. "It's moderately famous."

"Overblown, oversized early Romanticism," Indigo said. "It passes all understanding why different qualities in colour, on a two-hundred-year-old piece of canvas, should be worth going to such trouble to obtain. When you can obtain exactly the same patterns of colour and shading on a computer image . . ."

"Because the original is the original!" Kai retorted, stung by artistic criticism, whereas personal insults would have left him cold. "How can you compare a mere machine-read copy to the actual brushstrokes laid down by the painter?"

"Well, what *I* want is the original," Mr. Nemo cut in. "To be more specific, I want the canvas, whole and entire. You can leave the frame behind if absolutely necessary."

"Where is it currently located?" Kai asked.

"By our standards, the world is fourth-by-reticulation and seventh-by-response, with double marking," Mr. Nemo said. "Tina here knows the world and she'll be organising transport. Specifically, it's in Vienna, in the Kunsthistorisches Museum. I know from your dossiers that most of you speak German."

"That's usually one of the biggest museums in Vienna, if not *the* biggest," Irene said thoughtfully. "What time period are we looking at?"

"Early twenty-first century, where there's some sort of united Europe," Mr. Nemo answered. "If I *may* continue?"

"I beg your pardon," Irene murmured, retreating back to her rice. She had to remember that this wasn't a typical Library mission—and that she wasn't in charge of this team.

Though, she wondered, who *was*?

Mr. Nemo took another gulp of whiskey before continuing and Irene wondered at his stamina. "I've had a local agent arrange finance, accommodation, identity papers, and anything else you may need, which will be handed over when you arrive."

"Technical equipment?" Indigo demanded. "If you want me to do my job properly, I'm going to need suitable computers and tools."

"She's been instructed to obtain local high-end technology. Everything you could possibly ask for. You're working for *me* now,

Indigo, remember." His tone towards her was avuncular, but there was a vicious note beneath the pleasant surface. Irene wondered what had happened between them to merit it. "There are some things you don't need to worry about any longer."

Indigo visibly bristled but forced a nod, and Irene marked off another probable role on this team of theirs. Indigo, apparently, was technology and computer systems. Which was interesting. Kai had spent time on a world with a high level of technology and had experience in the area. But not all dragons were interested— or even enthusiastic—about that sort of thing. Ernst was obviously muscle. (Too obviously?) Tina was transport. However, what were Jerome and Felix meant to be doing? Or Irene herself?

"Are you going to want reports?" Jerome asked.

Mr. Nemo shook his head. "You're all experts in your fields. I intend to sit here in comfort till you return with the painting. Besides, frequent couriers might be . . . noticed."

Something that had been puzzling her resurfaced. "Mr. Nemo," Irene said, "when Kai and I came through the airport, at Paradise Island, there were a lot of your . . . fans there."

"Fans, my dear?"

"Enthusiasts with weapons, who turned the place into a war zone. They were desperate to find you. And the moment they discovered Kai and I were visiting, they targeted *us*. So I have to ask—just how secret is this job of yours? And is this exposure going to be a problem?"

Mr. Nemo leaned forward confidingly. His face was damp with sweat and pink from the heat, but it didn't make him look vulnerable. Metaphors flickered through Irene's mind: a poisonous toad squatting in its lair, a great wyrm curled up in its place of power, an octopus extending its tentacles. "Miss Winters, I assure you that nothing's known about *what* I'm after. However, while I was recruiting, it did become known that I was looking for people with very specific skills. You saw the results."

"Indeed," Jerome said, putting down his chopsticks. "You ended up with a mob on your doorstep, after the job and the reward. Perhaps you showed your cards too early?"

"They'll never find me. But if they did, they'd get more than they bargained for." Irene didn't like the look of Nemo's smile as he clapped his hands together. "And now for the next course. I do hope you all enjoy fugu sashimi."

The moon laid a trail of silver across the surface of the sea. Kai stood by the closed windows, sensing the deep pulse of the tides and the movement of the ocean. It was familiar to him in any world and any place, as much a part of him as the blood in his veins. He could always call on the waters to protect himself—and Irene.

She slept, but restlessly. He knew how concerned she was for the world where she'd grown up.

But as he was the one awake, apparently he was doing the worrying for her. He wondered if this was one of those things that nobody ever *told* you about relationships—or, at least, the sort that went beyond a single night's pleasure or a brief but passionate affair.

A year ago, he hadn't met Irene. He hadn't known that there could be someone—outside other dragons—who would be prepared to risk their own life for him.

Irene had said, truthfully and sincerely, *I am responsible for you, and you are under my protection.* And at first he'd had to suppress a laugh—after all, how could a human possibly have that sort of a relationship with a dragon? But then he'd realized she'd meant it. And she'd proved it, time and time again. Vale was a human too, but also a stalwart friend. And there were even a few Fae who might not be utterly worthless.

Kai reflected gloomily that it would be a relief to shed all these thoughts, thoughts that challenged his traditional upbringing at court. However, if he wanted to deserve his father's respect, he had to be an *adult*, rather than be trapped inside a cage of his own prejudices. But it seemed unfair that such a virtuous, *noble* resolution should be so hard to keep.

Light flickered in the room behind him and Kai turned to see that the television had switched itself on. Mr. Nemo was perched in the same chair, heavy-lidded eyes fixed on him. The glass window behind him revealed an octopus spreading its tentacles across the ocean floor, graceful in its delicate movements. In the bed Irene slept on, unmoving, peaceful at last.

Mr. Nemo put his finger to his lips, then gestured towards the suite door. A clear invitation for a private discussion. After a moment's hesitation, Kai accepted the challenge and noiselessly left the room.

A television screen on the wall opposite flickered on, resolving into yet another image of Mr. Nemo. It was as if the man were crawling round behind the walls of his lair, scrambling from screen to screen to keep pace with his guests. "Prince Kai," he said. "I hope I'm not disturbing you."

"Not at all," Kai replied warily.

The light from Mr. Nemo's desk lamp carved deep shadows into his face, bringing out the skull beneath the skin. "Don't worry, this doesn't concern Miss Winters—or the new truce. I haven't formally signed up to it yet, though I see its possibilities. But it's late, and I'd said we could . . . chat. Do you have any questions?"

Kai had been pondering dozens earlier but could only think of one now, under Mr. Nemo's hooded gaze. "You've made it clear this job is urgent. But you've insisted we stay overnight, rather than beginning immediately. Why?"

"It's the nature of the transport Tina's arranging. She'll be your driver throughout," Mr. Nemo answered.

"But why couldn't you have had it ready for earlier this evening?"

"I couldn't be sure that you'd all agree to the job . . . I might have needed to bring someone else in—and I couldn't have the transport sitting around waiting. Trying to keep Tina in one place is an achievement in itself. Logistics, Prince Kai."

For some reason, Kai wasn't entirely convinced, but Mr. Nemo had moved on. He leaned forward in his chair, unclasping his fingers. "You don't have any *other* questions?"

"Oh?"

"Concerning the other dragon who is my . . . guest. I thought you might want to air them, while we're in private? "

Kai felt the heat of anger in his belly, the prickle of nascent claws at his fingertips. He controlled himself. "That person is not my concern."

"Really? I would have thought that Princess Qing Qing is—"

Kai cut him off with a single furious gesture. "Do not refer to her by her original name! She has disobeyed her parents and broken with her family. She does not *deserve* the name her parents gave her."

"Dear me." Mr. Nemo chuckled again, his whole body shivering with morbid amusement. "I must apologise. I know that the lady—let's call her Indigo, shall we?—is on the outs with her family, but I hadn't realized it was that bad. It sounds positively criminal."

"It is," Kai said curtly. "And she fled the consequences of her actions."

He had never met Qing Qing, but he'd seen pictures of her in his father's palace, before they'd been taken down. She had shamed both her parents—Kai's father and her mother, the Queen of the Western Lands—by trying to raise open rebellion against their rule. Now her name was no longer spoken.

Mr. Nemo nodded understandingly. "I can imagine that her family might want her back under their control. She might be a danger to them . . ."

Kai had no intention of discussing his family any further with this Fae. He shrugged.

Mr. Nemo chuckled again at his stubborn silence. "You should remember, if you help out in this retrieval, I will owe you a favour. And there might be quite a large favour I could do you—and your family. One you'll have already paid for."

Kai felt the heat of anger again, and his eyes glinted red. "We have no need of your services."

"Then think of yourself," Mr. Nemo said, meeting Kai's furious gaze through the camera. "Wouldn't your father be pleased if you could place Indigo back in his care? I can help you with that."

The offer hung in the air like the shadow of an incoming tide: not yet fully present, but impossible to turn back. "What is she doing here in the first place?" Kai demanded, hoping for some answer that would allow him to say no.

Or did he really want a reason to say yes?

"The lady was imprisoned by a powerful Fae," Mr. Nemo said. "I knew of her talents—her technological talents—and I took steps to obtain custody. I have assured her that if she carries out my request, I will grant her freedom. Freedom from me, at least. Freedom from her family . . . well, that's another question entirely."

Kai bit his lip and tasted blood. He couldn't possibly accept an offer like this from a Fae. It was unthinkable. There was certainly some sort of trick involved. There had to be. Finally he said, "I have already agreed to cooperate in this theft. This late-night bargaining . . ."

But caution cut off his last few words before he could definitely say no. What if there was a way to make this happen? If he turned it down here and now, then would Mr. Nemo hold him to that later? Was it so wrong to make a bargain like this, when everybody stood to gain from it?

"There's no hurry," Mr. Nemo replied. His lips curled in a smile that bared sharp teeth all the way to the gums. "You can give me your answer when you return."

CHAPTER 9

Irene had seen dungeons, bloodstained theatres, battlefields, and conflagrations—but now she had truly experienced hell.

And it was inside a minibus with four Fae and two dragons.

She wasn't quite at the point of stepping out onto the motorway to play with the oncoming traffic, but it was *close*.

They'd left Mr. Nemo's island by private plane, with Tina piloting. Then they'd transferred to the minibus and Tina had taken the wheel. As Irene suspected, her talents lay in transport and motion: she was able to seamlessly transfer from one world to another while travelling, as some Fae could do.

What most Fae *couldn't* do was carry multiple people along with them. However, it seemed Tina could manage half a dozen passengers, including the dragons, with ease. They'd started in America. Now they were approaching Vienna. Roads had reeled by outside the minibus windows—desert plains, country fields, dark cityscapes, rustic villages—each of them there for a few minutes and then shifting to something else. The other Fae had treated this as merely a normal method of travel. Indigo had been silent, and Kai had muttered something about feeling travel-sick. But they'd been able to cope with the journey itself, as had Irene. The company was another matter. Everyone had retreated into a separate corner of the minibus, and given that there were only four corners, tempers were fraying.

Ernst cracked his knuckles. Repeatedly. Then he did it again. Jerome was unable to sit with his hands still: he was constantly practicing card draws or dice throws. In the enclosed space the rattling of his dice on the floor competed with Ernst's knuckle-cracking, like two clocks out of synchronisation with each other. Irene found herself hoping each time that they would find the same rhythm, and twitched with frustration every time they didn't. Felix sat in his corner, unwilling to talk, even to Jerome. Occasionally he twitched, looked as if he was about to say something, then retreated into silence again. Kai was brooding over something himself, and occupied a seat as far as possible across the minibus from Indigo. Indigo herself ignored them all with glorious disdain, fiddling with a small piece of electronics from a locked briefcase that she wouldn't let out of reach.

As for Irene, her main source of irritation was that there wasn't anything to *read*. Not even briefing documents. In fact, it was rather worrying that there weren't any. Possibly she'd been spoiled by her work for the Library, but she was used to having at least *some* background information when she went out on a job. They'd been given passports, credit cards, cheap burner mobile phones, and the address of their base in Vienna—and that was it.

She was in the front passenger seat, next to Tina. This wasn't actually a privilege. Tina was not a reassuring driver. She cut across other cars with casual disdain, in pursuit of some distant ideal of speed that existed somewhere off the far side of the vehicle's speedometer, responding to shouts or horns with a sneer and a gesture. Irene found herself constantly having to bite back gasps of panic. And Tina seemed incapable of any conversation other than the road ahead and how to handle it. She seemed immersed in her purpose, her mind full of speed and travel, and there was no room for anything else—no real *personality* was left. If Irene had needed a warning about what happened when the Fae abandoned their humanity for their archetype, then Tina was a living example.

"You *will* slow down to the speed limit once we reach Vienna?" Irene finally said, trying to sound firm rather than nervously hopeful. "We'll want to stay under the local cops' radar."

Tina shifted something she was chewing from one cheek to the other. "Not a problem. I'll be strictly one kilometer under the limit. Maybe half a kilometer? I don't want to overdo it. I'd have been there already, but with people in the back weighing us down like they are, it takes me a longer run-up to change spheres."

"Relax," Jerome called from his seat. "Tina knows her job. I've worked with her before."

And as the passengers either bickered or aligned themselves with old acquaintances, that was a big problem, Irene reflected. She didn't know any of these people. And Kai's clear distrust of Indigo was even more worrying. She trusted Kai's opinion, and—more to the point—his knowledge of other dragons. He hadn't wanted to discuss who she was, but he had been absolutely clear that she was treacherous.

It was shaping up to be a *wonderful* mission.

"Checkpoint ahead," Tina said, a moment before Irene spotted it. "You'll handle it?"

"I will," Irene agreed, readying herself in the passenger seat. It was time for her to prove that she could be useful too.

The minibus slowed as it drew into the queue for the roadside checkpoint. Though the uniform wasn't what Irene remembered for the Austrian police. It was grey and utilitarian, and the officers were all wearing cameras mounted on shoulder-straps.

The others in the back of the minibus fell silent as Tina drew to a halt, and one of the officers marched across. "Good day, ladies," he greeted Irene and Tina in German. "Sergeant Melzer, CEN-SOR." He flashed an identity paper at Tina: Irene could just make out the acronym CENSOR and the organisation's name in half a dozen languages. The English was worrying—*Combined European Nations Supernatural Observation and Response.* "Your destination and your reason for travelling, please?"

Tina shifted her gum from one cheek to the other and jerked a thumb at Irene.

Irene leaned forward. "We're on our way to Vienna—to join our co-workers," she said, in her best native-accent German.

"Co-workers?" the sergeant probed. He could see into the back of the minibus from his current angle, and his eyes narrowed at the assorted group.

"We're part of a new software start-up company which will specialise in cloud information gathering and storage, combined with rapid-response data retrieval and block-chain implementation, for specific search functions," Irene rattled off. She saw the man's eyes begin to glaze with boredom and continued with more tech-babble borrowed from marketing brochures, finishing, ". . . we have recruited pan-globally in order to obtain the most cutting-edge programmers and specialists—"

The sergeant's brow furrowed. He pointed a thumb at the heavy-set Ernst. "*He's* a programmer?"

"That is highly prejudiced comment," Ernst growled. His German had a noticeable Russian accent. "I am specialist in open-source development and libraries."

"Indeed," the sergeant said. He clearly wasn't entirely convinced but was prepared to file it as *someone else's problem*. "Now if you'll please take this disc in your bare hand one by one—that's right, madam—and let me observe for a moment. It's just non-allergenic silver."

Supernatural Observation and Response, the sergeant's papers had said . . . "Should we be worried about werewolves?" she asked, passing the disc to the others behind her.

"No more than usual, madam," the sergeant answered, watching the disc's progress. "There's no need for you to be alarmed."

Which might mean there was every reason to be alarmed. Irene mentally cursed Mr. Nemo once again: if there were dangerous supernatural creatures on this world, then he should have warned them.

Tina finished skipping the disc over her knuckles and returned it to the sergeant. "Thank you all," he said with a curt nod. "Please return to your business. Oh, and you might want to watch the speed, madam. Not that it's *my* job to pull you up on it, but there are speed traps nearer the city."

"We appreciate the warning," Irene said, as Tina hit the accelerator hard.

"Is this a problem?" Ernst asked, once they were on the move again. The snowy landscape outside sprouted warehouses and car parks as they approached the city, and the traffic clustered around them. Above, the sky was a mass of grey clouds, dismal and unpromising, as dark and ominous as the coats of a thousand massing wolves.

"In which sense?" Irene replied. "The werewolves? Or the fact that our faces and number plates are now on record?"

Indigo looked up from her tinkering with some gadget. "That camera he was wearing? Don't worry about it. Once I have my system up and running, I can hack into the police records and do whatever I want."

"I'd meant to ask you about that," Felix said, finally speaking. "How can you be sure that your knowledge will unlock this world's computer systems? This isn't some sort of science fiction movie, where you can plug a laptop into the alien mother-ship computer and hack into it."

Indigo was still for a moment, like a cobra considering the best angle for its strike. "The basic technology isn't the issue," she said, speaking slowly, as if to a child. "There are only so many ways that one can create a transistor, or a vacuum tube, or all the other pieces that are used to make a computer or tablet or cell phone. When it comes to computer languages and programming, there's plenty of parallel evolution across different worlds—just like spoken languages. Have you ever noticed how many worlds develop Windows?"

"I never thought of it that way," Felix admitted.

"Well, now you know," Indigo said. Again there was that note of condescension in her voice. "In my case, here, I have a variety of programs and hacking tools from different worlds. I'll be able to find something which will work with this world's computer systems or which I can adapt. I know my job." Indigo glanced at Kai as she spoke, and there was something almost . . . conspiratorial about it.

Her words to Felix did make sense—but was it really that easy to transfer technology across worlds? Irene recalled a Library seminar, a year or so back, that had said this simply wasn't possible. And Irene didn't like mysteries—at least outside of detective novels.

She glanced at Kai. He knew more about technology than Irene, so if there had been a flaw in Indigo's argument, surely he'd have pointed it out. Only Irene had noticed his silent exchange with Indigo, how his eyes had flashed what looked almost like a warning at her. But why should Indigo's skills provoke any reaction at all?

"If there are werewolves and other supernatural creatures here, then it's probably a Gamma world by the Library classification," she said, turning to more immediate problems. "By our standards, that means both magic and technology."

"Does magic appear in high-order worlds like this?" Ernst asked. "I do not visit them often, but I had not thought to find it here. Will it be a problem?"

"You can get magic in these environments, but it would be very highly organised magic," Irene said. "With laws and principles and so on. And if there *are* other supernatural creatures here—"

"Besides us," Tina interrupted cheerfully.

Irene supposed Librarians counted as a sort of supernatural creature. "Yes, besides us—then they'd obey consistent rules. Like silver always burning werewolves and vampires being allergic to garlic . . . In high-order worlds, you could practically write a guide on how to identify local unnatural creatures . . ."

"And in any case, CENSOR's hunting them," Indigo said. "That should keep them busy—and away from us."

"There are dragons in this world, by the way," Kai noted. "At least one, possibly more."

"How do you know?" Felix demanded quickly.

"It's a . . . dragon thing." Kai's lip curled at the term, but he spread his hands with a shrug. "I can't tell where they are or how many they are. The fabric of the world sings with it."

"Do you agree with him?" Jerome asked Indigo.

Indigo raised her wrist. The thick silver cuff round it was still there, even though there was no longer a chain attached. "While this is on me, I've no way of telling."

"So you can't do . . ." Felix waved his hand. "Dragon things?"

"No," Indigo said, her words as sharp and brittle as volcanic glass. "I can't do dragon things. However, I can do computer things—and that's what you need at the moment."

"As long as these dragons aren't in Vienna, they're not our problem," Ernst said. Straight to the point, as usual. "So. On to Vienna."

Oh no," Indigo said, looking around their new headquarters. "This will not do. It will not do at all."

Her eyes glittered with fury. Even if she wasn't showing any of the usual signs of a dragon's anger while in human form—her eyes weren't gleaming red, her skin was unmarred by scales—her rage was still palpable. Tina showed no sign of recognizing danger on or off the road. But the other Fae had backed away as rapidly as was inhumanly possible (without seeming too visibly intimidated).

Irene looked at the piles of boxed computer equipment on the shabby carpet. Power extension cords lay jumbled in disconnected patterns. A few battered desks had been pushed against walls. The run-down block had been described as having OFFICE SPACE TO RENT on the billboard downstairs, but was empty of other tenants. Maybe that had been a miserable attempt to attract investment—if so, it had completely failed. Unsurprisingly, given that this was an industrial district on the outskirts of the city.

"On the positive side," she said out loud, "we should be undisturbed. And our hotel rooms are just across the street. Indigo, forgive me if I'm being imperceptive, but are you complaining about our base or the equipment?"

Indigo spun to face Irene, her hair floating out behind her like smoke. "As anyone could see if they bothered to *look*, I'm complaining about the equipment. This is a complete joke."

Irene forced herself to stand her ground. She'd faced angry dragons before, but it never became any easier. "What do you want, and what will it take to get it?"

As Indigo paused to consider, Jerome fanned out his credit cards as if they were playing cards and sorted through them. "Is that your role in our team?" he asked her. "Procurement—you get what we need?"

"Procurement and organisation—just let me know what you want," Irene said confidently. She had to get them to trust her somehow, so why not with this? Wishful thinking about locking the lot of them in a hotel room while she and Kai got the job done would have to be put on hold. She had to take control of this operation now, while the situation was still fluid and before anyone else could try to assert their authority. There was too much depending on it. "And I suggest we get started, as we're on a deadline." *And the world that I care about, the reason I'm actually doing this, has only a day or two more than that deadline. At best.*

"I'm not averse to working as part of a team," Felix said. "I've done it before." He was perched on a desk, brooding like a raven. Irene still found it hard to be absolutely certain what he looked like, as her eyes always slid off him. No doubt he'd be impossible to pick out in an identification parade too. "I'm not even against working with Librarians or dragons. But I'm also prepared to show you the door, if I think you're not contributing."

"That seems fair," Ernst rumbled. "I too am open-minded about cooperation with traditional enemies. But do not disappoint me. You would not like that."

Kai shrugged, as if he hadn't vented about collaborating for an hour to Irene the night before. "I see no reason why we shouldn't cooperate. If we meet again, we can always pretend we don't know each other."

"That usually ends up with a gun duel at dawn, after a night trashing a casino, then chasing each other across town," Jerome added.

"That's oddly specific," Irene said.

"These things happen."

Indigo had been scribbling a list on a discarded notepad. "Here," she said, presenting it to Irene. "I need these items or their local equivalents. It's going to cost, though. I can start putting this pile of junk together . . ." She gestured at the boxed equipment.

"But I need better. And the sooner I get it, the sooner I can get our faces off those official computer records."

Irene took the list and stared at it blankly, then passed it to Kai. "Right," she said. "And I have some *suggestions* about a possible division of labour . . ."

Irene was a strong believer that if you could get people accustomed to obeying simple orders, under the guise of suggestions, they'd then do what they were told later when in horrible danger. This theory wasn't going to dazzle followers of Sun Tzu's *The Art of War* anytime soon, but the basic principle was sound. But would it work on this team, all of whom were experts in their own field?

A gratifying silence filled the room, as everyone waited for her to speak.

"We have three immediate needs," she said. "We need information on the painting and its security; information on the city; and cash. Does that sound reasonable?"

It was possible to guess at the team's alliances from the way people were glancing at each other for signs of agreement or disapproval. Jerome, Tina, and Felix were one axis: she and Kai were another. Ernst was unreadable and Indigo was wholly contemptuous.

"So who should do what?" Tina asked.

Irene resisted the urge to sigh in relief at this sign of agreement. "I'm making some assumptions about people's skills and knowledge here." *Mostly because you haven't actually told me what they are,* she added silently. "But I'd suggest that Felix survey the Kunsthistorisches Museum. On the cash front, I was thinking Ernst and Jerome might arrange some financing, and possibly check out the local criminal underworld while they're at it . . ."

"You think I am expert in such things?" Ernst asked. "You

think I am the sort who simply walks into bar, and all local criminals wet themselves and hand over wallets?"

"Nothing so crude," Irene said hastily. "But I do think that the two of you will be able to get the pulse of what's going on."

"You're not doing badly so far," Jerome said thoughtfully. He flashed a charming smile at her. "What do *you* plan to do yourself?"

"I want to find out more about this world," Irene said firmly. "Did Mr. Nemo say *anything* about werewolves, or that CENSOR organisation?" A general shaking of heads. "We're operating in the dark here and I don't want us to blow our cover. I'm used to researching this sort of thing, and doing it fast."

"And I'll be setting up this pile of junk." Indigo prodded the nearest box with the toe of her boot. "I want Kai here to assist me. I need another pair of hands, and he has more of an idea of what he's doing than the rest of you."

"Kai?" Irene queried, surprised.

Kai sighed. "It makes sense," he said.

"And me?" Tina asked.

"I was thinking you might like to map out this Vienna," Irene said. Incomplete knowledge of a city could lead to nasty surprises during a fast getaway. "Unless you feel you'd be more use doing something else?"

"No, that sounds good." Tina's eyes had lit up. She flicked another piece of gum into her mouth. "I can work with this."

"You are a little silver-tongued charmer." Ernst prodded Irene squarely on the collarbone with one meaty finger. "Do not think I will indulge you, just because I like you. But for the moment you talk good sense."

"Too kind." Irene rubbed the spot where he'd poked her. If he ever punched her, she wouldn't be getting up again.

Maybe this was actually going to work.

And once they were all busy . . . *she* could quietly check in with the Library. She had some very urgent questions to ask.

CHAPTER 10

The Austrian National Library was the biggest library in Austria (in most alternate worlds, at least). Situated in the middle of Vienna, in the former Imperial Palace, it was a glorious work of architecture. And the inside was decorated with paintings, frescoes, and mosaics that had been known to bring the viewers to a standstill in admiration. More relevant to a Librarian, it had a collection of manuscripts, incunabula, and papyri.

But practicality had instead brought Irene to the University of Vienna's library, where she was now sitting. Here she was anonymous, one among hundreds or even thousands of visitors taking advantage of the facilities. She'd been quite honest when she'd told the others that she wanted to make an assessment of this world—its history, its culture, and its current dangers.

But there had been one *other* thing she'd wanted to do first.

It had only taken Irene a few minutes to find a back corridor where she could open a temporary passage to the Library. Once there, she'd sent a desperate email to Coppelia, to check the possible implications of what she was about to do. Mr. Nemo might have sworn that they weren't breaching the treaty, but Irene was profoundly uneasy about the whole business.

As to what she was going to do if this theft turned out to be politically inadvisable . . . well, she'd have to improvise.

Outside, the wind whistled along the wide streets. Winter held Vienna in its grip, and while it wasn't actually snowing, it certainly wasn't warm. Grey clouds filled the sky and people walked with their collars turned up and their heads down, eager to escape the cutting edge of the wind.

And everywhere, the cameras. That had been an unpleasant surprise. With determined optimism, Irene reassured herself that if Indigo was as good as she claimed, they wouldn't be an issue.

If. If. If.

But inside the library's reading room, there was warmth and the silence of shared study. Students and the general public mingled along the long dark oak tables, which stretched the length of the room. Each person had their own nest of papers, laptop, or tablet. But everyone was hunched over their work, as if afraid that someone were about to point an accusing finger and blame them for something. There was a sense of nervousness in the air that even Irene, a newcomer, could sense.

Irene had found a corner and was combining web searches on a newly purchased laptop with paper-based research—leafing through the sheaf of newspapers and magazines she'd also acquired. And even if web searches were monitored, her computer was entirely anonymous.

One of her main discoveries was the high number of supernatural beings here, which was going to be a problem. The CEN-SOR organisation had adopted a number of aggressive practices when hunting said supernatural beings, which might also be a problem. And *The Raft of the Medusa* was about sixteen by twenty-three feet, which was *definitely* going to be a problem when it came to stealing it. That was rather larger than the average book.

She idly flipped through online photos of the Kunsthis-torisches Museum, trying to get a feel for the place. It was built on a large and luxurious scale inside, displaying the Hapsburg dynasty's power just as much as their art collection. It was also well-equipped in terms of electronic security. This was also not one of those places that skimped on guards because it had electronics.

Wait. In that stock photo of a gold sculpture by Cellini . . . was that a *dragon* in the background?

Irene leaned closer, her nose nearly touching the screen as she squinted at the expanded view. Yes, even though he was in human form, he was unmistakably a dragon. The lines of the face, the posture, the way he held himself. Here in Vienna, in the same building as their target, only a few years ago going by the date . . .

There was a whisper of air behind her, and a cylindrical metal object poked into her back. It was the third time this week.

"Don't make a disturbance," Felix said, his voice quiet enough that it was barely a purr in her ear. "I'd like a word with you, in private."

"This isn't very private," Irene replied equally softly. This was bad. And she didn't even know what she'd *done* to trigger this reaction.

"It will be, in a moment. Pack up your stuff. Keep it nice and casual. We're going to walk to the door over there and have a little talk, once we're sure nobody else is listening in." He didn't add any further warning; the steady firmness of the gun muzzle in her back was quite enough.

Irene shoved her things into her bag. The Language would be no help here: she'd never be able to finish a word, let alone a sentence, before Felix could fire. A crawling unease was forming in her stomach. Just how badly *had* she underestimated the situation?

Nobody looked up as they passed through a side door labelled STAFF ONLY into the unlit corridor beyond. Here, Ernst emerged from the shadows like a looming monolith. His hand clamped around her throat before she could even squeak, and he hoisted her off her feet, pinning her against the wall. Felix shut the door tidily behind them.

"So," Ernst grunted. "All those nice speeches, and you turn traitor before we even reach suppertime. I am disappointed in you."

Irene struggled desperately for breath. She held up her hands, trying to demonstrate peace, harmlessness, anything that might persuade him to release her.

"Careful," Felix said. "She's probably trying to use that special language of theirs."

"It is not her language I'm worried about. It is her silver tongue. If we let her speak, she will no doubt try to persuade us of her innocence."

Spots flashed in front of Irene's eyes, and she kicked at Ernst, but she didn't have the leverage or reach to do any damage.

"I don't know," Felix mused thoughtfully. "Perhaps she might have something useful to say?"

"Only one way to find out," Ernst said. He slackened his grip, letting Irene slide down the wall till her toes touched the ground and she could—just—support herself. His fingers remained clenched around her throat, a warning.

Irene sucked in gulps of air. "Not a traitor," she gasped, her voice raw.

"This is good," Ernst said approvingly. "I like it even better if you can prove it."

Irene rolled her eyes towards Felix. She guessed he would ask the awkward questions while Ernst applied the physical threats. She had miscalculated somewhere, and she needed to work out how, before it was too late. "Why say I'm a traitor?" she croaked.

"Because the moment you get away, you go sneaking off to your Library for further orders." Felix's tone was light and playful, but his eyes were cold. "Were you arranging to steal the picture with your other friends? Or were you making a deal to sell us out?"

Oh damn. He must have been following her from the moment that they'd left their base.

Irene looked from Ernst to Felix again. "All right," she said. "I admit I checked in with the Library. I'm not going to deny it." This was particularly annoying, as she could have told them beforehand and avoided all this. "I'm under orders to get a certain book from Mr. Nemo. That's why I agreed to steal the painting. But I had to confirm it didn't infringe the truce—"

"Ah yes, this so-called Fae-dragon-Librarian truce," Felix interrupted. "It's a nice story, but do you really expect us to believe in it?"

For a moment Irene stared at him. She'd been through hell and back to get the truce signed. "But Mr. Nemo himself confirmed it existed!"

Her disbelief must have shown in her voice. But Felix just shrugged. "I know you Librarians. You're all good liars. And it's not as if Mr. Nemo actually gave his word that he'd heard of it."

"I also know nothing of such a truce," Ernst rumbled. "It is good story. It gives you decent alibi. Now how about we get to real story and facts?"

"Tell me, Irene, which finger do you use least?" Felix asked. "We don't have to kill you, but we may need to apply some encouragement . . ."

Irene felt a cold sense of dread. She'd made a really, really *bad* mistake. She'd grown used to dealing with Fae who accepted that the truce existed. And she'd felt a measure of safety negotiating under its protection. She'd been spoiled, assuming these Fae would also treat her as a neutral, rather than an enemy or a competitor. And now she—and Kai—might be about to pay the price.

"Be reasonable. Please. I can answer your questions without all this." She knew her fear was showing in her voice. Maybe that would help convince them.

"Yes, but how can we trust you?" Felix shook his head sadly and somehow less theatrically than usual. He seemed more *human* now that he'd moved away from his archetype of shadowy thief. But worryingly, this felt like a very personal grudge instead. "How can we trust *any* of you Librarians?"

You Librarians, Irene thought. "You've met some of us before," she hazarded. "And it didn't go well?"

"That's putting it mildly," Felix said with quiet savagery. "You people are unprincipled monomaniacs."

"I'm not denying that," Irene admitted. "But if you know about the Language . . ."

"I do indeed, which is why Ernst is going to squeeze your throat until your head pops off if you try anything."

"Then you know we can't lie in it?" Irene met his eyes. "It's like you Fae—if you bind yourself by your word, then you have to keep it. If I give you my word, in the Language, then I have to speak the truth. I don't know what this other Librarian did to you. But I'm not them. I want this theft to succeed. I have something important at stake too."

She felt nervous sweat trickling down her back as Felix and Ernst exchanged glances.

"Ernst?" Felix finally said. "I'm not sure I trust my judgement here. What do you think?"

Ernst shrugged. Irene could feel the vibrations of his movement through his hand round her throat. "It is true, that if they swear in their Language, they must keep their word?"

"Yes," Felix said sourly. "But they're good at working round that."

"Then she should swear she's not going to betray us. That she will be as honest with us as she is with that dragon boy of hers. That seems fair enough."

"That's unfair," Irene said quickly. Her fear was still very real, but if she made the wrong promise, the Language could tear her apart. "I'm prepared to pledge 'one for all and all for one'—with one caveat—but you must do the same."

Ernst's hand tightened. "Caveat? You demand an exception, just for you?"

Irene coughed and made frantic gestures till he relaxed his grip. "The Library," she gasped. "If they tell me, back off and pull out, then I won't have a *choice*. But if I do, I'll *swear* not to interfere with your work on the job."

Everyone in the main reading room would have their heads down over their work, oblivious to her plight, she thought despairingly. It was like a theatrical farce, but deadly serious. Even if she screamed, nobody would reach her in time to help.

And, she wondered with a shiver, what else had she missed? She made a mental vow that she wouldn't be so careless again.

"Let's do this by stages, less room for error," Felix said slowly. "Give us your word that you haven't betrayed us—and that this side trip of yours to your Library was as you claimed. Then maybe we can negotiate what happens next on a more equal basis."

"All right." Irene swallowed and chose her words. **"I swear by my name and power that I have not betrayed you and I do not intend to betray you. I also swear that a truce has been signed between all dragon monarchs and a number of powerful Fae, and the Library is also a signatory."**

She looked up and Felix's face was set in hard lines. "And your side trip . . ." he prompted.

"My main motivation in returning to the Library was to check I wouldn't break the truce because of this theft."

Her words echoed in the shadowy passageway with a resonance that went beyond the physical and hummed in her bones. The Fae felt it too. Ernst released her throat and pulled his hand away as though it had been stung, and Felix twitched, glancing up and down the corridor nervously.

Irene wanted very badly to rub her throat, but that might have looked like weakness. "All right?" she said. "Convinced?"

"*Main* motivation?" Felix queried.

That was the problem with using the Language to swear truthfully: she had to be truthful. "I also asked if they had any information on this world which they could share. I don't know about you, but I'm feeling dangerously under-informed."

"So there is a truce," Ernst mused. "Maybe I will get work from dragon employers now. That would be amusing. But your problem makes more sense now. If your Library catches you breaking treaty they have signed, then they throw you out or have you publicly executed, or something like that?"

"At the very least," Irene agreed. She could feel that the balance of power had shifted. Even if Felix wasn't quite convinced, Ernst seemed prepared to believe her. She took a step forward. "So shall we discuss what *you're* both after?"

"From Mr. Nemo?" Felix asked.

Now that was deliberately obtuse. Irene could spot it half a mile away. "No," she said. "From *me*. If you'd wanted me dead, I'd already be dead. Which means you want something. Perhaps it's time for all of us to be honest about what we want here?"

Felix hesitated, then nodded. "All right. You tell me, Irene—just how many oddities have you spotted in this job, already?"

"You mean things which would be complete deal breakers, if there wasn't some bait I really wanted on the hook?"

"Yes," Felix murmured. "Just like that. I don't normally work with other people. Or if I do, *I'm* the one who picks them. No offence, Ernst."

"None taken," Ernst answered gloomily. "How nice to have such freedom!"

"And I'm not convinced people can hack into computer networks that easily." It seemed Felix didn't trust Indigo any more than he trusted Irene. "I'd like a sample or two of what our dragon 'colleague' can do *before* I rely on her to back me up."

"And Mr. Nemo didn't mention supernatural creatures—or that dragons visited this world," Irene said. "A *minor* point which would have been useful to know." For a moment she thought of pointing a finger of suspicion in Indigo's direction, but rejected it. That sort of accusation could be impossible to take back. And she didn't know enough about Indigo to know whether it was justified or not.

She didn't know enough about any of them.

"You say dragons, plural," Ernst noted. "In the van, dragon boy said he could sense them here. You have more proof?"

"There was a photo of the museum from about two years ago. I saw a dragon in the background. He was in human form. I know it's not current, but . . ." Irene shrugged. "I need more information. *We* need more information."

Felix had opened his mouth to answer, when suddenly a raucous clamour of alarm bells split the air—a sound that would have been bad enough in the large reading room but that was actively painful in the enclosed corridor.

Crashes and thuds came from the room beyond, and the sound of stampeding feet.

CHAPTER 11

Then the noise cut off. Abruptly the gun was in Felix's hand again, pointed squarely at Irene's forehead. "You *have* betrayed us," he snarled, his tone barely controlled.

"Before you jumped me, I didn't even know you were here!" Irene retorted. "And if that was a fire alarm, we should get out of here too!" There was no noise coming from the reading room now . . .

There was a crackle and a click as a loudspeaker came on. "Attention, attention," a man's voice said in German, harsh and echoing, as the broadcast repeated in other rooms within earshot. "This is CENSOR. We have a report of a vampire infestation in progress. Everyone is to leave this building immediately and submit to identity checks and blood tests, as required under CENSOR charter. Ignorance of the law is not an excuse. Any attempt to avoid testing is illegal. Please form an orderly queue and be prepared for your belongings to be searched." A pause. "Attention, attention . . ."

The barrel of Felix's pistol was still pointed right between Irene's eyes. She swallowed. "Felix. Pull yourself together." *Why did I use the word* pull? *It goes far too well with* trigger. "I haven't had *time* to invite CENSOR to stage a raid. You both know that. I'm on your side—and I've sworn it too. But we need to get out of here now."

Felix's hand didn't shake, but his eyes were unsettlingly wild. "I knew it," he crooned, half to himself. "I knew I couldn't trust you. Well, this time's going to be different—"

Ernst had moved in total silence. His hand came down hard across the back of Felix's neck, and the other Fae crumpled like a rag. His pistol went spinning across the floor till Irene stopped it with her foot.

"All right," she said. "Whose side are *you* on?"

"Side of common sense," Ernst said calmly. "Only a fool fights in a burning house—or with the police outside." He bent down and picked up Felix, swinging him over one shoulder. "We need the quickest way out of here without meeting police. Or CENSOR people."

Irene considered. She'd visited this library once, although it was in another world long ago. "Up's no use. We'd be trapped as they worked through the building. And no, I can't take you into the Library itself from here—I can't bring Fae inside."

"Down?"

"If they're hunting for vampires, they'll probably be checking the cellars. No, we need a side door somewhere. Or an excuse to mingle with the crowd."

"More difficult with a burden," Ernst remarked, patting the unconscious Felix meaningfully, though his tone was carefully neutral.

Irene considered his statement. "Is that a subtle moral test to see if I'd leave him behind?" she said. "Or are you just being prag-matic? Either way, you're the one who's going to be carrying him."

"Had to check," Ernst said with a shrug, though she noticed he hadn't committed to either explanation. "So how do we get out of here—with him? We may have a problem."

"We *do* have a problem. And we don't have identity papers, apart from our passports." Irene had a nasty suspicion that pass-ports alone might not suffice. She might pass, but who knew whether CENSOR's checks could detect Fae?

The view outside, from a dusty second-storey window, didn't inspire peace of mind. The street was swarming with a mixture of police and people in CENSOR uniforms. Crowds of civilians were being organised into neat queues, pointing towards checkpoints that looked like a combination of airport X-ray device and MRI scanner. Blood samples were being taken with neat efficiency—the sort that involved a syringe to the elbow. Though nobody ob-jected. Everybody was standing where they'd been told to stand, as if this were routine, and were eyeing the people around them with controlled nervousness. But people were still spilling out of the library into the street. That was good; it meant that there was still time for them to mingle with the crowd. If they could solve the Felix problem.

All the CENSOR people had shoulder-cams, just like the one they'd seen earlier, and carried walkie-talkies at their belts. *This city runs on fear,* Irene thought, *and CENSOR seems to have their hand on the throttle . . .* She frowned.

"You have idea?" Ernst queried.

"Yes," Irene said slowly. "But we'll need an exit where the CEN-SOR people can intercept us—without too many other people listening . . ."

+ + +

They were among the last to leave through the exit Irene had picked—one of the side doors out of the building. Both CENSOR guards stationed here had pistols slung across their backs and short truncheons (or whatever the technical term was for a short, heavy club) holstered at their belts. They looked much more military than a regular police force, and extremely dangerous.

Irene had situated herself and Ernst at the back of a group. Rather than carrying the still unconscious Felix over his shoulder, Ernst now supported him with an arm around his waist. He moved with artificial slowness, as though the other man actually weighed him down.

As the last stragglers filed through the exit, Ernst let Felix slide to the ground as though he could no longer support the other man. Irene gasped, bent over him, then beckoned to the guards. "Excuse me," she said in faultless German, "but can you help us? My friend is ill . . ."

The two CENSOR guards were well-trained enough not to come running into what might be a trap. However, they did take a couple of steps into the building, out of view of their colleagues. Which was all Irene needed.

"You perceive that we are your colleagues, reliable and trusted," she said.

The atmosphere lightened. While the two men didn't suddenly take off their weapons and start shaking hands, they noticeably relaxed. "Anything to report?" one asked, while the other bent over to check Felix's pulse.

"Yes, and it's urgent. Can you give me a channel directly to whoever's in charge of this operation?"

"No problem," the first man said, pulling a walkie-talkie from his belt. He hit a selection of buttons, muttered a code, and finished with, "Eisen, reporting in now," before passing it to Irene.

Irene had tried this once before, so she knew it was *possible*, but she wasn't sure how many she had to convince. And with the Language, the more people involved, the harder it became . . .

"**You perceive I am a trusted authority,**" she said into the walkie-talkie, "**and that I am telling you that this whole affair is a hoax. It's an attempt to distract you from the real vampire infestation, at the Spanish Riding School. You perceive that you need to take action and get there—now.**"

Blinding pain ripped through her skull, and blood began to leak from her nose. She swayed, holding herself upright by force of will, and tried to blot her nosebleed as inconspicuously as possible. Frantic babbling came from the walkie-talkie: she hit the switch that she'd seen the CENSOR guard press, and it cut off. "**Cameras, deactivate,**" she added, feeling faint.

Ernst had strolled behind the guards, his motions so casual that he hadn't registered as a threat. This was despite his being over six feet tall, with the sort of build and musculature that made him the archetype of an enforcer. Before the CENSOR guards could ask what was going on, he picked them up by their necks and banged their heads together.

"I used to think it was artistic license, when I read about that," Irene mumbled. This was a *bad* headache. There must have been at least half a dozen people on the far end of the connection. She fumbled for aspirin in her bag and dry-swallowed a couple.

"And I used to think sensible women took out the cameras *before* doing criminal things." Ernst kicked open a random door, grabbed each guard by an ankle, and dragged them both through it. He then shoved the door shut.

"If I'd tried that before using the Language on them, they might have shot me first." Her nosebleed had mostly stopped. Irene stuffed bloodied paper tissues back into her bag: she didn't want to risk leaving blood samples around.

Ernst peered around the edge of the doorway. "Mmm. They are dismantling the checkpoints now and the queues are almost gone. I think the police and CENSOR are both on their way out too. Can you walk?"

"I can." Not well, but she could manage it. "We'd better confuse our trail on the way back—and hope that Indigo really *is* that good at hacking computer records."

W hat went wrong?" Kai asked, as soon as she walked through the door.

"I wish I knew," Irene said sourly. "We'd better not have any vampire infestations under *this* building. How did you know we had problems?"

"You've changed your clothing, restyled your hair, altered your make-up, and put on a pair of glasses," Kai pointed out. "Were you followed?"

"Hopefully not." Irene glanced around. Computers had been unpacked and were arranged on desks in a complex configuration. Indigo was in the middle of a nest of keyboards and monitors, swapping in successive memory sticks before bursting into fusillades of typing. She hadn't bothered to look up.

Kai waited for further details with a rather too obvious patience. He might as well have shouted, *Hero nobly and patiently waits for the inconsiderate heroine to explain what's going on.* But she wasn't about to trigger his protective instincts by actually *telling* him. That could split the team apart—just after she'd managed to temporarily glue over the wobbly patches. She rubbed her forehead. Her metaphors were getting mangled, it was that bad. Instead she said, "Are Ernst and Felix back yet?"

Ernst strolled in from the tiny office bathroom next door, dripping wet and with a towel round his waist. His hair had changed colour to a muted brown, which contrasted obviously with the blonde mat of hair covering his chest. Apparently he didn't think it necessary to dye *that.* "I'm here. Felix went to research the museum. I told dragon boy we'd split up to avoid attention after dodging the CENSOR people. Knew you'd be okay."

It was difficult, sometimes, to decide whether to be more irritated by colleagues assuming she could handle anything, or colleagues fretting over her safety. Irene gave up and sat down. "Good." Her headache had gone down too. Sometimes she wondered if she should be taking so many aspirin. But the risks of sudden death tended to take priority. "Kai, the CENSOR situation has left us with a problem. It's now near certain that they've caught all three of us on camera. I'm hoping Indigo can sort that out."

"You have a high opinion of my abilities," Indigo said, not looking up.

"I hope it's justified. If CENSOR manages to track me down—track *us* down," Irene corrected hastily, in case they thought disposing of her removed the problem, "then we're going to be severely hampered. We have enough logistical issues as it is."

"Such as?" Kai handed her a cup of coffee.

Ernst leaned against a desk and began to rub his hair dry with another towel. "If you have a plan already, that is good."

"And if you disturb any of my computers, that is *bad*," Indigo replied, an icy expression on her face.

"Bah. You are not one of those fools who does not plug things in properly."

"Logistics . . ." Irene said quickly. "Firstly, the painting's big. It's about five yards high by seven or eight yards long. While I'm not saying it's *impossible* to get out of the museum, it's going to take some planning. Secondly, cameras are going to be all over the place, from what I've seen. Thirdly, CENSOR are on the lookout for paranormal business, *and* they have guns. While none of us are vampires or werewolves or whatever, if we get spotted doing anything . . ."

". . . inhumanly magnificent," Kai said with far too much enthusiasm.

Irene looked at him wearily. "Yes, that could be a problem. Fourthly, a dragon has been on this world—and in that museum—within the last couple of years. I saw a photo."

Kai picked up a spare laptop, ignoring Indigo's furious glare, and slid it towards her. "Can you find this photo? I might recognize them."

She typed in a quick search term and slid it back. So much for any hope that making Kai and Indigo work together might improve their attitude towards each other. "So. For inconveniences, we have a powerful supraregional law enforcement body that hunts down the supernatural. We have the supernaturals themselves, if they get in our way. We have standard law and order. We have an extremely large painting that we're going to need a similarly large vehicle to remove. Better add a lorry to our shopping list."

"Do you think Mr. Nemo knew the size of this painting?" Ernst asked thoughtfully. "He did say that we needn't bring the frame."

"I'd forgotten that," Irene said, cheering up a little. "That'll help."

"But it'll take hours to remove it from the frame, even for an expert like Felix," Indigo said. "An overnight job?"

"If necessary."

"Ah!" Kai said, frowning at the laptop screen. "Yes, I do know him."

"Another relative?" Ernst suggested gloomily.

"No, not at all. It's Hao Chen. He's from a minor family, not connected to me by blood at all—a lower branch to the Winter Forest family. I don't think he holds any court position."

"Hao Chen?" Indigo said, looking up from her computers. "Is he doing something *useful*?"

"If you were in touch with the family, rather than being hunted for high treason, then you'd know, wouldn't you?"

Indigo shrugged. "You may be as petty as you please. But me returning to our father, and bowing my head for the axe, is far more likely than Hao Chen finally being useful."

Irene deliberately forced her mouth shut. *Our* father? She'd gathered Indigo was part of Kai's family, but for her to be actually a sister—or half-sister . . . ? She suppressed visions of having unknown siblings show up on her own doorstep at some point in the future. Right now, she needed to break the stand-off. "Indigo. Are dragons still looking for you?"

"They've probably got bored by now," Indigo answered with a

shrug. Her hair quivered in long waves down her back, like a frozen waterfall briefly resettling.

"But are they still *actively looking*?"

Indigo raised both eyebrows, turning her attention from her computer screen to Irene. Her icy tone rivalled that of her uncle Ao Ji. "Do you have any justifiable reason to ask that, or are you merely the sort of person who loves to roll in scandal, as a dog does in excrement?"

Just like Kai, the angrier she gets, the more formal her diction becomes. Irene shrugged. "I do know dragons can track those they've met from world to world. I think that it's only reasonable to worry about a sudden descent by family members hunting you—especially as this world is aspected towards order rather than chaos."

"She has point," Ernst rumbled. "Me, I do not like to sleep when dragons may be about to rip the roof off. I end up sleeping badly and get wrinkles."

Irene was starting to wonder just how much of Ernst's persona—and accent—was genuine. "Cucumber slices for the eyelids, perhaps?" she suggested. "Or used teabags?"

"Neither helps," Ernst said sadly. "It is hard, being manly man."

"I will say this just once," Indigo snapped, "and I will not repeat myself. I have a token which shields me from dragon pursuit and observation. He"—she jerked her chin at Kai—"can confirm that such a thing is possible. Now tell us more about your research, girl."

"My name is Irene," Irene said steadily, although her temper seethed. But she'd expected a challenge from Indigo, sooner or later. "Or Miss Winters, if you prefer. I'll also answer to Librarian. But not *girl*, or *woman*." Memories of C. S. Lewis's Narnia came to mind. "I'll make an exception for *Daughter of Eve* . . . maybe."

"You think I read such childish fantasies?" Indigo enquired.

"I think you recognized the reference," Irene returned. "I'm prepared to assume that you called me *girl* out of habit. But now I've explained, I expect you to respect my wishes."

"Are you going to let your concubine speak to me like that?" Indigo demanded of Kai.

Kai's eyes flickered with the red of dragon anger, but there was also an element of sheer delight. Was he looking forward to a confrontation—where Indigo would lose? "Miss Winters is not my concubine," he answered, perfectly polished. "She is a Librarian, she holds the position of a Librarian-in-Residence, and she is also the Library's sole representative on treaty matters. You do yourself no favours by displaying your ignorance and lack of manners."

"And she clearly has you wrapped around her little finger," Indigo sniped back. "I could live with that, but she's also managed to get herself in trouble on her very first day here. I can tolerate favouritism, but not incompetence."

"That's not what happened," Irene said shortly. "Ernst, you were there. Did I actually do anything to cause the problem? Or were we—you, me, Felix—simply unlucky? And speaking of that mess, was the Spanish Riding School on the news?"

Indigo paused her and Kai's glaring match and checked one of her monitors. "Yes. They found a group of Epona-worshipping cultists among the grooms. All performances have been postponed till further notice."

That came as a total surprise. "Really?"

"Why are you so surprised?"

"Because I invented an incident there to distract the CENSOR officials. If they've actually found something there, it's a very strange coincidence. And if they're not publicising what *I* did, then . . ."

". . . then they are trying to hunt you down *secretly*," Ernst finished.

An unpleasant chill knotted Irene's insides. "What fun," she said. "This job gets more and more entertaining."

Or might there be another reason for them pointing to cultists at the school—other than covering up her involvement? If CENSOR were investigating, perhaps they *had* to find a culprit, or it showed fallibility on their part? Either way, CENSOR was a growing problem for the team . . .

"I think you'd better stay inside from now on," Kai said seriously. "And if you do go out, it'll need to be under heavy disguise— at least until Indigo can get into the police records."

Indigo nodded, grudgingly. "If you must research, you can do it here."

Staying inside and not being hunted might be appealing for some, but not her. There was too much to *do*. However, she could use the computer time. "That sounds a good idea," Irene agreed. "And since nobody knows *your* face yet, Kai, why not check out the Art History Museum?"

"I thought you'd never ask," Kai said.

CHAPTER 12

Kai leapt down the last few stairs and sauntered through the lobby. It was a relief to be *doing* something, even if it was only preparatory scouting. And getting away from Indigo was delightful in itself.

She treated him like a low-grade minion and it rankled. Though he wasn't sure whether it was because she had *no right* to behave as though she were still his older sister and deserved his respect, or because of her low opinion of his technical skills. Either way, it had left him with a headache and a number of silently drafted poems that had contained *very* expressive imagery.

Still, at least now he could make progress without the handicap of Fae "assistance."

He glanced around as he stepped into the street, conscious of the ubiquitous cameras, even in this run-down area of Vienna. And he was just in time to spot a group of men closing in on Jerome. They were being careful about it; they'd picked a location that wasn't under surveillance and they were quickly herding the Fae into an alleyway.

Was Jerome in trouble already? Those men didn't look like CENSOR officials or police. Without pausing, he readied himself for a fight. He strolled towards the alleyway, head down and collar turned up like any other passer-by.

He'd expected a lookout. What he hadn't expected was for the lookout to scrutinise him, then call back down the alleyway to where the three others surrounded Jerome, "Boss, it's another one of them."

"Send him over," one of the group responded. "They can both hear it at once."

Since he wasn't being manhandled, Kai walked across, assessing the threat. All four men wore clothing that tried to look expensive but had been made on the cheap, and now only succeeded in looking shabby. The two by Jerome had their hands in their pockets, and was that . . . why yes, it *was* the outline of a gun. Flat caps and scarves concealed their faces, plausible in the miserable weather. Except their faces, where they *could* be seen, were definitely identifiable, with the broken noses and scars that went with a low-grade criminal career.

Jerome leaned casually against the wall, with a light in his eyes that seemed almost dreamy, as though he was weighing odds in his head and liked his chances. "You didn't have to get involved," he said to Kai.

Kai shrugged. "I walked right into it. What's going on?"

"We're making an offer to your friend," the leader said. "And to you, since you're here as well." He used the impolite Germanic *du* for "you," rather than the polite *Sie* usual for strangers.

"I'm listening." But he could guess what the "offer" was. They were being shaken down by the local criminal gang for as much as could be gouged out of them. That was what happened when you set up on the cheap side of town—as he frequently pointed out to Irene, when justifying the cost of five-star hotel suites.

"Don't bother," Jerome said. "They just want money."

"How much money?" Kai asked, out of academic curiosity.

"Two thousand a week."

Kai pursed his lips in a whistle. That was a whole month of rent for their "offices." "High expectations."

"Yeah," the heaviest thug said, "and it'd be a real shame if we were disappointed."

Kai and Jerome exchanged glances. Kai was certain he could take out these men by himself. They might have guns, but he had speed. And Jerome seemed more than capable of handling himself.

But before they could make a move the leader said, "And since you're from out of town, I'm thinking you 'entrepreneurs' never had CENSOR call on you before?"

At this threat, Kai felt the cold whisper of uncertainty against the back of his neck. "Explain yourself," he ordered.

"I don't know where you're from—America? Hong Kong? Your German's good, but you can hear the accent. And yeah, I know you've got CENSOR or something like it back home . . . everyone has these days. But you don't realize how hard and *fast* they come down on you here. You better start making payments real soon and *regular*. Or CENSOR's getting a phone call outing you as vampires—or werewolves. Or saying you're hiding books of magic. Whatever."

He paused, and when neither Kai nor Jerome interrupted, he smirked. "Yeah. Thought that'd get you thinking. Perhaps you've got something upstairs you don't want CENSOR or the police getting a good look at, huh? Maybe there's a reason why you're here on the cheap, doing your shopping in cash instead of on credit?"

This was a problem.

"I'd like a word with my colleague," Kai said quickly.

"You've got five minutes," the leader said. "Don't do anything stupid."

Jerome watched the men as they strolled to the alley entrance, their posture making it clear just how confident they were. "You're the one who's been setting up the computers with Indigo," he said quietly. "Just how bad will it be if the cops turn the place upside down? Will they find anything?"

"Well, we *are* in the middle of planning a theft," Kai pointed out. "And no raid is a good raid . . . The more we show up on police files, the more complicated it gets. And the way they're putting it, CENSOR investigate a bit more in depth than the police."

"So we don't want a police visit. And we definitely don't want a CENSOR visit."

"No. It would be far too dangerous." Kai considered their options. These men were an inconvenience; some of his kin would have swept them away without a second thought. Kai wasn't *quite* that ruthless, but even so . . .

"We'll need them close up before we make a move," Jerome said, clearly following the same train of thought.

Then a light bulb went on at the back of Kai's mind. It was so simple it seemed too good to be true. "Jerome . . . what if we just pay them?"

"Seriously?" Jerome seemed personally insulted by the very idea.

So was Kai. But there were moments in life when one had to lower oneself to practices such as making deals with Fae, drinking poorly made tea—and paying off thugs. "It's a stopgap measure," he said quietly. "We won't be *here* the next time they come around. Besides . . ." There *was* a practical aspect, after all. "There'll be someone behind these people. If they all vanish, more will come, and then they'll know we're hiding something."

"Yes, but the *money* . . ."

"Indigo can sort that out."

"For someone who doesn't like her, you've got a great deal of confidence in her. You seem to think she can hack into *anything*."

Kai was suddenly wary. There were things about Indigo and her skills that he wasn't willing to share—not even with Irene, and certainly not with a Fae. "I don't like her, but she's very good at what she does."

"You finished over there?" the leader called.

"Just a moment!" Jerome called, before turning back to Kai. "I'm not asking *can* she help here, but *will* she? She's got your attitude."

"Excuse me," Kai said, highly offended. "She is *nothing* like me."

"If you say so," Jerome said. His smile took some of the insolence out of the statement—or, possibly, added to it. Kai wasn't quite sure. Jerome carried himself like an aristocrat rather than a gambler. It was hard to know how to read him. But Kai had to assume he was at least prepared to follow his plan.

Kai signalled the thugs over. "We're prepared to pay—or at least, discuss payment."

"There's nothing to discuss," the leader said. "Two thousand a week. Cash. First payment within two days. Or CENSOR gets a phone call."

"Okay," Kai said, with an inward sigh. He knew it was what Irene would have done, but having to concede to these petty criminals galled him. "How do we get it to you?"

"We'll give you a phone number. You ring it. We give you an address. And don't try anything stupid."

"We wouldn't dream of trying to fool geniuses like you," Jerome assured them, with a sardonic smile.

"Right. I've had just about enough of you sneering at us. Boys?" The leader jerked his head at the other thugs. "Let's give these two a little lesson in manners."

His hand slid into his overcoat pocket and emerged sheathed in a set of brass knuckles. The others smirked as they pressed in, each with their own favourite props—more brass knuckles and a flick-knife. In the case of the biggest one he had no weapon at all, just his own bare hands—his huge fists seamed with old scars. "Nothing permanent, boys," he said. "Just a reminder for next time."

"You think your bosses will approve, now that we're ready to pay?" Jerome asked.

"A few bruises never hurt anyone, and you've got to learn some . . . respect." He swung for Jerome's guts as he spoke.

But the punch never landed. Jerome caught his wrist, directing the blow into the alley wall. The man yelped in pain and Jerome tripped up the second as he dashed in to help, sending the thug sprawling to the wet pavement.

Kai had targeted the flick-knife wielder as the most immediately dangerous. They circled each other warily. Then the thug flourished his blade in what was *supposed* to be a threatening gesture. So it gave Kai great pleasure to block the move and twist his opponent's arm behind his back until he dropped the knife, before shoving him into the wall.

But while he was busy, the remaining man had grabbed Jerome by his shoulders, moving with surprising speed. The first thug moved in to punch the Fae, blood dripping from his skinned knuckles.

"Hey!" Kai rushed over to help.

But Jerome simply snorted and rammed his head backwards into the face of his captor. Then he wrenched free, not even breathing fast, ready to attack.

"Hold it!" the leader gasped, trying to look in control. "All right. You two can walk away. You've got the message. But it's going to be four thousand now."

"Worth it," Kai said smugly, watching them stagger away.

"Worth it to what—call off my fight?" Jerome said, a dangerous glint in his eyes. Abruptly, Kai remembered Jerome had never agreed to his plan to pay, and would clearly have been happier if he'd handled the thugs himself. It would have been . . . more of a challenge, more of a *gamble*.

"I didn't want him getting blood on your overcoat," he answered, trying to keep the tone light. "I don't care what they say; even with cold water, it never washes out."

"Fair enough." Some of the tension between them ebbed away. "Nice work."

"You too."

"Is your sister also that good, if you've had the same training?"

Kai bit back the words *do me a favour*—highly dangerous when the Fae could take it literally and demand a price in return. Instead he said, "I'd be happier if you didn't call her that. And probably, yes, but we've never sparred."

"Could be interesting," Jerome mused.

"Save that thought till after this is over." Kai stared at the gloomy sky without really seeing it. "Being shaken down by the local gang isn't much of a surprise. But the fact they used CEN-

SOR as a threat—that means the fear of the supernatural is far more embedded in this world than we realized. And where are these local supernaturals anyway? Could they help or hinder us?" They began to walk towards the Metro, the quickest way of reaching the museum—which had, after all, been his original target. Although public transport suddenly felt a bit too public.

"Who knows?" Jerome replied. "But if CENSOR have stirred up that much suspicion of those with 'powers,' we'll have to be really careful. The last thing we want is to trigger a lynch mob waving stakes, or whatever they do here."

"Keeping that gang happy, so they don't set CENSOR on us first, will help," Kai pointed out.

"Looks like we dodged a bullet, then. We only need to pay."

"It does make me wonder, though . . ." Kai gestured at the street, the city beyond. "If *we've* hit problems already, what's it like for people who actually live here, experiencing this environment of fear on a daily basis?"

Jerome's eyes were bleak, and his amused smile vanished. "There are more ways to control a land, or a world, than by dictatorship. And I think CENSOR's found one of them."

CHAPTER 13

Irene looked up from her monitor. The two of them were alone. "Could Hao Chen still be here? Tell me about him."

"He's worthless." Indigo was working through another set of computer memory sticks, doing some sort of tests on the contents of each before discarding them. Each had its own little labelled nook in a foam-rubber-lined case. Even when Indigo would have—by her expression—preferred to have thrown them across the room, she carefully put each one back in place before trying the next. "I don't have time for him."

"Worthless in the incompetent way, the libidinous way, or the frivolous way?" Irene asked, with a wry smile.

"Frivolous. He has no mind—no, that's not quite correct. He does have a mind, but he chooses not to use it. He spends all his time on gambling and betting and theatres—and he's led his sister into bad habits too."

"His sister?"

"Shu Fang. They have the same parents on both sides. They made a binding contract for life, would you believe it? Of course, they're low family, so they can do that sort of thing."

Irene knew that the royal dragons engaged in what Kai had referred to as "mating contracts." They didn't seem to go in for long-term or permanent marriages. But it seemed less powerful dragons had a bit more leeway. "If Hao Chen is still hanging around this world, does that mean we might expect his sister as well?"

"You should have asked Kai before you sent him out," Indigo said, unfairly Irene thought. "Why are you pestering *me* for details?"

"Because I thought you might know something useful," Irene said carefully. She wasn't here to make enemies.

"You seem to have dropped your bad attitude . . ."

"And you seem to have stopped calling me 'girl.'"

"I needed to know your limits," Indigo said. She slotted in a new memory stick. "Fae are manageable, once you've grasped their particular delusion, but humans are less logical. You're associating with Kai, for a start."

"You do realize that I'm curious about what's going on there with you two," Irene said, leadingly.

"And you do realize that I'm not going to discuss my private life with *you*."

Irene felt disappointed, but she was used to hunting down secrets. Indigo clearly had a few of them—and again, knowing so little about her teammates felt far too risky for comfort. "So why did you rebel against your parents?" Irene probed. "Is the rule of dragons really that bad?"

"No, not if you ask someone who accepts everything they're told by their father," Indigo countered. "But unlike Kai, if you really think about politics, about our monarchs' right to rule, about the gaps in our history . . . what then?"

"You tell me, Indigo—you're the one who would know. Is there something to hide?"

"Of course there is," Indigo said with casual scorn. "And people would kill to keep those secrets. Our so-called history is a shared fiction, agreed to keep those who are in power where they are. There is no such thing as genuine truth, only received truth. The winners write the history books in all cultures, as it serves their advantage. Parents tell their children the stories which paint them as heroes. Enlightened self-interest is the best that anyone can hope for."

"And I thought *I* was cynical."

Indigo leaned back in her chair. "So why don't *you* tell *me* something instead? This program needs a few minutes to run, so you might as well . . ."

Irene shrugged inwardly. Maybe if she talked, Indigo would be inclined to share in turn. "Let's start with CENSOR. It was founded after the Second World War—that happened in the forties here too. And it also shared the same standard Axis-Allies split which occurs in a lot of alternate worlds. But after the war, people discovered major-league supernatural interference. Secret cabals of vampires, packs of werewolves roaming the streets, hidden organisations of mages behind the scenes."

"That's curious," Indigo said. "If they were so secret, how did they get found out?"

"It seems new surveillance technology was invented during the war," Irene answered. "But CENSOR's archives would have more detail. Have you been able to access them?"

"Not yet," Indigo muttered, irritation in her voice.

Could it be that Indigo wasn't finding the local systems quite as easy to hack as she'd boasted? Probably not helpful to ask. "Anyhow, after that period there's a constant stream of supernatural incidents. An attempt by vampires to take over the Conservative Party in Great Britain, a rampage by werewolves down Las Ramblas in Barcelona, some sort of cabal of blood sorcerers in Belgium—"

"Something strange always happens in Belgium," Indigo interrupted.

"Why's that?" Irene asked, distracted.

"I don't know. Go on with the supernatural idiocy."

"There's an ongoing seething boil of lower-grade problems too; enough to keep CENSOR busy and everyone else paranoid. What I couldn't find was any public mention about what happened to the arrested paranormals *afterwards*."

"If I were in charge of CENSOR, I'd either use my paranormal captives to test new strategic initiatives, or I'd assemble them into my own private army," Indigo said. "Either way, I wouldn't welcome public interest in my activities. When you were researching CENSOR in the library, do you suppose you triggered an alarm that provoked the raid?"

"I don't think so," Irene said. "My research didn't suggest someone could be caught by an online search. All the same, we'd better be careful. And I hope you are very good at your job, if they *are* capable of that level of oversight."

Something flashed on one of Indigo's screens and she peered at it. "The whole thing seems messy. If there are all these supernatural factions, why haven't they seized control? And if CENSOR's so vigilant, why haven't they stamped them out?"

"It's only been sixty years or so since their rise," Irene said thoughtfully. "And it seems to be mostly a Europe-specific problem. America's a theocracy with very strictly controlled travel in and out. China, Russia, the Middle East . . . most of them have their own CENSOR equivalents, which seem even more effective than here."

"The United Kingdom?"

"Very strongly tied to Europe, which is why CENSOR has an English name and acronym. They did attempt to leave the European Union last year, but apparently that was prompted by demonic interference. A lot of politicians were subsequently tried for treason and beheaded at the Tower of London."

Indigo looked up and seemed to come to a decision. "Irene, between us, this hacking job may be slightly more difficult than I'd thought."

Irene's mental alarms went off. They were hardly on *between us* terms, and she sensed an attempt at manipulation.

"There's all this security. And now CENSOR to consider. What if we can't get the job done on time, with *this* limiting my powers?" Indigo lifted her right hand. The silver cuff gleamed coldly on her wrist.

"I don't suppose I could be of assistance with that?" Irene offered, to see what she'd say.

Indigo sniffed. "You honestly think you could do anything with those Librarian tricks that I couldn't do myself? Please, don't be ridiculous."

Was that reverse psychology, to get Irene to remove the bracelet? Or was it a test of Irene's commitment to the team? "As you like," was all she said.

And was the momentary flicker behind Indigo's eyes amusement, or disappointment at a failed gambit?

"So what *did* Mr. Nemo offer you?" Indigo asked, too casually.

"A book for the Library," Irene answered, equally non-committal.

"Good to know that we can count on you for anything up to and including murder, then, with that bait . . ." Indigo said, and turned back to her computer.

Irene was still wondering about Indigo's motives when her phone buzzed. A text from Kai.

We have a problem. Museum closes for renovations in two days.

Night had fallen. The once-empty office was filling up with a detritus of guide-books, maps, notepads, and crumpled bits of paper. If CENSOR did ever manage to find them here, they'd need to torch the place to conceal their plans, or hire an industrial shredder. Outside, lorries groaned and rattled past, following their nocturnal routes through the more industrial parts of Vienna.

Ernst rolled his shoulders thoughtfully. "I think we need more pizza."

"If you can think at all, then you should be thinking about *this*," Felix snapped, marking locations on a tourist map of the museum's second floor.

"At least ordering in food fits our cover as a tech start-up company," Irene said, leaning over to study the exits. "Staying up working, living off pizza, coffee, and takeaways . . ."

Kai had returned, then been sent out again on a shopping mission by Indigo. He was now installing technical bits and pieces at her direction. Rather to Irene's surprise, he seemed to be enjoying himself. She sometimes forgot that he'd spent time in a high-technology world. "Night work is essential," he said doggedly, "if we only have two days."

"Two days counting tomorrow, or two days starting from today—when they shut the place down?" Tina asked. She was scrawling illegible markings on street maps of Vienna. She'd also obtained some miniature cars, which occasionally came whooshing down the main table and into the planning session. She was clearly a woman deeply in touch with her archetype.

"The first, unfortunately," Jerome said. "I still think we should go in post-close-down. If there are going to be builders and security people all over the place, it could give us the perfect cover."

"That's true," Felix agreed, "but we don't know exactly how it's going to work. If we move now, we can expect their regular security and guard patrols . . . more of a known quantity."

"But if we move after, we can do as much damage as we like," Ernst suggested. "We can have a big fire—or explosions—and blame it on terrorists or even evil mages. There will be so much destruction that there will be no evidence we took the painting. Nice and tidy for us. Messy for them."

"We are *not* burning down the Kunsthistorisches Museum," Irene said flatly. The very thought of destroying so many creative works made her flinch. Even if they weren't books. "Nor are we blowing it up. Overkill is not an option here with the threat of CENSOR hanging over us." Some Librarians would have considered the cost—in lives or artworks—a reasonable price to pay. But while there were still other options, she'd use any excuse to get the others to back down.

"I still can't believe they didn't have the planned closure online," Indigo muttered. "It's blatant incompetence."

"It's certainly odd." Irene scribbled on a sheet of paper, trying to work out which aspect of the building was most amenable to illegal entry. Unfortunately for their purposes, the museum had wide-open spaces all round it: roads on three sides, and a park area facing the Natural History Museum on the fourth. The roads would be convenient for a rapid getaway, but they were well-lit and covered by multiple cameras. And having their getaway vehicle park there for half the night wouldn't be an option.

"They're closing because of subsidence," Kai interjected. "Isn't that what the notices said—"

"Still, the timing is suspicious," Irene continued. "We show up. Later the same day, they announce that the museum's going to be closed for renovations. Maybe I'm being paranoid?"

"No such thing as paranoia when on a job," Ernst said. "But at the moment no clear evidence to support it. Let us return to planning. Will computer technology be able to help us?"

"There is a *minor* problem," Indigo said, reluctantly.

"Ah, if it is minor, then you can explain it easily."

Indigo's glare could have been used to polish diamonds. "I can explain the consequences easily enough, but unless you want to go back to school, not to mention university, I can't explain *why* it's a problem. Not to you, at least."

Ernst looked amused, but Felix seemed annoyed. Irene hastily said, "What's the problem?"

"The CENSOR networks have unusually tight safeguards." Indigo pushed her long hair back irritably. "The easiest way of getting round them would be to insert physical interrupts into their systems. The problem with that is that it involves breaking in to insert them."

Kai frowned. "Into the central network systems, under the Vienna International Centre?"

"The UNO City buildings, yes. North-north-east of the

Prater—the amusement park—on that curve of land between the Danube and the Danube Canal." She pointed it out on one of the maps. "And if you thought security around the museum was high, security around CENSOR's own nerve centre is going to be *very* high indeed."

"What one man can invent, another can break into and steal," Irene said thoughtfully. "Perhaps we could hire locals to arrange a distraction? More hands would be useful."

"Didn't you have your own crew, Felix?" Tina asked. She sent a car whizzing down the table to do a ramp jump off an angled pizza box lid.

"Not any more," Felix said, in tones that shut off any possibility of raising the question again.

Irene decided a change of tactic might be an idea. "Indigo, is there a particular point where you need to put your physical interrupts, or are there options?"

"Multiple options, but none of them particularly good."

"What I'm wondering is—whether any of them are under the river?"

"What does that have to do with it . . ." Indigo followed Irene's gaze towards Kai. "Oh," she said, then with more interest: "*Oh*. Well. I didn't know you had that level of control."

Kai sat back. His expression could not be defined, even by the most charitable, as anything less than extremely smug. "It's not as if you *would* know, is it?"

Felix sighed. "Does this mean that we have an option besides scuba-diving and wet suits?"

"It's certainly possible," Indigo said. "Though in that case, if Hao Chen *is* in the city, we might have a problem."

Kai's smirk slipped. "That's true. His element is also water. While he's certainly not as strong as I am, if I use my strength, then he might feel something."

Jerome frowned. "Wait, did you just say Hao Chen?"

"Does it mean something to you?" Indigo asked.

"Because I saw that name this afternoon."

"Details, please," Irene said, trying to repress a groan of frustration.

"I was making the rounds of local casinos, to get the hang of the underground scene here. One of them—one of the less legal ones—was touting for a big event tomorrow evening. I managed to see the guest list. One of the names listed was Hao Chen."

Silence fell briefly as everyone considered this.

"You said he was a gambler," Irene finally said to Indigo. "Do you think it's really him?"

"Well, there's an easy way to check. What's the place's name? I may not be able to hack into CENSOR yet, but I can certainly manage a cheap local casino."

"An *expensive* local casino," Jerome contradicted her. "And one with an illegal side—the security's likely to be good."

"Yes, yes, whatever," Indigo agreed dismissively. "The name?"

"Casino Nonpareil. Founded by a French gambler somewhere in the seventeen-fifties." He shrugged at people's gazes. "Look, it's my business to know these things. She knows libraries." He nodded towards Irene. "I know casinos."

"Give me a moment." Indigo lowered her head towards her monitors like a cobra swaying towards its prey.

"Assume a worst-case scenario." Irene turned back to Kai. "If Hao Chen's in the area and might notice you messing with the Danube, then what would it take to distract *him*?"

"Being drugged?" Kai suggested. "Knocked over the head? Or maybe some really intense emotions."

The smile that drifted over Jerome's face was a thing of beauty. "I believe I can arrange some . . . strong emotions."

"In that case," Irene said, "we need to organise the division of labour—and agree on our timing."

She glanced around. Even Felix was listening. But she had to be careful. She couldn't afford to lose their trust again. "Now, if I may make some suggestions . . ."

CHAPTER 14

I think I'm suffering from Stendhal Syndrome," Irene murmured, looking around wide-eyed at the paintings. The syndrome wasn't recognized by orthodox medicine, but it perfectly described her current art-inspired ecstasy. "This place is just . . ."

"It is, isn't it?" Kai agreed approvingly. "That veined black marble they've used for the pillars is perfect. And that central hall with the cupola and the marble stairs . . . beautiful use of light."

"I didn't know you knew so much about architecture."

"I've been reading the guide-book," Kai admitted.

The two of them were making their way round the Kunsthistorisches Museum, in the role of a pair of besotted tourists. Irene had changed her appearance again and so far hadn't set off any obvious alarms.

And when taking a photo, one could include all sorts of interesting details. Doorways, for instance, for later comparative height references. Inconspicuous background alarms throughout the building. Even *The Raft of the Medusa* itself.

Irene had to admit it was a striking painting. Its portrayal of the survivors—and corpses—on the raft was painfully convincing—with the remains of the frigate *Méduse* in the background. The musculature on the bodies, both living and dying, seemed real enough to touch. Waves swept over the edges of the raft and rose through gaps between the planks. And while the raft's jury-rigged sail strained in the wind, the ocean surged in the background as storm-clouds gathered overhead. A couple of desperate men waved ragged clothing towards a ship—barely visible as a dot on the horizon. But others—men and women alike—bowed their heads in despair or knelt hopelessly beside the bodies of the dead.

It was also *enormous*. It was one thing to read the measurements written down, but quite another to see the painting stretching nearly from floor to ceiling. This was not going to be easy. The Language was too unpredictable to risk using it to remove the painting from its frame without damaging it, unless Irene had a very definite understanding of what she was doing. And even if she were to free it and they rolled it up, it wouldn't fit through any of the windows—ground floor or first floor—without entirely dismantling said window.

There weren't any significant collections of books in the museum, either. She wouldn't be able to drag it into the Library and then drag it out again later somewhere else. Even if the Fae on the team had trusted her to walk off with it.

". . . not that there's much of a French collection here anyhow," Kai said, interrupting her thoughts. They wove their way through the rooms—all interconnecting chambers of various sizes, no corridors. "It's an astonishing display."

"It's the result of the Hapsburgs collecting such things for centuries," Irene noted. "I expect your uncles do the same. What was that line from the guide-book, about Rudolf II? 'What the Emperor knows about, he has to have'?"

"Sounds more like the Library to me," Kai said with a straight face.

Irene couldn't help herself. She smiled. "Let's go and talk strategy, before we visit the Prater."

Vienna had wonderful coffee-houses. Unfortunately they all had security cameras. But surely it was only natural that two tourists should stop off for coffee, after a morning at the Kunsthistorisches Museum?

Irene dabbed away her whipped cream moustache and cut into a slice of Sachertorte. "We needed a chance to talk, away from the others," she said, her voice lost in the hum of other conversations.

"I won't claim I like anything about this job, but then I don't have to *like* it," Kai replied. His expression was guarded.

"But if I apologise for getting you into this, you'll just remind me you chose to come. Am I right?"

Kai's mouth quirked a little. "You are. And I have my reasons for coming."

"Really?" Irene stole a fragment of his apple strudel. "What are they?"

"Oh, building bonds with the Fae, given that we have a truce with them now. Gaining future favours. That sort of thing. And if you eat my apple strudel, madam, I'll devour your Sachertorte."

"You'd better not say that in front of our new colleagues," Irene said primly. "They might get entirely the wrong idea." As he choked on his coffee, she went on, "What do you make of them—our colleagues?"

Kai frowned. "Tina's the one person on the team we can't afford to lose, as she's the only one who can find her way back to Mr. Nemo's hideout. Either Mr. Nemo really trusts her—or he has some sort of hold over her."

"What about Ernst?"

"I don't think he's as simple as he pretends to be."

Irene nodded. "Yes. At least part of that 'big ox' routine is an act. What about Felix?"

"He's probably the best-equipped of this whole team for the job we're undertaking," Kai said slowly. "He's a thief to his bones. But at the same time I have the impression he's the least interested in working with the rest of us. And I don't think he likes you at all."

"Apparently a Librarian thwarted him in the past, and he holds a grudge," Irene said. "Who knows if it's justified? I also think Felix was expecting to be in charge."

"Ernst said Felix has his own team. I wonder why he's not using them here."

"Interesting question." Irene doodled with her fork in the remains of her Sachertorte. "So why did Felix accept this job and why was he hired? This is a Fae master thief who's failed on at least one job in the past, who's no longer working with his usual crew, and who's taking a commission—not stealing for his own pleasure. It doesn't feel right . . . but I wish I knew *why*."

"He'll be after *something*," Kai said, accurately but unhelpfully.

"And what about Indigo?"

"She's bad news," Kai said, his good mood gone. His tone discouraged further discussion.

"Morally or politically?" Irene didn't want to pry, but the situation was too dangerous for her to remain ignorant. Plus, against her better nature—which mostly existed because of her school's lessons in morality—she *was* curious.

"Both."

"What, does she eat baby seals or something?"

"There's no point in being offended about eating baby seals, when there are worlds where there are so many seals that it's positive population control."

"I appreciate you don't want to talk about this, but I'm going to keep asking." If the Library's reputation, or a world's safety, depended on exactly what Indigo had done or might do, then sensitivity would have to wait.

There was a pause while conversations went on around them. Yet it was all hushed. Even the most innocent speeches were delivered in the knowledge that someone might be listening, that a camera could be watching, and that a potential accusation was only a moment away.

Finally Kai said, "If I tell you some of it, you mustn't share it with the others. You can tell the Library if you absolutely have to, but not Fae."

"I can promise that," Irene agreed.

"Indigo outright rebelled against both my father and her mother." The disgust in Kai's words was palpable. "She raised public dissent against my father's rule, Irene. She tried to persuade other dragons to join her. She claimed our monarchs had covered up matters which fundamentally undermined their right to govern. That they were dictators, and she had no intention of being their slave for the rest of her life. When she couldn't get support, she fled. And there was something worse . . . but it was bad enough that even *I* don't know what it was, and I'm my father's son. Whatever she did, that knowledge was placed under seal at the highest levels. I can't tell you more than that, but you must believe me, Irene. Don't trust her. She may be my own sister, but I'd believe a *Fae* before her."

Irene felt a surprising ache of pity for Indigo. Imprisoned, co-opted into working for Mr. Nemo . . . and completely disowned by her family. She knew dragon culture worked differently—to them, honour, lawfulness, and fealty *was* familial love—but even so, it had to be painful to be cut adrift from everything she'd known. Irene couldn't count the times she and her parents had disagreed, occasionally to the point of barely withheld rage, but she'd never once questioned her parents' love for her.

Yet she still nodded slowly. "Thank you. I appreciate the warning. In fact, going with the *not trusting anyone* thought, I'd like to share this idea about what we should do if things go badly wrong . . ."

Outside, the clouds had drawn in. Inside the café, the ubiquitous surveillance cameras continued to watch over the citizens of Vienna.

The Casino Nonpareil was located in a large and gracious building about the same age as the Kunsthistorisches Museum. It was the sort of place one had to be in the know to find—and have the money to be allowed in.

Inside, the rooms were segregated by game. There was a Roulette Room, a Poker Room, and others that Irene hadn't had the chance to investigate. They were currently in the Baccarat Room, which might once have been a ballroom. There were chandeliers still hanging from the ceiling, but now they overlooked a dozen or more card tables. Further signs of modernisation were dotted around inconspicuously: a fire alarm, sprinklers, more security cameras . . . A sign near the door of the room stated: IN THE EVENT OF A CENSOR RAID, ALL GAMES WILL BE CONSIDERED NULL AND ALL STAKES RETURNED TO THEIR ORIGINAL OWNERS. It was repeated in several languages, presumably so no gambler present could claim ignorance.

"The fact that they bother to have that sign there at all suggests an unfortunate frequency of CENSOR raids," Irene said softly. She'd changed her appearance again—chestnut hair dye, a different hair-style, make-up suitable for a rich gambler's arm candy, and a little black dress. The operative word was *little*, and it only just covered the Library brand on her back. And she was ready to give an *all systems go* text to Kai, as soon as Hao Chen was here and suitably distracted.

Jerome followed her glance. "Oh, they have that sign in all the serious casinos in town," he said. "Get me another whiskey sour, will you, 'sweetheart'?"

"Of course, 'honey,'" Irene answered, dimpling, and headed towards the bar.

Jerome was accompanying her here. Kai, Ernst, and Tina had been assigned to the river job, to insert the technology Indigo had given them. Meanwhile, Felix was on the move, watching for signs of CENSOR alerts. Indigo herself was back at their base, ready to activate the interrupts remotely.

Irene's nerves twisted themselves into knots as she waited to collect Jerome's drink, sweeping a casual glance across the room. None of this would be worthwhile if Hao Chen didn't turn up. It was past midnight now. If he wasn't here by four in the morning, they'd have to go ahead with the plan anyway—trusting to luck that neither he nor any other nearby dragons noticed Kai meddling with the river. Jerome was enjoying himself, playing endless games of baccarat. But Irene . . .

Irene was deeply worried. If this world *was* claimed by a particular dragon as his territory—for example, this Hao Chen—then she was about to be put in an impossible position. She *couldn't* risk being caught stealing from a dragon—and if this world was his, anything on it would be considered his too. She would therefore be breaking one of the major stipulations of the treaty. The *no thefts from signatories* clause might have been primarily intended to refer to *books*. But any dragon or Fae would apply it to any or all of their property. And if she couldn't steal the painting, she wouldn't get the book. The world she'd known and cared about would slip into chaos . . .

If only she could slip back to the Library to check. But she'd almost lost her life, as well as the team's trust, last time.

She made her way back to Jerome and slipped the drink into his hand with an affected giggle. They'd discussed what sort of role she should assume. Jerome had ruled out professional gambler the moment he saw her handle a deck of cards. And Irene had rejected bodyguard on the grounds that she preferred to be underestimated. So that left "companion"—which also gave her an excuse for murmuring in his ear.

"More people are arriving," she whispered. "Are these the serious players finally turning up?"

Jerome nodded. "It's like a party. The big names won't arrive too early."

The people drifting into the Baccarat Room didn't necessarily look fashionable or expensive, though they had all donned evening wear. The occasional piece of heavy gold jewellery or Rolex suggested money, but that didn't tell her whether the gambler was skilled or just well off.

She scanned the room, looking for any sign of a dragon in human form—or even said dragon's minions. But a question from earlier was teasing at her. "By the way—what did Tina mean, when she said Felix had people he worked with?"

Jerome shrugged. "It's no secret. He's always been the sort of thief who has . . . associates."

Irene could think of several fictional tropes that might apply to this archetype. "Was he the master of countless devoted minion thieves? Or the acknowledged leader of a friendly group, with expertise in different areas?"

"Ah, you know the sort of thing. It was the second option. Half the time they were feuding, and the rest of the time they were pulling off heists."

Irene swirled the soda in her own glass. She wasn't touching alcohol under these circumstances. "If they were that good, why didn't Mr. Nemo hire *them*?"

"Things went wrong," Jerome said. The room's chandeliers trembled under the impetus of some distant traffic, and for a moment the shifting lights made his expression seem actually sympathetic. "He messed up. Then he messed up again. And a man in his position can't afford to make mistakes. You know how things work, with me and my kind. Once we start slipping from what we are, who we are, it all goes wrong. His crew sort of . . . drifted away."

Irene remembered Felix's very personal animosity towards her. If one of her fellow Librarians *had* interfered with a theft and caused him to lose touch with his archetype in the process, she could understand why he was bitter. "I see," she murmured. "And yet Mr. Nemo still hired him."

"Felix will do anything to get his reputation back." This time there was clear warning in Jerome's eyes. "Don't foul up here, 'Carla'"—her pseudonym for the evening—"and don't get in his way."

A stir by the doorway broke the tension. Irene's eyes narrowed as she caught sight of a profile she recognized. It really was impossible to mistake a dragon for a normal human, once you'd met one, however much they tried to dress down. And Hao Chen had scarcely bothered to hide what he was. His dinner suit was nicely cut, but his presence was unmistakable. His black hair was swept back in loose waves that tumbled over his shoulders, and his eyes were the same deep blue as Kai's. A set of silver rings pierced his left earlobe, running from bottom to top—and the seal-ring on his right forefinger was also heavy silver. He didn't have an entourage, unlike many of the other gamblers present, but he smiled and greeted people graciously as he passed.

"The croupier said that he usually plays at table two," Jerome said softly. "Give it a moment and we'll drift over. This may go better than I'd thought."

"Why so?"

"Because, 'Carla sweetheart,' you Librarians don't know *everything*." Jerome was positively grinning now. He finished his drink and passed her the empty glass. "Get rid of this, get me another, and we'll stroll."

Hao Chen gave Jerome a pleasant smile as the Fae approached. His eyes slid over Irene, but not quite in a dragon's usual judgement of *human, therefore unimportant*—there was something more nuanced to it. "I don't think we've met?" he enquired, his German perfect.

"Afraid not," Jerome said, and offered his hand to shake. "But I wouldn't be surprised if we met again. You look like a gentleman who likes to play baccarat at odds of forty to one."

Hao Chen paused for half a second before taking Jerome's hand. His smile widened to match Jerome's own. "What a delightful surprise. You know, it's been simply ages since I had the chance to match myself against a *proper* player." He glanced back at Irene. "I don't suppose your friend . . ."

Jerome patted Irene's rear possessively. She controlled her first reaction—to stab her high heel through his shoe—and lowered her eyelashes. "Oh no, honey," she said. "I'm just here to hold Mr. Town's drinks for him while he's playing. And his winnings, of course." She even managed another breathy giggle.

Hao Chen nodded and turned back to Jerome. He had clearly written her off as irrelevant. "So, any preferences?"

"Chemin de fer or macao," Jerome replied. "More interesting than punto banco."

"Macao," Hao Chen said without hesitation. "Just the two of us, I take it?"

"For the moment, at least." The two men were staring at each other like duellists about to draw blades. The rest of the casino might as well not have existed.

"Good enough." Hao Chen looked at the glass in his hand as though he'd forgotten its existence. "Let me get some chips. Are you provided for?"

"Of course," Jerome said. He tapped the side of the bulging handbag hooked over Irene's elbow. "But I let Carla here carry them. Wouldn't want to spoil the line of my suit."

Hao Chen flashed his smile again and moved towards the inconspicuous desk near the door where a cashier sat.

Jerome eased himself into a chair at table two, leaving Irene to stand. "Any thoughts?"

"He's probably checking up on you while he gets his tokens," Irene answered, leaning close. "And your 'forty to one' thing is clearly some kind of password, though I have no idea what."

"It's a particular betting system in baccarat," Jerome said. He flipped open her handbag and began removing chips. "It's known as 'Dragon 7.' And among certain gamblers, from both sides, it's a recognition flag to let the other guy—or girl—know that we're here to *play*. Just because you've got a fancy formal truce going doesn't mean that there weren't dragon-Fae truces before that."

His grin took some of the sting out of his words. And it left Irene wondering, with a hint of annoyance—just how many smaller "private arrangements" were out there, beyond the scope of politicians and royalty.

"Any last instructions?" Irene asked. She could see Hao Chen making his way back.

"Let us play two hands before you buzz the others. That should be enough to keep his eyes on the table. Otherwise, just keep lighting my cigars and fetching my drinks. I'll be the interesting one tonight."

"Suits me," Irene agreed.

"Any preference over who starts as banker?" Hao Chen asked, slipping into a facing chair. One of the quietly omnipresent croupiers hurried over with two decks of cards.

"You first," Jerome said. "We'll see how it goes."

And they began to play.

CHAPTER 15

As Irene watched, she wished that her knowledge of the rules extended further than Ian Fleming novels.

Hao Chen laid down a bet. Jerome matched it. Hao Chen dealt Jerome a card, then himself, both face-down. They inspected their cards as tension built in the air.

A pause.

Jerome tapped the table with one finger, and Hao Chen slid him a new card, face-up: the jack of diamonds. When Jerome shook his head, face impassive, Hao Chen dealt him another: the eight of clubs. Jerome sighed, flipped over his face-down card—the four of hearts—and slid his counters across the table to Hao Chen. They both smiled at each other, and it began again.

Around her, other games were going on with the same degree of intensity. Outside in the streets of Vienna, the city moved to the rhythm of late-night business—the opera, restaurants, street stalls, the hum of traffic, and the throb of the Metro. But in here there was silence except for the slap of cards on tables. Even the onlookers, like herself, kept quiet while the players focused on the truly important matters—the cards and each other. No doubt it was the same in the other rooms of the Casino Nonpareil. The legal and illegal game rooms . . .

Hao Chen dealt a third hand. Jerome raised a finger for a momentary pause and reached inside his jacket for a cigar case. He snapped it open and offered it to Hao Chen—and when the dragon refused, he selected a cigar for himself. Irene was ready with her lighter.

And when she slid her lighter back into her handbag, she tapped the button on her phone that would send the pre-typed message: *Go ahead.*

The phone buzzed in response. Then a moment later, buzzed again.

As casually as she could, Irene slipped it out of her handbag.

It was a message from Kai, and as she read it, she was seized by the familiar feeling of a plan coming apart.

F not answering phone.

Felix was supposed to be watching for CENSOR alerts, but what if he'd encountered some actual CENSOR agents? And if so, was there a risk to the mission? Jerome knew Felix better than she did; he might be able to explain the Fae's current behaviour. Yet she couldn't interrupt the game now. Hao Chen would suspect something. And it was too late to abort Kai's side of the operation. With a silent curse she tapped in, *Carry on—be careful.*

The last bit was redundant, of course . . . but she was only human.

The third hand went by. A fourth. A fifth. The stakes were rising, but Irene couldn't see any clear signs of either man winning or losing. They were both professionally expressionless. Hao Chen crooked a finger at a passing waiter and was provided with a gin and tonic. Clearly they knew his tastes here. Jerome drew on his cigar as Hao Chen dealt them both face-down cards.

And then the crowd split open in a sea of murmurs. A young woman came striding through, her fringed skirt hissing round her legs with every step, and she headed straight for their table. Her hair and eyes were both slate-grey, the colour of a rainy sky. And like him, she was a dragon.

Hao Chen jolted upright. "Shu Fang! What are *you* doing here?" he asked. He clearly intended to demand an answer, but instead he sounded plaintive, almost querulous.

"I'm here to get you out of trouble again, ninny," she snapped. Her gaze flicked to Jerome and judged him for what he was in a single moment. "Not *more* baccarat . . . No offence, but we have trouble incoming and you don't want to be caught in it. Get the hell out of here, now."

"But the hand's dealt," Hao Chen complained. "We can't just . . ."

The woman glanced over her shoulder—nervous, almost panicked—then back to the table again. "Then someone *else* can play it. *You.*" Her gaze drilled through Irene. "Chair. Sit. You, Fae, take a few steps back and hide in the crowd. Trust me, it's for your own good."

Hao Chen bit his lip. "It might be best, just for this hand," he agreed reluctantly. And Irene realized he knew what—or who—was coming. Jerome rose, swapping places with Irene. He patted her on the shoulder as condescendingly as possible and faded back into the crowd.

Someone else was approaching their table, the crowd parting before her, and silence flowing out across the room in her wake.

Irene stared, and she was hardly breaking her cover in doing so; even the other gamblers had abandoned their cards to goggle at the newcomer.

The woman was the first dragon Irene had ever seen who actually looked *old*. She was thin rather than slender, her face drawn into long wrinkles, white hair knotted back in a complicated bun. A heavy pair of wraparound dark glasses covered her eyes from brow to cheekbones. While her stick rapped against the ground with every step, she wasn't leaning on it—and Irene could recognize a sword-cane when she saw one. She wore a champagne-gold evening dress and diamond brooch like an aristocrat, but her arms were corded with muscle under the cloth and her hands were seamed with scars.

Hao Chen swallowed and rose to his feet. "Lady Ciu," he said, with a graceful half bow. "You do me too much honour by visiting—"

"You will address me as aunt!" the elderly dragon snapped. "And what are you *doing*? Having failed to gamble away your entire allowance on slow horses, you're now wasting it on fast women? And dragging your sister into it as well?"

Her head turned to fix Irene with a glare that was quite palpable despite her dark glasses. "And could you find no better opponent than *this*?"

Irene fought the urge to slide under the table and stay there. She'd been in the presence of powerful dragons before, who could manipulate the elements and even summon up storms. Lady Ciu was dangerous in an entirely different way. She didn't have the powers of a dragon monarch, but Irene had absolutely no doubt that she was lethal—and quite ready to dispose of irritating humans. "*Gnädige Frau*," she said, raising her address to an extremely formal level—*gracious lady*—"if you will excuse me . . ."

"Hm? She speaks!" Lady Ciu's cane flicked out and rapped Irene painfully on the shoulder, as she tried to rise from her chair. "How curious! Well, if I've come all the way here, perhaps I should see how my nephew gambles. Hao Chen, you may finish your round."

Hao Chen shrank back into his chair. "Do you want a card?" he asked Irene.

Irene realized she didn't even know what the card in front of her was. Carefully she lifted up the edge to peer at it, doing her best to imitate Jerome's style. It was the four of spades. What would James Bond have done? What were her odds of getting nine or less if she started with a four?

Lady Ciu hissed between her teeth. People who'd been drawing closer to watch retreated a pace and then tried to look as if it had been pure coincidence. "What's this? A gambler who can't even remember her cards from one minute to another?"

Irene's mouth was almost too dry to speak. "*Gnädige Frau*, your nephew had only just dealt the cards. I hadn't had a chance to look at them yet!"

"Is that so." Lady Ciu stalked round the table to stand directly behind Irene. From the way Hao Chen flinched, she was fixing him with her gaze. "Very well. Are you going to ask for a card? Get on with it!"

Irene's hands trembled, but not just from the natural fear of having an apex predator behind her. It was the knowledge that only a couple of layers of cloth lay between Lady Ciu and the Library brand across Irene's back. If she discovered that, it would ruin Irene's chance of remaining anonymous. And the odds of Lady Ciu believing a Librarian just *happened* to be playing cards with her nephew . . . She bit her lip. "Card," she said to Hao Chen. "Please."

He flipped a card across the table, face-up. Six of spades. With the four she held, that made ten. She'd just lost the hand—she knew that much.

A huge wave of relief filled Irene. "Sorry," she said, and flipped over her four. "My loss."

Hao Chen reached out quickly to scoop up the counters. "Good game," he said insincerely.

"Yes." Lady Ciu's cane tapped Irene's shoulder again, more gently, but on exactly the same spot—or same bruise, rather—where she'd rapped earlier. "Good try, girl. But I can tell you're working for someone else. *You're* no gambler. So . . . where's your patron?"

For a moment the room was still. Then Jerome came walking out of the crowd, his cigar still in his hand. "You'd be referring to me, I think."

Hao Chen and his sister had both frozen, visibly counting down the seconds until violence erupted. But Lady Ciu simply sniffed. "One of your type. I *expected* as much."

"I've got no argument with your nephew, ma'am," Jerome said easily. "And I don't think you've got any with my Carla there."

One of the advantages—or disadvantages, Irene reflected—of the casino's *illegal* side was that nobody even suggested calling the police, or moved to intervene. Everyone was staying well out of it.

But at least, she reflected drily, *we have Hao Chen's full attention . . .*

"That may be so," Lady Ciu said. "However, I have nothing *but* arguments with you. Your presence here . . . offends me."

Jerome took a long puff of his cigar. "Well now, I hadn't heard that this place was your private holiday home, ma'am. Perhaps if I had done, I wouldn't have come."

"And now that you are here?"

Make your excuses and go, Irene thought desperately in Jerome's direction.

"I'm here to gamble." Jerome lowered his cigar. "And if you don't care to have your nephew bet against me, ma'am, then perhaps you'd like to play a hand yourself."

"Ha!" The old dragon's eyes were invisible, but her mouth curled into a smile. "Very well. I accept. Let's see how you play the game."

Hao Chen and his sister stumbled forward simultaneously. "Aunt, but—" "Aunt, you can't possibly—"

Lady Ciu rapped her cane hard against the ground, ignoring the younger dragons. "Girl—Carla—let your master take your seat. And don't try anything to help him."

"Now that's uncalled-for," Jerome remarked, as he took the seat that Irene had hastily vacated. He emptied her bag of all their casino chips before passing it back. "I'm not the sort to try to stack the odds in a fair game."

"We'll see." Lady Ciu took the seat that had been Hao Chen's. "You may be banker. Shuffle and deal."

As Jerome shuffled, Irene noted one of the casino employees—a senior one, by her clothing—sidling across to Hao Chen. Irene caught a few desperate phrases. "You *promised* she wouldn't come here . . . last time she . . ."

And then the phone in Irene's bag buzzed. It could be an emergency. But the whole room was looking at the baccarat table right now, and she couldn't risk drawing attention.

She took a deep breath and ignored her phone.

"The stakes?" Lady Ciu asked.

Jerome toppled his entire stack of chips across the table. "I wouldn't be satisfied with less, ma'am."

"Hao Chen!" she ordered. "Match his stakes."

Hao Chen swallowed. The word *but* hovered mutinously on the tip of his tongue and was bitten back. He stepped up and pushed his own chips forward.

With an inclination of his head, Jerome slid a card face-down across the table and then dealt himself one. He lifted the corner of his own, but his face was of course unreadable.

Lady Ciu did the same, her face equally impassive. "Another."

The four of diamonds slid across the table towards her. She nodded but didn't ask for a third.

Silence draped the room, the scene stifling noise better than the room's velvet curtains. Jerome considered, smiled, and dealt himself a card.

It was the five of spades.

Still with the same smile, he flipped over his face-down card. The six of spades. "Your game, ma'am," he said.

With a hiss of indrawn breath, Lady Ciu exposed her two of hearts. She'd only had a total of six.

"You're reckless," she said. "If you hadn't drawn that second card, you'd have won. Banker's hand."

Jerome shrugged. "I thought it was worth the risk, ma'am. That's how it goes." He pushed the counters towards her. "Your winnings."

Lady Ciu stared back. "You've had your gamble. Now get out of here and count yourself lucky."

Behind her, Hao Chen made a tiny *walk away now* gesture with his fingers.

Jerome's mouth curled into a lazy smirk in response. "I look forward to our next gamble, ma'am." He rose and offered Irene his arm. "Shall we?"

And then an alarm went off. It wasn't the usual whooping of a fire alarm: it was the mixture of sirens and alarm bells that Irene had heard before—in the university library. The tension broke and people began to shuffle rapidly towards the exit.

But they were blocked as men and women in uniform entered. "Will everyone here remain *calm*!" their leader demanded, and her voice was anything but soothing. "This is a CENSOR raid! Any attempt to resist will be grounds for immediate arrest."

CHAPTER 16

The room instantly dissolved into uneasy groups of people eyeing one another dubiously. A couple of gamblers were surreptitiously ignoring the house rules and scooping their stakes off the tables.

The CENSOR group's leader pulled out an ID card and addressed the room. "Lieutenant Richter here . . . We've been tracking vampires from yesterday's university raid and have information suggesting one of them is here." Her tone softened a little. "Ladies and gentlemen, please sit down. When we've finished our sweep of the building, you'll be free to go."

A fist of ice closed round Irene's guts. Next to her, she felt Jerome go tense. Was it pure coincidence that they'd shown up here, or did they have some way of tracing her or intelligence about the gang? And even with her new disguise, if they had photos from the university library incident and took a *good* look at her . . .

"I expect better treatment than this," Lady Ciu muttered.

"Let *me* handle it," Hao Chen said, clearly keen to mollify the older dragon. Ignoring his recent opponent, he walked across to the lieutenant, his aunt and sister in tow. Hao Chen murmured something to the woman, then flashed some sort of ID. That bought him a nod. Then the CENSOR people parted without another word, and the dragons left.

"Curiouser and curiouser," Irene murmured. She wasn't the only person who'd been watching. Half the room had had their eyes on the interaction. A couple of men tried to repeat the effect, but flashing cash—or threats of *I know your superior*—didn't work, and they were turned back into the crowd.

"Save the chat for later," Jerome answered. "I can probably leg it, but I don't know about you. Got any plans?"

"Maybe I do. But you're pretty certain of yourself," Irene couldn't help commenting.

He shrugged. "I'm lucky, 'Carla.' It goes with the territory."

"Well, you did lose that draw with Lady Ciu . . ." Irene assessed her options as she spoke. She couldn't use the Language too publicly, but a few surreptitious words would be lost under the din of conversation. "Give me a second, then drift towards the bar."

But first things first. She slipped out her phone, checking the messages.

Job done. On move, being followed. Need to lose them. Still no word from F.

She tilted the phone so that Jerome could see, biting back a sigh of relief. Apparently everything had gone all right, even with Felix absent—and what *had* happened to him, anyhow?

"Felix dropped out of sight. Hm."

"Any thoughts about him?"

"Let's get out of here first."

He had a point. They moved casually towards the bar. And as they walked under the fire alarm, it was simplicity itself for Irene to say, **"Fire alarm, sound at full volume."**

It was sheer perfection. It blasted out loud enough to deafen the room, and it was also connected to the lighting system. The bright chandeliers abruptly dimmed, and strips of neon light appeared over the door. Time for the finishing touch. Irene sparked up her cigarette lighter, telling it, **"Remain lit and fly into the nearest sprinkler system head."**

Irene had never previously appreciated quite how *thorough* water sprinklers were. The effect was like being drenched by a dozen cold showers on full. Water filled the air.

CENSOR could either hold back the crowd—now a yelling, wet, panicked mob—by force, or give way and let everyone into the corridor. They gave way.

Outside, the corridor was a heaving mass of people, shouting to be heard over the alarm. Jerome locked a hand round Irene's wrist, and together they followed the soaked crowd into the street. The couple of guards at the door failed to maintain a cordon—and within a few minutes Irene and Jerome were streets away, innocently waiting to be served at a late-night sausage stand.

So, about those dragons," Irene said quietly. "If this place *isn't* claimed, as Mr. Nemo said, then what are they doing here? And why has Felix vanished? There are too many unanswered questions."

There were other couples chatting to each other in the queue, ranging from students in jeans and duffel coats to people in evening wear. Hot dog stands made no class distinctions—and anyone could also be a CENSOR operative.

A police car drove past, sirens blaring loudly and lights flashing. But it wasn't heading in the direction of the Casino Nonpareil. Irene could only hope that Kai and the others weren't its target.

Jerome shrugged. "I guess Felix had his own business."

"Like what? That's not very helpful."

"I can see you're annoyed, but I don't know why you're annoyed at *me*."

"I'm annoyed because—"

"Sweet or spicy?" the stallholder asked, holding up mustard.

"Sweet," Irene said, annoyed at the distraction.

"Spicy," Jerome said with a grin. "Because?" he prompted as they strolled away, local cuisine in hand.

"I'm annoyed that you revealed yourself as Hao Chen's partner back there," Irene admitted.

Genuine surprise showed on Jerome's face. "You know, I thought that you'd be *thanking* me for stepping in."

"All right," she admitted. "Perhaps that was ungrateful. But still . . . you put yourself in unnecessary danger."

"I wouldn't have missed a game like that for the world," Jerome answered.

"It was a *huge* risk!"

"Honey . . . I *like* risks. I want risks. That's how I roll." He considered her with a frown. "By the way, I'd have thought you'd have been prepared to lose me back there, as long as you got the job done."

Irene took a bite, considering her answer. "There's two ways of looking at that. The first is that we haven't got the job done yet. You're still useful."

"And the second?"

"I don't play that way," Irene said slowly. "This isn't a game show or a zero-sum situation where only one person wins. I don't see why we shouldn't *all* get what we want."

And yet he was right: why should she care about these total strangers? Being a Librarian and a spy meant being cold-blooded. She didn't have the luxury of choosing between her mission and the safety of casual acquaintances. It wasn't something that her parents had taught her. Yet the morality ground into her at school wouldn't be silenced. Plus she hated losing.

She felt a pang at the thought of her childhood refuge. Whatever she'd thought at the time, in retrospect it was a haven where ethics had been practical, trust had been possible, and she could still believe virtue would be rewarded. Even if it now seemed like fiction . . . And now Gamma-17 was in danger and she *still* didn't have the book she needed to save it.

"You're asking me to accept a lot," Jerome was saying.

"But we need trust if we're going to work together. Think of it as a gamble . . ." Then Irene paused. "And what *are* all these police cars doing? That one's the third to pass us!"

"Okay. Before we go any further," Jerome said, "I need you to promise not to lose your temper . . ."

T he. Imperial. Regalia." Irene spoke through gritted teeth as she inspected the items in front of her. "Sword. Crown. Orb. And sceptre. That agate bowl was supposed to be the Holy Grail at one point, wasn't it? And that emerald salt cellar is bigger than my fist." At this precise moment, it would have given her great pleasure to throw it through the apartment window. "I'm . . . lost for words."

"I can probably think of a few," Felix said, reclining smugly on the lounger with a glass of wine. "Furious. Shocked. Jealous. I don't think any *Librarian* could have pulled this off, could they?"

Irene forced herself to back away from the cliff edge of her anger. They still needed him. And she had promised Jerome—who clearly knew everything—that she *wouldn't* lose her temper. Even with some of the Hofburg Museum's most valuable items spread before her. "Oh, all right. I admit it. I'm impressed."

"As you should be."

"Don't push your luck." Irene looked around the bland apartment. "So what do you plan to do now?"

"I haven't decided yet." Felix took another cheerful sip of wine. It was the most relaxed—the most *friendly*—that Irene had seen him. The successful theft had filled a nagging hole in his self-esteem, and for now he was the affable gentleman thief through and through. "Sometimes one just has the urge to steal a thing because it's there, if you know what I mean?"

Jerome clinked glasses with him. "That I do."

Irene counted down from five to one silently, trying to control her exasperation. Felix was clearly unreliable. But . . . if the group agreed that he needed to be shut out of the operation, could they count on his non-interference? What if he decided to steal the painting himself, hiring a new gang, now that he was on a high? But if they kept him with them, how long before he started boasting and said too much about the other people involved, such as Irene and Kai? If they really were infringing the treaty, she didn't like to think of the consequences.

"Let me call the others," she said, needing a moment to think. "I want to be sure they're all right."

"Be my guest," Felix said with a lazy wave. His gaze returned fondly to the emerald salt cellar. It was sitting casually in a pile of crumpled newspapers on the coffee table and somehow seemed larger than life, almost too big to be real.

Irene wandered over to the window. The phone rang, twice, and then Kai's voice said, *"Irene?"* In the background she could hear the screech of wheels and the sounds of furious driving.

"All secure here," Irene said. "Are you *okay*?"

"Yes. We're somewhere—" He broke off. "No! No, the car won't *fit* through there!"

"Easy-peasy," came Tina's distant voice. There was a grinding noise of metal against metal.

"Give me the phone." That was Ernst's voice. "All is well. We are escaping. Dragon boy is back-seat driver. Is bad habit."

"I usually let him do the driving," Irene admitted. "Jerome and I are with Felix. He's looted the Imperial Treasury ... which is why all the cops are buzzing round the Hofburg Palace. Avoid that area."

"So that is where he is. Tell him we will be talking later, him and me."

"Have you had any word from Indigo?"

"Only to confirm that the interrupts did their job."

There was a painfully loud crash and a thud, then the squealing of wheels again. "Are you all right?!" Irene demanded, wincing.

"No," Kai snapped, back on the call. "I just nearly swallowed the damn phone, that's all."

"Good. See you back at base," Irene finished. The phone went dead without another word.

Irene turned to face the two Fae. "They're all right—I hope."

She'd come to a couple of conclusions. Someone needed to pull this so-called team together—not just to give orders, but to convince them to cooperate as well. And who knows, maybe it could even be good practice in getting dragons, Fae, and Librarians to work together? Not that she'd ever be able to tell anyone about it . . . *"We need trust,"* she'd told Jerome. Now she had to trust them all, as she couldn't do this alone. They really *needed* Felix too. The thief was *good* at what he did. But if he wasn't with them, and could even act against them . . . she was going to face a very unpleasant choice.

"When I took the job, I thought everyone on the team was as, shall we say, invested in the job as I am," she said. "I was wrong, wasn't I?"

"I wouldn't say you were exactly *wrong,*" Felix said. "I just like to have my cake *and* eat it."

The pile of gold and jewels on the table drew Irene's gaze. "That's a pretty big cake," she admitted. "So are you sure you really *need* the Mr. Nemo job now? The risks are stacking up. CENSOR is breathing down our necks. And there's not just one, but *three* dragons in town."

Felix frowned, emerging from his haze of pleasure a little. "*Three,* you say."

"We ran into the others while we were at the Casino Nonpareil. Of course, they probably won't get in the way of our heist. But given the level of danger, I wouldn't blame you if you walked out . . ."

She was hoping Felix and his archetype couldn't resist a challenging theft. It wasn't just about the money for him. And the greater the threat, the more tempting it would be.

"Are you trying reverse psychology on me, Irene Winters?"

"I am," Irene admitted. "Good catch." She tried to channel her training. *When an opponent spots your negotiating tactic, admit it, and openly admire them for their intelligence in noticing it.* "But . . . don't you want to be the thief who stole *The Raft of the Medusa* from under the nose of three dragons? The man with his name in Mr. Nemo's private address book, on speed-dial for the most important thefts of all?"

"It's a gamble," Felix said. But she could hear the waver in his voice, the temptation tugging at him.

"We're all gambling," Irene answered. "So—what is *your* plan for the painting? I'm sure you already have something in mind."

And as Felix leaned forward, eager to display his cleverness, she knew she had him.

CHAPTER 17

We have a loiterer," Indigo said.

Irene looked up from the detonator that she was assembling under Ernst's guidance. "Whereabouts?"

"By the main entrance." Indigo turned one of her screens so the rest of them could see the door to their building. She'd tapped into all the local cameras after the gang incident. "He's been past twice and now he's standing there, checking the list of tenants. Of course, he might not be here looking for us, but . . ."

"But worst scenario is probably true," Ernst agreed philosophically. "If we dump his body a good distance away, it may take them longer to find us."

"Or it might lead people directly here, if he's supposed to be investigating and goes missing," Felix pointed out. "If he's one of that gang, he may be calling early for payment?"

Irene stared at the grainy black-and-white picture on the monitor. Indigo's new equipment might be top-of-the-line quality, but the camera in the building's lobby was cheap tat. Still, there was something familiar about him . . . "Can you get me a better image?" she asked.

The camera zoomed in—and the man turned to reveal his face.

Irene and Kai looked at each other in shock. "It's Evariste," Kai said.

"If you both know him, then he's a Librarian or a dragon. Which?" Felix kept his tone casual, but Irene could sense the caution beneath it. Last night's confrontation and discussion seemed to have brokered a truce between them, but it wouldn't take much to break it again.

Indigo sniffed. "Not a dragon. Certainly not a dragon."

"He's a Librarian," Irene said quickly, "and he may have an urgent message." She was remembering her email to Coppelia and her need to know whether the treaty clashed with this job. And since she hadn't gone back to the Library . . . the Library had come to her.

Felix put down the paperwork he'd been forging. "Are you backing out?" he asked quietly.

"I need to know what he has to tell me," Irene said, instead of answering his question.

Felix was silent.

"I go down to get him," Ernst suggested. "Stay in room while they talk. I am neutral third party. I have no grudges. I crush anyone's head if necessary, whoever they are."

Irene reminded herself that Ernst was no more trustworthy than any other Fae in the room. Even if his "friendly thug" attitude was easier to live with than Felix's caution—or outright hostility. Then another thought struck her. "Indigo, can you get sound down there?"

"Easily," Indigo replied.

"There you go," Irene said. "You can listen to what we have to say. And I won't need to bring him up here and expose you all."

Felix looked as if he would like to object, but nodded. "That sounds fair enough."

"I'd better go down too," Kai suggested, ". . . just in case he tries anything."

"Well, of course. Anyone can see that you and Librarian girl are partners in crime." Ernst patted him on the shoulder. "Is rather cute, no?"

In the corridor outside, Irene took a deep breath. Even if she and Felix had negotiated a temporary peace, the room had been tense all morning. Kai and Ernst had both been very unhappy— and that was putting it mildly—about Felix dropping out for his own private schemes *and* Jerome abetting him. It would have been even worse if Indigo had not commented that it was *"typical of all Fae,"* thus uniting most of the room against her instead.

Kai looked sideways at her. "Any thoughts?"

"Only that I'm counting the hours till this is over," Irene confessed.

"I still don't see why Lady Ciu would have retired *here*," he said, not for the first time.

"Perhaps she likes the local Sachertorte," Irene offered.

"No, she doesn't look the type to have a sweet tooth," Kai said seriously. "And it can't be the art. I was told that the eye injury left her nearly blind."

"She could see well enough to play cards last night," Irene pointed out. "Kai, she seemed . . . comparatively reasonable. Why are you so disturbed?"

Kai hunched his shoulders in a familiar gesture of discomfort.

"She wouldn't have been interested in the game. She couldn't care less what cards she drew. She was simply playing with her opponent, like a cat with a mouse."

That wasn't comforting. "And you said that she was a senior courtier before her injury, even if she wasn't as powerful as some." *"Of a lesser family,"* Kai had said, meaning that Lady Ciu didn't have the elemental affinities of the more powerful dragons. So— thank goodness—she couldn't raise earthquakes or storms, or bring down blizzards that would wipe whole cities off the map. But she was still a dragon, which made her very dangerous. And Kai had said she was part of the Winter Forest family, as well—a group of dragons who had good reason to have a grudge against Librarians in general, and Irene in particular. "Where did she get that eye injury? You said she'd been a famous duellist?"

"I don't know," Kai said. "I was told in a war, but I don't think that was the whole story . . ."

And then they were in the lobby. Evariste was in local garb but Irene would have known him anywhere. A dark-skinned man, his hair was growing out and clubbed back in a short tail. His overcoat was heavy and his shoes scuffed, an unobtrusive match for the local area. He carried himself with a learned wariness, light on his feet and ready to bolt.

He suppressed a twitch as he saw them. "Hi," he said nervously. "Look, we aren't in immediate danger, are we? Should I be hitting the sewers and hiding till we can get out of town?"

"It's not that bad," Irene said. "And thanks for coming." She remembered Evariste had little experience with fieldwork on other worlds. In fact, after their mission together went bad, she'd assumed he'd hole up in the Library for a few years. At least until he'd learned better skills.

Evariste leaned against the deserted lobby desk. "Oh no, no trouble at all. Do you realize that the Library entrance to this world is in *Japan*?"

Irene winced. When Evariste emerged from the Library into this world, he would then have had to travel all the way to Vienna. "I really am sorry," she said guiltily. "I came here via Fae transport. I don't even know the Library's classification for this world."

"A-327," Evariste said promptly. "There's no Librarian-in-Residence either. And to get right to the point, no, nobody's claimed this world according to our records. If you're stepping on someone's personal fief, you'll have a problem with *them*. But it won't have wider implications. And you're looking different. What happened to your hair?"

Irene sighed in dizzying relief. Safe. She wasn't risking the peace treaty by stealing from anyone here. She relaxed, touching her purple-streaked, gel-spiked hair. "A disguise. I've already been on too many cameras on this world." Then she frowned. "Wait a moment. If our classification is A-327, it would mean this world is technology-oriented, with no magic."

"I've seen the technology—cameras everywhere. This is not what I'd call a safe place."

Kai was frowning too. "I see what you're getting at," he said. "This world's supposed to be crawling with supernatural entities. Werewolves, vampires, mages, whatever. And yet the Library designates it as non-magical—or at least, not magical enough to be significant."

Irene nodded. A or Alpha worlds were aspected towards technology, with little to no magic. Beta worlds had magic as the norm—with any technology being pretty unimportant. Gamma worlds had both. Perhaps the Library's information was out of date, and supernatural creatures were a recent development? But this didn't match with what she'd read about the world. "Curiouser and curiouser," she said. "But the most important thing is—"

"Is to ask how Evariste's daughter is," Kai said firmly. "I'd been told that you got her back safely. Is everything going well?"

Evariste's face lightened. "Miranda Sofia's fine, but confused. Anyone would be—after being kidnapped by dragons." He glowered briefly and quite unfairly at Kai. "But we're settled on a new world now, very high-technology, helping a Librarian-in-Residence who's nearing retirement. I only popped back to the Library to do an errand for her."

"Is that where you saw Coppelia?" Irene asked, feeling sorry for him.

"Yes. She grabbed me and said that you'd requested some information. She gave me a token to find you. She also said—go ahead, walk off with the whole museum and everything else in it, just don't miss your deadline."

"Sounds like her," Irene said with a sigh.

"Good. Then I'm out of here. I'm hunting down a set of archaeological detective stories for Accidie about Prester John."

Irene wished her own mission were so easy to explain. "Please let Coppelia know I'm being as proactive as possible."

"I will," Evariste promised. "Good luck with your mission, then . . ." He was clearly on the point of leaving, but curiosity prompted him to ask, "How are you handling all the surveillance?"

"We've got a techie. She's hacked into the local systems."

Evariste blinked. "That sounds like something out of a bad movie."

Irene shrugged. "Apparently programming languages are somewhat transferable between worlds."

Evariste's expression was dubious. "Irene, do you hang out much in high-tech locations?"

"Not as much as some," Irene admitted.

"Don't take this the wrong way, but . . ." Evariste was clearly nerving himself up to disagree. "You want to be careful. Programs and exploits *don't* transfer that easily. There are too many variables. If someone's telling you that it will work, then watch out. Maybe they're just telling you what you want to hear."

Irene glanced to Kai, but his expression was guarded. It wasn't shock or disagreement, but a studied neutrality. Her heart went cold. *What has Kai not been telling me?* She knew that he kept secrets from her; that was fair enough—she kept secrets from him. But if he was hiding mission-critical information, it had to be private *dragon* business. She didn't like to think about the implications. "I see," she said. "We'll be careful."

"Was there anything else?" Evariste asked. He was clearly keen to leave as soon as possible.

"No . . . I mean yes." A thought sparked in Irene's mind. "I apologise for reminding you of Qing Song," she said, "but he was of the Winter Forest family, wasn't he? Did he ever mention someone called Lady Ciu, when you were his prisoner?"

Evariste frowned, but at least he didn't flinch at the memory. "In what context?"

"Probably approving," Kai said. "She used to be a respected warrior . . ."

"There was a Ciu," Evariste said slowly. "He didn't talk about her as lady or anything, though. She'd worked for his family, though—I think it was teaching the kids sword-play. The way he talked about it, it was a century or so ago. He said she retired.

Something about getting hurt in a fight. But her retirement wasn't because of the injury, it was because she'd lost. He said she'd been taken care of, I seem to remember. *Putting her out to pasture*, that was it. But I got the impression that he'd liked her."

So was this world Lady Ciu's private retirement home? And were the two younger dragons her servants—or her nurses and keepers?

The phone in her pocket buzzed and she answered.

"Tina here. We have a problem."

"What sort of problem?" Irene demanded.

"Felix says he's going to shoot Indigo. Jerome's backing him up. You interested?"

"Tell everyone to stay calm, we're coming now," Irene said, ending the call. "Evariste, Kai, there's trouble upstairs—got to go. Take care, safe journey, thanks for the help—"

"Whatever," Evariste agreed. "See you around."

He was already heading out of the door as Irene hit the stairs running, and Kai followed. "What is it?" he said.

"Felix pulled a gun on Indigo," Irene panted. "Don't know why."

Kai sped up, racing ahead. Visions of what might happen if the team indulged in an open confrontation—bloodstained visions—flipped through Irene's mind like ratcheting film frames. They could say goodbye to the job if that happened. She kicked into a final burst of speed, dashing up the last stairs in Kai's wake.

Indigo's hands were curved open in a gesture that would have revealed claws if she'd had them, and though her eyes might not be dragon-red, they glittered with anger. Across from her, Felix held his gun in a marksman's grip. Jerome had his gun out too, and though his grip seemed almost careless, the Fae had it aimed squarely at Kai, holding him motionless. Ernst still sat at a table, half-assembled bombs and detonators scattered across it in a dangerous detritus.

"You were quick," Tina remarked.

"Will someone kindly tell me what the hell is going on," Irene said, her tone ice-cold.

"Your Librarian gave it away," Felix said. "I was looking in the wrong direction when it came to betrayal. I should have gone for the obvious candidate."

"What do you mean?" Irene asked. It *had* to be Evariste's comment about programming. Inwardly she cursed having let the others listen in.

"What she's doing with those computers is flat-out impossible. Your friend said so." His paranoia was visible in the tense lines of his body. "So how come she can manipulate this tech so easily, if she's never even been here before? How come she's doing the impossible?"

"Because I *am* that good," Indigo snapped, with a harmonic to her voice that should have made the monitors tremble where they stood. "So what if the Librarian couldn't manage it? *I* can."

"But why's it so easy for you?" Felix demanded, nearly hysterical as his paranoia blossomed. "Is someone helping you? Are you planning to sell us out? And Mr. Nemo too?"

Indigo tilted her arm so that the light caught the wide silver bracelet that still encircled her wrist. "I'm bound, fool. I need Mr. Nemo to take this off. I'm one hundred per cent committed to the job. More than *you* are . . . Do you think I'd really be cooperating with creatures like you if I had any other choice?"

Irene saw Felix's finger tighten on the trigger. "I don't think she is getting help," she interrupted, suspicion dawning slowly. "At least it's not what you think . . . Want me to make some guesses?" Pieces fitted together now.

"Like what?" Felix demanded.

Irene walked farther into the room, Kai just a step behind. She could sense his anger, his readiness to move against any target that presented itself. Which might be her in a minute. "Contrary to what some of you may think," she said, "Kai doesn't tell me everything. So I need to do some hypothesising."

Jerome shifted position. Now his gun might have been pointed at anyone—or everyone—in the room. This was no better. "Go on, then?"

"I've noticed that the dragons are far more organised than the Fae—it's one of your known strengths. It was evident during the treaty negotiations, when both sides were flexing their muscles. The dragon delegation argued that their superior organisational powers brought more to the table, and so justified the grant of wider concessions. But organisation's considerably easier when you've laid the groundwork in advance . . ."

Indigo didn't move, but her eyes burned. Irene knew that she'd struck gold. She felt a bit sick; this betrayal cut deep. And when she glanced at Kai, he looked like thunder, confirming her suspicions.

"So tell me, Indigo—how does this work exactly? Laying down top-secret infrastructure for the dragon empires in secret, subverting human power structures? Do tech-savvy dragons like you grease the wheels of dragon commerce across a spectrum of worlds? It might sound mundane, but by making sure human and dragon software is compatible, you could control any world that uses technology—Alpha *and* Gamma worlds. Maybe even high-tech worlds where chaos rules and the Fae are stronger . . . is that right,

Indigo? So can any dragon access the local computer networks, whatever world you're in, whenever and wherever you want?"

Every Fae in the room looked ready to kill someone. Ernst's hands froze. He carefully put down the tweezers and wire he'd been holding. "Surely that is not possible. The sheer numbers of worlds . . ."

"I'm not saying they've done this in *every* world," Irene answered quickly, looking at the Fae, poised for action yet still hanging on her every word. "Maybe just the ones where dragons live full-time? Like this one, where Lady Ciu's been a permanent resident for decades. And I'm not saying that every world's going to have exactly the same operating systems. But perhaps with enough dragons 'influencing' their target worlds, they can make sure the right sorts of technology get developed? All added up, it could be enough to allow an *expert* to carry a briefcase full of memory sticks and expect to hit the ground running, if she went to a high-order world . . ."

The pieces were all fitting together. She couldn't believe the scale of it. Dragons made everything look so effortless—power, control, wealth. And they always managed to place themselves in positions of high authority and stay there. This sort of sustained, covert, multigenerational campaign to infiltrate the software infrastructure across multiple worlds . . . She'd never even considered such a thing would be *possible*. It was like the old proverb about swans—floating gracefully on the surface of the water, but paddling away underneath like a mill-wheel. "Am I right, Indigo? And has there been draconic influence in this world's software development?"

Indigo's face was neutral, but her eyes flickered. Perhaps she was running through decision trees as logically as any computer,

Irene wondered. Then Indigo finally sat down. "If anyone were to take this seriously, you realize that you've endangered yourself and everyone in this room?"

"Well, of course," Irene said. And that was as good an admission as any Irene had ever heard. The thought of bursting into manic laughter was very tempting. As if this job weren't messy enough. "This must be a *huge* dragon secret. Maybe their biggest. Naturally we're all in danger of death—permanent death, inescapable death, death raining down on us in storms of fire—if word gets out that we know about this." She looked around the room. "Note that I said *if* word gets out."

"And if dragon boy talks?" Ernst asked, his voice a quiet rumble of threat.

Kai picked up a discarded mouse from one of the tables. It splintered in his hand as he tightened his fingers around it. "You said it yourself, didn't you? Irene and I are partners in crime." His voice was bitter.

Felix looked at Indigo. "I'd love to shoot you now. But we need more answers. And you're hardly in league with your kin any more." Then he lowered his gun, sliding it back into his jacket. "So why *were* you on the run from your family?" he asked.

"Emptying my father's bank accounts, on multiple worlds, to help finance revolution," Indigo answered. "Now are you going to help me with this theft, or not?"

"I like your style. Any chance of future collaboration?" Felix suggested.

Irene suppressed a sigh of relief as the tension coming from the Fae started to ebb away. Maybe no one would die today.

"I think *not*," Indigo snapped. "My feelings towards my father don't make me like *you* any better."

"Needs must when the devil drives," Felix said philosophically.

Then Kai stormed out, slamming the door behind him. Irene wondered if she'd hoped for peace—at least local, better-than-nothing peace—too soon.

"You'd better go after him," Indigo said, a malicious edge to her voice. "You wouldn't want him to slip his leash . . ."

Kai was pacing up and down the landing outside. He grabbed Irene's arm the moment she emerged, dragging her into one of the empty offices. "Thank you, Irene. Thank you *very* much."

He was genuinely angry. "There is a big difference between having a truce and actively *giving away* sensitive information to those creatures! How could you? How could you *do* such a thing—"

"I didn't ask you about this, so your loyalties weren't compromised," Irene retorted. "I took great care *not* to ask you. I asked Indigo—and *she* confirmed it."

Kai's temper wasn't abating. "It doesn't matter where it came from—you *know* I can't let that sort of information get out. You've made it impossible for me to tell my father that the others know, without admitting that you do too. Was that deliberate? Were you putting your own life at risk, out of some foolish camaraderie with Fae who have been *threatening to kill you*? Irene, whose side are you on?"

"I'm trying to keep everyone pointed in the same direction till we've stolen that damn painting!" Irene snapped. "I hadn't decided to say anything—but Evariste forced my hand and the others were out for Indigo's blood. I needed to say something. And what about Mr. Nemo knowing too? Why else would he have hired Indigo as his hacker, in a team of *Fae*? The Fae have mad scientists, or urban coders, or other archetypes too. There must have been a reason why he chose a dragon."

Kai muttered a sharp curse. "This grows more and more complicated. My father would have accepted the necessity of this mission
at the beginning, to secure the book for the Library, but now . . ."

Irene was aware that *then don't tell him about it* wasn't much of
an answer—or at least, not one that would satisfy Kai. "I'm sorry,"
she said, "but that's the problem with you taking the initiative and
coming with me on a mission. I have my own priorities. But you're
not under my authority any longer. I don't want to do this without
you—but if you honestly feel that you can't stay any longer, I will
understand."

"That's emotional blackmail," Kai accused. "You're trying to
make me feel guilty."

"No." Anger was receding now, leaving Irene exhausted. "No,
Kai, it's honesty. I can't make any promises about how this mess is
going to work out, but I *have* to go through with it. If I don't, a
world I care about falls into chaos—and we'll never get it back.
That world made me who I am, perhaps just as much as my
parents."

"Aside from the mission . . . Did you hear what she *said*,
though?" Kai interjected. He was clearly still very angry. "How Indigo *admitted* to stealing from our lord father?"

Well, Irene thought, *it does explain why nobody was willing to
talk about the details of her crimes. It might have given other dragons
ideas.*

Not for the first time, she wondered if there were such a thing as
a universal standard of morality. Her old school had claimed that
some lines should never be crossed. This seemed simplistic, but
maybe they had a point. And how would it feel if her *own* parents
could never forgive her for committing a particular crime? Or if
she couldn't forgive them?

But actual laws only applied to human beings. Everything in dragon society came down to custom—including family obligations, personal standards, and ties of loyalty. Indigo had irrevocably broken those ties. And Fae society was driven by personal ambition and the perfection of an individual's desired archetype. If a Fae took on the role of a fictional mass murderer, they could be an ally or an enemy, but not a *criminal*—unless their actions inconvenienced someone more powerful. And Librarians routinely stole books as part of their job. However, the only real crimes amongst them included betrayal of the Library and other Librarians, or failure . . . So was it actually possible for all these factions to share a morality? For this job, for the treaty, and beyond?

But Kai was looking at her, expecting an answer. "You know my mission must be my priority. I'm not trying to manipulate you."

Kai snorted. "Maybe not, but you're succeeding."

Irene gave up and ran her hands through her hair. "Look," she said, "I'm going back in. Will you be all right?"

Kai raised an eyebrow. "Do you think I'm just going to stay out here? Don't worry, I'll behave myself. And I know you can look after yourself. But I promised to keep you safe, Irene . . . even against my family, no matter how angry I am."

CHAPTER 18

It was early evening in the Vienna Naschmarkt, and all the food stalls and mini-restaurants along the long street were up and running. Delicious odours tempted the prospective diner—fish and garlic, steak and sausage, curry and mustard and falafel. They all combined into a mélange that would have been unthinkable in an actual meal, but that lured the nose and set the salivary glands flowing.

"How much farther does this market go on?" Kai asked, half glancing at Irene. Things were still a little tense between them. "We don't want to be late."

He had a point. They were off to deliver the gang's "protection money," and their instructions had been clear. Show up at seven o'clock on the dot, under the stall with a blue awning at the far end of the Naschmarkt—Vienna's old market. While technically Kai and Jerome were the contacts for the gang, Irene had invited herself along. Ernst and Felix were holding the fort with Indigo—ready to evacuate if CENSOR showed up. Tina was circling the Naschmarkt area in a small van, in case emergency pickup was needed.

"It shouldn't be much farther," Irene said. The stalls along the street became more run-down and displayed shorter menus as they continued. The ones where they'd started, near the Ringstrasse—the circular boulevard at the heart of old Vienna— were good quality, tourist traps, or both. But farther down, they grew seedier and cheaper. Not so much as to be dangerous—well, Irene reflected, perhaps not a place to be walking alone late at night—but perfect for illicit dealings.

"There." Jerome nodded at a blue awning flapping in the rising wind. "That one, I think."

The three of them perched on rickety stools at the stall's single bench. It advertised Middle Eastern food, but it neither looked nor smelled appetising. Irene checked her watch just as a young woman laid an acquisitive hand on Kai's arm.

She was strapped into tight Lycra and far too much fake leather. Her hair was a mix of blue and purple that gleamed under the street lights, and her eyes were generously smudged with eye shadow. "Hey, handsome. You here for the dog racing?"

"We are," Jerome said, before Kai could wrench his arm away. He slid a small-denomination bill across the counter to the owner. "For your trouble."

"Not a problem," the man said, clearly used to that sort of exchange. Tucking the note away, he began serving another customer.

Irene watched the young woman carefully. It didn't seem as if she *could* be concealing a weapon; everything fit too snugly. "Straight handover?" Irene asked.

"The boss would like a word first," the young woman said.

Under her bravado and the heavy eye shadow, she looked more than uneasy; she seemed spooked.

"And if we don't want a word?" Kai asked. He removed her hand from his arm gently but firmly.

"He said it'd be a good idea—for all of you," she said hastily, almost stuttering. "That he could do a deal with you."

"We're already working a deal," Jerome replied.

"He said . . ."

Irene had been on the alert while they talked. There was no way anyone would trust this young woman to negotiate on her own. But there was nobody else close enough to jump them if they walked away, the people farther down the counter were all busy with their food, and . . .

. . . there was a red dot of light on the counter between her and Kai. It was the laser sight of a rifle.

She glanced behind them, at the row of old houses that edged the street. There was no way of working out the origin of the rifle sight. And there was no way of knowing if this was the only gun trained on them, which ruled out her counting on shielding herself or the others with the Language. They were sitting ducks out here—which was, of course, the idea.

"I think we should go with the nice lady," she said calmly. When Kai turned to frown at her, she indicated the red light on the counter. "It seems that her boss wants to talk to us *urgently*—and how can we say no?"

If the building they were led to had been a person, it would have been a criminal leading a double life. Neighbours would say, *But he was such a nice man!* after the police had finished their investigation and removed the bodies. On the front it was a cheerful reseller, offering tickets for the latest shows and visits to surrounding attractions. But inside . . .

Past the main door and the front office were dull grey walls and uncarpeted flooring. There were dark stains in the corners, and Irene imagined washdowns that hadn't managed to get rid of all the blood. She could almost see people coming in one end . . . who didn't necessarily come out the other. And there were absolutely no cameras. What happened inside the ticket resellers would stay inside the ticket resellers.

Several large men had taken custody of them as they walked through the front door. They'd been searched, and Jerome's gun removed. The girl had been sent away with a packet of something pharmaceutical. If this had been a high-chaos world, it couldn't have conformed to archetypes more perfectly. And it had all been done with the bare minimum of speech.

Irene hadn't tried resisting, and the others had followed her example. She was very curious about what was going on. If the gang had simply wanted them dead, they could easily have shot them from a distance, or put explosives under their office, or . . . really, it was rather depressing how simple it was to kill someone. So what did they want?

They were bustled into an office, where the man behind the desk was best described as *grey*: grey hair, grey suit, grey eyes, grey teeth. He even had a grey slimline laptop, and his grey coffee mug was resting on its discreetly closed surface. He looked them over, an insultingly slow assessment. "So you're the new boys in town," he finally said.

Irene decided this was not the moment to stand up for female representation. "You wanted a word?"

"I'm looking for some new hackers and coders. I thought I'd offer you the job."

Irene, Kai, and Jerome exchanged glances. "Oh, we wouldn't want to step on the toes of your current people," Kai said.

"That won't be an issue."

Which suggested that said toes had been turned up, and said people would never be heard from again. "But why us?" Irene asked. "We're new here."

"Right. Which is why I know you haven't got any local connections."

"We're just block-chain entrepreneurs—" Irene tried.

"Shut it." He pointed a split-nailed finger at her. "I had people at the Nonpareil last night. You and that guy were there when it all went down." His finger shifted to Jerome. "And then afterwards, you weren't on the police or casino records. No names, no photos—nothing. Someone cleaned up after you real good. Well, I want that someone on my payroll."

Wonderful. We've shot ourselves in the foot by being too *good at our jobs.*

"So who's in charge?" he demanded.

"Her," Kai said, before Irene could suggest anyone else.

"Is that so . . ." The grey man sat back in his chair.

"I can talk a machine into anything," Irene bluffed. She could guess why Kai had chosen her. As long as the grey man wanted a computer expert, he'd keep her alive.

"Helpful attitude. I like it. All right. I'm going to want you to get into police records. I'm also going to want a, what do they call it, Bitcoin thing. And we handle a lot of file distribution. You'll be doing that too. Don't worry, you'll get paid. But your team's working for me now."

"We've got commitments elsewhere," Jerome put in. "You can't expect us to drop out on jobs that we've already agreed to."

"So you work overtime. I'll buy you coffee. They do good coffee here in Vienna."

"And for that you pay us a lot of money . . ." Kai said. "And you *don't* report us to CENSOR."

"Yeah, that'd be nasty. For you. Glad you're getting the idea."

Irene's back itched with the knowledge that four men with guns were standing behind her and the other two. This was the sort of situation where the wrong word could result in gunfire and casualties. None of them were immune to being killed by a stupid gunshot from a stupid thug, in a situation that had absolutely nothing to do with their real job. "Just give us our priorities," she said.

"The police records come first," the boss said. "And as for CENSOR . . . you could say we have a certain *understanding* with them. We do them favours, they make it worth our while. If you cross me, my sources would be *very* interested in suspicious individuals like you."

A very risky idea suddenly struck her. If the gang were loyal foot soldiers, they'd be finished. But if they survived it, they could gain invaluable intelligence from almost an inside source. The possible information justified the gamble. "CENSOR really seems to rule in these parts. You wouldn't want us to hack them, would you, to gain an edge? Just say the word." Irene mentally crossed her fingers.

The grey man narrowed his eyes, his expression indicating Irene had managed to suggest something that was both completely unthinkable *and* extremely tempting. She breathed a sigh of relief. It was the sort of reaction that she'd have, if someone simply offered up a copy of Shakespeare's First Folio.

"You think you really could?" he finally said.

"Yes," Irene said confidently, wishing she had Jerome's poker face.

Jerome chose this moment to say, "You can't turn us in to CENSOR *now*, can you? They'd ask us questions, and now we could give them certain answers—about you."

"We would have just paid up and left," Kai chipped in, in support. "You can't blame us now, for protecting our interests."

"Are the two of you collaborating to say the worst possible thing?" Irene demanded in disbelief. She'd get *nothing* on CENSOR at this rate.

"I feel attacked," Jerome said.

"I *definitely* feel attacked," Kai answered.

They were bonding, which was good—how often did a Fae and a dragon manage cheerful banter?—but Irene *really* wished that they'd chosen some other time and place to do it. She sighed and turned to the grey man. "We're going to cooperate."

"You two are lucky you've got one sensible woman on the team. You, kid." He was talking to Irene again. "You find out one thing for me from CENSOR, and I'll let you off your first fortnight's fees..."

"And what's that?" Irene asked. If it seemed useful, maybe Indigo could pluck it from CENSOR's databanks, not that they'd bother to hand it over...

"Something happened yesterday. CENSOR raided the university library, then the Spanish Riding School right after. They are all stirred up and my sources tell me something bad's going down. Find out what it is."

Irene felt her heart skip a beat. What if CENSOR really had been following their trail at the library and at the school? It could risk the job—in which case, Indigo really needed to do more digging. And if the grey man had sources inside CENSOR, then he could tell her more about them. But this back-and-forth was simply too slow. She had to know. Time for a better lever.

"I'll see what I can do," she said, holding his gaze. "In the meantime, **you perceive I'm trustworthy, and you need to tell me everything you know about CENSOR.**"

There was a sudden babble from the room as all the thugs tried to speak at the same time. Pain spiked inside Irene's head—the penalty of using the Language on so many.

"Shut up, the lot of you!" the grey man ordered, and his flunkeys went quiet. "I guess you need to know, if you're going to do the job right," he continued. Self-rationalisation based on a Language-induced shift of perception was a wonderful thing. "It's like this. CENSOR pays us for information. We pass on anything weird that we pick up, and they tell us what to listen out for too. And if we slip them a few extra names to 'deal with,' that's just how we do business. But since the university and school raids, we haven't heard from them—and that's really unusual. Maybe someone's been bad-mouthing us, and if so, I need to know who. But if it's because something huge is going down—I want in."

"Thank you, that's very helpful." So CENSOR had connections on both sides of the law—within the police *and* organised crime. Their task was looking harder by the minute. Irene gave the grey man her most appreciative smile. "Did CENSOR mention any keywords or other data? Something I could use in my search of their records?"

The grey man shrugged. "They said to listen out for anything about libraries or librarians. Maybe someone at the university library's implicated."

Pure dread clutched at Irene's throat. That was one explanation, but the *other* possibility had dire implications for their mission. On first contact, the thugs had threatened to turn Kai and Jerome over to CENSOR if they didn't pay up. And their list of fake accusations had included *"hiding books of magic"* . . . But was the Library really on CENSOR's watch list—or was this just an uncomfortable coincidence? Who was actually behind them?

"Thanks," she said. "I'll do my best."

Perhaps he'd sensed that she was giving in too easily, for his eyes narrowed. "I'll send someone to check on you."

Well, that would be unfortunate for whoever the someone was.

"Piet, show them out," he said. "And get me more coffee."

Mercifully, Jerome and Kai hadn't made any further attempts to interfere. Irene quietly thanked any nearby deities as she headed for the door. They'd need all the time they could get to evacuate their base.

Then one of the quieter thugs frowned. "Boss?" he said. "Why did you just *tell* her all that?"

"What?" the grey man said.

Irene bit back a curse. The *you perceive* Language trick only lasted for a short amount of time, but it didn't usually wear off *this* fast. She felt Kai go tense next to her, and nudged him towards the door. **"You perceive that there's nothing to worry about,"** she tried again.

The sudden headache made her stumble, and Kai caught her elbow. Jerome ushered them out of the room, before closing the door. "Lock it," he barked.

She bit her lip, focusing. **"Door, lock. Lock, jam."**

The woman standing guard in the front office looked at them suspiciously. "Something wrong?"

"Not a problem," Jerome said cheerfully, but her hand was now resting on her gun. "We've got our orders—"

The guard collapsed as Kai delivered a swift blow to the back of her neck.

"I hope that was worth it," Kai said, dragging the unconscious woman behind the counter. "The moment the Language wears off again, they'll be after us."

"They're looking for a *Librarian*," Irene said, and dry-swallowed a couple of aspirin.

"So?"

"Who else knows about Librarians, besides dragons and Fae?"

Jerome had flipped his phone open, but he paused mid-text. "So *that's* why CENSOR gave Hao Chen a pass at the casino. Of course the dragons are in with them." His gaze shifted to Kai. "Your sister's got a point."

"About?" Kai queried, bristling.

"About what happens when dragons are in charge."

The door crashed open, and thugs spilled out. Behind them, the grey man yelled in a tone of genuine panic, "Shoot the witch!"

All that liaison with CENSOR, and you never expected to run into a real witch? Irene ducked behind the counter. "**Guns, jam!**" she shouted.

Jerome and Kai were dealing with the thugs. She slipped past them into the room they'd just left. As she expected, the boss was shaking his phone and cursing. "No phone signal in here, right?" she asked.

He flinched, looking at her as if she were an abomination out of an X-rated horror film poster. It took him a moment to remember his gun, and he pointed it at her with a shaking hand. "Stay away from me, witch!"

"You've put me in an unfortunate position," Irene said. "I don't suppose I can persuade you to keep your mouth shut about all this?"

"Stay back or I'll shoot!"

"Your gun's jammed," she reminded him. He'd been within earshot when she'd used the Language. "Work with me here. I don't want to have to kill you."

He pulled the trigger, but nothing happened. His nerve broke, and he made a bolt for the other door.

She grabbed his flimsy chair and threw it. It hit him in the back, and he stumbled, giving her time to close in. He dropped the gun and pulled a knife from an inner pocket. She dodged sideways, avoiding his slicing blow, and kicked him in the knee. He sank to the ground, the knife skittering away.

"Finished playing with your prey yet, madam witch?" Kai enquired from the doorway.

The grey man made a wavering reach for his knife, so Irene stepped on his hand and turned to Kai. "You've got all the others?"

"Down and unconscious."

"All right. We've got work to do."

Ten minutes later, the thugs, guard, and boss alike were tied up in the interview chamber. Irene sealed the doors with the Language, bonding them to their frames. They wouldn't hold against significant exterior assault, and the rooms weren't airtight—the prisoners wouldn't suffocate. But it would keep them all usefully out of the way for the next few hours.

"So we're blown," Jerome said, his tone cheerful rather than depressed. "But are you thinking what I'm thinking?"

"Maybe," Irene said. "I'm thinking that we've been very lucky."

Kai frowned. "I don't follow. As far as I can see, we've been massively *unlucky* to have these idiots try to blackmail us, unlucky that they spotted us in the first place—"

"And unlucky that dragons are involved with CENSOR?" Jerome asked, with mock innocence.

Kai levelled an icy glance at him, a glint of dragon-red in his eyes. "CENSOR could have captured a Librarian in the past. That could well be why they know *Library* and *Librarian* mean something."

"You don't believe that, and neither do I," Jerome said.

Irene took a deep breath, focusing herself. She didn't believe it either, though she could understand why Kai wouldn't admit the obvious. "We're lucky," she said, interrupting their exchange, "because the grey man thought he could extort money from us, so he hadn't reported us to CENSOR yet. We still have the advantage."

"But the moment they get out of there, they'll tell CENSOR—and everyone else."

"Then we move up the timetable." Irene flexed her fingers. "We don't have time to wait. We'll make the run tonight."

CHAPTER 19

Felix slapped his ID card down in front of the museum security guard. "CENSOR," he snapped. "We have a report of possible demonic manifestations on the second floor, near the French Romantic painters. What do your security systems say?"

The security guard's gaze flicked nervously from the ID card to Felix, then to Irene and the others behind him, all of them stern in their stolen CENSOR uniforms. "We haven't had any disruptions yet," he stammered. "All systems are normal . . ."

"We have our locational readings," Felix answered. He tapped one of the devices hanging at his belt. "We may still be in time to prevent a full-scale manifestation and threat to life."

The security guard perked up, clearly visualising a future that *didn't* have him dismissed for missing an outbreak. "Can I do anything to help, sir?"

As they'd planned, Jerome took over. "Sir, it might be possible to resolve this with minimal disruption. This late at night, there shouldn't be many possible targets to remove. If we stake out the gallery now and run the new e-warding programs, we can leave the rest of the museum undisturbed . . ."

"I don't know," Felix said dubiously. "We can't risk *any* danger to the public. Even if we're talking just a few staff, with the museum closed for the night . . ."

"Let me call my supervisor over, sir," the security guard said, eagerly taking the bait. "He'll tell you if it's possible."

Felix nodded. "Very well. Lang, report in to headquarters. Give them a sitrep."

"Yes, sir," Irene responded. She took a step away, raising one hand to shield her mouth as she murmured into her headset.

The security guard's supervisor arrived in less than half a minute. He and Felix broke into a rapid discussion about how best to handle things. And most importantly, how the museum took absolutely no responsibility for anything that might go wrong. Kai, Jerome, and Ernst adopted poses of casually menacing professionalism. Ernst's uniform was visibly straining, designed for someone a couple of sizes smaller. Irene hoped that it would survive the night—or at least, long enough for them to get out of there.

"All okay so far," Irene muttered. "How about you?"

"Acceptable," Indigo answered, live from their getaway van. Irene could hear the hum of traffic through the phone, and the distant ebb and flow of CENSOR transmissions being monitored. "So far nobody's noticed my taps into the network—or picked up on the squad you intercepted for their uniforms. Tina should have us in position to collect you in ten minutes. Let us know if you need more or less time."

"Understood."

Felix broke off his conversation and signalled them over. "Herr Vogel has approved the investigation. You all know the procedure. Lang, anything to report?"

"Central says all under control and to go ahead, sir," Irene responded. "They say call back in ten minutes if there are any issues."

"Very good," he said, acknowledging their code for pickup time. "Bauer, you stay here a moment—see if you can link their security cameras to our system. The rest of you, follow me."

Herr Vogel insisted on accompanying them up the twin flights of marble stairs, prattling nervously all the way. The regular lighting was off at this time of night, but the security officer had passed round torches. Marble lions crouched at the bottom of the staircases, their muscles smooth curves that gleamed in the torchlight. Painted figures peered down from the ceiling, eternal and unmoving. The entire museum seemed to be on guard, waiting for a moment's slip. Irene felt a trickle of sweat run down her back under her stolen uniform. So many things could go wrong, so many people might make a mistake. This was why she preferred operating on her own . . .

"I hear there are problems all over town," Herr Vogel said tentatively. "People are saying on social media that CENSOR patrols are making widespread arrests?"

"I can neither confirm nor deny this," Felix answered, in tones that confirmed it very clearly indeed. "With any luck this won't take long. Naturally we don't want to cause unnecessary panic here as well."

"Oh, absolutely," Herr Vogel said quickly. "We'll try to keep things under control. If something happens . . . should we assist?"

"I appreciate your devotion to duty. But the answer is no. Our policy is containment. If this *is* a demonic manifestation, anyone unprotected may be subject to possession. We can't risk your staff infecting the general population."

The little colour in Herr Vogel's cheeks drained away. "I had no idea the risk was so great."

"To all Vienna." Felix gave him a grave nod, one serious man to another. "Fortunately there's no sign of anyone hanging around outside the museum."

"Fortunately?"

"Cultists." Felix looked into the middle distance for a moment, haunted remembrance shadowing his face. The torchlight caught his expression at just the right moment to emphasise his battle-weary air. He was every inch the professional CENSOR officer, someone who'd devoted his life to fighting horrors beyond imagination.

Irene had to admit that Felix was doing an excellent job. And, as far as she could judge, thoroughly enjoying it. She suppressed a jealous thought that she could have played the squad leader just as well. The important thing was getting the job done.

"Ah, I see. No, the area seems quiet tonight. Nothing on our cameras."

Hopefully it would stay that way. So far things had gone according to plan. They'd triggered CENSOR raids across Vienna, based on false information, via Indigo's links to their network. They'd then ambushed a CENSOR team with a conveniently sized van and mostly conveniently sized uniforms. And they'd now infiltrated the Kunsthistorisches Museum—while Indigo and Tina remained in the stolen van. Indigo and Tina were currently circling Vienna, ready to return for the pickup—it had been judged far too dangerous to keep the van sitting outside the museum.

"Here we are," Herr Vogel said, gesturing round the gallery.

The walls were dark grey, the floor tiled wood, and a long skylight in the ceiling gazed up at a cloud-filled night sky. Though it was empty, the paintings were full of human faces that seemed to stare at the group from the shadows.

Kai came jogging into the room. "I've linked up the museum cameras to CENSOR central command, sir. They'll be able to analyse the feed and pick up anything that we can't."

"Excellent," Felix said. "Benz, get out the scan tech. Herr Vogel, I must request that you leave this room now. There may be high-energy discharges, and while the paintings will be safe, I can't answer for your physical integrity."

Herr Vogel hesitated, then nodded. With an inclination of his head he strode away, leaving them together in the darkened room. Just the cameras left to take care of now . . .

Felix turned to Irene. "Check with central command, Lang. Are you getting the camera link feedback?"

"Can you access the cameras?" Irene murmured into her headset.

"Got it and setting a feedback loop," Indigo answered. "Walk around a bit and gesture with your equipment. I'll record it and play it back, to distract security."

"Central says to run full scans, sir," Irene answered Felix. "They have full access."

Irene wandered around, pointing pieces of appropriately mysterious equipment at the walls and paintings. Then Indigo said, "That's enough. Synching—three, two, one, *mark*. You're good to go."

"We're clear," Irene said, putting the equipment away.

"Are we?" Felix asked.

"We'll know if they come in here, I suppose," Kai answered.

"Damn. I've *got* to get Indigo to sign up with me one of these days. I never knew dragons could be so useful." Felix moved briskly over to where *The Raft of the Medusa* hung. "Irene, Ernst, give me a hand. Jerome, Kai, you're on watch duty."

Irene bumped fists with Kai in congratulation, before joining Felix. Felix scrambled onto Ernst's shoulders, peering at the upper edges of the frame. He drew in a hiss of breath. "This is going to be as much of a nuisance as we'd thought. There's tech behind this."

"What kind?" Ernst asked.

"Security alarms, what else? But far more than any of the other paintings seem to have. More than the Imperial Treasury had, even."

"So there *is* something unusual about this one," Ernst commented. "Then again, this is the one Mr. Nemo wanted. Ours not to argue." He shrugged, making Felix protest and clutch at the wall for balance. "Will this stop you getting it down?"

"Of course not! But I can't be sure exactly what I'll set off."

"Hopefully it's part of the main alarm system," Irene said. She touched her earpiece. "Indigo, are you picking all this up? Can you deactivate it?"

There was an uncomfortable pause. "That might not be quite so simple," Indigo said slowly. "There's security in this system which I hadn't expected. Fiddling the cameras is one thing, but turning off the alarms is something else. In fact . . ."

"'In fact' what?" Irene asked. That didn't sound encouraging.

"Oh, don't worry, it's nothing. But it'll actually be easier if you handle the alarms at your end."

Irene reported that back to the team. She decided to keep the *Oh, nothing* to herself. Hopefully it *was* just nothing, and if it wasn't . . . they'd find out soon enough.

Felix laughed, glancing at the busy team—and it was infectious. Irene herself had to chuckle at a Fae, dragon, and Librarian team working so effectively. "Let's do it," he said. "Irene, as we planned: first alarms, then detach the painting." He leapt off Ernst's shoulder, landing like a cat. "Ernst, be ready to hold the painting."

Irene swallowed. This was where the theft made the final jump from plan to actuality. No time for nerves now. She stepped forward to lay a finger against the frame. **"All alarms attached to the painting I'm touching, deactivate."**

Her voice echoed in the gallery, amplified by the harmonics of the Language. She frowned at a brief twinge of head pain, but it didn't last. Next step. Felix had explained the mechanics of how the painting would be connected to the frame and the wall, from his prior "acquisitions" experience, and she'd worked out the most efficient vocabulary. **"Fastenings holding up the painting I'm touching, detach and release; painting, slide gently to the ground without damage."**

The painting shuddered as screws unwound themselves from brackets and bolts detached themselves, then came free. Then the whole thing slid down the wall like water down a pane. Ernst caught it with barely a grunt as it started to topple, gently lowering it to the floor.

Felix looked at the wall where it had been and whistled. There was a wide array of circuitry there—far more than one would have expected. "This is serious paranoia," he said.

"Irene!" Indigo's voice was sharp.

Irene winced and put a hand to her earpiece. "What is it? And please don't shout."

"Whatever you've just done has triggered alarms which I *can't* shut down—and they don't just flow to CENSOR, but somewhere else as well. You need to speed up."

"We're out of time," Irene reported to the others. "Alarms have been triggered that Indigo can't intercept. We need to get out—now."

Felix let out his breath in a thoughtful whistle, playing his torch along the lines of the frame. "And the other shoe just dropped . . ."

"Speak plainly," Ernst demanded.

"There's two canvases here. One's fastened over the other. What was it Mr. Nemo told us again?"

Irene restrained the urge to correct him to *there are two canvases*. This was unfortunately not the time to be a grammar purist. Instead, she cast her mind back. "Mr. Nemo said he wanted the canvas, whole and entire, and we could leave the frame behind. I suppose 'canvas' could apply to both paintings, at a stretch, as an uncountable noun . . . ?" But why was this hidden painting guarded better than the Imperial Treasury? Just how much more didn't they know? "Shall I detach the frame now?" she asked briskly, substituting efficiency for panic.

"Go ahead." The shadows hid Felix's face, but his shoulders were tense. "And call in Indigo for immediate pickup. Ernst, get the packaging ready."

Ernst slipped off his backpack and pulled out a large piece of fine, clean canvas. He unfolded it as though shaking out bedsheets, and it fluttered to the gallery floor in a ghostly drift.

Irene was grateful for the time they'd spent beforehand going through the plan. She didn't have to waste precious seconds looking for the right words. Bending down and touching it, she said, **"Frame and struts of the paintings I am touching, come apart, detach, and roll away."**

The wood, gilding, and ornamentation fell apart immediately in a dry rattling of antique pieces. Irene's imagination supplied images of ancient bones scuttling across the floor. **"Paintings I am** touching, float over to the plain canvas lying on the floor, and rest on it face-down."

She leant back as they drifted into the air and wished that there were some way to make them move faster. Tension knotted her shoulders, mingling with an incipient headache. All her instincts told her that this was about to go badly wrong—if it hadn't already. And the unexpected extra security was also a fairly good signifier of probable disaster.

"I feel as if you're using me like a blunt instrument," she remarked, trying to wall away her nerves.

"Yes, but you're so good at this," Felix answered. "Normally I'd take more time and enjoy the process, but we need to move. Roll it up."

"Paintings and canvas on the floor, roll yourselves gently into a tube." As they obeyed, curling into an ungainly Swiss roll, Irene switched to her headset. "Indigo, get ready, we're about to exfiltrate."

There was a muttered exchange of words at the other end, then Indigo said, "We'll be at the museum entrance in a couple of minutes. We think."

"Think?"

"Roadblocks. Don't worry about it." Tyres squealed.

Irene tried not to do just that. Indigo and Tina would be there. Because if they weren't, after all she'd been through, she was going to drag the paintings through the streets of Vienna herself and use them to bludgeon anything that got in her way.

Felix fastened the roll with packing tape. "Almost ready to go," he said.

A few seconds later, Irene and Jerome were leading the way to the great staircase, torches turned off. The others followed, carrying the hefty canvas roll between them. While Ernst could have just managed the entire weight on his own, the carefully packaged roll was unwieldy and cumbersome. The museum was silent, and dim light filtered in through the skylights—not enough for them to appreciate the décor, but enough to find their way out. Irene's stomach began to unknot slightly as they approached the staircase. From here it was a straight run to the exit. *Almost there, almost there,* she reassured herself. The wide stairwell beckoned, a white marble statue of a man with a raised dagger shining corpse-pale at the bend in the stairs.

"Stop sneaking around," Lady Ciu's voice said. "You're not fooling anyone."

She glided out of the shadows at the bottom of the stairs, tall and whipcord lean, as poised as any of the museum's fine statues. Her dark glasses were a band of pure blackness across her face. While she carried her sword-cane in her left hand, she wasn't leaning on it now; her right hand rested on the handle, ready to draw the blade.

Jerome put a restraining hand on Irene's arm and stepped into the light. He reached for his gun. "How convenient," he said. "I'd been hoping to see you again."

CHAPTER 20

Irene quickly ran through half a dozen things she could do with the Language. Order the floor to swallow up Lady Ciu . . . Drop the cupola on her head in a shower of glass, gilding, and fresco . . . Break the sword-cane in her hand.

Yet every single one would tell the dragon that a Librarian was involved. This world wasn't protected by the treaty, but her and Kai's reputations as ambassadors were at risk. And she didn't want to *think* about what would happen if Lady Ciu discovered the dragons' top-secret computer conspiracy had become public knowledge. All the more reason to have Felix take charge of the actual theft . . . and the *blame*.

Perhaps the elderly dragon would be willing to negotiate. But too many things didn't add up. The extensive security behind this particular painting. The alarm Indigo hadn't been able to shut off. The fact that dragons happened to be in Vienna, right where the painting was—and now Lady Ciu happened to be here. There was clearly *something* shady afoot.

But she still had to have that painting.

Not for the first time, Irene cursed the size of their target. Shoving it through a window simply wasn't an option. Even if they could risk damaging the canvas that way, they couldn't expect Lady Ciu to just stand there while they did it. And if Irene used the Language to help somehow, then that was again undeniable proof that a Librarian was involved . . .

Jerome was still smiling at Lady Ciu. "Is it time for another gamble?"

"I knew you were that sort," Lady Ciu answered. Her voice dripped contempt. "No self-control—and you can't resist the thrill of a mortal risk."

"I may not be able to resist a bet," Jerome replied, ". . . but you can't resist a challenge. We're well-matched."

Out of Lady Ciu's line of sight, the canvas-carrying team had come to a halt. In the lead, Felix hesitated.

Irene raised a hand in silent instruction for them to stay where they were.

"I can hear your confederates scuttling," Lady Ciu said. "So what now?"

"You let me come down to the foot of the stairs," Jerome said, "and then we draw. This is between the two of us."

Irene wished she could see the dragon's eyes and read her expression—but Lady Ciu's dark glasses were as opaque as the black stone of the pillars, as dead as a shark's eyes. And a bullet *could* kill a dragon who'd taken human form. So if Lady Ciu was willing to go up against someone with a gun, armed only with a sword, then either she was suicidal—or she was very good with that sword. Impossibly good. Legendarily good.

"I agree," Lady Ciu said slowly, to Irene's shock. "But your friends? Will they interfere?"

"No." Jerome glanced towards Irene. "What happens between us is between *us*, all right? This is on me. I signed up for the risk of it. Nothing more." He was already walking down the stairs, each sharp footfall on the marble steps like the ticking of a clock. "Whoever survives this can discuss next steps."

"Gambler," Lady Ciu accused.

"It's what *I'm* doing here. I'm not ashamed of that. But what about you? Sitting like a spider, waiting for challengers?"

"I'm doing my duty . . ." Lady Ciu paced backwards as he approached, keeping the same distance between them. "When my lady queen commands me to guard a world, a place, or an item, then I do so. My sword has always been enough."

"So far." Jerome was nearly at the bottom of the stairs. "Should I turn up the lights? I wouldn't want you to miss your cue."

Lady Ciu snorted. "My eyes are my least important sense. Don't waste your last thoughts on such a thing." She pulled a long blade from the neck of her cane. It gleamed like a strip of moonlight in the near darkness. "But what do you mean, you 'signed up'? Who hired you?"

"Does it matter?"

"It might make the difference between whether I keep you alive or not."

Jerome chuckled, deep in his throat. "The stakes are all or nothing, lady."

"I'll be a little more precise." She shifted her wrist. Light flickered on the steel. "It makes a difference to me whether you were hired by a dragon or a Fae."

"To do what?"

"Don't be ridiculous. We both know why you're here."

Jerome shrugged. "I don't roll over on my employers."

"I can appreciate loyalty." Lady Ciu lowered the tip of her sword. The two of them were ten yards apart. "On three, then?"

"Very well." Jerome let his hands fall to his sides. "On three."

Silence filled the museum. It seemed to clutch at Irene's throat. She couldn't see a way out of this without revealing a Librarian was involved—or without someone being killed. And while she had never claimed her hands were clean, she certainly didn't believe in casual murder. But this was what Jerome wanted. She glanced over her shoulder at Kai and the others, and for a moment she saw the same tension in Kai that she had seen in Lady Ciu: the same eagerness for a challenge, the same readiness for a life-or-death duel. He wasn't going to offer any convenient way out of this. None of them were.

Neither Jerome nor Lady Ciu spoke. If they were counting to three, then they were doing it to themselves, listening to their own heartbeats.

And then they moved. There was no signal, no word spoken, nothing—but they both slid into action at the same second. Lady Ciu dashed towards Jerome even as his hand fell to his holster. Her sword rose as he aimed. The movements were almost too quick for Irene to see.

Lady Ciu's sword blocked the bullet.

The crack of the gunfire mingled with the sound of bullet against steel, and the shot ploughed into the marble floor. Lady Ciu's blade cut from high to low, as Jerome fired a second time.

They stood for a moment like statues. And then Lady Ciu sagged, her hand clasped to her shoulder; but Jerome fell. Blood pooled around him, black against the white marble floor.

He shuddered as he lay there. "Not quite . . ." he whispered.

Lady Ciu took her hand away from her shoulder. It was dark with blood. "You are the first man in sixty years to have wounded me," she said. "I salute you."

Jerome smiled weakly. And then he went still. His fingers lost their grip on his gun.

Lady Ciu turned to Irene and the others. "Well? Will you surrender, or must I come after you?"

Irene turned away from Jerome's body, as if in shock—which was genuine enough—to whisper unobserved into her headset. "Indigo, when I give the word, turn on every single alarm in the building at top volume. Can you do that?"

"If I do, people will come," Indigo said.

"Do it anyway. And we need the truck here. Right away." Then she locked eyes with Kai, mouthing, *Get everyone to cover their ears. Now.*

Below, Lady Ciu sighed. "Very well," she said. She strode towards them, blooded blade naked in her hand.

"Now," Irene said into the headset, and ran forward, urgently beckoning the others.

She'd underestimated the sheer volume that the entire building's alarms could produce. Urns trembled in their niches. The statue of Theseus stabbing a centaur shook. Dust came loose from the ceiling, showering down in a choking mist. The noise was deafening: it shivered her bones and drilled into her skull. These alarms weren't designed to go off all at the same time and at this volume—especially not with humans present.

Or Fae.

But especially not dragons.

If it was painful for Irene, it was that much worse for Lady Ciu. She sank to one knee, her hands pressed against her head—though even in her pain, she didn't let go of her sword. Her dark glasses came loose and fell, and for a moment Irene saw the wide band of scarring across her face, like an old-fashioned domino mask. *"My eyes are my least important sense . . ."*

But there was no time to gawp. Staggering in the turbulence of sound, Irene and the others charged down the stairs, clipping the statue of Theseus with the canvas—Irene winced—then they were down the final flight, and out into the central hall. Kai was worst hit by the noise, his keen draconic senses doubly punished by the volume, but he was somehow still upright, still moving.

There was no time to stop for Jerome's body. Irene could only hope that he'd been telling the truth when he'd said this was what he'd wanted—and that he hadn't been disappointed by his final gamble.

But even through the noise, Lady Ciu stayed alert. Her voice was inaudible as her lips moved in curses, but her fury was obvious.

Light pulsed around her.

She's going to take dragon form, Irene realized in horror. *And in an entrance hall this big, she has the space to do it . . .*

The canvas-carrying team faltered. Felix and Ernst had possibly never seen a dragon assume their natural form before. Kai of course had, which gave him all the more reason to hesitate before advancing. But Irene grabbed Felix by the shoulder, dragging him on. The sound of screeching wheels was just audible over the shriek of the alarms. "Keep moving!" Irene gestured and shouted, loud enough to make her throat hurt. "Don't stop!"

Lady Ciu's shape resolved as they stumbled past—a *dragon*, huge and serpentine, great tail lashing as her wings strained outwards. Her natural colour might have been the dull yellow-brown of sandstone, but in the thin moonlight she was a mass of shifting shadows, a flow of muscle under rippling skin. Scars marked her face in this form as well, an intaglio of silvery lines like watermarked silk. She lowered her head, her long neck sweeping round as she tried to locate the smaller figures scrambling past her.

They had bare seconds until Lady Ciu gave up trying to find them and blocked the exit instead. Irene threw herself against the barred entrance and called, **"Doors, unlock and open!"** The doors heard her, even if no one else did, and undid themselves and swung wide open. She could only hope Lady Ciu hadn't noticed over the alarms.

But the boom of heavy wood as the doors slammed open couldn't be missed. With a thundering snarl of pure fury, the dragon twisted her body to strike.

Irene threw herself through the doors and down the steps outside, into the cold night air, almost falling as she slipped on the smooth marble. Their truck was there, engine running. Felix was a step behind her. Ernst, carrying pretty much the full weight of the canvas, staggered out like a javelin-thrower with the world's biggest spear. It sagged at either end as he charged down the steps and dragged it towards the back of the lorry.

Good, one of us has the sense to keep to the plan, Irene thought. But she couldn't look away. Not till Kai was out safely.

A great coil of dragon body slid past on the other side of the doorway, and Irene thought of boa constrictors tightening around their prey. She still couldn't see Kai.

"Come on!" Felix yelled.

She'd pulled Kai into this. He'd only come on this mission because of her. She was *not* going to leave him in there. The words in the Language for *brick, mortar, marble,* and *come apart* tumbled through her mind as she prepared to demolish the museum's entrance to get him out of there. Whatever it took.

And then Kai launched himself over Lady Ciu in an acrobat's smooth jump, rolling head first down the stairs in a graceful somersault.

Irene bit back the commands that she was forming, just waiting to be spoken. Her relief was too huge for words, which for a Librarian was huge indeed. She ran to where Felix was scrambling into the back of their vehicle, and leapt up beside him, holding her hand out for Kai. They crowded into the confined interior, already full of Indigo's computers, with the great roll of canvas propped crossways like a huge inconvenient cigar.

Lady Ciu's draconic cry of thwarted rage drowned out the alarms and rattled the glass in the windows. The bronze statue of the empress Maria Theresa in the square outside shivered on its plinth. Then the dragon slid through the wide-open museum doors, her wings tight against her body.

Tina hit the accelerator, and the truck lurched into desperate speed, jolting along the park's paths and out onto the road.

There was chaos on the streets of Vienna. Traffic surged through the main arteries of the city, spurting at top speed when it could—slowing to an aggrieved crawl when it hit police or CENSOR barricades. Their stolen CENSOR vehicle gave Irene's group some leeway—police waved it through without hesitation. But it also made them terribly conspicuous.

Irene squeezed Kai's hand, beyond grateful that he was out safely, then turned to Indigo. "Are we being followed?"

"By CENSOR? Not yet. By Lady Ciu? Look out the window and tell me yourself."

Tina was hunkered over the wheel, jiggling in her seat as she steered the truck between two cars and into an impossibly tight gap in the traffic. In a momentary glare of streetlights, Irene could see she was chewing gum as if her life depended on it, with a manic grin on her face.

Felix scrambled into the front passenger seat. He lowered the window, letting in a blast of street fumes and noise, and cautiously poked his head out—then yanked it back in. "We've got trouble," he said. "There are *two* of them up there."

"Is the other dragon blue or grey?" Indigo asked.

"Greyish? I wasn't exactly holding up paint samples to match its colour . . ."

"It's Shu Fang, then. We could have a problem."

"The wind's picking up," Felix replied hopefully. "That should inconvenience them, right?"

"The wind's picking up *because* Shu Fang's out there," Kai said, cutting in. "It's her element. And even if Lady Ciu can't spot us among the traffic, Shu Fang definitely will. There can't be that many CENSOR trucks near the museum."

"Well, damn." Tina jerked the lorry into a right turn, and all of them grabbed something to hold on to. Indigo cursed under her breath as she steadied her keyboard. Horns outside screeched in protest, and voices emboldened by the night and the anonymity of traffic yelled insults at the CENSOR vehicle. "We'll never make it to the Kaisermühlen Tunnel if they're right on top of us. It's another ten minutes across town . . . at least."

The first draft of the plan had involved Tina simply driving the truck between worlds, in the same way as they'd arrived. But if they were being actively followed by dragons, then either the dragons would pursue them from one world to the next, or the dragons' metaphysical "weight" might tether them to this world. So they'd decided to use a large tunnel, where Tina could shift worlds unobserved. The problem with this was now becoming clear; it relied on having a head start.

Irene glanced at Felix. He was looking uncertain, indecisive, as if he wanted a place to hide. If the lorry hadn't been rocketing along the road at eighty miles an hour, he'd probably have jumped out and made a run for it. *All right. I can do this . . . time to take charge.* "Indigo, can you report the dragons to CENSOR as a major supernatural threat? They could actually do their *job* for once."

"You think I haven't already tried?" Indigo spat. Her rapidly typing fingers gleamed in the light from her monitors, and her eyes flickered red. "Someone's in the system and actively working against me. I'm having enough trouble stopping anyone putting our truck's number plate out as stolen."

"But who . . . Hao Chen? Or his minions?" Irene said, remembering Hao Chen's links to CENSOR. They'd simply let him go, during the casino incident. "It could explain why he's not up there with Lady Ciu and Shu Fang." She realized another unwelcome fact. "And if you try to clear the traffic between us and the tunnel electronically, CENSOR will spot that? If the dragons *are* in league with them, they'll know where we're going . . ."

"So do something about it!" Indigo demanded. "I'm doing *my* part of the job. You do yours and buy us some time. Otherwise we'll be trapped here—they'll have stopped us and spotted us before we can get out of here."

"'Spotted us and stopped us' is the order I would expect," Ernst pointed out.

"Do *not* contradict me!" A glare of streetlights showed the snarl on Indigo's face. "And I will not be taken alive."

A gust of wind hit the lorry side-on, strong enough to make it sway on its wheels. And then in a great fanfare of car horns and screaming, something came down on the roof. The lorry shook under its weight, and Tina muttered curses as she struggled with the wheel. Long rasping shrieks of claws against metal came from the roof as the dragon began to slice her way through.

Irene grabbed for the Taser at her belt, and Ernst pulled out his gun. "Hold steady!" Irene called to Tina. At least nobody would get in the way of a truck with a dragon perched on its roof, but it was small consolation.

Something in the lorry's roof gave with a crack, and a limb tipped with steel-bright claws ripped through.

Tasers were only made for incapacitating humans, as Irene knew. However, the Language could get round that. **"Electroshock weapon in my hand, deliver your full charge into that dragon's flesh!"**

The flaring discharge lit the crowded lorry interior with a flash of blindingly harsh light. It outlined everything and threw black shadows against the floor. With a scream the dragon clinging to the roof dragged herself loose, shaking the battered vehicle so hard that it nearly came off its wheels. They rocketed forward as Tina slammed on the accelerator.

"It is only due to pure luck that your idiocy hasn't fried all my computers," Indigo said between her teeth, with the careful control of a woman inches away from severing heads. "Why didn't you *warn* me?"

"No time. Sorry." Irene looked around at the motley crew. "Any thoughts about what to do next? We're still not out of this world."

Then one of Indigo's computers chimed. And Hao Chen's voice came through loud and clear. "Good evening to those of you hacking CENSOR. We wish to talk." He paused. "Unless you'd prefer to die instead."

CHAPTER 21

How's he talking to us?" Felix demanded.

"Broadcasting on a CENSOR channel," Indigo said.

"Are we going to answer?"

"Can't you counter-hack his computer and make it blow up or something?"

Indigo's expression of scorn could have been used to etch diamonds. "Hacking doesn't *work like that.*"

"Well, sod hacking, then," Felix muttered. "Anyone got any other bright ideas?"

Kai's eyes were on Irene. "If I go out the back and take my proper form, I could distract them," he suggested. "My colour wouldn't be enough for them to identify me . . ."

But Irene couldn't take that chance, for the sake of the treaty—and for Kai's sake. And why had Lady Ciu been so eager to learn whether Jerome was employed by a dragon or a Fae? Why would dragons want to steal such a thing? If Kai *did* confirm to her that a dragon had been involved, he wouldn't get away easily—if at all.

"No," she said firmly, assembling her thoughts. "Tina—you need a long run-up to get away because of the load you're carrying, right? Two dragons and a Librarian, as well as three Fae and the truck itself?"

"Yeah, pretty much," Tina replied, swerving round a pair of cars that had collided in the centre of the street. "No offence, but you've got weight."

"I know, I know, it's all the Sachertorte." Irene swivelled back to Indigo. "Can you give me a temporary channel to Hao Chen, and cut it off whenever I signal, so that he can't hear us?"

"Easily," Indigo said.

"Here's a new idea," Felix suggested. "If we can get up to a high place and have Tina drive off, would she be able to make a transfer to the next world—before we hit the ground?"

"Not in a lorry," Tina said, without turning a hair. "Could do it in a plane. Have done it in a hang-glider. But not in this. Besides, it wouldn't sort out the problem of dragons following us."

"Okay," Irene said. "Felix, we need to buy time. Can we play good cop, bad cop over the audio connection? I'm the hardliner, you're the reasonable one who wants to negotiate . . ."

Felix nodded. "I can do that. But what are we buying time *for*?"

"We need to get to the nearest underground garage. I know there's one nearby—"

"There is, but once in, we wouldn't have enough run-up to escape through it," Tina said. "Even if it gets us out of sight of the dragons."

"It would," Irene countered, "as long as some of us get out first."

"Connection made," Indigo said, hitting a key. "You're through."

The wind outside shook the truck again. Irene raised her voice. "Hello, CENSOR! We are the independent association of mages and supernatural beings, and we demand that you immediately cease all operations against our kindred!"

There was a pause. "You're *what*?" Hao Chen said.

"Independent association of mages and supernatural beings . . ." Irene repeated. "We don't have a cool acronym yet. We demand immediate release of all our colleagues from your prison camps—and law reform!"

Hao Chen snorted. "Don't be stupid. We know what you really are. I'm here to negotiate your surrender. Or death."

"Wait!" Felix managed to interject real panic into his voice. "We can be reasonable about this. I know the painting's important to you. How about we make a deal?"

"Fool!" Irene snapped at Felix, doing her best imitation of an irritated aristocrat—Lord Silver would have been proud. "These people won't listen to anything except strength. We should burn the painting. Now."

"Someone hold her down!" Felix told the empty air. "Look, whoever you are, you said you're willing to discuss terms. What can you offer us?"

"Well, your lives, for a start," Hao Chen began. "And if you've been paid for this attempted theft, then—"

Irene gestured to Indigo to mute the connection.

"Right," Indigo said, as Hao Chen continued to offer freedom, money, and possible employment opportunities. "He can't hear you. What do you mean, some of us get off first?"

"You, Kai, and I leave the truck as soon as we're in the garage. Would that lighten the load enough, Tina?"

"Piece of cake." Tina turned a harsh left, directly against the oncoming traffic, and shifted her gum. "But what about you?"

Outside, in the windswept night sky, one of the dragons roared. The noise rang across the city, echoing in the bones of the humans below. A panicked howl of vehicle brakes and alarm bells answered, and all the Fae in the truck winced.

Irene looked around at the unlikely team. Tina, only interested in the road ahead; Kai, unreasonably trusting, utterly reliable; Ernst, inscrutable as ever behind his thuggish archetype; Indigo, focused on her work, as bright and brittle as lightning; and Felix, jittering in his seat. "Kai and Indigo can fly me out. They won't be looking for three people on foot—and we can leave once we've lost the dragons. But you'll need to wait for us. And your word on that would be really reassuring."

"We've already identified your vehicle," Hao Chen declared over the open channel, unaware that his audience had stopped responding. "We're moving in CENSOR forces with roadblocks right this minute. You can't keep driving round Vienna forever. You should really consider making a deal, while we're still prepared to talk to you . . ."

"Your plan's fine by me," Tina said. When Felix turned to stare at her, she shrugged, eyes still on the road. "I'm not saying I'm happy about it, but there's a limit to how well even I can drive this thing, if a dragon hitches a ride on top again. How long do you want us to wait—and how will you find us?"

"Kai will do the finding," Irene answered, glad that at least one person could stand the idea of *trust*. "Six hours should be more than enough time."

"I can stomach this idea," Ernst muttered, "which is to say, I don't like it. But it makes sense. How will you find us, dragon boy? Do you have our scent in your nose?"

"It's more metaphysical than that," Kai said with dignity.

Indigo lowered her gaze to her monitors again. "I approve your plan too," she said.

Felix's expression was shadowed, and for a moment Irene thought he would refuse. But then, astonishingly, he laughed. "The thing I most regret is that we won't see the expression on their faces when we've vanished. It's a deal, Irene. Give me your word in your Language, and I'll give you mine."

"I swear that this isn't a betrayal, and that I intend to join you later, after you're safely out of here—so that we can all escape," Irene said. A twinge of caution made her add, **"And claim the reward Mr. Nemo has promised us all."** The words echoed, carrying more weight than they should have done.

"And I swear by my name and nature that once we're in a safe location, before we take the canvas to Mr. Nemo, we'll wait six hours for you to join us," Felix said. "You have my word. Ernst?"

"It'll do. I pledge as well." He offered his hand to Kai. "Here, dragon boy. Get a good grip on my hand and be sure you can find me again. We don't want you getting lost."

Kai had a slightly mixed expression on his face as he took Ernst's hand. "By now I think I could find any of you," he said, "wherever you were. But I appreciate the gesture." There was something in his eyes that seemed to give the moment an extra significance. *An offered hand, a gesture of trust between Fae and dragon . . .*

"Hello? Hello . . . Will you do a deal? I'm waiting for your answer," Hao Chen said over the connection.

"Let's do it," Irene said. "How long to the car park, Tina?"

"Three minutes," Tina said. "Might be two."

Irene made a *turn the audio back on again* gesture at Indigo, who nodded. "How do we know we can trust you?" she asked Hao Chen. "This could be just one more trick."

"You're the ones who broke into the museum," Hao Chen responded. "How do we know we can trust *you*?"

"Aaaand roadblock ahead," Tina said, her tone deadpan. "Hang on, this is going to be bumpy."

Felix yelped and covered his face with his arms. Irene glimpsed the road beyond—the marshalled police cars, the men with guns—and dropped to the floor. Out of the corner of her eye she saw the others doing the same. They were all clinging on to something. Even Indigo.

The lorry hit the barricade of cars and careened through with a bone-shaking crash. The windscreen smashed to pieces: Tina ducked her head sideways as a bullet smashed through the glass, pinging off the back wall. They slowed, the lorry listing to one side, and then accelerated again, glass and metal crunching in their wake. The sound of bullets receded behind them.

Irene reflected that just as they'd kept Hao Chen talking while they escaped, *he'd* been setting up a roadblock while he "negotiated." She glanced around. No casualties. Good. "You think that's going to make us surrender?" Irene said into the link.

"Think of it as a warning shot," Hao Chen said. "You've been marked from the air. You won't get past the next roadblock. Surrendering now is your *only* chance of getting out of this alive."

"You really think CENSOR's going to shoot us, rather than shoot actual *dragons*?" Felix demanded. "What happened to their priorities?"

"As far as CENSOR knows, you're a group of terrorist mages who summoned the dragons yourselves," Hao Chen answered. "Once you're stopped, the dragons will magically disappear."

"Yes, but they're attacking *us*!" Felix pointed out. "How does that fit with your stupid narrative?"

Irene could almost hear the shrug on the far end. "Everyone knows mages are insane and evil. So who cares if their own weapons turn upon them? I should really thank you for the pro-CENSOR publicity, by the way. It's the best we've had in years. The main problem with keeping it funded is the lack of genuine supernatural activity here. But you know that, don't you? You're not from this world either . . ."

"So just how long *have* you been running CENSOR?" Irene asked. The revelation was less shocking than it might have been, now that she put the pieces together, but she still found herself disgusted by it. All that fear, all that paranoia, and all of it based on a lie simply to keep convenient control of this world. Maybe there were no universal standards of morality—but this was still just plain *wrong*.

Hao Chen laughed. "Getting me to betray myself over an open channel? I'm not that stupid. This channel's secure. And even if you distributed a recording, who'd believe you?"

Tina made a *cut audio* gesture to Indigo. "Five seconds," she said. "The next turning."

"Look where you're driving, woman!" Ernst growled.

"Yeah, yeah. Everyone who's getting out, be ready to do so." She spun the wheel abruptly and hit the brake. The truck turned with a ferocious squeal, rocking to the right. One of Indigo's monitors finally came loose from its brackets and went flying. She cursed in fine archaic style.

Irene snatched up one of Ernst's explosive packages. It might be useful: there were still enemy dragons *and* CENSOR to deal with, after all.

Kai scrambled to the back of the vehicle, keeping his balance in spite of the vehicle's contortions, and held out a hand to Irene. "Let me go first," he suggested, "and I'll catch you."

"No offers to catch me?" Indigo demanded. She picked up her ever-present attaché case, swaying in the dim interior as she rose to her feet.

"You are tough dragon," Ernst pointed out before Kai could say something regrettable. "You will break less easily than puny Librarian. Dragon boy has his priorities right."

"There'll be a barrier gate up before the garage," Felix said. He was still curled to one side, his arms protectively in front of his face. "It'll be closed this time of night."

"Twenty-four-hour parking for us!" Tina answered, and the lorry charged down the slope into the car park. The barrier pole bowed under the vehicle's momentum, then gave way and went bouncing loose, shuddering across the concrete. From behind them came the furious roar of a dragon seeing its prey escaping.

The car park was well lit inside—Irene could see flashes of it through the shattered window screen, over the shoulders of Felix and Tina, momentary glimpses of the sort of concrete and painted pillars that seemed universal to all worlds that had developed cars and needed somewhere to park them. Then there was a crunch from above, and the lorry jerked mid-movement as something low-hanging hit the roof.

"I'll turn left and drop you," Tina said, totally focused on her job, "then we're free to go."

As she spoke, she spun the lorry into another jerking turn, and the tyres screamed again, an accompaniment to the roaring dragons outside the building. Briefly, the vehicle slowed. Kai pushed the rear doors open and leapt out, landing with barely a stagger.

Irene's jump was much less graceful than Kai's—or Indigo's. But she landed without breaking anything or spraining an ankle, underrated hazards when leaping from moving vehicles. The back door was still swinging open as Tina gunned the lorry into motion again. Ernst flipped a casual wave in their direction. The lorry charged between rows of parked cars, leaving a trail of glass and a shattered wing mirror behind it.

But the noise of its passage was drowned out by the sounds coming from the entrance. Irene and the two dragons turned to look, then broke into a run, with the operative direction being *away*.

Shu Fang was writhing through the entrance in a long coil of rain-grey scales and muscles, her wings pressed tight against her sides. Wind came with her, gusting blasts that whined against car windows and sent random pieces of rubbish rattling along the floor. Dozens of car alarms started jangling at the disturbance, adding new tones to the cacophony. Shu Fang moved with surprising speed, not at all slowed by the confined quarters.

Indigo was in the lead as they ran for it, her precious case swinging as she sprinted. Kai had Irene by the wrist in the sort of grip that would leave bruises later, dragging her along behind. They were going in the opposite direction from their truck, dodging behind one row of cars and then another. Irene desperately wanted to know what Shu Fang was chasing—the lorry, or *them*—but she wasn't waiting around to find out.

And then between one moment and another, the constant squeal of wheels on tarmac was gone—as was the truck. Indigo paused mid-step, eyes wide with sudden fear, and gestured for Kai and Irene to stop.

The three of them crouched to hide behind the nearest car—a sleek Renault, Irene noticed with the distraction of terror, and owned by someone with a family, judging by the scatter of toys in the back seat. They waited. They could hear the heavy grinding of Shu Fang's movements, her belly rasping against the concrete. Her claws and wings scraped on the pillars and random cars, and the wailing of innumerable car alarms made for an insufferable accompanying dirge.

On the positive side, Irene reflected hopefully, *there's only one dragon in here, so maybe both wouldn't fit? Or maybe Lady Ciu just disliked the noise ...*

There was no way she was going to stand around and wait for an elevator, with a rampaging dragon in the vicinity. But this sort of place usually had fire exits. The stairwell it was, then.

Kai tugged wordlessly at her arm, then pointed at one of the farther columns. There was indeed a fire exit sign on it, and the outline of a door. She nodded, then prodded Indigo.

But they all froze as Shu Fang's voice echoed through the underground car park. It carried above the car alarms, echoing with a cadence that rattled human bones and made Irene's breath catch in fear. "Little ones ... why do you waste your time running? I already have your scent."

Irene hadn't thought of that. No chance that she'd lose their trail, then.

"Surrender," Shu Fang said, her voice a cascade of deep-toned wind chimes, "... or I'm coming to get you."

Irene drew the pistol from its holster on her purloined uniform.

"Slide across the floor when I throw you, and keep going until you hit a wall," she whispered to it. Then she pitched it under the nearest row of cars. It skidded across the floor, moving with an impetus beyond anything her throw could have supplied. And it kept on moving out of her line of sight.

Wind plucked at their clothing and made car aerials quiver and hum. Behind their sheltering car, they watched Shu Fang slide past, following the noise of the gun on concrete. Her eyes were like onyx, her body a length of storm-cloud that gleamed under the neon lights like a winter river in flood. She should have seemed ridiculous in the concrete surroundings, but instead she was utterly terrifying, a creature out of mythology that could rip the modern world apart.

Now, before she realizes it's a diversion and destroys us all . . . Irene twisted Ernst's explosive's detonator to five seconds and slipped it under the fuel tank of the adjacent car. *Then* they bolted for the exit.

Shu Fang was right behind, lunging towards them like an express train. Wind blasted ahead of her, slamming into Irene's back and making her stumble. Panicked, Irene wondered if she should have set the explosion to go off sooner, or later, or if it would have any effect at all . . .

And then it went off. The noise in the confined space was devastating; it drowned out the alarms, and even Shu Fang's roar of fury. Flames crackled behind them as they all piled through the exit—thank heavens for fire doors and regulations. They could hear cars exploding as they ran up the stairs.

"What if CENSOR's out there?" Indigo demanded.

"Then you're 'under arrest' and we're taking you in for questioning," Kai answered, his gesture taking in Indigo's civilian silk top and jeans. "Just be yourself and it'll look convincing."

Indigo snorted. "Did he learn that sort of deceit from you?" she asked Irene.

"Yes," Irene panted, wishing she were as fit as the dragons. "I believe he did. Good job, Kai. Let's *go*."

CHAPTER 22

Following the rest of the team's trail had taken them reassuringly far from the world of Alpha-327—and its hostile dragons. And winter in the desert was colder than winter in Vienna: the wind licked across empty hills and valleys, cutting through Irene's coat as if it weren't there. The landscape beneath them was divided by the single road that ran through it—like the stroke of a pen, where the ink had dried from glossy black to dusty grey. On either side of the road the land rose in successive ridges, in shades of pink, grey, and orange. The only landmark was the single building in the distance, with a very familiar truck parked outside it.

Riding on Kai—something that Irene had done less than half a dozen times—was still a thing of wonder. In his true form, as a dragon, he was a shimmering marvel of dark blue. His scales shone like sapphires, his voice thundered but was still recognizable as his own. She sat in the hollow of his back, behind his shoulders, as he cut through the sky, his flight more supernatural than physical. He didn't beat his wings but glided through the air, as fluid as a shark in water. Despite the rushing of the air, they could hear each other well enough to talk.

"You're supporting an unjust regime," Indigo said with passion, not for the first time. She was parked behind Irene on Kai's back, seated with a graceful nonchalance that indicated just how little she worried about falling off. "Your treaty does nothing more than rubber-stamp the draconic status quo. And if political allegiances do shift, then why should a new regime honour its commitments? To the Fae *or* the Library?"

"Would you argue the dragons' political regime was unfair, if you were one of the ones in power?" Irene asked wryly.

Indigo didn't lose her temper. "If I'd wanted to be in power, under my father and mother, then I could have been. It would have been easy. But have you ever been in a situation where you felt you *had* to do something about the status quo? That your ethics demanded it? Or don't Librarians care about that sort of thing?"

"You've yet to tell me what you're actually standing for," Irene countered. "It's all been about what you're standing *against*. But if you're disputing the authority of the monarchs, what do you plan to put in their place? Or are you an anarchist?"

"An elitist," Indigo said. "And I'm not alone. Far from it."

"So you and your allies are planning a situation where dragons still hold power over humans—just with *different* dragons in charge?"

Indigo looked unapologetic. "The definition of elitist, as I understand it, is that those who are superior should hold power. I'm a reasonable person. Show me humans who are as competent or intelligent as dragons, and I'll bring them into government as well."

Irene somehow didn't expect Indigo would find *any* humans whom she considered "superior." Even Kai, who was prepared to admit that Librarians, humans, and even Fae could be competent or useful, wouldn't have argued for democracy—for the will of the people to choose their own government. As for herself . . . well, she'd willingly sworn to the Library. She'd bound herself to serve a hierarchical organisation in the process. And if she disobeyed her orders, she'd be punished.

But Indigo seemed determined to challenge her own kind.

"What if you *can't* change the status quo?" Irene demanded.

Sparks flickered in Indigo's eyes like a foreshadowing of lightning. "Anything can be changed if you really put your mind to it, Irene. If you're strong enough. You and I are both strong. If we don't achieve our desires, then we have nobody and nothing to blame except ourselves."

Abruptly Kai banked, dropping from the sky in a smooth plummet. "We're here," he said, his voice a deep rumble that Irene could feel in her bones. "You were so busy arguing, I didn't like to interrupt."

"We should be careful when we draw near," Irene said. "We never described your true form to the group. All they'll see is a dragon . . ."

"Land at a distance and approach on foot," Indigo suggested.

Kai descended towards the ground, and Irene tried not to think about how fast the road and earth were rising to meet them. She *really* didn't like heights. It was impossible not to think about falls, and impacts, and messy splashes.

But Kai settled gently on the ground beside the road, about fifty yards from the building.

At this distance Irene could see it better. It looked like a disused diner in the middle of nowhere. Maybe the area had once been inhabited. An old sign above the main entrance was so smeared with dust that it was impossible to make it out, and the broad window was shielded by tattered drawn blinds. If the Fae were in there, then they were hardly rushing out to greet them.

Behind her and Indigo, light flared for a moment, briefly casting a pair of harsh shadows across the dusty earth. Then Kai clasped her shoulder, human once more. "Which of us goes in first?" he asked.

The question was answered by Ernst cautiously appearing in the doorway of the diner. He waved to them.

"About time," Indigo muttered, and strode ahead. Irene and Kai followed at a more leisurely pace.

Kai didn't seem disposed to hurry. He waited till Indigo was out of earshot. "I'm glad that you weren't falling for her ridiculous anti-monarch propaganda," he said softly.

"I have no intention of signing up to her crusade," Irene said. "To anyone's crusade."

Kai looked reassured. "I knew you had more sense than that. And we shouldn't have to associate with her for much longer."

Which means I'll soon be away from her dangerous influence? Irene thought wryly. But out loud, she said, "I know what you're *really* annoyed about . . . We didn't have to pretend to arrest her. So you missed out on ordering her around, in handcuffs."

Kai snorted back a laugh as they joined the others. "Well, when you put it like that . . ."

Ernst had discarded his CENSOR uniform jacket and was now

wearing a battered but equally stretched check flannel shirt instead. "Good job! Though next time, describe your dragon form, so that I am not hunting for missile launchers."

"They've been tried," Kai said briefly. "It didn't go well."

It probably came down to the size of the target, Irene thought to herself. She'd seen missiles employed quite successfully against smaller dragons, as it happened. But was it her job to give either side a better understanding of each other's respective military capabilities? No, it was not. "Are Tina and Felix all right?" she asked.

"Well enough, but Felix will have a hangover when he wakes. The owner of this place stored whiskey in the cellar. So Felix and I tossed a coin as to who should keep watch—but I prefer vodka, so I did not mind when he cheated."

Irene's curiosity finally boiled over—now that they seemed almost out of danger, with the end of their journey within sight. "Ernst . . . may I ask you a question?"

"Certainly," Ernst said gloomily. "Everyone asks it, eventually. Let us walk aside so that I will not be overheard."

Kai gave them a speculative glance. "I'll go and see if there are any other supplies in this place. I wouldn't mind a cup of coffee."

"Tea for me," Indigo said, and followed him inside.

Irene mentally crossed her fingers that the kitchen would survive their joint presence, and turned to Ernst. "Please understand that I don't intend to insult you . . . but your whole 'Russian' ambience—the vocabulary, the attitude, even the reference to vodka . . . it feels a little overdone, even given the principle of Fae archetypes. I was wondering why."

"The fact that you see it means that I must work on it further," Ernst rumbled. "You see, Librarian girl, there are certain patterns which must be respected. I was originally from . . . well, you would not know the name. It was a small town in a country that no longer exists, in a world which has little except wars to make it interesting. Can you guess my way out of this?"

"The Russian mobs?" Irene theorised. "The, um, Bratva? The *vory v zakone?*"

"Precisely. And in such a place, it was better to act the insider than be an outsider. Better to be Russian than . . . well, where I was once from."

"I understand," Irene said. "But did you always know that you were Fae?"

"No. But after ten years I was working for a Fae boss, and he saw my potential. He showed me the different spheres and how to walk between them. He told me that I must have the proper blood somewhere in my family, because I found it easy to become . . ." He looked for words. "What I was. What I am . . ."

"Thank you for the explanation," Irene said.

Ernst shrugged. "A small thing. You didn't ask what I was expecting."

"Well, I don't want to get *too* intrusive, but what was that?"

"To ask why I was doing this. Everyone else already has. Even dragon boy, though I did not tell him. It entertains me to tweak his nose a little."

"I wouldn't want to be left out, then . . ." Irene raised an eyebrow. "I'll tell you my reason, if you'll tell me yours."

They began to stroll towards the building. "I am under orders," Ernst said. "My boss, he has an arrangement with Mr. Nemo, and so I do as I am told. It is not for my sake alone. My husband is not well, and my boss pays for his medical care. We all do what we must, no?"

"I'm sorry to hear that." Irene was surprised that the burly Fae had any emotional entanglements at all, but she had better manners than to say so. "I'm doing this for a book Mr. Nemo has, and that the Library wants . . . and since we're being honest, or I hope that we are, the book's important to the stability of a world I care about. A place I went to school. Somewhere from *my* past."

"It is never simple," Ernst agreed. "Always there are complications." He paused. "Thinking of complications, I am reminded—before he began to drink, Felix unrolled the canvas. He was wanting to see the second painting, the one behind the first. It is in the side room there—the garage." He nodded towards it.

"Didn't you want to see it?"

Ernst rubbed his nose thoughtfully. "I wanted to, yes. Then I thought, what if my boss says to me, did you see this mysterious painting, and I tell him yes. And I find myself being shot in the back many times? You know how these things can go."

"I . . . see your point," Irene said. And she did, far too well.

But the choice to *not* look was also problematic. Why was the painting so important to the dragons? Important enough for them to take over CENSOR—or perhaps they'd even created CENSOR?—and station *three* representatives on that world to watch over it, and be willing to kill to keep it. They hadn't even listed it on the treaty as a world under their protection, perhaps in case anyone wondered why . . .

For the Library's sake, she told herself, she had to know.

"Did Felix say anything to you about the canvas, after he'd looked at it?"

Ernst shrugged. "He said it meant nothing to him. And Tina was not interested. She could not *drive* it, after all. Perhaps it will mean something to you or the dragons. Shall I tell dragon boy to bring you some coffee in there?"

"That'd be very kind." Irene smiled at him. "And the job's almost over now."

"It has been a smoother caper than most so far," Ernst agreed. "Even with Jerome lost to us. Still, without his diversion, we might not have made it out so cleanly. I will turn down a glass for him later."

She'd been trying not to think about Jerome. "So will I."

The garage door opened with a squeal. Of course there was no *need* for silence—they were in the middle of the desert, with nobody around for miles. But some impulse made her want to tiptoe and hush, as though it would let her erase her presence later.

Perhaps my subconscious knows something it isn't telling me . . .

Irene flipped the light switch and blinked in the sudden glare. The canvas was spread out on the floor before her. And then she blinked again, in shock this time, as she saw *what* was on the second canvas.

CHAPTER 23

At first glance the canvas seemed to be a rough draft for *The Raft of the Medusa*, with only the people fully completed. She could see a group clinging together, on an incomplete raft that was barely a sketch of timbers, with a churning ocean and a thunderous sky. But these people weren't the ones in the original painting. (Could it really be called original, though, Irene wondered? Which of the two was older?) There were only nine figures, not the dozen or more on the "public" painting—which would do for a term. Their faces were instantly recognizable too, as dragons in human form. More than that; Irene *knew* some of those faces. The Kings of the Eastern, Southern, and Northern Oceans. The Queen of the Southern Lands. The unfamiliar faces showed enough of a family resemblance to the ones she *did* know that she guessed they might be siblings—the fourth king, the other queens . . .

And who was the ninth figure, a man with the same family look as the four kings, but older? He was staring into the distance, with a look somewhere between resolution and despair.

Stormy waves curled over the edge of the vaguely sketched raft, and the sky beyond was full of clouds that seemed to reach out for the pitiful vessel, attempting to pull it back to whatever it was that they'd escaped from. That was it, Irene decided—this wasn't just a painting of a desperate group of survivors, it was a picture of them *fleeing* from something. But what? And why?

She leaned in to examine the swarming clouds in the background, and the figures hidden within them, only visible when one looked closely. More dragons, pursuing . . . but somehow wrong. She'd seen dragons several times now—she might, in fact, be one of the Library's experts on the subject—and the ones in this painting seemed somehow more *primitive* than the dragons she knew. Their eyes held no expression, no intelligence, nothing but blank ferocity. Their outlines seemed to merge with the swirling wind and water from which they came. And maybe she was being fanciful now, but they seemed to represent the uncaring forces of destruction that threatened the few pitiful escapees on the raft. It seemed as if they were trying to reach these few to drag them down, tear them apart . . .

Irene shivered at her emotional reaction to the picture. But wasn't that what true art was supposed to elicit? She tried to analyse her perceptions of what was depicted here as objectively as possible. The people on the raft weren't just trying to escape the ocean; they were clearly fleeing from other dragons. A different breed, perhaps? Or . . . an older variant? And while Irene would have liked to think that it was just fiction . . . why had the dragons gone to such lengths to keep it hidden?

The whole point about draconic power was that it was absolute, unchanging, and utterly unquestionable. The dragon monarchs themselves were immortal; nobody even raised the possibility that they might someday die. By definition (their own, at least), dragons were too powerful to have weaknesses as such. And if this judgement included all dragons, their rulers were perfection personified. So this painting was either a gross insult to the entire set of dragon monarchs, or it represented a truth that they would never willingly have revealed. But if it was the latter, was it a metaphor for some past state of distress and disaster, or a genuine depiction of a real escape? There were no immortal kings and queens here, but a group of desperate travellers, struggling together and in mortal peril. They were running for their lives from something that reached out to destroy them.

Sometimes historical truths slipped into fiction over time. And a story might contain a reference to long-forgotten facts. As a Librarian, Irene knew this better than anyone. She even remembered a fairy tale by the Grimm brothers that had directly referred to the Library's history. That had contained a secret that people would have killed for too.

Of course, this painting might be no more than a carefully crafted slander. A suggestion that the dragon monarchs had once struggled for their thrones, or had faced a threat dangerous enough to threaten even them. But in that case, why preserve the evidence? Why not burn it, rather than keeping it hidden away, guarded and watched?

Irene knew almost nothing about dragon history. Kai had occasionally dropped the odd mention of wars with chaos—past and present—and the rise and fall of certain great families. But that wasn't the same thing as a definite chronology. And he'd made it clear that deeper questions were actively discouraged among dragons too. They were expected to accept what was and not ask for further details. In human history, the rulers all died eventually and were replaced by new and theoretically more progressive generations. But how did it work with near-immortal dragons? What *had* there been, before the dragon kings and queens came to power?

And how dangerous might it be to know?

The door creaked behind her. Irene turned, catching Indigo's silhouette against the morning light. Another half-dozen pieces of the puzzle came together in her mind. She waited for the dragon to speak.

"Aren't you going to say anything?" Indigo asked. "You're usually so quick to give your opinion."

"I hadn't realized that it annoyed you so much," Irene answered. "Then again, I'm *only* human." She considered her options as if they were a deck of Jerome's cards. Pretend ignorance of the situation? Or admit her suspicions and accept the consequences? "Kai's taking his time with the coffee."

"Don't expect him anytime soon." There was a savage smile in Indigo's voice. "It's just the two of us."

"Should I worry about him?"

"Does he matter to you? Besides politically, that is?"

"Let's just say, whether or not he's in danger will affect my response to the situation." Irene kept her tone as calm as her face, not wanting to give Indigo the advantage of knowing just how *much* Kai being in danger meant—and how it might affect what Irene would do to her.

"Oh, relax. I've seen you're fond of him, and he of you. It gives me hope for him." Indigo moved closer. "Not *immediate* hope, but I think in the long term. So tell me, when did you start noticing things weren't adding up about the job?"

As if I would tell Indigo everything, just because she asked . . . "The problem with having a reputation for intelligence is that people *assume* I know everything. You're demanding full details. But all I know is that you've confirmed *something* dubious is going on. Thank you for that, by the way."

"Come on. Use that mind of yours. Point out something you spotted, something I failed to hide, that roused your suspicions."

"Well . . ." Irene hesitated artistically. Why did Indigo seem to be in a hurry, pacing impatiently around the garage—did it mean Irene should play for time? "I should have noticed something odd right back at the start, when Mr. Nemo had those passports made for us. Only someone hooked into this world's computer systems could have prepared them—and we know how difficult that would be for an outsider. You were the only person on the team who could have done it. But you claimed you'd never visited this world before."

"It could have been a Fae," Indigo countered. "Someone with expertise. I'm sure that such creatures exist."

"In that case, why not hire them for this job, rather than you?" Irene walked around the edge of the canvas, putting space between her and Indigo. "And why did we have a gambler on the team? We all assumed it was because Jerome was lucky, and used to handling high-stakes capers. But *someone* knew all about Hao Chen and wanted a gambler on hand as one of the things most likely to distract him. The most likely person to know his weaknesses would be a dragon. And then there's the fact that you know what *this* is," she said, gesturing to the painting. "You weren't surprised when you saw it just now."

Indigo shrugged. "Perhaps I'm better at hiding my emotions than you are."

"At seeing your *own parents* in this picture?"

"Ah." Indigo paused. "You've met them, then?"

"Your father, and not exactly by choice." Irene would far rather have avoided Ao Guang's attention for the rest of her natural life. Being an object of interest to dragon monarchs wasn't safe. Especially if they thought you might be useful.

"So you have some idea of the stakes that we're playing for here. You've been a pawn." Indigo walked up to the edge of the canvas, facing Irene across it. "Wouldn't you rather be a player?"

Irene restrained the urge to roll her eyes. Why did everyone assume she wanted to be a devious mastermind and puppet mistress—and put it in terms of *chess*? It was so . . . clichéd. "Is this where you offer me a position on your side, for when your aunts and uncles are cast down from power?"

"That'll do for a start." Indigo wandered around the canvas, and Irene matched her, keeping it between them. "Running from me, are you?"

"Maintaining my independence," Irene said.

"And that's what you'd be doing if you accepted, on a larger scale. Maintaining the Library's independence *and* status. Keeping my faction as an ally. Imagine your position if I did rise to power, and you *weren't* among my allies. We can manage a truce with the Fae on our own. Wouldn't it be better for us and the Library to be . . . friendly?"

Irene looked at the circling dragon and had a very strong flashback to her memories of Mr. Nemo's sharks. "That's true," she agreed carefully. She didn't think a fervent declaration of *No, I will never work for you!* would go down too well. "Being on good terms with you and your friends certainly won't break our oaths. I can work with that—and so can my superiors, if I put it to them in the right way."

"The benefits of a meritocracy." Indigo gestured down at the canvas between them. "As opposed to the stagnation caused by mere accidents of birth. Immortal slavery which will *never* change."

"Is this painting 'real'?" Irene searched for the right phrasing. "In the sense of representing something that genuinely happened? Or is it symbolic of some sort of past disaster?"

"That . . . is something I don't know. Though I know more than most, having two royal parents, and being an inquisitive person. I have no shame about how far I've gone and what I've done to trace the past to its roots. At times at my family's expense. You should sympathise with curiosity, I think—surely you must understand how it feels to want to *know*."

Indigo gazed at the picture as if she were a burning-glass and it was her tinder. "Very few dragons go that far back. The official story is that the kings and queens are eternal, immortal, whatever— that they were the children of some incredibly ancient First Dragon, or something similarly cosmic and inexplicable. Apparently all the legends of immortal dragon rulers in mythology are retellings or misinterpretations of their reality. And of course, my beloved parents and their siblings write our history books, so they can say what they want. Wasn't there a story about that? He who controls the present controls the past."

"And he who controls the past controls the future," Irene completed the quotation. It was true. Those in power were able to dictate what "truth" was passed down—and their children then grew up believing it. "And you intend to prove that the accepted versions of the past are incorrect?"

"Money wasn't the only thing I stole from my father. I took information too, and that is much more valuable. Information on what *this* was and where it was hidden. If he'd known how much I knew . . . well, fortunate for me that he didn't. I had to bargain with Mr. Nemo to get the resources and the backing for this job. But you and I both know that sometimes one must deal with the enemy, when playing for high stakes." Indigo pointed at the canvas. "This is a can of worms. I intend to open it."

"That's a rather mixed metaphor," Irene pointed out.

"I didn't spend my life studying metaphor. I occupied myself far more usefully." Indigo shrugged. "And by the way . . ."

"Yes?"

"You may be thinking that we dragons are curiously ignorant about our own roots. But how much do you know about the history of your own Library?"

"Point taken," Irene admitted. "But do you think that a—well, an artistic impression like this—carries the same weight as a genuine historical record? You were the one who argued that a painting was no more than patterns of colour and shading on a piece of canvas."

"Unfortunately not everyone sees things my way. But fortunately, it's those who don't see things that way who *will* believe the story represented in this painting. And as for artistic impression versus historical record . . . maybe I'll never find out exactly what happened thousands of years ago. But this painting will show that it wasn't the eternal peace of a glorious reign that *they* claim." She practically spat the pronoun, and her eyes glinted dragon-red. "And that's the only way we can trigger change. It is time for us to ask questions. It is time to *demand* answers."

"I'm not your audience," Irene said, before Indigo could go into a speech she'd obviously practiced. "What I would like is to stay well out of this." Others might not care or believe that the painting represented dragon history in some way. But Indigo clearly thought *dragons* would, and that it would have a seismic effect on their society—and she should know. This painting was a bomb, and Irene wanted to be far away before it exploded.

"*I'm* not stopping you from disappearing," Indigo said calmly. "Take your payment from Mr. Nemo. Then go home."

It was a tempting offer. This wasn't Library business. But there was one tiny problem . . . "And what happens when people start asking *who* stole this, once the painting's exposed and it has the effect you're anticipating?"

"Ah." Indigo examined her fingernails. "Yes, I suppose it might be inconvenient for you, if I said a Librarian was involved. Some people might even trace the crime back to the Library itself. Collusion with the Fae, to get hold of an object which damaged the dragon monarchs' reputations . . . I don't really need to go into the possible consequences, do I?"

Irene might have thought that Indigo was bluffing. But she knew the dragon wasn't—and Indigo knew that Irene knew it. Even if the Library saved itself by claiming Irene had acted on her own and without permission (and it would), the smear would still cling. Fear and fury knotted together in Irene's stomach, as she realized just how bad this could be. "You are gambling with the Library's reputation, and even its survival," she said, her voice as calm as ice. "And you are making yourself a dangerous enemy."

Irene *had* to find a way to stop Indigo. This situation had blossomed out of nowhere and was getting worse by the minute. The recently forged peace was fragile and there were people on both sides who'd be glad to believe the worst of the Library. But Irene also had to bring the canvas back to Mr. Nemo, or she'd lose the book that she so desperately needed. The world of her childhood was at stake. So threats to destroy the painting were off the table.

And would the Library expect her to somehow silence the dragon, permanently? She winced at the thought. And finally there was Mr. Nemo . . . how much did he know and what was his real involvement—in charge or Indigo's partner in crime? Could he trigger the same rupturing of dragon society as per Indigo's crusade—even if she wasn't there to inspire it? Or was this his goal too?

"Good," Indigo said, unmoved by Irene's implied threat. Maybe to a dragon, it was no more than the yapping of an angry puppy and she only needed to move her ankles out of the way. "You're taking this seriously."

"I assure you that I'm taking it *very* seriously." Irene shifted her focus to practicalities. If she couldn't dispose of the painting, she could perhaps immobilize Indigo, and then seek help from the Library—or even from her immediate "colleagues." The Fae members of the gang would be on Irene's side. While they might even welcome dragon revolution and/or regicide, she suspected they really wouldn't like having been used as pawns. And they *definitely* wouldn't like having targets painted on their backs, for their involvement in the theft. "I think the next stage in this dance is for you to state your demands."

"I don't have any . . . yet." Indigo began moving towards her again, and Irene again retreated. If Indigo got her hands on her, Irene could forget saying anything in the Language besides *argh*. "I'm prepared to keep your involvement under wraps—if you do me a future favour. Or two."

"Or many," Irene noted. "That sort of agreement tends not to have a formal end date."

"You'd be a valuable asset . . . I wouldn't *waste* you. That would be stupid."

Perhaps she was telling the truth, but being *used* at all didn't sound exactly good for the asset. "How kind of you," Irene murmured.

"You're very well trained," Indigo said. It wasn't a compliment. Coming from her, it was a simple statement of fact. "That school of yours, I suppose. Did they teach you to spy and pick locks there too?"

Irene blinked in shock at this sudden reference to her old school. How could *Indigo* know about it? The only time she'd spoken freely about her past had been to Ernst just now, or . . . to Kai, on Mr. Nemo's island. When they would have been under surveillance. *That* was it. Indigo had been the picture of sullen resentment at that dinner, but she must have been getting a full briefing from Mr. Nemo behind the scenes. And this reference to it was just a demonstration of how much Indigo knew about Irene—to show how much power she held in the current situation.

She couldn't let Indigo see her feelings, so she simply shrugged. "Something along those lines." But her most important lessons had involved learning to trust other people, to cooperate with them, to accept that people who weren't Librarians could deserve respect and fair treatment—whether they were humans, Fae, or dragons . . .

Indigo looked a little disappointed that her jab hadn't had any effect. "It's a better offer than many other dragons would give you. Would you rather be *my* ally—or *their* slave?"

"I hate to think how much surveillance video you have of us all planning the heist," Irene said instead of answering Indigo's question, her heart clenching at the thought. This wasn't just blackmail material against Irene and the Fae—it was blackmail material against *Kai*. "No wonder you wouldn't let go of your attaché case."

For a moment Irene thought she saw irritation flicker in Indigo's eyes. Perhaps she hadn't expected Irene to think of that. "At least I didn't leave anything on that world. Don't fret about Lady Ciu and her servants. They can't prove anything. They don't even suspect Library involvement. Yet."

Just how strong am I? Irene wondered. *Strong enough to kill her to shut her mouth? I'd rather not . . .*

But if she had to, the colder part of her knew she would.

"I need an answer now," Indigo said. "A general expression of your willingness to cooperate with me will do."

"If I want to keep the Library's involvement secret, I'll have to fall in with your plans . . ." Irene said, preparing for something she'd never attempted before. "And I'm forced to admit it. I can only say that **you perceive that I am standing here and agreeing to your terms for the next five minutes**."

The effort of using the Language manifested in a streak of pain across her temples, and pulsed in her chest. She'd never tried the Language's *you perceive* trick on a dragon before. They were creatures of order given form, so affecting them with the Language was like making water run uphill. Very, very difficult.

But not impossible.

She managed to step backwards, though her head ached as though it were going to split. Indigo kept looking at where she'd been standing—and, more to the point, didn't indicate she'd noticed Irene sidling towards the door. The smile on her face suggested her imagination was supplying all the details she could possibly want of Irene's capitulation. But when it wore off . . .

Irene stepped outside into the bitingly cold wind. Priorities. Destroy Indigo's attaché case and her computers. They hadn't visited anywhere Indigo could upload her information, yet. Find

Kai. Somehow rally the Fae to her side—and make sure that Indigo didn't have *any* leverage left. And all within five minutes.

Ernst was inside the diner's main room, nursing a mug of black coffee. He blinked in surprise. "Is all well?"

"A few minor hitches," Irene said. "There's something we all need to discuss. But first, have you seen where Indigo left her attaché case?"

Ernst nodded glumly and put down his coffee, gesturing behind him. "Always things must get complicated. I was afraid of this. The case is behind the counter."

Irene nodded in thanks. The sooner she fried everything in the case, the happier she'd feel.

"Irene?" Ernst said.

"Yes?"

His fist took her in the stomach, knocking the air out of her before she could say anything. Another blow on the back of the neck sent her spinning down into unconsciousness.

But she thought, as darkness closed round her, that she heard the word *sorry*.

CHAPTER 24

I rene woke up to a surge of self-condemnation.

Worse still, she was wearing a bikini. And high heels.

She tried to assess her surroundings with her eyes closed, something that seemed annoyingly familiar, pushing aside the urge to scream and throw things. The most worrying aspect—of many—was the weight she could feel against her throat. There was some sort of collar around her neck. It was difficult to think of any possible circumstances under which this could be a *good* thing.

Other than that . . . wherever she was, it was quiet. Though in the background she thought she could hear the faint buzz of air conditioning. The air smelled of disinfectant and she was lying on something padded, but it didn't feel soft enough to be a bed or mattress. The quality of the light, through her closed eyelids, suggested a fluorescent light overhead.

Deciding she had more to gain if she looked around, she opened her eyes and slowly sat up. She was in a padded cell. No bed. No furniture. A fluorescent strip stretched across the ceiling, out of her reach. The door too was padded, on the inside, and there was a spy-hole in it—which, given her luck, probably allowed a full view of the whole room. No convenient standing out of view and then jumping the guard when they entered. Damn.

A panel in the wall—also padded, of course—slid back to reveal a television screen. Well, that answered the question of where she was. As if she hadn't suspected.

Mr. Nemo appeared. He was sitting behind a heavy ebony desk with a pile of brochures stacked on it. Behind him, a window looked out onto the depths of the ocean. An octopus flexed its tentacles as it glided through the water with the slowness of a ballerina. It was far too symbolic for Irene's tastes.

"Miss Winters!" Mr. Nemo said cheerfully. "How pleasant to see you up and around. Please don't try to say anything: that collar around your neck will give you an electric shock if you do. And that includes speech in your Language."

Irene raised her fingers to explore the collar. Unfortunately the television screen didn't allow her to see her reflection. She could feel the smooth links of metal round her neck, like an oversized watchstrap, and a more complicated disc was lying at the hollow of her throat.

It could all be a complicated and hilarious bluff. Or then again . . . his claims might be true.

Mr. Nemo seemed to take her silence as acceptance, although her options for responding were limited. "Now I suppose you're wondering what you're doing there. Well, I assure you that it won't be for long. I'm in the middle of organising a highly exclusive auction. Fae nobility, dragon monarchs—I did *think* of sending a catalogue to the Library, but they might have felt obligated to interfere. And since I'm not signed up to your peace treaty, I can do precisely what I like. The next few days are going to be very interesting. Naturally I can't have anyone coming here or meeting me personally, despite this auction being *particularly* important, but there are ways round that."

Irene pulled herself to her feet. She sketched out a large rectangle and mouthed, *The painting?*

"Precisely! And a few other bits and pieces too. It seems a shame not to take advantage of the occasion." He tilted his head to one side, beads of sweat glistening in the wrinkles of his face. "Now, I suppose you're wondering why you're in a high-security prison . . ."

Irene made an exaggerated *go on* gesture with one hand.

"My little auction may have some consequences." He shrugged, the picture of a man saddened by all the dreadful things that could happen. "I'm not a signatory to this treaty of yours, so I have no constraints on *my* behaviour. But *you* might feel that you should do something anyway, even without input from your superiors. So I'm temporarily removing you from the situation. Think of it as a summer holiday, Miss Winters! A little vacation from responsibility . . ."

Irene began to say something, but as the first word escaped her lips the collar round her neck tightened, and an electric shock jangled painfully through her body. She found herself on her knees, fingers trying to pry the collar off, gasping for breath. *All right. Not a bluff.* But one part of her mind was taking cold mental notes, even as tears rolled down her cheeks. *It'd stop me managing more than a word . . . but could that be enough?*

"I really hoped that wouldn't be necessary," Mr. Nemo said. "Please try to relax, Miss Winters. You shouldn't have to stay here for more than a day or two. I'm sure you're worried about Prince

Kai too, but he's in perfectly good health—although under similar conditions. You'll both be under constant surveillance, of course. My camera network stretches island-wide. Even if you could leave your room, there is absolutely nowhere you could go where I couldn't find you."

Irene noted that Mr. Nemo had slipped into full-on gloating. But every Fae archetype, including master criminals, had its weaknesses as well as strengths. Keeping enemies captive in the middle of a secret base wasn't a good move, for a start . . . Resorting to American Sign Language, for want of any better ideas, she signed, *What about your promise to us?*

He cupped his chin in his hands thoughtfully. "You're probably asking me about payment for the picture. Very unfortunately, I can't understand a word you're signing. But don't worry, Miss Winters, I always keep my bargains. As soon as you present yourself to me and ask for it—in some manner that I *can* understand—I'll be glad to hand it over and let you go. But . . ." He waved his fingers in her direction. "Ta-ta for now, my dear."

The television screen went dead, and the panel began to slide across it again. But Irene was already moving. And her first priority was getting something sharp. She lashed out at the television screen with one foot, heel braced. There had to be some point (no pun intended) to the ridiculous high heels she was wearing.

The heel punched squarely into the glass screen, sending a spider-web of fractures racing across its surface. The panel was still trying to close, blocked by Irene's foot, and fortunately safety systems stopped it from attempting amputation. Balancing on one leg, Irene tugged off her right shoe, then dragged it out of the ruined screen, detaching some fragments of glass in the process. A couple of small shards fell to the floor as the panel finally closed.

Irene set her teeth, so as not to make any noise that might trigger the collar, and used one razor-sharp shard to slice into her forearm. Using her finger as a stylus and her blood as ink, she managed to scrawl a single word in the Language on her collar: **Deactivate.** Of course there would be cameras watching, but she should still have a few seconds. Kicking off the remaining heel, she tensed and addressed the door: "**Unlock and open.**"

To her relief, she remained unshocked as the door swung open.

Now she had one last trick to play. The camera watching her would be linked to all the rest of them. Symbolic links, physical links, the Language was *good* with links. And if even one camera was watching and listening to her right now . . .

She took a deep breath, braced herself, and spoke clearly. "**Surveillance devices in my presence, and all surveillance devices linked to them, malfunction!**"

The Language worked easily in high-chaos worlds—in a way, it worked *too* well, fulfilling its user's wishes to an almost over-enthusiastic degree. Unfortunately, it then demanded a price. The shard of glass fell from Irene's hand as she swayed, and she had to prop herself up against the wall to stay upright. Blood trickled from her nose, and she blotted it with the back of her hand. She'd managed exotic things in high-chaos environments before—exploding a boat, warping a staircase, freezing a canal—but she hadn't tried to mess with anything as widespread as a whole hidden island's surveillance network. She shut her eyes for a moment as afterglow-images tracked across her vision. But if her command had taken so much energy, then it must have done *something*. In the absence of any signs of success—the cameras were hidden, after all—she could only trust that her splitting headache meant she'd succeeded.

More blood trickled down her arm as she staggered down the corridor, her pace speeding up as her sense of urgency grew. *Must find bandage,* she thought. She wasn't desperate enough to use her bikini yet. *And watch out for pools of sharks or piranhas.* This was a Spartan, behind-the-scenes sort of place, unlike the more visited parts of Mr. Nemo's lair. And each new hallway looked just as interchangeably grey as the next. If it had been a film set, one corridor could have represented the entire complex. She could imagine James Bond protagonists being chased through here by the villain of the moment, heading for disaster. She just hoped she was on the winning side of that particular Fae archetype.

She ran.

Ten minutes later, she was hiding behind a corner as the third pair of guards so far marched past her. Their flowery sarongs might be pretty and colourful, but their guns looked all too genuine. Fortunately they weren't very good at conducting searches. The problem with successfully hiding your island from everyone else—your guards never accumulated any experience with genuine enemies.

But Irene needed information. She stepped out once they'd passed, and coughed in an official way. As they spun round, trying to work out where to aim their guns, she said quickly, **"You perceive I am your superior officer."**

They snapped to attention. "Report!" she added. "What is the current situation?"

The man on the right looked embarrassed. "Subject L is still on the loose, sir. All other guests are still in their holding locations."

"I see." Irene needed more—but it would be hard to explain certain questions. Such as *Where precisely are these holding locations?* "Good. New orders, men. You're to accompany me to visit the guest Tina. Mr. Nemo has a new job for her, and with Subject L on the loose, we need to make sure she's safe."

"Sir!" Both men saluted again and set off at a trot. Irene followed, feeling extremely conspicuous in her bikini. She hoped that the Language's influence would hold for however long it took to reach Tina. Of course, she *wanted* to get to Kai. But Mr. Nemo would expect Irene to head straight for him. Their friendship . . . attachment . . . was an open secret. It was probably on their files in a dozen secret locations, from Fae to dragon spy headquarters.

They eventually reached what Irene considered the "public" face of the island—including the corridors she and Kai had wandered through previously, with their huge aquarium-type windows. The door into this section was obvious from this side but formed an unobtrusive wall panel on the public side. And really they'd come much farther than Irene had thought possible, by the time one of the guards paused, shook his head, and said, "Wait a moment . . ."

Irene kidney-punched him, hit him on the back of the neck as he folded up, and pulled his gun out of his holster. She was quite pleased with their progress so far; the Language perception trick could wear off inconveniently fast. "All right," she said, as the other guard boggled at her. "Where are the Fae guests being held?"

"Sir? But . . ." He blinked, trying to come to terms with reality, and went pale. "Oh my god, you're *her*. You're Subject L."

Irene wondered exactly what they'd told the guards about her. His reaction seemed unnecessarily dramatic. "I asked you a question," she said, capitalizing on his fear in tones of quiet menace.

"I won't tell you anything," the guard muttered. "I am a loyal and faithful soldier."

"Look," Irene said patiently, "the camera system's still down.

Nobody can see *or* hear you, and there's nobody here except you and me. And your friend. Who's unconscious. Wouldn't you prefer it if I went away and left you in peace? Rather than shooting holes in you? Or twisting your mind into knots?"

"You're sure the cameras are out?" he asked tentatively.

"If they weren't, then we'd have a dozen more guards with us and I'd be back in my cell," Irene reassured him. "I give you my word. Tell me what I want to know, and I won't kill you—or even torture you . . ."

"Down that corridor, turn right, then take the third left, and the three Fae guests are in rooms next to each other," the guard said, so fast that he was practically babbling. "Madam Tina, then Mr. Felix, then Mr. Ernst."

"Good job," Irene said. "Now tell me what you see down the corridor there."

"I don't see—"

Irene hit him on the back of the head mid-phrase with the butt of the gun. That wasn't prohibited by any promises she'd given, after all . . . And as he collapsed, she started running.

There were no guards outside the indicated doors. Mr. Nemo must be assuming that she wouldn't go to the Fae team members for help. Well, she certainly wasn't going to ask Ernst, and Felix wasn't of any immediate use, but . . .

Irene mentally crossed her fingers and knocked on the door that she hoped was Tina's.

"Go away!" The snarl from inside was definitely Tina's. "Unless you're here with permission for me to get the hell off this island, in which case come the hell in."

Irene tried the handle. It was locked. So much for them being "guests." The Language took care of that.

Tina was crouched in an armchair facing the door. Cigarette butts, wads of chewing gum, and paper planes littered the floor. There was a curious sense of poised expectancy in the way that she sat there, almost like a car with its engine idling, ready to crash into movement. Her eyes widened as she took in Irene.

"Has Mr. Nemo given you your reward yet?" Irene asked.

Tina twirled a set of shiny new car keys round one finger. "All ready to be picked up. You wouldn't appreciate it."

"And yet you're still here."

"I am kind of grinding my gears here, waiting to hit the road," she admitted grudgingly.

Irene nodded. "In that case, I might be able to help . . . I'm here about something Kai discussed with you earlier. A paid job?" This was something Kai and Irene had discussed as one of their backup plans, days ago, when they were sitting in Vienna eating Sachertorte. She prayed to any gods of the open road that they'd be on her side in this negotiation with their acolyte.

Tina slowly smiled. It was like watching a landscape light up as the sun rose. "You know, I was kind of hoping you would say that." She was practically vibrating now, clinging to the edge of her chair, fingers white-knuckled with the effort of holding herself in position. "So what am I taking and who am I taking it to?"

Irene breathed an inner sigh of relief. "I'll give you a name and an address . . ."

CHAPTER 25

I rene had congratulated herself on getting *one* thing done as she and Tina left the suite. It was a mistake. No sooner had the thought begun to coalesce than the two other doors in the hallway opened.

Ernst was the first to step out, his eyebrows rising as he took in Irene's outfit. "Perhaps I missed something?" he asked.

Felix stood in his doorway, a gun dangling loosely in his hand. But despite its support, he looked worn and anxious—as if he still hadn't quite reclaimed his archetype.

"I'm leaving," Tina said. She stepped out from behind Irene and waved at the two men. "Night-night, sleep tight, don't let the bedbugs bite. I've had enough of this place. You going to stop me?"

"Thinking about it," Ernst rumbled.

"I don't think so," Irene said. She tried to appear imposing, despite her bikini, but she couldn't help recalling how fast and hard Ernst could hit. "What was it Mr. Nemo said to us? He'd allow us to leave, free and without constraints, at our own chosen time? Surely you're not going to stop one of your own doing that."

Ernst shrugged philosophically. "Mr. Nemo isn't always right. Sometimes best solution is to knock everyone down and sort it out later. Great thinkers put it more elegantly, but I prefer my way. Also, my way is less lethal."

Ernst was obviously a lost cause. But Felix . . . Irene could think of bait that he wouldn't be able to resist. "I'm glad you're all right," she said to him. "I really wasn't sure about your master plan at first, but everything seems to be working out just as you said . . ."

Felix's glare shifted into a slightly confused frown, though he did his best not to show it. No master schemer could ever admit to not knowing what was going on. "It wasn't much," he said after a moment, all false modesty.

Ernst hesitated, caught between possible targets. "Explain," he suggested.

Irene shrugged, affecting to ignore Felix's gun and Ernst's balling fists. Behind her back, one hand made frantic *escape now* gestures at Tina. "You've probably noticed that the surveillance cameras are all out of action," she said to Ernst. "That was *my* part of the job." She nodded to Felix. "And you did *your* bit of it by making sure I could infiltrate the heart of Mr. Nemo's stronghold as a harmless prisoner. Or should I say, apparently harmless?" She forced herself to smile. "And now we're at the stage of the plan where there's no surveillance, everyone's running around like panicked gerbils, and Mr. Nemo's own extensive collection is up for grabs." She looked Felix square in the face. "Like I said. Good plan."

It was like a reverse of that moment when she'd been in the Vienna University Library and had been confronted by Ernst and Felix. Except that this time Felix was prepared to listen and Ernst was the suspicious one. And Felix *was* listening. She could see the kindling excitement in his eyes at the thought of a caper on this scale.

Ernst coughed, reminding everyone of his looming presence. "Felix. This is *not* a good idea. What is the plan? Where is a map? Where is an escape route? Where is *anything*—other than Librarian in front of you with silver tongue?"

Felix whirled to face him. In the background, Irene could hear Tina retreating at a run. Good. "Ernst. Remember you owe me a favour—from Galway? I'm calling it in."

Ernst's face settled into lines of severe disapproval. "You're going to regret this," he said, dropping his usual speech pattern for a moment.

"Maybe so. But sometimes you've got to do the regrettable thing. Give us fifteen minutes, Ernst. Not more than that. That's my favour. Then we're even."

Ernst looked between Felix and Irene. He sighed. "Fifteen minutes. Then I take no responsibility for what happens next." He stepped back into his room and shut the door behind him.

Irene could hardly believe it had been that simple. "You must have done something very impressive for him," she commented.

"I picked a lock," Felix said briefly. "It was an important lock. Now are you with me on this raid, or do you have your own target?"

"My own target," Irene answered. Tina had told her where to find Kai. "Tell me, did you see what was on the second canvas?"

"I did," Felix admitted. "I was the one who unrolled it. But it didn't mean anything to me. I'm guessing it's blackmail material, or similar?"

"Similar," Irene agreed. She was tempted to walk away and get on with rescuing Kai, but an inner prod of morality made her pause. "A word of advice, between temporary colleagues. I know you'll want everyone to know how you stole it from under the noses of three dragons. But that wouldn't end well. At all."

"Fair warning," Felix said gaily, and Irene knew that he hadn't listened to a word that she'd said. "See you around."

He took off at a sprint, and Irene did the same.

Several corridors away and a couple of levels higher up, she found the area Tina had described. It was a combination of prison cell system and sick-bay. The first locked door opened on an empty room. So did the second. But the third . . .

Kai lay on a hospital trolley at the centre of the room, unconscious. There was a medical mask and gas tube strapped to his face, and he was connected up to a couple of monitors that beeped regularly. There weren't any guards, or trip-wires that she could see, or infra-red alarm beams, or pressure pads in the floor . . . though of course, the point of such things was that intruders *wouldn't* be able to see them.

There weren't any *obvious* guards either. Surely any competent guard captain, on Irene's escape, would have assigned additional security to her possible targets. However, if she wanted to get Kai out, she was going to have to risk it.

Irene picked her way silently across the floor, her bare feet silent on the concentric tiling, and reached Kai's side. His breathing was calm and undisturbed. She suppressed a sigh of relief. Carefully she removed the breathing mask from his face, stripping off with a sympathetic wince the surgical tape that held it in place. She checked his pulse. Steady. Good. She had no idea what they'd been giving him, and she wasn't going to sniff the gas to find out.

When a hidden door slid open in the opposite wall to the entrance, it did so in dead silence. It was the change in the air that alerted Irene, as a cold draught brushed her bare skin. She looked up to see Indigo standing there, smiling, a remote control in her hand.

The dragon touched a button.

The floor under Irene fell away. She grabbed desperately at empty air; then her fingertips caught the edge of the panel she'd been standing on—which had retracted. As she swung over a gaping darkness below, her arms were already trembling with exertion. She didn't know how long she could hold on.

The room had been a trap, and she'd walked right into it.

Irene struggled to pull herself up, but she didn't have a good enough grip on the edge of the floor; she needed time and leverage, and she didn't have either.

Then Indigo loomed over her, silhouetted against the light. "Well?" she said.

"Well what?" Irene retorted. Now she could see various cunningly intersecting panels and trap-doors covering the entire floor—their edges outlined by the light from Kai's room. She hadn't stood a chance. She could also hear the sound of water, deep beneath her. Memory unhelpfully supplied a full-colour replay of the last person who'd dropped into one of Mr. Nemo's shark pools. "Am I supposed to beg you to get me out?" Sweat slicked her hands.

"Are you deliberately trying to provoke me?" The words were mild enough, but Indigo's eyes burned with fury.

"You're not Fae," Irene said through gritted teeth. "So I'm guessing that you're not here to gloat. If you're going to offer me a hand up, what are your conditions?"

"Ah." Indigo rested the panel's remote on the sleeping Kai's bed. "Normally I would play along. Gloating over a helpless victim is the sort of petty, time-wasting, inefficient thing that Fae get up to at their worst moments."

"Normally?" Irene echoed. That didn't sound good.

"You made mistakes." There was a glint of red in Indigo's eyes. "Firstly—and *don't* try it again—you used your Librarian abilities to delude *me*." The room in the air prickled with static electricity, and Indigo's hair shivered and crackled with it. "You dared to interfere with the functioning of my mind. You *dared*."

Irene's heart sank. Apparently she'd escaped in precisely the way most calculated to infuriate the dragon. "You're the one associating with Fae," she said, her fingers aching with the strain of holding on to the edge. "You know what they can do to emotions and perceptions. Why are you so upset with *me*?"

"Because I thought better of you," Indigo said coldly. The toe of her shoe came down on the fingers of Irene's left hand, and she began to press.

Irene bit back a gasp of pain. She was forced to let go, leaving her suspended by just one hand over the drop. The waters below her sounded louder now. Hungrier. Could the Language help? But Indigo would never let her complete a full sentence. "Mistakes . . . plural?" she forced out, her right arm burning.

"You came to find *him*." Indigo pointed at Kai behind her. "You could have gone looking for the canvas. You could have escaped. Both actions would have been logical uses of your time and energy. But instead, you chose to come crawling to his side, a pathetically *emotional* display. He's not that powerful—you couldn't expect him to save you. You would have known that Mr. Nemo would keep him safe too, as a bargaining counter. He's not in mortal danger. And yet . . . you're here. It was a waste trying to cultivate you with logic and reason. You aren't worth my time."

"Yet you're still here, gloating. Like a Fae."

"I think it's therapeutic to explain to someone else how badly they got things wrong." Indigo smiled. Her toe moved towards Irene's other hand.

"Aren't you going to offer me a chance to join you, in exchange for my life?"

"No. You'd just lie."

Irene had to admit that Indigo was absolutely right on that point. She definitely had the upper hand. The upper hand, the higher ground, and the lethal foot.

When the opponent completely controls the chessboard and things can't get worse for you, sometimes the answer is to make it worse for everyone . . .

"I'll find a more cooperative Librarian to support our faction, somewhere else, if I need one," Indigo went on. "You won't be missed. In fact, with you *gone*, you'll be that much easier to blame."

"Tell me," Irene gasped, "what's the thing you know?"

Indigo paused. "What do you mean?"

"You knew about. Painting . . . You have some idea—what it means. What came before . . . dragon monarchs?"

Indigo's mouth curled into a cruel smile. "You're thinking that because you're about to die, I'm going to tell you all my secrets. Mistake. I'm not a Fae. I'm a dragon. And very soon I'm going to be a ruler."

Her foot came down.

Irene couldn't hold on. The pain was too great. But as her grip slipped, she shouted, **"Panels, trap-doors, open!"**

Indigo's eyes widened in shock. She was already moving as

Irene finished her second word, throwing herself towards the door. But she'd come too far into the room, and all the floor panels and trap-doors opened at once. And with the floor effectively gone, everything in the room dropped into darkness—Irene, Indigo, Kai, trolley and all.

As she dropped, Irene hit some kind of chute and she could hear Indigo screaming in fury above. There were scrapes and a thud, perhaps from Kai's trolley—and the light above vanished as the floor panels closed again. Irene could guess what would come next. She held her breath.

There was light—a blaze of it, electric, violent, eye-searing—and open air. And then water.

The impact was disorientating. Irene felt herself sinking, but she was too dizzy to be sure of anything else. She forced her eyes open and spread her limbs to slow her drop downwards. She was drifting in sea-water—the open ocean? No, a confined pool, though a large one—and above her she could see two other blurred figures in the water. One had long hair that drifted around her, the other was tumbling like a rag doll in slow motion. In the distance, sleek shadows moved through the water, sliding ever closer.

The cut Irene had made in her arm gaped open, scraped in the fall, and a slow trail of crimson oozed from it. And the Language wasn't much use underwater: speech wouldn't work if she couldn't breathe.

She kicked desperately towards Kai, managing a pace that would have impressed the most enthusiastic lifesavers at her old school. Indigo was swimming towards him as well, but clearly water wasn't her element. And for once Irene's unwelcome outfit worked in her favour. It was far easier to swim in a bikini.

She could see the sharks gathering out of the corner of her eye.

They moved closer now, huge and lethal in gun-metal grey and stark white, their eyes dead coals that watched her and assessed her value in flesh and blood. Perhaps they were used to having prey dropping by for dinner, and knew they could take their time about it.

Their circuits narrowed. One passed behind her, close enough that she felt its passage in the water, a physical force shoving her to one side. She moved, terror giving her strength and speed. It wouldn't give her armour, though, and any second now . . .

Her hand closed on Kai's arm.

His eyes opened.

Under the influence of his will, the water embraced the pair of them, while another wave swept outwards in a pulse that threw the sharks back. A tentacle of water rapidly coiled around them to raise them to the surface, then carried them just as swiftly to the shore. Kai slid an arm round Irene's waist, supporting her as she coughed for air. A thin pattern of scales marked his skin, as elegant as fractals and as perfect as frost.

They found themselves at the edge of a wide pool of sea-water, at least fifty yards across, inside a low-roofed cavern. A hatch above showed where they'd entered, and electric lights, strung across the roof, blazed with actinic power. The air had a coldness to it that made her shiver, and suggested that a heavy thickness of rock stood between them and the warmer tropical air outside.

"Are you all right?" Kai asked. He swung himself up onto the side of the pool, then helped her climb out. His brows drew together as he noted her clothing and condition.

Irene opened her mouth to speak, but as she began to answer, the collar suddenly activated. She choked, attempting to pry it away from her neck, and an electric shock raced through her body as she crumpled to the ground. *Oh no,* she thought through the pain, *the water must have washed off . . . the Language . . .* For a moment she thought she'd pass out from the combination of water and electricity.

Then Kai was on his knees beside her, his face a picture of worry as she shuddered in pain. But as the spasms wore off, Irene noticed Indigo was also pulling herself out. Fury blazed in every line of her body and her hair clung to her in a sodden mass. For once she was less than elegant. "Son of Ao Guang," she spat, "you have chosen a very bad time to wake up."

Kai rose to his feet. "If I'd been able to convince everyone else that you were as faithless as you are dishonourable, we wouldn't be having this conversation. *What have you done to Irene?*"

"I?" Indigo spread her hands. "It was Ernst who hit her. It was Mr. Nemo who had her dressed in that ridiculous bikini. I've done little more than offer her advice, which she didn't have the sense to take."

Kai snorted. "I woke up to find all three of us swimming in a shark pool together, so I'm going to assume you had *something* to do with it. And you were right behind me when I was tasered earlier. I suppose you had nothing to do with that, either?"

Irene touched Kai's arm, then motioned towards a passageway set into the rock. Hopefully Mr. Nemo's surveillance system was still malfunctioning.

"Leaving so soon?" Indigo said softly. "I don't think so."

Kai gestured loosely, his hand opening in a martial artist's invitation to spar, and the water rippled in response as if some unseen wind had touched it. "You still have Mr. Nemo's binding on you. And even if you didn't, I don't fear your storms down here. Water is *my* element. The advantage is mine, not yours. But please—go ahead. *Try* me."

So that was Indigo's power—storms, or possibly rain. But Indigo would have to actually break through the roof to affect them. And she was still wearing that metal bracelet . . . Which she'd *said* blocked her powers, Irene realized with slow dread. She'd lied about so many other things. Why assume she was telling the truth about that?

Irene glanced up at the cave's roof to reassure herself it was still there. It was. And so were all those high-powered electrical lights, strung across it to provide a perfectly lit view of victims being eaten by sharks. A worrying suspicion began to stir. How did an elemental affinity with storms actually work?

Indigo smiled, but it wasn't pretty. She spread her hands as if to demonstrate how empty they were, and Irene felt a sense of dread.

The lights all blew together in a fusillade of explosions like gunshots. Glass rained down, spattering on floor and water alike. Then lightning leapt from the electrical wiring above to sheathe Indigo in a blaze of blue-white fire. Two balls of lightning hovered above her open hands. "Well, Brother?" she taunted. "Who has the advantage now?"

CHAPTER 26

Irene was painfully conscious that she was soaked and standing on a wet floor, and that water was an excellent conductor of electricity. Kai hesitated, perhaps coming to the same conclusions. Then he gestured. A wave spun upward out of the water, swirling to hover above them like a cobra's hood, a shield between them and the other dragon.

Indigo's face was illuminated by her flaring power, like a classical mask carved from alabaster. She pointed her hand towards them.

But before the lightning could leap out at her command, the water folded round Irene and Kai, dragging them into the passageway in one great gush. It carried them perhaps twenty yards down the tunnel before it ran out of force, washing to a gentle standstill. Kai caught Irene's arm and they ran, following the tunnel downwards.

The fluorescent lighting was clear enough for them to see where they were going—and this was a practical tunnel for island staff, rather than one of the more opulent guest tunnels. They turned several corners and finally stumbled through an open door into a guardroom. Here two of the sarong-clad guards had seized a moment to have a quiet cigarette.

Without breaking step, Kai caught one guard's wrist and spun him into a table, then knocked him out with a crisp blow to the chin. Irene grabbed a chair and thwacked the second guard before he could draw his gun. Kai caught him on the rebound and sent him to join the first in temporary slumber.

"All right," he said closing the guardroom door. "I see it's one of *those* days."

Irene shrugged. *Again* . . . she signed, relieved that they had trained in the same sign language. So very useful on covert missions. *Do you think she'll follow?* she asked.

"Not on her own. She wouldn't have the advantage here. Besides, the farther in we go, the stronger the chaos becomes, and the weaker we both are . . ." He properly looked at her, now they could catch their breath. "Is that collar the thing that's stopping you talking?"

Irene nodded and Kai reached into a pocket for his lockpicks, then blinked, realizing for the first time that he was in evening dress. Wet evening dress. "This is ridiculous," he said. With a gesture he forced the water from their sodden clothing—one of the less grandiose but still useful aspects of dragon elemental powers.

There wasn't actually a formal sign in ASL for *Fae*. So Irene nodded again and made a sympathetic face. As lockpicks were likely thin on the ground, she looked around for other implements—and purloined a paper clip from a stack of reports.

"I can think of a simpler method. Turn round, please?" He fiddled with the collar. "Ah. Thought so. There's a lock here at the back where you can't see it. It's an incredibly complex and expensive volume-sensitive gadget . . ."

There was a snap. The collar came loose.

"And then they put it on a cheap catch," Kai finished smugly. "So tell me what's going on?"

Irene updated him with relief, finishing with the painting and Mr. Nemo's upcoming auction. "And Indigo's working with him because she wants to go public with it to bring down the monarchs."

"I told you she couldn't be trusted," Kai muttered.

"I admit you were right," Irene said. "Entirely right. But you didn't predict she was actively working with Mr. Nemo, rather than being his prisoner . . ."

Kai took off his jacket and draped it round Irene's shoulders. She realized that she'd begun to shiver from the cold, with her impractical clothing. She gave him a smile of thanks. "But we *need* to get that painting back. You know dragon politics better than I do, but I get the impression that the painting could be grounds for a civil war. And I'm sure there are some dragons who'd want one. Indigo hinted that she wasn't working alone. Then, treaty or no treaty, the Fae would take advantage of any perceived weakness. And even if the Library avoided taking sides, open conflicts between chaos and order would put Librarians in danger as they'd try to stabilise multiple worlds. It could last for years. For generations, even. All our work on the treaty would come to nothing too."

Kai frowned. "Have you actually seen this painting?"

"Yes," Irene said. "And . . . look, please accept my word that if it went public, it would be devastating. You don't need to see it to trust me on this point. I mean, wouldn't it be *easier* in some ways if we could deliver it back to the monarchs and honestly say you'd never even looked at it?"

His frown deepened. "Irene, is it really that bad?"

To Irene's mind there was no shame in being desperate, but many dragons would never agree. "It suggests there was a time when the monarchs were weak. That the history they've passed down might even be a lie—and who knows what truth it actually conceals? And Indigo thinks she and her allies can use it." There was a silence. "I'm not asking you to look away from the painting, if you really want to see it. But given how much trouble we may already be in . . ." She didn't want to think about that. "Can't at least one of us truthfully say *I only ever saw the back of that canvas* . . ." She'd drawn him into this; now she had to protect him.

"Anyhow," she said, as if he'd agreed, "can you reattach this thing, so that it looks as if I'm helpless? Then we need to find Mr. Nemo." She rapped the electronic collar on the table, hoping to hear something essential snap. But Kai plucked it from her fingers with a superior look, squeezed it until a crack formed, then dripped in a few drops from the puddles on the floor. It might have survived a drop into a shark pool, but the interior circuitry wouldn't survive *that*.

"Where should we search?" Kai asked, as he bent the catch back into shape. His inhumanly strong fingers locked the collar around her throat again. "Mr. Nemo could be anywhere on this island."

"Let's start with down," Irene answered. "Every time we've seen him on video, he's had a view of the seabed behind him . . ."

Kai nodded. "Why not? And he must be on this island, there's too much localized chaos here for him to be elsewhere."

"If we can at least reach him, then we can try to make a deal . . . and get our payment."

Kai bent against her for a moment and murmured into her ear, "What about Tina?" They were both keenly aware the surveillance could be back on at any time.

With her cheek against his, she whispered, "I sent her away as we planned. But we can't depend on that."

"I know." He was still for a moment, then said, "There was something I didn't tell you earlier. Mr. Nemo made me an offer, after we first came to the island—"

And it was at precisely that instant that the guards came swarming in, drawn guns a harsh contrast to their flowery sarongs. And someone was yelling, "They're in *here*, Captain! We've found them!"

Irene gritted her teeth at how inconvenient life was sometimes. What *was* the deal that Mr. Nemo had offered Kai? And how come he'd never mentioned it before?"

But at least it was clear the guards *hadn't* expected to find them here. Which meant that the surveillance system wasn't up and running yet and their previous conversation hadn't been caught on camera. So she kept her mouth shut, feigning dumbness, and glared at the guards.

Kai smiled lazily at the guards, ignoring their guns. "Just the people I wanted to see. I would like to speak with Mr. Nemo. At once."

The techs finished tinkering with the large video screen, which covered half the wall, as the guards marched Irene and Kai into a conference room—guns still drawn. Indigo sat in a wide cupped armchair beneath the screen, hair now miraculously dry, clothing unmussed, no longer bothering to wear the bracelet that she'd claimed bound her powers. But the glint in her eyes suggested she would like to drop the island and all its inhabitants—especially them—into a shark tank. Ernst loomed behind her with his large arms folded, his expression somewhat weary.

The screen fizzed and came to life. Mr. Nemo was still sitting behind his desk, but he looked significantly less at ease with the world. "Prince Kai," he said shortly. "You wanted to speak with me."

"There have been a few irregularities," Kai said, ignoring Indigo utterly. "I thought it might be easier to sort them out person-to-person—as it were."

"Irregularities, you call them . . . My communication network is barely operational. A *thief* is loose in my personal store. And some of my favourite aquatic pets have been traumatized. Traumatized, sir! By you!"

"Ah," Kai said cheerfully, but with steel beneath. "And I might have something to say about being attacked by your servant here—"

"I am not his *servant*," Indigo broke in. "I am an ally of convenience."

"There you have it," Mr. Nemo said. "I can't be held responsible for anything my ally might have done of her own volition."

And what about you? Irene signed, glaring at Ernst.

Ernst shrugged. Either he could understand ASL or he could guess what she meant. "Not officially affiliated," he said. "Acted on my own behalf, based on personal opinions. Besides, it was not so bad as it might have been. If I had wanted to hurt you, you would have been hurt."

Irene had to admit that was true. Whereas Mr. Nemo and Indigo didn't care whether they hurt people or not, when ruthlessly pursuing their goals. And Indigo was precisely the sort of person who would declare that a just revolution was worth a million deaths. As long as *she* wasn't one of them, of course.

"So what do you want to say to me?" Mr. Nemo demanded, folding his hands in an echo of his earlier calm.

"My reward . . ." Kai said. "You promised that after we returned with the item you'd sent us to steal, we would be allowed to leave with—what was it? Our respective prices, there and then, without hesitation or delay or cheating."

The tension in Mr. Nemo's shoulders eased. "Now that's reasonable. So what's your price?"

"Irene will want her prize too, before we leave. But I want *her*," Kai said, and pointed at Indigo.

Indigo stiffened in her chair. "Are you mad?" she demanded.

Kai's smile was as cruel as Irene had ever seen it. He was a dragon prince, free from the fetters of human morality. "Mr. Nemo said that he could give me the means to keep you prisoner. I'm calling in his marker."

Irene forced herself to stifle her expression of shock. Could *this* be what he'd wanted to say, when the guards interrupted? And was his plan even viable? If Indigo was off the metaphorical chessboard, then she couldn't use the painting in her attempts to trigger revolution . . . It would give them time to hide it again and avoid the whole political deck of cards coming tumbling down—with all that meant for a spectrum of worlds. *Then* they could deal with Mr. Nemo.

"You drive a hard bargain, Prince Kai," Mr. Nemo said softly. "But I accept your deal."

Indigo rose to her feet, eyes glittering. "Are you handing me

over to this child like a *slave*? As if you even have the power . . .
And what other bargains have you been making behind my back?"

"My dear Indigo!" Mr. Nemo replied, after an inaudible command to a guard off-screen. "Or should I say, Princess Qing Qing?
As you've said yourself, you're not my employee—we're allies of
convenience. We're both at perfect liberty to make deals with anyone we choose. I admit that I may have had some discussions with
Prince Kai here about the future, in a broad and undefined sense.
He seems to have made an extremely specific choice based on
them. And my word, madam, is my bond."

"You're babbling," Indigo said calmly. She began to pace,
moving—Irene noted—several steps away from Ernst. Was she
more worried than she wanted to show? "I'm not your property.
You can't just hand me over. And if you try, then not only is our
deal broken, but I will destroy your computer records. You think
that *she* damaged your systems?" She pointed at Irene. "All she did
was mess with a few of your peripherals. When *I've* finished, you'll
have nothing but a pile of virus-ridden slag. And where will all
your blackmail information be then? Not to mention records of
your precious one-of-a-kind valuables?"

The threat was delivered with a deadly calm that made it somehow more impressive. Mr. Nemo, however, merely smiled. "I'm
fully aware of your capabilities, madam. That *was* why you went on
the job, after all, rather than spending your time here. And we
both know that I could make a similar barrage of threats regarding
all your technological secrets and data keys. We both know that
we're not going to betray each other at this point."

Kai had gone still at the mention of Indigo's secrets. He was
probably envisaging sensitive information on his kind—in the
hands of a Fae who'd sell them off to the highest bidder. Irene

wasn't that thrilled with the idea herself. "And your promise to me?" he asked.

"I always keep my word," Mr. Nemo answered. "But you're going to have to allow me a minute or two, while one of my staff retrieves something from storage."

An uneasy silence settled over the room. On the screen, Mr. Nemo sipped his whiskey. Indigo watched Kai and Irene, as motionless as a painting herself, but with a glint in her eyes that promised violence. She seemed poised on a hair-trigger, ready to snap if Mr. Nemo's reassurances proved worthless. Ernst—and all the guards scattered around the room—stood and waited, with the stance of soldiers who were well used to waiting.

Irene considered. If Kai's plan *did* work, and Mr. Nemo was retrieving her promised book too, it might snatch success from the jaws of failure. Though Indigo didn't seem too concerned about this reversal of fortunes—or was that just a refusal to show fear? Should Irene be more worried about the fact that Indigo *wasn't* worried?

Their mission had changed. Now she had to not only save a world for the Library, but also rescue hundreds or even thousands of worlds from a dragon civilization at war with itself. But if this gambit failed, she couldn't rely on Tina fulfilling her mission in time. There was one other card that Irene could play, but if she did . . .

Just as she was beginning to seriously consider flooding the entire base, the doors opened behind them. One guard was carrying a heavy briefcase, while two more dragged a beaten-looking Felix between them and a fourth carried a large sack.

It was an utterly stereotypical burglar's sack. Irene couldn't even imagine where Felix had procured it. But it was bulging full, and she had to admire how far he'd managed to get in the time he'd had.

"Allow me to kill two birds with one stone," Mr. Nemo said, looking more cheerful than he had for a while. "Prince Kai, I have your payment here. And I have Miss Winters' prize as well. I'm not sure exactly how Felix here knew to take it, but he found it. As well as a few other highly valuable items."

Felix shrugged, dangling between the two guards. "I have my ways. Perhaps you mentioned it, or perhaps you weren't as discreet as you'd thought." Battered, bloodied, and captured as he was, there was still a smirk to his voice. Even if he was temporarily inconvenienced, it was all part of his master thief role. Perhaps, Irene reflected, being caught and dragged in front of the authorities was an *essential* part of it . . .

But she was too distracted by the thought of her own prize to spend time analysing Fae narrative tropes. If the book *was* in that bag, then salvation for the world she cared about was five yards away from her. The world was a haven in her mind, the only place—other than the Library—where she'd ever felt truly safe. She was so close she could almost taste success.

"And did you intend to sell the book to Irene, before we caught you?" Mr. Nemo asked. "Or simply keep it so she couldn't have it?"

It was as though masks flickered across Felix's face—Ambitious Thief, Practical Thief, Callous Thief—and were discarded again without any of them solidifying into reality. "I'm still thinking about it," he answered.

"Well, your thinking time has run out." Mr. Nemo turned back to Kai. "Here's your payment, prince. I hope we can now consider the matter settled." His words had an air of formality to them.

The guard with the heavy briefcase flipped it open, offering the contents to Kai. Inside, on a thick lining of black velvet, lay a heavy silver collar linked by chains to a pair of cuffs. Unlike Indigo's fake cuff, this reeked of power. The metal glistened as fluidly as frozen mercury, but as Irene looked closer she thought that carved traceries of words swam beneath the surface.

Kai flinched before he could catch himself. "Those *things* are your payment?"

"I promised you the means to keep Princess Qing Qing prisoner. I didn't promise you any more than that." Mr. Nemo put his glass down, a smile of pure satisfaction curling across his face. It was as sincere as Felix's earlier self-fulfilment. Both Fae were utterly satisfied with how well they embodied their archetypes. The non-Fae present were merely convenient secondary actors to them, only valuable because they provided feed lines or situations allowing the Fae to take centre stage.

"But . . ." Kai looked between the restraints and Indigo.

"Catching her is your problem," Mr. Nemo said. "Not mine. I believe the phrase is, *Who will bell the cat?*"

Indigo seemed unimpressed. "Very nice. I admit it. Now can we throw these hangers-on out of here? We have other matters to arrange."

"Of course," said Mr. Nemo. "And here's Irene's reward—*The Tale of the Shipwrecked Sailor.* Enjoy it, my dear. I think that concludes our business?"

Irene took a deep breath. She felt Kai tense at her side, being uncertain of what she had in mind but ready to back her.

"No," she said, her voice echoing in the room. "It doesn't. I've changed my mind about my choice of prize." Her stomach churned with despair at the thought of what she was giving up, and the risks she was taking with others' lives. But if she didn't do this, more than one world was at stake . . . Though that world was so precious to her, the collapse of the draconic status quo would cause shock waves across the cosmos and a war that could last a thousand years . . . This was her last chance to resolve that mess. "For my payment, Mr. Nemo . . . I want the painting."

CHAPTER 27

Irene had rarely managed to reduce a room to quite such stunned silence. (Well, there had been the occasion with the robot impersonator and the levitating corgis. But the silence hadn't lasted long. There had been corgis involved, after all.)

Indigo was the first to recover. "Out of the question," she said.

But in Mr. Nemo's hastily concealed shock and the momentary trembling of his hand, Irene saw hope and possibility like big neon signs. This had seemed almost too ridiculous to work. But technically this was a permissible request. There was nothing in the deal about not changing one's mind, and she hadn't actually been handed her prize yet. And when dealing with Fae promises, technicalities were the very soul of the deal.

"Possibly we've misheard Miss Winters." Irene didn't miss his attempt to curry favour with the polite form of her name. And the smile working its way across his face tried and failed to convey geniality. It was the sort of generous grin that went with classic pictures of Father Christmas, and it was grossly out of place in this context. "You wanted a very specific edition of *The Tale of the Shipwrecked Sailor*? I made some enquiries, and the world in question has been shifting towards chaos, has it not? I know how you Librarians are about that kind of thing. Naturally I would be pleased to assist you . . ."

Irene took a step forward. "Let me be precise," she said firmly. "I request and require that you give me a specific item from your collection—the canvas which I helped steal from Vienna yesterday. The hidden canvas which shows the dragon monarchs. That is the item I choose. I want it now, and I want to leave with it now—as agreed by you, 'without delay or endangerment.'"

Mr. Nemo looked as if he had swallowed one of his catfish. "Are you quite certain?"

"Absolutely," Irene replied.

"You do realize that if you make this request, I'll have absolutely no incentive to give you the book that you're interested in? The book which I've discovered is one-of-a-kind." Steel entered his voice. "In fact, I can promise you that it will not be sold or traded to the Library under any circumstances."

Irene didn't need to close her eyes to see memories of the world where she'd spent six years at school—a world that she'd loved. To be perfectly honest, she had hated it occasionally too. But it had made her who she was in her most formative years, nurturing her just as much as her parents. She'd never needed to go back there: it had been enough to know that it was safe. A private refuge in her mind, whenever she'd needed one. And now, because of an even greater battle for power, it might be lost in the flow of chaos. Its inhabitants would become nothing more than background characters for visiting Fae to use in their narratives, or perhaps they would be twisted into Fae themselves. Archetypes rather than human beings, stories rather than real people—as unable to change as Mr. Nemo was now unable to break his word.

I'm sorry, she thought. *I'll try to find another way. There has to be another way.*

She wouldn't let herself think about what would happen if there wasn't.

"I'm quite certain," she said. But the steadiness in her voice required all her training. And she wouldn't let herself look at the sack of stolen goods in front of Felix.

"You can't be *seriously* considering letting her have it," Indigo said.

Mr. Nemo looked pale and in pain, his face twisting under the pressure of his vows. "I don't have a choice."

"You can do better than this," Indigo urged him. "Behaving this way is illogical. It's no better than being an animal. Or a human. You're not like my parents—you're capable of thinking round the situation, finding some other way of handling it. Don't let one single human spoil everything—just because she's playing with the letter of your promise to her."

Beside her, Irene felt Kai stiffen at the comparison of his father to a Fae. Any Fae. But he had the sense to keep his mouth shut.

"I'm not surrendering," Mr. Nemo muttered, his face ashen. He took a harsh, gulping breath, like a drowning man seizing a chance at oxygen. "I can't refuse her request, now that she's made it. And I would be breaking my word to take action against her myself, or order any of *my servants or allies* to take action . . ."

Indigo blinked, her eyelids flickering like a serpent's. Then she moved, sliding through the air like a knife. She grabbed a gun from the nearest guard's holster, levelled it at Irene, and fired.

It was Kai's superhuman speed that saved her, rather than her own reflexes. He slammed sideways into her, and the two of them rolled across the floor. In the pinwheel of violent motion, Irene caught sight of the guards raising their guns, uncertain whom they should be shooting.

There was very little cover in the room—just the big conference table, the flimsy chairs surrounding it—and nowhere to hide. A bullet clipped Kai's arm, drawing blood, and he gasped in pain.

But Irene was ready this time. **"Guns, jam!"** she shouted.

Indigo's gun clicked. She cursed and threw it to one side.

Kai rose to his feet. "If you want Irene, *Sister*, you're going to have to go through me."

"As you wish." Indigo stalked towards them like a thundercloud. Even if she and Kai couldn't take their dragon forms due to the local chaos, there was something inhuman about the way they faced off. Looking at their faces, Irene could see their resemblance: their father's likeness was unmistakably stamped on both of them.

Physically, at least. Mentally? That was another question.

Indigo leapt onto the conference table, seemingly without effort, lunging towards them. Kai sprang onto the table to meet her, ripping through the air. She swung into a kick, foot heading for his chin, but he caught it on his crossed arms, throwing her backwards. She flipped, landing on her feet, and struck at him again, but he blocked—their motions speeding into a blur, becoming as fluid as a well-practiced demonstration, rather than a lethal fight.

Irene backed away, safely out of reach. She was no expert on martial arts. However, Indigo's pattern of movement was clearly aggressive, while Kai was focusing on holding her back. But how could she use the Language to help him, without it backfiring on him?

"Miss Winters." Mr. Nemo sounded as if he were strangling on his own unfulfilled promise, but he was still breathing. Unfortunately. "I will regard . . ." He coughed, hands clenching. "Regard any attempt to attack my men or damage my property as opening hostilities between us. And will take any necessary . . . counter-measures."

In other words, he'll feel free to have me killed out of hand.

"And you, Ernst . . ."

"*I am not your servant,*" Ernst grunted. His body language screamed a heartfelt desire to be somewhere else. "If you give me orders, then that would *make* me your servant, and you break your bond."

Mr. Nemo gave a choking snort. "Your boss is my friend . . . Ask yourself what he'd want you to do." He sagged over the table, hands going to his temples, like a man trying to ward off a stroke by force of will.

Indigo dropped to sweep a wide kick at Kai's ankles, hair floating out in a fan behind her. He leapt, leg coming down towards her throat in an axe kick. But she blocked it, catching his foot in midair and twisting, sending him rolling across the table. He pivoted and sprang at her as she came to her feet. The two of them closed briefly to deliver a sequence of short, harsh blows before circling each other like predators.

There was a spatter of blood on the table, from Kai's wounded arm.

Ernst reached into his pocket, then pressed something small into each ear. Irene realized with a sudden sinking feeling that he was using earplugs. That greatly reduced what she could achieve with the Language. And he made his choice clear, however reluctant it might have been, when he slung a chair at her—knowing she was bound not to destroy Mr. Nemo's property.

Irene dived sideways, past a couple of the guards. They stood still, awaiting orders, the guns in their hands almost an open invitation to be grabbed and used. Felix watched the room with narrowed eyes, waiting for a convenient moment to act. *I suppose in his personal narrative as master thief, this is where most of the secondary characters get into a conveniently distracting brawl, allowing him to make his escape . . .*

But as far as Irene was concerned, *she* was the protagonist here. She wriggled out of Kai's jacket, balled it in her hands, and tossed it at Ernst as she backed away, shouting, **"Suit jacket, wrap around Ernst's head and smother him!"**

The garment obeyed, giving Ernst a headdress worthy of any haute couture model. His great hands rose to get a grip on the fabric, and he simply tore it away, ripping the seams apart as he pulled it from his face.

Indigo flowed through a set of movements that ended with her slamming her bare hand into Kai's chest. He jolted back, whole body shuddering for breath, and barely managed to parry her follow-up stroke to his throat.

"Wasting time," Ernst commented as he tossed away the jacket's remains.

Irene didn't bother answering. He wouldn't have heard it. And she'd got what she wanted: she was close enough to the briefcase containing Kai's prize. Before the guard holding it could react, she grabbed the case and plucked out the shackles.

"You can't do that!" Mr. Nemo shouted.

They were heavy in her hands, as solid and weighty as if made from pure silver. But the metal seemed to squirm as she touched it, as though there were something in her flesh that it found antithetical to its purpose. She controlled her instinctive repulsion, took a deep breath, and flung them through the air at Indigo, grateful that she knew the dragon's true name. "**Shackles, bind Qing Qing!**"

Indigo heard the words. Her eyes gleamed red as she flung herself towards Kai and knocked him into the path of the chains. But Kai converted his motion into a backwards tumble and ducked underneath them as they rippled through the air. The collar and twin cuffs clamped round Indigo's neck and wrists.

She shrieked. The sound rose through the normal octaves, and beyond an opera soprano's highest C. Many of the guards winced, raising their hands to their ears; a crack split Mr. Nemo's television screen. And even on-screen, his bottle and glass both splintered. Indigo's back arched and she fell to her knees, writhing in pain, her chained hands clawing at the collar around her throat. Gradually her motions slowed, her eyes glazing over.

Irene and Kai had both covered their ears at Indigo's scream, Kai falling back a cautious few steps to the edge of the table. Irene thought she could see shock in his expression; was it the memory of the time that he himself had been a Fae captive, bound and shackled? Or was it simply the sight of any dragon so reduced?

And then Ernst rushed forward with a quickness that belied his weight. His hand locked around Kai's ankle and he yanked, slamming Kai down onto the table in an ungainly belly-flop. While Kai struggled to catch his breath, Ernst grabbed his wrist, twisting it behind the dragon's back. He locked his free arm around Kai's throat, restraining him with an impossible strength.

Silence filled the room. Even Felix was still, too transfixed by the drama taking place in front of him to seize the moment to escape. "Now," Ernst said. "You surrender, Irene? Please? I do not want to have to snap dragon boy's neck."

"If you kill Kai, his family will destroy you!" Irene said desperately. Then she remembered that Ernst had his ears blocked.

The twitch of his shoulders showed that he had at least noticed her mouth moving. "You know I cannot hear you. Raise your hands to show you give up. And no big sentences in the Language. I do not trust them."

Kai struggled for breath. His eyes were furious; he wouldn't beg for mercy. But he knew how real his peril was. Here in a high-chaos location, away from water, he couldn't call on his element, couldn't take his true form . . . he was trapped like a human—and could die like one. But if she surrendered, could Mr. Nemo interpret this as her giving up the painting too?

A couple of thoughts formed, like a bridge across an ocean of desperation. The Language was powerful in high-chaos areas. What Kai couldn't do for himself, Irene might *make* him accomplish. If, that is, the presence of two dragons had forced just enough order into the area. She'd done it once before elsewhere, in another world and with other dragons . . .

"Decision," Ernst said. His arm tightened round Kai's neck. "Now."

Irene slowly began to raise her hands as if she was complying with his order. But the Language wasn't about accepting reality. It was about *changing* reality. **"Kai,"** she ordered, **"take your true form!"**

Light burned through the room as Kai shifted and *changed* in Ernst's grasp. The Fae tried to maintain his grip. But the archetype for that sort of fairy story—where a protagonist held on as their prey switched between lion, swan, serpent, whatever—wasn't strong enough here. With a shudder and a flex of his sapphire-scaled wings, Kai tossed Ernst to the ground. He uncoiled and the table collapsed under his weight as he threw his body across it, eyes burning. His great horned and bearded head turned to inspect the room. And for a moment there was nothing sentient in his eyes.

Irene was on her knees. She didn't have the strength to stand. A fragment of Kai's dinner jacket lay within reach and she groped for it, pressing it against her nose to staunch the flow of blood.

"Kai," she whispered. "I'm sorry." What she'd done to him might have been necessary, but that didn't make it right. It was still a violation of his body and his power.

Kai focused on her, and she saw self-awareness grow in his eyes. He recognized her. And she saw him note the unconscious Indigo, surrounded by a loop of his serpentine body. He swept a gaze across the room, wings folding against his body, and turned to glare at the television screen. "Are there any more *objections*?" he demanded in a voice like thunder.

Mr. Nemo held up one trembling hand, speaking as if each word was an effort. "I accept Irene Winters' claim. I will give her what she wants."

And then the whole room seemed to shake. The guards abandoned any last attempts to be efficient and broke and ran. On Mr. Nemo's screen, another guard shot into view. "Dragons, sir! Dragons above! Circling!"

Mr. Nemo pointed a finger at Irene and Kai. "Do you know anything about this?"

Irene would have liked to rise elegantly to her feet. Instead she crawled across to the table and dragged herself upright. "Really, Mr. Nemo—are you suggesting that we expected some sort of betrayal on your part? So we deliberately sent someone with the location to Kai's family, to come and find us here?" She looked the

Fae in the eyes. "And as a result, the dragons now know exactly where you are?"

Now that Mr. Nemo had accepted her claim, its power had loosened its grip and the palsy was leaving him. He no longer looked like a patient on the verge of collapse. Now he simply looked like a very worried man trying—and failing—to hide his fear. This made him suddenly less archetypal and more human, for some reason. "Are you calling your allies in to attack me? Is *that* what you're doing?"

Irene wished her head didn't feel as if it were about to fragment. Shakes racked her body. She needed the table to keep herself upright. It might have made these negotiations simpler, but the Language always extracted its price. "*I'm* making no threats. What the dragons do is up to them." She left that part open—hurricanes, storms, tidal waves, earthquakes . . . "However, if *you* want to take this opportunity, here and now, to sign up to the dragon-Fae truce, then Prince Kai and myself would be pleased to witness it. We can testify to the new arrivals that, as a truce signatory, they can't attack you or take any action against you or your possessions." She left a meaningful pause before continuing. "Before we leave. With that canvas . . ."

Mr. Nemo took a deep breath and for a moment he closed his eyes. The crack in his screen fractured his face, making him look like a surrealist painting. Then he nodded. "Done and done. I will order the painting brought to you at once. Please, Prince Kai, take human form—it'll make it easier for you to leave. Will a simple signed declaration of my intention to join the truce be sufficient? My word will bind me."

"Yes. And we'll inform the dragons on our way out," Irene promised.

Felix came sidling up from behind. "Any chance of a lift out of here?" he asked hopefully.

Mr. Nemo glared at him. "I'll let you leave in one piece, as long as my guards can search you first."

Felix smirked. "Deal."

Kai's body flared with light again, and then he was human once more, his shoulders sagging with weariness. "What about Indigo?" he asked quietly.

Irene didn't have any good answers to that. If Indigo remained unconscious, and they handed her over to the dragons above, they were quite possibly handing her over for execution. And while Irene would have been prepared to kill her in an outright life-or-death fight, some morality—something that dated back to those distant schooldays—flinched at the idea. Even if Indigo had been quite prepared to kill Irene.

"Princess Qing Qing is my guest," Mr. Nemo announced, cutting through Irene's thoughts. "And if my territory is protected, because I've signed up to the truce, you have no right to force her to leave. Am I right? I only promised the prince the means to keep her captive—nothing more."

Irene and Kai exchanged glances. Leaving Indigo here, powerless and an effective prisoner, might not be any kinder than handing her over to the dragons. She'd be a pawn in Mr. Nemo's schemes—or the schemes of any Fae he traded her to—unless she came to some new arrangement. But Kai didn't look any keener to hand Indigo over for execution than Irene. Perhaps working with her for the last few days had changed his perception of her. Or perhaps he was simply tired. "Acceptable," he said. "The painting?"

"Is being brought to the beach entrance," Mr. Nemo said. "My guards will escort you there. As quickly as possible."

"One thing," Ernst broke in. He'd removed his earplugs and had been listening to the conversation. "My reward? I too have changed my mind."

Mr. Nemo sighed. "Yes. What do *you* want?"

Ernst walked over to Felix's sack and emptied it out. Various items bounced across the floor—an alabaster statuette, a clay cup, two jewellery boxes that spilled their diamond contents out in a flashing stream, a folded cotton sheet, a small wooden puzzle box, and a wrapped scroll in a transparent plastic case. "This," he said, bending to pick up the scroll. "*This* is the book you were all talking about, yes? The Egyptian one, *The Tale of the Shipwrecked Sailor*?"

Mr. Nemo's eyes widened. "It is. What do *you* want it for?"

Irene felt her heart jump in her chest. Having it waved under her nose like this was torture, and this turn of events was not something she had remotely anticipated. If Ernst wanted to give it to his boss, then perhaps she could bargain with him? There might still be a chance to get hold of it and to save the world it came from . . .

"For myself," Ernst said, "for my own reasons. Do you accept it as my payment?"

"Done," Mr. Nemo said. A nasty smirk touched his lips. "I suggest you take good care of it. There are thieves everywhere these days."

"Very true," Ernst agreed. "But my boss trusts my judgement. And when I say to him I have used it to buy goodwill with the Library—and that in return I have promised him a visit from a Library representative to discuss this truce, I think he will agree I acted sensibly." He offered Irene the scroll. "Deal?"

Irene knew her hands were shaking as she reached out to take it, but she couldn't help herself. Her mouth was dry. "A visit from me?" she said to Ernst. "Or someone else?"

Ernst shrugged. "Either. Though if it is you, Library girl, I will tell him to be careful. You could talk him into giving you the shirt off his back. Deal?"

"Deal," Irene agreed, and her hands finally closed on the scroll.

"Now will you all get out of here?" Mr. Nemo demanded. He paused and added, ever the entrepreneur, "And if you have any future requests, my door is always open . . ."

Outside on the beach, a pair of white flags—attempts at signalling peaceful intentions?—streamed in the wind, the fabric snapping like gunshots. Two dragons circled in the sky above, distant flashes of crimson and light green against the growing mass of dark clouds. Kai's uncle Ao Shun walked the beach, his impeccably crafted shoes leaving prints a little too heavy for a human. Their friend Mu Dan, the dragon equivalent of a judge *and* private investigator, kept a careful pace to his rear. Ao Shun wore a suit, one that might have come from the Vienna they had just left—assuming the wearer was a millionaire and only had a taste for black. Mu Dan was still in an outfit appropriate for Vale's world, a deep crimson gown—with enough room in the sleeves and skirt for hidden knives and guns. A hovering group of the sarong-clad guards had sensibly left their weapons inside and were offering deck-chairs and cocktails.

Kai stepped hastily forward and went to one knee, touching right fist to left shoulder. "My lord uncle! I apologise for the inconvenience that has brought you here."

"Rise," Ao Shun said. His tone was not quite annoyed, but there was a barely hidden note of impatience behind it. Irene knew that this dragon monarch, at least, was prepared to accept some freedom of thought from his servants. She hoped that he was in an open-minded mood today. "And you, Irene Winters . . . I came here because I understood you had chanced across a . . . certain item."

Irene rose from her own bow. Curtseying while wearing a bikini would have looked stupid.

"Your Majesty," she said respectfully. "Your nephew and I believe this item might belong to you. The Fae who rules this island was shocked to learn he might have been a receiver of stolen property. He asked us to return the item to its proper owners as quickly as possible."

"I'm told he signed the treaty. How recently did this happen?" Ao Shun enquired. The sky above was darkening further. In the absence of direct sunlight, he could have been an ebony statue come to life. The glitter of ruby in his eyes indicated the state of his temper, even if it was controlled. In his shadow, Mu Dan faded into the background, despite her elegant gown and vivid presence. But Irene knew that she'd be listening like the dragon judge-investigator she was.

"About ten minutes ago," Irene admitted. "Possibly five."

Fortunately, before any further explanations could be demanded, a group of guards came onto the beach, bearing the rolled canvas between them with great care. Ao Shun's gaze moved to it. "Is that it?"

"Yes, Your Majesty," Irene answered.

"I will inspect it. You may remain here." It was an order, not a suggestion.

As Ao Shun ordered the guards to unroll the canvas, Mu Dan moved closer to Kai and Irene. "I have the most extraordinary feeling that I should be investigating . . . *something* here," she confessed. She glanced around the beach, her sharp eyes narrowing as she considered each detail. "No doubt it's that accursed Fae influence."

"I'm just grateful you both made it here in time," Irene answered softly. "Things were getting a little awkward."

Mu Dan shrugged. "It wasn't the *most* unusual summons I've ever had, though it was close. And I *certainly* wouldn't have expected to receive your note via a Fae. It's a good thing *I* knew *you* knew Lord Silver, as I'm not sure I'd have believed it came from you otherwise."

Kai was processing a train of thought. "Why did you send Tina to *Silver* with our message?" he asked Irene. "Couldn't you think of someone more reliable?"

Irene shrugged. "The problem was choosing someone she knew, who'd do her a favour—who could then contact a dragon we knew, who could get *us* the help we needed. Tina couldn't have gone to your uncle directly. The forces of order in his court would have been far too high for a Fae. And she'd never have been allowed in to see him, anyhow." It was the sort of last-ditch gamble that Fae story forms loved. But whether their plan had been helped along by Fae influences or not, it had worked.

"I'm glad we arrived when we did too," Mu Dan continued. "But you seemed to have almost resolved the problem . . ."

"I was only here in the first place to collect a book," Irene said self-deprecatingly. She lovingly patted the bundle under her arm. Again, she felt a thrill—and she still had time to get it to Coppelia. "Did you get to meet Tina yourself?"

"Yes. A very interesting person. I may use her in the future—despite her Fae nature." Mu Dan smiled at the expression on Kai's face. The diamond pins in her mahogany hair glinted in a sudden burst of sunlight; overhead the storm-clouds generated by the dragons' arrival—or Ao Shun's temper—were beginning to dissolve and separate. "As Irene keeps reminding me, our situation is fluid, but hopefully changing for the better. And I'm prepared to recognize useful talent when I see it." She looked thoughtfully at the rise of the cliffs behind them. "By the way, who *is* the Fae who lives here?"

"Mr. Nemo. An . . . interesting character."

Mu Dan's lips tightened, and her eyes glinted dragon-red. "Are we talking about Mr. Nemo the information trader, the thief, the blackmailer, the criminal, the trader in stolen goods, the . . ." She shut her mouth before more pejoratives could boil out, but her hands twitched, perhaps with an urge to tear the place down to the ground.

"Peace treaty, remember?" Irene said.

"You didn't tell me who he *was*!" Mu Dan seethed. "Have you any idea of the criminal secrets his hideout conceals? The ways in which he might be connected to past cases?"

Irene looked to Kai for help, but he was busy staying well out of the discussion. Mu Dan's reaction wasn't down to any Fae-versus-dragon sentiment, either: it was that of an investigator hearing that a notorious criminal was within arm's reach. "I really am sorry I can't hand him over," Irene said. "But he's under the treaty—and for now, he's behaving himself."

"For now," Mu Dan muttered darkly—making Irene rather curious about their past interactions.

Kai stretched. "The sooner we can get away from all of this, the better."

"I hope that *we* holds for all of us," Felix commented. He had appeared from nowhere, and the fact that they hadn't noticed was really rather embarrassing. "You did promise me a lift out of here."

"You asked for one, which isn't quite the same thing." Irene glanced at Kai, and he nodded. "But I don't see why not, under the circumstances. A word of advice, though. Don't inconvenience His Majesty Ao Shun."

"I don't need to be told that. And thanks. I owe you one. Both of you."

Ao Shun brusquely gestured to the guards to roll up the canvas. Briefly he was still, as though considering some private cost-effort analysis, before striding over to join them. "Nephew. Miss Winters. Your service is noted and appreciated. I will have my servants take charge of that painting." He raised one hand in signal, and the two dragons above came spiralling down. "Mu Dan, you have been of assistance. Li Ming, my private secretary, will speak with you later. You are all free to go."

From a dragon monarch, the phrase *your service is noted and appreciated* was as good as Irene could possibly hope for. It also suggested that she and Kai—and the Library—had come out of this without a stain on their characters, which was better than she'd *dared* to hope. She bowed again, as did the others, but Ao Shun was already turning away to supervise the painting's transport.

"I'll bear you and Irene away, until we can put you down elsewhere," Kai told Felix. "The sooner I shake the sands of this island off my feet, the better."

"And I need to reach the Library as soon as possible," Irene said, patting the book under her arm. "This won't wait."

CHAPTER 28

A knock at the door disturbed Irene's concentration, and she looked up from her computer. "Come in!" she called. Her mother entered. Her eyes fell on the pot of coffee on the table. "Interesting," she said.

"What is?"

"That instead of running directly back to your assigned world and your work—and your prince—you're staying in the Library for long enough to have coffee. And not just a cup, but a whole pot. Has it been a bad few days?"

"It's been . . . hectic." Irene propped her chin on her hand. "Is this going to be a slightly longer discussion than last time, or will one of us have to run off on a job again?"

"It's certainly a very convenient excuse for getting out of inconvenient conversations," her mother admitted. She found a book-occupied chair close to Irene and moved its contents onto the floor, taking a seat but not actually meeting Irene's eyes. "And neither of us really make conversations easy, do we?"

"It's been that way for a while," Irene said—neutrally. She wanted her mother to stay and talk, this time. "How's Father?"

"Already on a new job. Hunting down an expanded copy of the *Lokasenna* in G-39. I'll be joining him there."

"That sounds interesting." It was quite true. After the last few days, a simple book retrieval sounded heavenly.

Her mother took a deep breath, then let it out. "There's something I wanted to discuss with you."

All sorts of nasty potential surprises came to mind, but she tried to swallow her fear. "Please tell me it's only about Father's birthday—I know I need to get him something other than a dictionary this year."

"Well, that would be a good idea, but that's not for another three months." Her mother leaned forward. Her hair, Irene noticed, had streaks of full white among the grey. "This is difficult, Ray . . . Irene. I'm trying to be honest, and god knows that we find that hard. We spend too much time being good liars, and that's part of the problem."

"Go on," Irene said. She wasn't sure where this was going, but it already felt uncomfortable enough.

"Your father and I love you." Her mother's hands twisted together in her lap. "But we weren't necessarily good parents to you. And as the years have gone by, the more we tried to get close to you, the more we made things worse."

"I understand," Irene said, not knowing what else to say. She'd wanted them to talk, but she didn't want her mother to bare her soul in *this* way. It was raw and undignified and it made Irene want to cry. "It wasn't your fault. It's how we both *are*. We need to know what's going on around us, we need to control it, and that's part of being a Librarian and a spy, but—"

"But we never gave you a choice," her mother interrupted. "Not a real one. We always assumed that you would *want* to be a Librarian, as we had."

"But I *did*," Irene insisted. "Did want to, that is."

Her mother sighed, stooping forward in her seat. "The way you grew up, could you have really wanted anything else?"

Irene looked for words that would convince her. "You could say that to any child who admired their parents' work. The answer would be the same. It's not a *bad* thing to know that your parents do important work. It's perfectly valid to use that, when you're deciding what to do with your life."

"Because you've been brainwashed from childhood into believing it's the most important thing you could possibly do?"

"Now you're the one who's deliberately choosing emotive words." Irene leaned forward. "Mother, please, hear me out. If there's something I've learned over the last few years, it's that *everything* people do is important. I happen to have chosen this particular thing to do with my life, and I was lucky enough to have the choice. Because of you. Do you understand? Never say that you forced me into this. You didn't. I *chose* it, and because of what you and Father taught me, I chose it with full knowledge and consent." She tried to remember where that phrasing came from, and then it hit her: the Catholic definition of mortal sin. Oh well. "You're welcome to beat yourself up about things like searching my rooms—but please, *please* don't feel guilty about me choosing to be a Librarian."

"In a single year, you have put yourself in more danger than your father and I managed in a dozen. I didn't want a child just so she could get herself killed!" For a moment her mother's careful composure slipped, and Irene saw the naked fear in her face.

Irene took her mother's hands in hers. They felt . . . fragile. "Mother," she said softly. "I think all parents have this problem. Whether they're Librarians or not. And all children. I want you to be safe too. But we can't lock each other away in a tower somewhere. That would be a new take on an old fairy tale, wouldn't it? The princess locks her *parents* in a tower . . ."

Her mother bit her lip. "You're trying to distract me."

"I think it's reflexive. I'm used to avoiding this sort of thing."

"I know. You never tell me *anything*."

"Well, you always want to know *everything*," Irene started, then bit it back before the complaint could assume its habitual shape.

"We taught you not to depend on technology or magic, but to rely on yourself and what you know. We have this belief that knowledge can keep us safe. That knowledge leads to control." Her mother's hands tightened on Irene's. "And we believe it for the people we love too . . . But don't make the same mistakes that we have, Irene." Her mouth quirked in a smile. "Make some new ones."

The momentary door that had opened between them was closing again. Yet Irene was content with that. They'd both said enough. It was something they were both going to have to come to terms with in the long run—that neither of them *could* keep the other safe—and it wasn't going to be resolved by one conversation. But it was really important to her that her mother had actually *said* it.

Her mother let go of Irene's hands and looked at her computer. "What are you working on? That looks like Middle Egyptian hieroglyphs. Your father would be pleased to know you're studying them."

"Unfortunately I've forgotten the little I ever knew," Irene admitted. Whereas her father was one of the Library's experts on Egyptian and hieroglyphs, all the way through from the archaic to the Coptic. He'd always been disappointed that Irene had never been interested in that area. "This is a section from the text I brought back, *The Tale of the Shipwrecked Sailor*. It's from a bit where the mystical serpent ruling the island talks about his past. I had to hand in the text, of course. But I checked first to find out which bit diverged from other versions, and scanned it to study later." She shrugged. "I was curious. But I overestimated my powers of translation."

"Would you like me to ask your father to have a look?" her mother offered. "He'd probably be interested himself, and he can send you a translation when it's done."

"That would be marvellous," Irene said warmly. "Thank you. I'll email you the scan."

"Why *are* you curious about it?"

"It's from the world where you sent me to boarding school. I'm not sure what grabbed me about this. Maybe it's because I've never come across any unique books from there before." Perhaps it was because of all the trouble she'd gone through to get the text. It would be nice to have some sort of personal reward—even if it was only a new story.

Although to a Librarian, no new story was ever *only* a new story. It was always worthwhile.

"Well, I'll pester him till he gets it done." Her mother rose, shaking out her skirts. "Take care of yourself, Irene. Remember that I worry."

Irene had a lump in her throat, and she swallowed. "You can still call me Ray," she said. "I won't mind."

Her mother smiled. "You will mind . . . but I appreciate the thought. Give our regards to Prince Kai. Get back to him before *he* starts worrying."

"Life was much easier before I had to worry about everyone else worrying," Irene muttered.

"It's called growing up, dear. It comes with staying alive."

K ai was brooding over his own pot of coffee when she returned, sprawled in his favourite armchair by the fire. He greeted her with an absent nod.

She settled into the chair opposite. "Which of our many problems are you thinking about?" she asked.

"I could just be thinking," he said archly. "Planning for the future. Considering diplomatic issues."

"If you were, then you'd be drinking tea. You only drink coffee when we're eating out—or when you're upset." She waited. "Am I wrong?"

"Not wrong. Just not completely right. I'm not upset, I'm . . ." He looked for the right words. "Conducting some self-examination."

"Do you want to tell me about it?"

Kai sagged gratefully. "It would make my mind easier. I know I'm not your apprentice these days, Irene. But you've got more experience than I have. And better judgement."

"I dropped us into that mess because I didn't take your word about how dangerous Indigo was," Irene pointed out. "My judgement's hardly that reliable. Perhaps your uncle could help . . ."

"I've been speaking to him too. He dropped by earlier."

"Oh." Irene had thought that might happen. Ao Shun would

have wanted a more detailed account of events. But she didn't think he'd have been pleased. "Ah . . . how did it go?" It couldn't have been that bad—Kai was still here, after all, and so was London . . .

Kai stared at the fire rather than at Irene. "He agreed we had no way of knowing that the painting was an item of personal value to him—and the other monarchs. He didn't blame us. He thought that we'd done well to force Mr. Nemo to sign the truce. But—he was *amused*." Now the note of bitterness in Kai's voice truly became clear. It was the tone of a child—no, a teenager—who'd been through self-perceived hell and back. Then he'd been patted on the head by an adult and told that the whole thing hadn't been that important. "He thought we'd been playing around. He said how charming you looked in a bikini. He—"

"He was lying," Irene said flatly.

Kai stiffened. "Do not say that about my lord uncle," he commanded.

Irene tried to think how to explain herself in a way Kai wouldn't automatically reject. "I meant he'd have been lying for political reasons," she said. "Not personal ones."

That drained a little of Kai's anger. "Explain?"

"Kai, consider his actions—rather than what he said after the fact. Based on a message from *me* about the painting, brought via a *Fae*, your uncle dropped everything and came immediately to investigate. He was ready to level the place if we hadn't managed to resolve things . . . just five minutes earlier. Does that sound to you as if he thought it was unimportant and amusing?"

"No," Kai admitted slowly. He frowned, thinking it through. "Then it *was* that important. And that dangerous."

Irene thought of her own parents, and knowledge, and control. "And perhaps your uncle believed that the best way to protect you was to keep you ignorant of how important it was."

"What was on the painting?" Kai asked. "You know I never got to see it."

Irene could have said *Are you sure you want to know?* But that would have been putting off the inevitable. They both knew that he really did. "It was a bit like *The Raft of the Medusa*," she said, "but not quite. It was a raft, on the ocean, but the figures on it were all the dragon monarchs—your father, your uncles. And another man I didn't recognize, but who looked like family—also Ya Yu and three other women. They were all in human form, but quite recognizable. They were escaping from, well, *other* dragons."

Kai was very still. "My lord father and the other monarchs have *always* ruled. It is said that they are the true source of stories of heavenly dragon kings, in some countries. Why would anyone claim differently? Or paint a picture that suggested otherwise?"

The truly significant question lay between them like an unexploded grenade, with neither of them willing to touch it. *And why should a picture like that be so important—to Ao Shun, to everyone— if there weren't an element of truth to it?*

Irene took a deep breath. "The job's over. If your uncle would rather you forget about it, then that might be the safest thing for you to do." She saw the mutinous glint in Kai's eyes at the word *safest*, and hastily revised her suggestion. "It might be what he would *like* you to do."

"Both of those things might indeed be true," Kai agreed. "But that doesn't mean I'll agree to just leave it."

"That's between you and him," Irene temporized. It wasn't her problem, and she couldn't give him ethical advice. She wasn't even sure that she had any for herself.

"Though one point comes to mind . . ."

"Yes?"

"You *do* look charming in a bikini."

Irene snorted. "I don't consider that relevant here."

Kai relaxed, and his mouth twitched into a smile. "Maybe I need a rest from work-related thoughts. And there's something I've been wondering."

"What's that?"

"A minor question that's been nagging at me. If your parents left you at boarding school, what sort of cover identity did they have on that world? Travelling book collectors? Diplomats? Scientists?"

Irene felt her cheeks flush. "You have to promise not to tell anyone."

"Oh, *interesting*." Kai leaned forward himself. "Spies? Adventurers? Mysterious masked men and women of mystery?"

Irene took a deep breath. "Actually . . . missionaries."

Kai was silent for a moment. Then he began to laugh.

"It was a perfectly valid cover by local standards!" Irene protested. "It got me into the school with no questions asked . . . Memorising a lot of Bible verses was good mental training!"

Kai just looked at her. "Missionaries."

The doorbell rang.

"Your sins shall *not* be forgiven," Irene muttered. She rose. "Try to get yourself under control before I bring anyone in here."

There was a minor delegation on her doorstep. Lord Silver. Sterrington. And Vale too—and their detective friend was looking surprisingly cheerful. If the Fae had dragged him along for their own purposes, she'd expect him to be irritated. The only thing she could think of that would put him in a good mood would be an interesting murder investigation. *Oh no, not another one . . .*

"You might as well let us in, Miss Winters," Silver said cheerfully. He was fully awake—as it was four in the afternoon—and dressed to kill, or at least to party. "We have good news!"

With some reluctance Irene allowed them all to enter. "Is anyone dead?" she asked nervously.

"No," Sterrington said, shrugging off her cape and passing it to Irene. "Should they be?"

"Generally speaking, I find people much more entertaining alive," Silver noted. He added his cloak and hat to the growing pile in Irene's arms. "Do we have somewhere to talk? I was being quite serious. I think you'll like what we have to say. And your princeling should be there as well."

"Right this way," Irene said, redistributing her bundle onto the hat stand.

The looming presence of Fae had brought Kai back to his usual mannered self. "How may we be of assistance?" he asked, falling into a diplomatic role as everyone took seats.

Silver waved a hand at Sterrington. "Would you like to start?"

"No, no . . . be my guest," Sterrington said. She looked . . . pleased, Irene decided. As if she'd come out the better in a bargain. Paranoia raised flags in Irene's mind and threw up fortifications.

Silver opened proceedings. "You may be aware that there's been some minor argument among my kind about which of us should take the third role in our little treaty triumvirate."

"We could hardly have missed it," Irene said drily. "In fact, I raised the point vigorously with you just a few days ago." This sounded like a prepared speech on Silver's part—and one for an audience. Was that why Vale had been brought here?

"I don't think you appreciate quite how difficult my position has been, my little mouse. Of course, both of the main groups involved had perfectly reasonable points of view." Silver glanced sideways at Sterrington, then continued. "Having—reluctantly— found myself leading one group, I personally didn't *want* the role that you two have so virtuously accepted. But at the same time, a seat on the treaty committee carries weight. The person who holds it will have . . . influence."

"And nobody wants to give up influence," Sterrington agreed. "Fortunately, we have been able to find a solution which satisfies all parties."

"All *Fae* parties?" Kai asked.

"Well, naturally," Silver drawled. "Though I don't think you'll be too upset with the result. Madam Sterrington, would you like to explain?"

"I wouldn't want to interrupt your flow," Sterrington said.

Vale snorted. "I, on the other hand, am absolutely delighted to interrupt Lord Silver. They have an offer for you, Winters, Strongrock—though I admit it depends particularly on Winters accepting it."

"How did you get dragged into this?" Irene asked curiously.

"I believe I'm here as a witness." Vale shrugged. "And you know I like to know what's going on. Since I have no cases at the moment, I thought I'd make myself useful."

Silver's expression had been souring at the interjection, but he leapt into the conversational gap before Vale could get any further. "Kindly ignore the detective. My—no, *our*—offer is this. Sterrington here will take the Fae chair on our treaty liaison group. Her patron the Cardinal's agreed to it. But at the same time . . ." He smiled. It was, as usual, a mortal sin. "Miss Winters here will take my niece as her apprentice."

There was a pause as Irene turned the idea over in her head. Unfortunately, her mental process kept on coming up with the same conclusion. "Your niece is, I assume, Fae like yourself?" she queried.

"Well, of course," Silver said smugly.

"And you want her to be my apprentice?"

"Exactly. I'm glad to see you're so quick to grasp the essentials." Silver tilted his head, and Irene felt his regard like an intimate touch against her skin. "But I can imagine one point that's troubling you. I assure you that she's nothing like *me*, my dear little mouse. She's far less interested in the flesh. And far more interested in books. And much younger."

It made sense, politically speaking. Both Silver's and Sterrington's factions gained something from the deal, though Silver's investment might be more long-term. Yet Irene could see one major problem. "I don't want to shoot down this compromise out of hand," she said. "But Fae can't enter the Library."

Silver waved a lazy gloved hand. "Oh, I'm not expecting miracles. At least, not immediate miracles. I'm prepared to give you time to work on it. Months. Years. But I do expect you to try. Just because it hasn't been done previously doesn't mean it can't be done."

"He has a point," Kai put in unhelpfully.

Irene turned to him. "What do *you* think of this?" After all, he didn't like Sterrington—could he manage to work with her?

"I think it might work," Kai said slowly. "I believe Madam Sterrington here is willing and able to cooperate with us."

Sterrington inclined her head gracefully. "And let's be honest—*not* having a Fae on the liaison team is a serious problem. If Lord Silver's niece is genuinely willing to commit to the Library, rather than being a pawn in his service . . ."

"Once you get to know her, you'll see she's far more loyal to anything she can read than to her family," Silver said. "And having her as an apprentice would be helpful—blocking insinuations that any Librarians had inappropriately *close* attachments to dragons." His gaze strayed from Irene to Kai. "Of course, if I *had* chosen to take a position as a liaison, I suppose we could have managed something suitably bipartisan. Or rather tripartisan—and *thoroughly* inclusive . . ." He was now looking suggestively at them both.

Irene could almost feel Kai stiffen in his chair with rage. "Lord Silver," she said mildly, "you're not helping your case." She needed a moment to think. "Madam Sterrington, you'd be happy with this arrangement?"

"Entirely so," Sterrington said crisply. "I wouldn't share accommodations with you two, but I would take lodgings nearby. I'd support weekly meetings to discuss current issues, unless there are matters of more urgency. General sharing of information. I believe we can make this work. I would *like* to make this work."

And now the onus was on her. She'd demanded an answer from Silver and Sterrington—and now she'd got one. "All right," she said. "I am prepared to accept this deal. With one caveat."

"Which is?" Silver asked.

"My superiors have to agree."

Silver nodded. "I expect you to do your best to get that approval. I'll accept those terms, and hope we won't need to renegotiate."

"Witnessed," Vale put in. "Don't look so harassed, Winters. You'll enjoy training his niece, once you get down to the job. I've often thought you have the soul of a born teacher."

Irene couldn't work out where *that* deduction had come from, but decided to take it as a compliment. She sighed. "Thank you all for coming. I'll let you know as soon as I have an answer . . ."

Once they were all out of the door, she turned to Kai. "I didn't expect you to support that quite as much as you did."

"Oh, *her* I can work with," Kai said with surprising cheerfulness. "After all, she's the cunning agent of a devious spymaster. At least we know what we're dealing with there."

"And this apprentice?"

"Why are you asking me? You're the one who'll be training her. And if you can help her be something other than like Lord Silver, even my lord father would agree that's a virtuous and meritorious action."

Clearly she could expect no help from that quarter. "Oh, very well," Irene agreed, and found herself smiling. "It should certainly be interesting—if it *can* be done . . . Fae living in the same house as dragons? Fae becoming Librarians?"

Kai squeezed her shoulder. "Just because something is impossible has never stopped you before. You taught me that too."

EPILOGUE

Dear Irene,

I'd like to say all the usual things about hoping that you're well and asking about your friends. But instead I strongly recommend that you delete this email after reading it.

You were right: there *is* something unusual about *The Tale of the Shipwrecked Sailor*—the version that you retrieved. The section about the sailor and the serpent . . . well, to cut to the chase, it's described as a *winged* giant serpent, rather than a normal giant serpent (and yes, there are "normal" giant serpents, ask your mother about that trouble in Iceland sometime). And what does *winged giant serpent* suggest to you? Right. Exactly.

In the *usual* version, the serpent tells the sailor about a personal tragedy—a star fell on the island and all his family are burned up, though sometimes his daughter survives. She isn't mentioned any further in the usual story. Rather unfair on the daughter. I'd have been interested in a variant that gives her an appearance and her own perspective . . .

Your mother is leaning on my shoulder and telling me to get to the point.

In *this* version, the "winged serpent" (I'm avoiding certain words here) says that he and his four sons (note the number) and others of his kind fled to the island to *escape* a catastrophe. The language is rather opaque here—it's difficult to separate accurate description from semi-supernatural hyperbole.

But this is my best guess at translating that catastrophe: *The air became crystal and the earth closed its hands around us where we stood. Our bodies changed till we are as you now see me. Had we not fled, our spirits would have become as the wind and water and earth.* (The word for spirit here is *ba*, meaning the part of the soul that gives a personality its unique aspects.) *We left the land behind and crossed the limitless sea and sky, on newly fledged wings, to find a dwelling elsewhere. We were pursued by others who were also afflicted, but could no longer take human form* (this is extraordinary!) *and would have torn us to pieces. They no longer recognized us as their friends and kinsmen; their hearts were as stone.*

If there is truth in here rather than fiction, I'm not sure how much it has been mangled by my translation. Issues with the narrative could be due to problems any human might have, when trying to understand what someone non-human— or non-human *now*—is telling them. Or my problems with decoding the text could simply be due to the effect of multiple retellings of a story. The transmutation of an originally oral history? Or perhaps my translation is entirely accurate.

We then pretty much revert to the standard version, with the winged serpent advising the sailor to have courage—and promising at least he'll get back to his family again. At this point (in another change from the usual version) the sailor asks about the winged serpent's own family. The serpent says that his four sons have gone forth to become kings, and that they and their mates (or co-rulers? Queens? Four sisters?) will rule over others who have fled identical disasters. The term here is the same as the one used for the earlier *catastrophe*.

But the serpent says that he himself has a different task. He must establish an alliance with their utmost enemies, for the restoration of balance. (The phrasing is *the restoration of Maat*. The part that follows is complex, as normally in Egyptian mythology, this would be referring directly to the goddess Maat, so indicates *her* restoration. But she personified concepts such as honour, balance, and justice. So this might *not* have been about the restoration of an actual goddess, but about the qualities she represented. Could this be an attempt to translate whatever the winged serpent has said into the local terminology?) The serpent says that he will not return to this island, but will be reborn in a different form. He finishes with, *My fate shall be preserved by the scribes*, so perhaps there is still a further record out there. There was clearly more to this story once than just this document alone.

I agree that this text raises huge questions. However, they're questions that shouldn't be asked unless we have no other choice. Everyone deserves a bit of privacy, even "winged serpents." (I'm highly disturbed by these revelations myself— but you had to know as soon as possible, and a Library-routed letter seemed the safest method of contact.)

Your mother is pointing out (over my shoulder, again) that firstly, this appears to be a case of genuine history reported as fiction. Secondly, this is something we might want to bury six feet under and never mention again. It might be extremely dangerous to have any "winged serpents" find out that we're researching this part of their history. We're not telling you to forget what I've just said—after all, knowledge is control, knowledge is safety—but at the same time, I suggest you delete this email. And don't mention the contents to Kai—for his own safety too.

Much love,
Your father (and mother)

Don't miss the next installment in
the Invisible Library series . . .

THE
DARK
ARCHIVE

Coming Winter 2020 from Ace!